Robert Malachi McWade

The uncrowned King

The Life and Public Services of Hon. Charles Stewart Parnell

Robert Malachi McWade

The uncrowned King
The Life and Public Services of Hon. Charles Stewart Parnell

ISBN/EAN: 9783337065324

Printed in Europe, USA, Canada, Australia, Japan

Cover: Foto ©Raphael Reischuk / pixelio.de

More available books at **www.hansebooks.com**

THE UNCROWNED KING.

THE LIFE AND PUBLIC SERVICES

—OF—

Hon. Charles Stewart Parnell.

COMPRISING

A GRAPHIC STORY OF HIS ANCESTRY; ALSO FAMILY REMINISCENCES, RELATED BY HIS
AGED MOTHER,

DELIA TUDOR STEWART PARNELL,

AND A BRILLIANT HISTORY OF HIS PUBLIC SERVICES IN THE GIGANTIC MOVEMENT
EXTENDING THROUGHOUT IRELAND, AMERICA AND ENGLAND FOR
THE RELIEF OF THE SUFFERING IN IRELAND; ALSO,
A BIOGRAPHICAL SKETCH OF HIS GREAT
CO-LABORER,

RT. HON. WM. E. GLADSTONE.

By ROBERT M. McWADE, ESQ.,

Ex-President of the Municipal Council of Philadelphia, &c.

PROFUSELY ILLUSTRATED.

EDGEWOOD PUBLISHING COMPANY,

1891.

PREFACE.

Any effort, however well directed, will fail in preserving in a perfect form the illustrious career of Charles Stewart Parnell. A life so full of self-sacrifice for his countrymen, so devoted to the fundamental principle essential for manhood and progress — self-government, self-control — in a word, home rule, for the man and the nation, cannot be adequately portrayed.

The man who teaches this principle as Parnell did, loses the slaves of his will and the servants of his pride, but gains the confidence of true men, and the love and esteem of all mankind. It may be a loss of ease, it may be a loss of position, it may be a loss of property, but it is a gain of manhood, a broadening of the intellectual sympathies, an enlargement of the spirit of brotherly love. These principles, properly set in the heart and life of man, cannot fail to produce action. Let not the proud and lofty skeptic say it is for effect—hypocrisy—let him give us the same and we will believe there is a heart of love for man that prompts and inspires to such noble acts of self-sacrifice and duty. You cannot have these consecrated lives for mankind from a selfish and proud spirit. Can we appreciate the devotion of Washington and Lincoln to the cause of mankind? So then we may appreciate Swift, Flood, Grattan, O'Connell, Parnell. These leaders of the race struck for life, liberty, equality and opportunity for all men; they have not yet gained the victory. Brave must be the men who seeing every effort of their forerunners defeated—some meeting death by cruel tortures, others exhausted in the strife—with hearts that never fail, take up the banner of truth and cry, "All men are born free and equal," entitled at birth to equal opportunities of life, liberty and happiness. Why should the race be taxed to support the son or daughter of royalty? If elected to serve the people they should be paid a salary for the service until their term expires or they prove unfaithful. But why should the people be taxed to support the example of gambling, drunkenness and what is worse? It is only a God-fearing, government-loving people that will stand these things that they may escape bloody revolution.

But it is a peaceful revolution that is going on in Great Britain and extending East. The kingdoms of this world are to be the kingdoms of our Lord Jesus Christ. Every man is to be clothed and in his right mind, and to cast his ballot for those who make the laws that govern his own country.

If any desire to make the laws for the country in which I live they must come and live with me under those laws. The right I claim for myself I must grant to others: if I wish laws made by myself and my fellow-countrymen to govern me, then why should I think others incapable of self-government, when they are, and have been struggling for it and demand it?

The leader of this party in Ireland, Charles Stewart Parnell, and William E. Gladstone, in England, have given to this movement an impulse which makes it nearer realization than at any time in its history. The effect will be to lessen the burdens of the industrial classes, by legislation more favorable to the toilers, and to lessen the opportunity of the royal classes for excessive luxury and debauch, taking from them the hours of lounging in heated rooms, eating exciting food, without the exercise of hand and brain, and giving them the glorious opportunity—the opportunity of necessity to do something for themselves that will produce both brawn and brain, then life will be worth living.

Alas! these extremes, suffering at both ends, one starving for bread, the other decaying from excess of stimulants, without proper exercise, the bearers of the burdens grinding and crying, good Lord, deliver us, for they are very great. It is to remove these excrescences from the body politic that so many of our brave men and noble women have died at the stake, on the field of battle, or fell, exhausted in the conflict. Parnell's sun does not set because a cloud for a time came between him and the people whom he lived for and loved. The race, especially the Anglo Saxon, never has allowed the men who served it well, to perish. We must preserve the lives of those who have made sacrifice for the welfare of others. In this laudable undertaking, Robert McWade is to be encouraged and congratulated.

REV. J. GRAY BOLTON.

1906 Pine Street,
Philadelphia, Oct. 22, 1891.

CONTENTS.

CONTENTS.

CONTENTS.

CONTENTS.

CHAPTER XIX.

CHAPTER XX.

CHAPTER XXI.

CHAPTER XXII.

CHAPTER XXIII.

CHAPTER XXIV.

CHAPTER XXV.

CHAPTER XXVI.

CHAPTER XXVII.

CHAPTER XXVIII.

CHAPTER XXIX.

CONTENTS.

CHAPTER XXX.

CHAPTER XXXI.

CHAPTER XXXII.

CHAPTER XXXIII.

LIST OF ILLUSTRATIONS.

LIST OF ILLUSTRATIONS.

ROBERT M. McWADE.

CHAPTER I.

How oft has the Banshee cried !
How oft has Death untied
Bright links that Glory wove,
Sweet bonds entwined by love !
Peace to each manly soul that sleepeth !
Rest to each faithful eye that weepeth !
Long may the fair and brave
Sigh o'er the hero's grave.

We're fall'n upon gloomy days ;
Star after star decays :
Ev'ry bright name, that shed
Light o'er the land, is fled.
Dark falls the tear of him who mourneth
Lost joy or hope, that ne'er returneth ;
But brightly flows the tear
Wept o'er the hero's bier !

Oh ! quench'd are our beacon-lights,
Thou, of the hundred fights !
Thou, on whose burning tongue
Truth, peace, and freedom, hung !
Both mute—but, long as Valour shineth,
Or Mercy's soul at war repineth,
So long shall Erin's pride
Tell how they lived and died !

As the immortal poet, Tom Moore, apostrophized "Con of the Hundred Fights," an ancient Irish warrior whose victories the harpists and sagamores of the *Insula Sanctorum et Doctorum* also lauded in song and story, so do we, the expatriated sons of the Clan-na-Gael, mourn the loss of our matchless hero, Charles Stewart

17

Parnell. Tears for his death, sighs over his grave, sad, fond and lasting remembrances in the hearts of his people of his patriotism, his indomitable energy, and his glorious and hard-won victories, are the tributes paid the wide world over to his memory—one of the greatest apostles of human liberty that ever graced God's footstool. When the news of his sudden death was flashed to the New World by the Atlantic Cable, it was received with mingled expressions of fear and incredulity. Not a word of his illness had reached either his friends or his enemies. Like all great men, he had many of both. Doubt soon gave way to certainty, as the startling announcement posted on the bulletin boards of the newspapers throughout the country was supplemented by corroboratory despatches from some of his Irish Parliamentary colleagues. The great Leader was no more. His name, so magnetic in the cause of his beloved country, had now become a memory. Later intelligence told us that he had died at his summer home, Walsingham Terrace, Brighton, England, at half-past eleven o'clock on Tuesday night, Otcober 6, 1891, of rheumatic fever, hyperpyrexia and failure of the heart's action, at least so declared the certificate of the surgeons, not physicians, who were called in to attend him. These surgeons are R. J. Jowers, *pere et fils*, men of some admittedly local reputation in Brighton. He died in the arms of the woman he loved, Mrs.

Parnell. Mr. Parnell's step-daughter, Miss O'Shea, the elder Mr. Jowers and a faithful Irish servant girl were the only persons present at the end. He had been in bed since the previous Friday, suffering very great pain, but no one thought he was in danger of death.

Before I quote Mr. Parnell's intimate colleagues, my own personal friends, on his character and attributes, it is eminently proper that this biography of

THE UNCROWNED KING

should tell my readers what I have learned of his birth and ancestry. He was the fourth son of John Henry and Delia Tudor Parnell, and was born at Avondale, County Wicklow, Ireland, in June, 1846. In his early life he studied under Protestant Episcopal clergymen in Oxfordshire and Derbyshire. He studied at Cambridge, and a characteristic anecdote is related of his career at the University: When he was an undergraduate at Magdalen College he was caught in some peccadillo by one of the proctors and his "bulldog." He promptly knocked down the "bulldog" and ran for home. He thought he had been recognized, and feared that he would be suspended for a year, so he went to an old fellow who kept a chemist's store opposite the gate of Magdalen College, and asked him if he could imitate a black eye.

"Well, Mr. Parnell, I might, but I can't put it on in fast colors."

" But I must have a black eye."

" Well, sir," the old chemist replied, " the only way I knows of is the old-fashioned one."

"All right," said Parnell, " let her go." Thereupon the embryo Irish statesman braced himself, and the old fellow let him have it straight and hard between the two eyes. The next morning young Parnell had not only one, but two beautiful eyes of the desired color. When he was hauled up before the Dean of the college for his encounter with and ill treatment of the " bulldog," Parnell claimed that it was he himself, on the contrary, who had been subjected to ill treatment and who had got the worst of it; and as he looked as if he had, the Dean let him off scott free, reprimanding the " bulldog" for being too free with his fists. His pluck and readiness of wit thus served him in good stead, as they likewise did at subsequent portions of his career.

There's scarcely a man or woman, in this country, interested in any way in the desperate struggle made by Ireland's distinguished son and his courageous and able lieutenants, inside and outside, for that matter, of the Irish Parliamentary Party, who has not seen or heard his noble mother, Mrs. Delia Tudor Stewart Parnell, discussing with the people of the great cities of the United States the rights and wrongs of the Irish nation.

Her words were always full of life, of force, of energy, and her appearance was greeted everywhere with storms of applause. A few words from her own lips as to her personal experiences in "the great struggle" and the ancestry of her family will, I know, be most agreeable reading. Here. is what she says of herself and her family:

CHAPTER II.

The Tudors hailed from Wales. The first member of this family that ever came to this country was undoubtedly, as I heard from my grandmother, Delia Tudor, a Colonel Tudor in the British Army, during the time of the American Colonies. He is said—although I will not vouch for the accuracy of the statement—to have bought all the land on which South Boston is now located. His widow disagreed with her husband's relatives, and embarking at Plymouth, Devonshire, came to Boston with her only son, John. In those days every one did something to get a little means, to buy a few delicacies and some necessities, both of which were scarce. Mrs. Tudor had learned in Wales to make white breakfast rolls, an accomplishment of which she seemed to be the sole possessor in her vicinity. Her fame in this capacity soon spread, and by selling her rolls among her friends and neighbors she provided herself with all necessary money, and no doubt introduced the art of first-class bread baking in Boston.

My grandfather, William Tudor, was son to this boy, John Tudor. He, John Tudor, married a

24

very remarkable woman, dark-haired, dark-eyed, handsome, dignified, full of character and intelligence. John Tudor had also a beautiful sister, Elizabeth, who married a Mr. Thomas. Their married life was quite unhappy, and she died young.

My great-grandfather, John Tudor, was very close,—in fact, miserly and penurious,—but perhaps excusable in part for it, on account of the hardships he and his mother had to undergo in their early struggles, which taught him the value of money. His love of the "almighty dollar" would doubtless have deprived his own family of many necessaries of life, had not that excellent woman, by her intelligent management, been able to maintain and educate her children, to whom she was a devoted mother, self-sacrificing and generous to a fault. Her memory is revered by all her descendants. Her portrait in oil is preserved by the Tudors in Boston.

Her excellent qualities of mind and heart were strongly impressed upon her son, William Tudor, my grandfather. His public life and services have given his name honorable mention in many Biographical Dictionaries, where the reader may look them up, if desired; but they do not tell his daily and extraordinary excellencies. He was a devoted son, son-in-law, brother, husband and father. He married a half-orphan, Delia Jarvis, who is said to have been of Huguenot ancestry, of which Lord

Pomfret was the chief. She was a sprightly, beautiful and highly accomplished woman. She wrote poetry with facility, and was a skillful musician and a lovely singer. At the age of ninety she still sang sweetly. She was a delightful conversationalist, full of intelligence, anecdote and wit, with a wonderful memory. Her hair was dark auburn, her eyes deep blue, her face lovely and beaming with kind feeling for every one. Her superb and erect figure retained its commanding grace to old age. Indeed, when she had passed her ninety-first birthday she was one day walking down Pennsylvania Avenue, in Washington, when a gentleman walking behind her expressed to his companion a desire to see the face to which that exquisite figure belonged. Imagine his surprise when she suddenly turned back, and lo! it was that of his old friend, Mrs. Tudor.

No doubt her great age was attained and remarkable health preserved by the care that had been taken of her, and the sunny, happy disposition with which she met and looked upon everything. Boston was much of a seafaring town in those days, and her father, Mr. Jarvis, was so careful of her that she was not permitted to even look out of the window on certain occasions, lest she should see a drunken man or brawl. (I had never seen a drunken man, either, until I married and went to live in Ireland, and could not for a long time discover when a man was drunk.)

My grandmother sang and danced naturally, I always thought because she had French spirits. Many are the old Revolutionary songs she sang me, and the wonderful stories she told me. One ran thus :

A bow which from campaign he brought,
Herself and all beholders taught,
Though her the fairest nymph he thought
Of all that graced the plain.

Another ran :

Pretty little Cupid,
Give thy bow a twang,
Sink it in her bosom,
Let her feel some pain,
Then she'll be delighted
To be loved again.

She had also picked up some sailors' songs as the sailors passed through the streets and sang, though she could not look out at the window.

One of her own poems which made an impression upon my sympathetic, childish mind I remember. Some one had caged some birds and hung them up out of the way of the rats in the dining-room, but one after the other was killed until only one was left,—the one hanging highest on the wall. Every morning as the people came in to breakfast it would pipe plaintively, evidently pleading to be removed, but this was not understood until one morning its little cage was found empty, and grandmother wrote:

Poor little bird ! thy plaintive call,
Each morning reached the ear.
" Take me ! oh, take me from this wall,
My mortal foe is near."

Thus spoke each day thy note discreet,
   Had it been understood
Kindness had sent thee forth to greet
   Thy kindred in the wood.

———

Many who linger here below
   Surrounded by the good,
Alas! till death has laid them low
   Are never understood.

She also wrote some patriotic pieces, which were published, but generally without identity as to the author. Her nature was to accomplish good without personal notoriety. Such a contribution was published in the *Continental Intelligencer* on the occasion of the old Revolutionary soldiers assembled in the Capitol to hear John Quincy Adams' Fourth of July oration. It began:

Yes, brave old men, the story of to-day,
By one whose life-blood flowed from patriot veins, etc.

My mother, entirely ignorant of the authorship, brought in the paper, saying, "I rarely see a piece of POETRY in the newspapers, but here at last is one," and much to my grandmother's amusement and delight read the verses.

When a girl, Delia Jarvis, she was so fond of dancing, that notwithstanding the Puritan ideas of the times, she was one Sunday caught dancing a *Regodoon* to the air and words of

Neighbor, neighbor, lend me your purse,
   And I'll lend you mine to-morrow.
Neighbor, neighbor, keep your purse,
   I neither lend nor borrow.

Her oldest daughter, Emma, married Robert Hallowell Gardiner, of Maine. He took his mother's name, Gardiner, after his father's, on account of the property left him through her. His father was a near relative of Sir Benjamin Hallowell, of the British Navy, and was one of the Commissioners sent by the Governor of Massachusetts to represent the cause of the discontented States and Colonies before the British Government. During his absence the war began and the first battles of the Revolution were fought. Mr. Hallowell had immense landed estates in Maine, and prudently remained away on leave of absence until he could safely return, swear allegiance to the new Government, and thus save his extensive property.

My grandfather, William Tudor, was a Revolutionary soldier, and used to write to my grandmother from the battlefields as " My fair loyalist," (as she was opposed to the war), and subscribe himself at the close as " Your ever faithful rebel." Later, however, she espoused the cause of the " Faithful rebel."

On account of the Revolutionary War the engagement between my grandparents lasted seven years. While he was in the army, first with General Lee and then on the staff of General Washington. He was also Judge, Advocate-General of the Revolutionary Army, as he was a lawyer, trained in the office with John Adams,

His legal papers and books were burned at Washington by the British. He was opposed to all ideas of federation, and believed only in the complete independence of this country. Personally, while so good, he was impetuous and sometimes absent-minded. A story is told of him, that on one occasion when a disagreeable visitor was announced, he fled into the garden, but right through the glass of a door which he forgot to open. I spoke in the preceding pages of his being a good son in-law,—something remarkable for a special fondness to exist in this relationship, but it was so with him. He gave his mother-in-law a beautiful country home, and I had among letters preserved by my grandmother some to her while he was in Europe, in which he speaks of his desire to have the grounds beautifully arranged and planted for her. She was then the widow of Captain Young. He also spoke of the presents he had collected for the family.

On this tour he journeyed through Ireland on his way to England and to Europe, and his observations led him to predict the Irish rebellion of '96. He then spoke of the wretched clothing and the gaunt, starved look of the Irish people.

On the day that the Battle of Bunker Hill was fought, my grandmother, then a young lady, stood at the gate of her country home near Boston, and as the wounded British soldiers were being carried by, she had them brought in and attended and

comforted as best she could. Such was her sympathy and humanity that she could not bear to see
even an enemy suffer. Her lover, William Tudor,.
had been absent three days, and she thought was
in the fray; she was greatly concerned for his
safety. Imagine her fears, when a British officer,
in answer to her inquiries, and thinking she *must
be* on their side, said, "Never mind about them,
my fair young lady, we have peppered them well."

For her brave and sympathetic conduct upon
this occasion she was afterwards poetically referred
to as "the ministering angel at the gates of Boston ;" and from the day she stood there, receiving
and waiting upon the wounded patriots and
soldiers, until her death, at ninety-two, her life was
spent in serving others, regardless of the cost or
sacrifice to herself. But with all her noble-hearted
goodness and tender sympathy, she was the soul
of independence, and resisted every form of coercion, popular or personal. When the inhabitants
were forbidden to use tea in Boston, and it was
dangerous to do so, she regarded it as an invasion
of her personal rights, and got some tea by "*hook
or crook*" and openly gave a "tea party."

Notwithstanding the fact that she was so strong
in her womanhood and old age, she was so delicate
when a child that her mother and step-father, Mr.
Young, who was devoted to her, scarcely expected
to raise her. At nine years of age she was so
slight that she could easily be held out in a man's

hand.   Seldom has so strong an attachment existed
between a father and his own daughter as existed
between herself and step-father, Captain Young.
She idolized him.   He was so good to her and her
mother.   Her descendants cherish her memory
with pride and reverence.   Her portrait in oil is
with the Tudors in Boston, as is also that of my
mother, a beautiful work done by Gilbert Stewart,
soon after her marriage to my father.

The Life and Letters of John Adams contain
references and letters of my grandfather Tudor,
and letters from John Adams to John Tudor (my
great grandfather), the miser, eulogizing the great
goodness and promise of his son William, and
urging him to be more liberal toward him.

My uncle, Frederic Tudor, was called the "Ice
King."   He first discovered a means of preserving
ice so as to send it to the East Indies.   It was only
after many trials that he succeeded.   He established, with great difficulty, a trade with the West
Indies, and for many years practically controlled
the exporting of ice to Cuba.   In trying to establish this trade he first sent his cousin, then Henry
Tudor, his brother, but they failed in creating any
demand for ice.   Then my uncle Frederic char-
tered a vessel, put both himself and ice into it and
sailed for the West Indies.   I saw a letter of his
mother, beseeching him not to go, as "she was
afraid the ice would begin to melt and slide about,
from side to side, and upset the vessel!"   When

he began this ice trade, his mother, who was between sixty and seventy years of age, by her letters, written in Spanish to the Governor-General of Cuba, interested him in her son's enterprise. Frederic Tudor was afterwards presented with the thanks of the East India Company, as the ice he had shipped there proved such a boon in treating fevers in that climate.

Mrs. Tudor, his widow, in her large, elegant home in Boston, hospitably entertained my son Charles and others with him when he was in Boston, and the funeral of my daughter Fannie started from her house for the Tudor vault in Mount Auburn Cemetery. My other uncle, William Tudor, was widely known, because of his public services as soldier, statesman and journalist. He died, unmarried, in the prime of life, as Charge d'Affairs at Rio Janeiro. It is said the Emperor, Dom Pedro, consulted him more than he did his own ministers,—and Lord P. and others of the diplomatic corps said that had William Tudor lived the Emperor would not have lost his crown. One of our consuls said he could never forget his magnificent appearance. He was over six feet high, had coal black hair, and "the renowned large, dark blue, brilliant Tudor eye," as it was called in New England, which my brother and myself did not inherit.

The house of my grandparents was the daily resort of the officers of the French fleet during our country's early trials. Madame Tudor was often eulogized in Count de Segier's memoirs, who also declared the American young ladies very fascinating, and especially so Misses Emma and Delia Tudor, who had both received a finished education.

MY MOTHER, MISS DELIA TUDOR,

prior to her marriage, was called "The Belle of Boston." She mastered several languages, and spoke five of them fluently. She learned drawing and painting, composed music, and became a brilliant performer on the piano and harp. She also studied history with extraordinary avidity, and it was said by a writer in describing her, "became as familiar with abstruse sciences as the ordinary girl is with the intricacies of a spring bonnet." After finishing her school days in Boston, she went abroad, and became a recognized belle, and was quite an attraction in London society. Her piano and harp performances were pronounced superb by the best critics, and she became the guest of the best families in Europe. The sons of George the Third crowded around her piano, and were charmed no less by her music than by her native wit and independence. Her ready command of the languages may better be understood from the following story related by the wife of an English nobleman: "One evening. at the theatre in London, some gentlemen were trying to divine Miss Tudor's nationality from the different languages she spoke to the different members of the diplomatic corps and other foreigners around her. First they concluded she was Italian, then Spanish, then German, then French; and when she finally began conversing in English, one of them exclaimed, 'By Jove! she speaks English, too.'"

In the midst of this brilliant social career in London, the news of her father's financial troubles reached her and made her so unhappy that she broke away from every thing and sped back to Boston to him.

My father, Charles Stewart, is well known to history. He was born of Irish parents in Philadelphia. His mother was the niece of the Lord Mayor of London, who disinherited her when she eloped and married his father, who was a captain in the Merchant Marine, the Lord Mayor conceiving that his dignity had been compromised by this step. At twelve years of age my father was introduced to President Washington. The next year he ran away from his parents and entered the Merchant service as a cabin-boy. He rose rapidly, and when he was twenty-one he owned two vessels, which he afterwards presented as a free gift to the National Navy, which was much in need of ships. In 1798 he was commissioned a lieutenant in the navy, and two years afterwards succeeded to the command of the schooner *Experiment*. In September, 1800, he captured the French schooner *Deux Amis*, and soon after the *Diana*, besides recapturing a number of American vessels which had been taken by the French. From 1802 to 1812 he performed important services, but it was in 1815, while he sailed in command of the *Constitution*, that he covered himself with glory. He happened to fall in with the French ships-of-war, the *Cyane*, of thirty-four, and the *Levant*, of twenty-one guns, and captured them after a desperate conflict. On his return home, the Legislature of Pennsylvania presented him with a gold-hilted sword, and a gold medal was ordered for him by Congress. He had a world-wide fame, and was the only naval officer ever named for the Presidency of the United States. So much did he love active life that when placed on the retired list in 1857, on account of his advanced age, he petitioned Congress to be allowed, by special legislation, to be allowed to continue at his post, which was granted. During President Lincoln's administration he was made Admiral, and finally retired, retaining that rank. The remainder of his life was spent at Bordentown, New Jersey, where he died at the age of ninety-two.

CHAPTER III.

The occasion of their first meeting was while the *Constitution* was in Boston Harbor refitting. Grandmother gave a reception, and Captain Stewart was naturally invited. He was fascinated by my mother's beauty and accomplishments, and, as he was a man of action, lost no time in proposing, notwithstanding the fact that a note which he had confided to a friend, was then on its way carrying a proposal to the lady whom General Scott afterwards married, but, happily for my father, the bearer, "just like a man," kept the letter in his pocket and forgot to deliver it.

Naturally enough, my mother refused him; she liked him, but grandmother did not. It was said that a Duke and more than one Lord had sought her hand in vain, and perhaps grandmother was looking for something in the line of titled blood that would give her opportunity to enjoy and display her social culture. Be that as it may, my father persevered, and carried off the prize, as he always did. Delia Tudor gave her hand and heart to the young American sailor, who on more than one occasion proved himself an unequal match for John Bull. A fortune teller—now don't

37

laugh—long before had told him that he would marry the "Belle of Boston." But he could not long remain in port to enjoy the society of his charming young bride. His ship was ready all too soon, and he must tear himself away. "What shall I bring you on my return?" he asked his young bride. "Bring me a British frigate," was the reply. "I'll bring you two." Soon after this he kept his word by capturing the two vessels.

I was my father's favorite child and the oldest, being born in 1816, one year after the capture of the *Levant*, and was brought when about one year of age to his home, Montpelier, at Bordentown, New Jersey, afterwards familiarly known as "Ironsides." I had a younger brother Charles, to whom the estate descended, and after his death came to me. As children he and I were very devoted to each other and happy together, but an unfortunate occurrence which separated my father and mother, resulted in our being parted for years, he going to live with father and I remaining with mother. It happened about this way: It was during the war between Spain on the one side and Chili and Peru on the other. Father was commanding an American vessel which was supposed to be entirely neutral. Mother was on board with him. By some means a Spanish officer got aboard to save his life from the enemy, and brought letters from some one to my mother begging her to hide him, and save his life if possible.

MRS. CLAUDE PAGET.

Through the assistance of some one of the ship's officers, she was enabled to place him under the butler's charge to wash dishes and help in that capacity.

This was all without father's knowledge, and out of sympathy on the part of my mother to save the poor man's life. But the facts got out, and my father was summoned to Washington and court-martialed for violating the neutrality law. He wanted my mother to go personally and appear with him and vindicate him. She was so beautiful and eloquent that he was very proud of her, and wanted to have her defend him personally, knowing that she would have great power by her presence, but she was of a nervous nature that could not bear the shock of so appearing, and instead of *going* she wrote her vindication, which completely exonerated my father, but he could not forgive her at the time, and they separated.

Myself and Charles were thus absent from each other seven years. Soon after the occurrence I brooded much over the sadness thus occasioned, and though only ten years of age, wrote the following little song and set the words to music:

> Dost thou not think of days gone by
>   When we did play together?
> Dost thou not hear the tender sigh,
>   And oft those days remember?
> Ah, yes, I know full well that thou
>   Art thinking ever, ever
> Of happy days that did ere now
>   So cheer us all, my brother.

MY BROTHER CHARLES.

Brother Charles when he grew up engaged in extensive business pursuits, both in this country and in Europe. Early in life he became a civil engineer, and assisted in building the Reading Railroad. After his death this is what a magazine article said of him:

"While his father commanded the *Home Squadron*, he acted as his private secretary. He was also a member of the bar and had a lucrative practice. For breadth and integrity of character, manly, bearing and goodness of heart it would be hard to find his equal. He was entirely the artificer of his own fortunes and idolized by his family and friends."

My mother took me to Washington about the age of ten or eleven. We spent our winters in Washington after that. Our summers we usually spent in New York, Boston and Maine, at my mother's sisters. When I grew older we spent some summers at Newport. This is in the earlier days of Newport, when it was just beginning to be fashionable. There was not a cottage there. Everybody lived in boarding-houses. Newport people were very easily satisfied then. We got rye coffee; always got hot cakes; everywhere we went we had good buckwheat cakes. Mr. Parnell was induced by his friend, Lord Powerscourt, to travel. He was his cousin. On the steamer coming, they met Mr. and Mrs. Thomson Hankey. Mrs. Hankey was related to the Biddles of Philadelphia. The whole party came to Washington together. My mother called on Mrs. Hankey, and when the two young men heard there was a young lady in the drawing-room, they also put in an appearance. This was early in 1834. Then the whole party came to see us. The two young men were sure to come too, and on the occasion of that very first visit to us, Mrs. Hankey astonished me by beginning to quiz Mr. Parnell about his admiration for me. This was something like Benedict and Beatrice, and probably it laid the first stone, for Mr. Parnell was very shy, like many a young Englishman. His friend was not. Both were very handsome young men, but Mr. Parnell was the handsomer by far. Then they went away on different visits together, but soon separated. We went to West Point as usual. I was a great favorite with the proprietor of the West Point Hotel, and Mr. Parnell and his cousin came to West Point, too, immediately after our arrival there. I was a great favorite with the cadets. I helped them play tricks on their superior officers, and got one of them under arrest, which shocked me horridly, for I was very sensitive. I induced the proprietor of the hotel to give a ball to the cadets. I got very few dances with them, because of the persistent attentions of Lord Powerscourt and Mr. Parnell to me. Right in the midst of the dancing, which I was enjoying very much, Mr. Parnell said to me, "I hate this dancing; won't you come into another room?" However, I went into another room, as he wanted to get out of the ball-room. Well, we got into another room, where there were several other couples; so then he dragged me off to another room, with a similar fate. Then he got me out onto the piazza, and there were several couples; and then he gave vent to a John Bull oath, " Damn it," which I had not heard since I left my father's ship, which astonished me exceedingly. I began to think he was very bad tempered and became a little afraid of him. So the next morning he went out to smoke with his cousin, but soon left him smoking and hurried up to the hotel and asked me if I would not like to see Kosciusko's Retreat. Of course, as I had never seen it, I was glad to go and see it. There he proposed,—asked me to go to Ireland with him; and going away from the Retreat, we met his cousin hurrying to find out where we were. I hardly took Mr. Parnell to be serious, so I said to Lord Powerscourt very frankly, " Your cousin has just asked me to go to Ireland with him, but I don't like being lost in an Irish fog, and I am afraid he has no house there." That was my idea of Ireland. Lord Powerscourt laughed and said he "thought his cousin had a mud cabin." That was all the encouragement he gave me. Well, we had parties on horseback and different things, and they left, and we went to Lebanon to see the Shaking Quakers ; but the whole of this business at West Point gave me a violent headache which lasted for a week. This is but the beginning of the history of his perseverance, which ended in our marriage at Grace Church, New York, Dr. Taylor officiating, the 31st of May, 1835. My mother was very much opposed to the match, and she would not consent to it herself until he promised to bring me back every year to see the family. Yes, but he did not keep his promise, as he did not promise to bring the children and I was not willing to leave them.

CHAPTER IV.

IN THE VALE OF AVOCA.

Our home was made in Ireland at Avondale, County Wicklow, except when we were visiting among his friends, and when I went to Paris for the education and social advantages of my family. My mother and brother had a beautiful home in Paris. My husband was pleased to have us go there on account of the great advantages it afforded to me and to my children ; but he would not let them go to school unless I was near them.

We had eleven children born, five sons and·six daughters, all born at Avondale except Theodosia, who was born at Torquay, the place where the family first landed in England; and Henry, who was born in Paris. All born in the same room at Avondale except Anna. Five of the eleven children are now living, three daughters and two sons. Ten of them grew up to majority. Hayes died of pleurisy and an affection. of the liver at fifteen ; and I lost an infant son five months old, William Tudor, through bad vaccination. All the daughters married but Fanny and Anna, and all the sons married except John and Hayes. William died as an infant. Of those now living, Anna

AVONDALE.

is the only one that was prominent in the Land
League in Ireland.   My son John was also a
quiet worker in this country, but on account of a
nervous defect in his speech, he did very little
public speaking.   My daughter Anna usually re-
sides near London.   She has not been active in
Irish matters for some time.   Her work was prin-
cipally in the Ladies' Land League in Ireland
during the imprisonment of the members.   My
son John is now residing in Atlanta, Ga., engaged
in business in that city.   My daughter Theodosia
married Claude Paget, who is in the employ of the
British Navy, and is now with his ship in the
British Fleet at Hong Kong.   His wife, with her
infant son, is visiting among his relations.   Lord
Anglesea, the head of the family, is a cousin of
the husband of Minnie Stephens of New York.
There was not a family in England that would not
have been proud to be allied to the Parnells.   The
wedding of Mrs. Paget took place from my
daughter Delia's house in Paris, and all the near
relatives of his family went from England to it,
and thought themselves fortunate in being allied
to the ancient family of Parnell.   In this connection I wish to say that my son's family is one of
the most ancient in Great Britain, going back to a
Norman Duke, who was killed at the battle of
Hastings, on the Norman side, and, on the Eng-
-lish side, going back to the Lord High Stewarts
of England, and by marriages to the Stewarts of

Scotland and the Howards of England. My cousin, the Rév. Samuel Stewart, a missionary, who was connected with the Lispenard Stewarts of New York, used to say that the Stewart family were descended from Banquo's ghost. In the story, you know, Fleance, the son of Banquo, was saved. He fled to Paris and there he married a princess of the house of Tudor, so that the Stewarts were descended from the Tudors.

My daughter Emily married Captain Robert Dickinson, of the British Army. It was she who went to Mrs. O'Shea, immediately after her brother's death, and persuaded Mrs. O'Shea to let Charles be interred in Ireland. Mrs. O'Shea, as was very natural, did not want to part with the corpse. My daughter Emily accompanied the funeral to the cemetery, the Glasnevin, near Dublin. It is the Catholic cemetery where O'Conner was buried; though my son was buried in a piece of ground which was given to the poor.

CHAPTER V.

Speaking of my son in particular, he was born at Avondale, on the 27th of June, 1846, and was my sixth child. Very early in his life he manifested those peculiar traits of mind and character which afterwards led to his distinction. One prominent characteristic seemed to be to take the part of the oppressed. He was always ready to fight the battles of even his older brothers and sisters. In connection with this I remember an anecdote. One day he thought the nurse was too severe with his sister Anna. He got up on a table and seized his big stick and put his sister on a table, placed himself in front of her and fought off the two nurses. He was about seven or eight years old then. Another time, when I punished his sister Anna, he gave himself and me no rest until he got me to stop punishing. He kept saying, "O mamma, she'll die, she'll die!" Anna was very resolute, and Charles thought she would not yield while there was a spark of life in her.

Religiously, my son was a Protestant. His father belonged to the Church of England, and Charles was much with very religious and pious people.

My mother was Puritan on one side and Huguenot on the other.

His education was begun at home by his mother,
governess and tutor at Avondale ; afterwards he
was at school in Summersetshire, kept by a lady.
Then he was sent to a clergyman in Derbyshire,
whose wife was a very excellent woman, and took
a great pride in the education of the pupils. Then
he went to the Rev. Dr. Whiseshaw, who prepared
him for Cambridge. He then said he was the
only boy in his whole establishment whom he
could trust. The whole country bore witness to
the fidelity of his promises even when he was a
lad. He was sent to Cambridge on account of
his father having been sent there ; besides, he had
a great talent for mathematics, and that is a great
mathematical college. He said he owed to me
whatever facility he had for speaking or writing
English, and not to schools. I gave great care to
his education, requiring him to make accurate and
fine translations from the original into the English,
both in Caesar's commentaries and Virgil.

But, unfortunately, he did not have this care
from me so long as his sisters had. This possibly
explains their greater fluency in expressing themselves. I think he did not remain at college the
full term for graduation, on account of a disagree-
ment between himself and one of the professors.
He left of his own accord, as his self-respect prevented his yielding, and asking pardon where he

thought he had been unjustly treated. After
leaving college he had another private tutor at
home. He grew very rapidly, and his health was
delicate. He would have outgrown his strength
entirely but for the care I took of him. He was
always very nervous, of which I might recite many
instances but for lack of time. He afterwards
traveled in America and in Europe. After entering
upon public life his history is well known to the
world. One of the strongest traits of his character was indulgence and love of his friends. An
affection once formed with him must always remain. This is clearly shown in his course and ad-
herence in his friendship, especially towards
William O'Brien, as is shown by the following
letter, which he wrote O'Brien after the celebrated Boulogne controversy, which the world
thought had made them enemies :

FEBRUARY 11, 1890.

My DEAR O'BRIEN :—I desire to express to you
how deeply I feel the kindness and gentleness of
spirit shown to me by you throughout the negotiations. I have felt all along that I had no right
to expect from anybody the constant anxiety to
meet my views, the intense desire that all proposals claiming your sanction should be as palata-
ble as possible to me, which so distinguished your
conduct in the communications which passed between us. I know that you have forgiven much

roughness and asperity on my part, and that you have made allowances for some unreasonable conduct from me, which to anybody gifted with less patience and conciliation than yourself would have been most difficult.

I appreciate intensely the difficulties which surrounded you during these negotiations, the constant daily anxiety which would have been overwhelming to anybody possessed of less courage and devotion than yourself.

I fervently hope and believe that the prospects of Ireland are not so dark as you fear, and after a little time, having passed through the clouds and darkness, we shall again stand on our former footing—when in happier days we were comrades in arms in behalf of a united Ireland.

Dearest O'Brien, I am always yours,

CHARLES S. PARNELL.

Another instance in this connection, I might also relate. When I went to London to stop with him in 1886, I took him a poem I had written about the evicted tenants and asked him "if he or I should publish it?" He said, "Give it to dear William O'Brien to publish," which I did.

Another instance of his tenacious affection and disposition to sustain others, is shown by his relations to his wife when she was Mrs. O'Shea. Her sentiments to him were those of admiration and enthusiasm for his work, in which Captain O'Shea did not agree, he being a Liberal Unionist, while my son was a Nationalist. My son was naturally of a very chivalric character, and he had great pity for Mrs. O'Shea, as well as great admiration of her talents and of her love for his country. No Irishmen should lift a stone against Mrs. O'Shea, for she served Ireland faithfully, and that is what made Captain O'Shea so "mad."

It is but a repetition of the history of David and Abigail. Abigail went out and fed David and his men when her husband was cursing and seeking to destroy them; so Mrs. O'Shea came to the rescue of my son and his friends, whom her husband detested. Captain O'Shea was particularly angry with all the Nationalists, and being a Liberal Unionist, particularly anxious to break up the whole movement. He tried to hit what he thought was the bull's eye, other things having failed. In this connection I wish to say that I do not believe Charles could have done what he did, nor endured with his weak physical condition the eternal harassment of political life, the rigors of imprisonment, the jealousy and treachery of friends and foes alike, had it not been for the sympathy of a few women, the nearest one being Mrs. O'Shea, whose sustaining force gave him courage and helped his little remaining strength to do the mighty deeds of his last days for Ireland.

It is a matter of regret that he was not able to carry out the plans he formed in 1886 for himself, sister Emily and me to have a home near London, where we might have spent together our remaining days and assisted him in his labor. In summing up the public work that he did, I take pleasure in referring to the following facts published in 1880: First, he compelled the English government to make a grant of £170,000. Second, he caused the passage of the Seed and Potato Bill, and the Irish Relief Bill. Third, he saved the Irish tenants about ten million pounds by abatements of rent. Fourth, he called into existence the Mansion House Committee, the Marlborough Committee and the Land League Committee, by whose exertions £225,000 have been collected and spent in relieving the distressed people of Ireland. Fifth, he checked the increase of distress by the timely supply of food, fuel and clothing, thus saving hundreds of thousands of lives. Sixth, by neutralizing the Eviction Laws he prevented thousands of poor cottiers from being cast out of their hovels to die in the ditches. All this he has done in Ireland.

Then crossing the waters to America, he made Ireland known as that country was never known before, and awakened public opinion to English misrule and its direful results among the Irish farmers. Second, by his character and pure patriotism he was able to address himself to the intelligence of America, speaking in the Capitol at Washington and in the Legislative Assemblies of most of the States, thus elevating Ireland and its cause in the esteem of the best classes of the American people. Third, he raised for the relief of the suffering Irish near three million of dollars, which was forwarded through the Land League and other patriotic organizations to the sufferers. He called into existence the societies of this country which have aided Ireland. Fourth, he induced the Federal Government to send a naval ship laden with provisions to Ireland and to propose an appropriation of three hundred thousand dollars.

CHAPTER VI.

HER DAUGHTERS' LITERARY ATTAINMENTS.

Speaking of the literary attainments of my daughters, let me call attention to the *Celtic Magazine* of June and July, 1880, in which my daughter Anna wrote a continued article on "How they do in the House of Commons." In the February number of 1881 is a picture of the birthplace and old homestead of my son Charles. In the same magazine, of September, 1882, are a portrait of my father and a biographical sketch of Fanny, together with a number of her poems. Here is the most striking one of them all, one which Mr. McWade published in "The Great Irish Struggle:"

HOLD THE HARVEST.

Now are you men, or are you kine, ye tillers of the soil?
Would you be free, or evermore, the rich man's cattle, toil?
The shadow on the dial hangs that points the fatal hour—
Now *hold your own!* or, branded slaves, forever cringe and cower.

The serpent's curse upon you lies—ye writhe within the dust;
Ye fill your mouths with beggar's swill, ye grovel for a crust;
Your lords have set their blood-stained heels upon your shameful heads,
Yet they are kind—they leave you still their ditches for your beds!

Oh, by the God who made us all—the seignior and the serf—·
Rise up! and swear this day to hold your own green Irish turf!
Rise up! and plant your feet as men where now you crawl as slaves,
And make your harvest fields your camps, or make of them your graves!

The birds of prey are hovering round, the vultures wheel and swoop—
They come, the coroneted ghouls! with drum-beat and with troop—
They come to fatten on your flesh, your children's and your wives';
Ye die but once—hold fast your lands and, if ye *can*, your lives.

Let go the trembling emigrant—not such as he ye need;
Let go the lucre-loving wretch that flies his land for greed;
Let not one coward stay to clog your manhood's waking power;
Let not one sordid churl pollute the Nation's natal hour.

Yes, let them go!—the caitiff rout, that shirk the struggle now—
The light that crowns your victory shall scorch each recreant brow,
And in the annals of your race, black parallels in shame,
Shall stand by traitor's and by spy's the base *deserter's* name.

Three hundred years your crops have sprung, by murdered corpses fed—
Your butchered sires, your famished sires, for ghastly compost spread;
Their bones have fertilized your fields, their blood has fall'n like rain;
They died that ye might eat and live—God! have they died in vain?

The yellow corn starts blithely up; beneath it lies a grave—
Your father died in " Forty-eight "—his life for yours he gave;—
He died that you, his son, might learn there is no helper nigh,
Except for him who, save in fight, has sworn HE WILL NOT DIE.

The hour is struck, Fate holds the dice; we stand with bated breath;
Now who shall have our harvest fair?—'tis Life that plays with Death;
Now who shall have our motherland?—'tis Right that plays with Might;
The peasant's arms were weak indeed in such unequal fight!

But God is on the peasant's side—the God that loves the poor:
His angels stand with flaming swords on every mount and moor;
They guard the poor man's flocks and herds, they guard his ripening grain—
The robber sinks beneath their curse beside his ill-got gain.

O pallid serfs! whose groans and prayers have wearied Heav'n full long,
Look up! there is a Law above, beyond all legal wrong;
Rise up! the answer to your prayers shall come, tornado-borne,
And ye shall hold your homesteads dear, and ye shall reap the corn!

But your own hands upraised to guard shall draw the answer down,
And bold and stern the deeds must be that oath and prayer shall crown;
God only fights for those who fight—now hush the useless moan,
And set your faces as a flint and swear to Hold Your Own.

MISS FANNY PARNELL.

There is also published in the *Celtic Magazine*, a beautiful picture of "The Meeting of the Waters," celebrated in Moore's poetry, which was the first piece of poetry that I ever learned. The scene is on our place, Avondale, and just at the beginning of the vale of Avoca. I remember it is "where the bright waters meet." Avoca is formed by the meeting of Avonmore and the Avonbeg. In the August number of the magazine of 1881 is published a sketch of Kilmainham Jail, Dublin, where my son was confined, and where about eleven hundred Irishmen were imprisoned on different charges, without trial.

MY OWN PUBLIC SERVICE.

Since the beginning of my son's parliamentary career, I have interested myself deeply and actively in the Irish Land League and all Irish national movements. In fact, from the time I first placed my foot upon Irish soil in 1835, as the bride of John Henry Parnell, my heart and actions have been in sympathetic accord with all movements for the liberty and prosperity of the Irish people, for liberty and prosperity are essentially linked. But my first real public action was a public speech, that I made in Dublin, and I was nearly scared to death. I had started a series of musical and dramatic gatherings, which were called "Originals," because everything was to be of original Irish talent, even including drawings,

paintings and dance music. The ladies who came
to play brought their own original quadrilles,
waltzes, galops, etc. We had dancing after
the reading and elocution. It was in 1861, I think,
and they were to be held on Saturday afternoons.
My part was to deliver the address of welcome
which opened the series. Fully three thousand
people were present, many of them being from
the Viceroyal households. Lord Carlisle, though
unable to attend in person, was represented by
many of his aides-de-camp, whom the Irish
called "eighty-scamps" in those days. They had
a great way of changing names to suit themselves.
For instance, the *sick* and *indigent* in the hospitals
who were hard to please, used to be called the
"stiff and indignant." Besides my opening address,
I selected a portion of Emerson's poems to recite,
for I thought not only the sentiment was appropriate, but also that my opening speech was original enough for me to give them at one time.
In my speech I referred to the poem and to our
American Republic, telling the people that "it
was characteristic of the Americans to 'go ahead,'"
and that "I wanted the Irish also to strive to 'go
ahead.'" I astonished my audience, and the aides-
de-camp looked nervous. This series of literary
and dramatic readings led to the establishment of
a society of a similar nature in Dublin, particularly
for the encouragement of literature, which is still
flourishing there.

My first appearance in this country was on the occasion when Davitt was in New York, just before his return to Ireland. The gathering was held under the auspices of the Ladies' Branch of the Land League, and I, as President, had to make the first speech. The audience numbered several thousand, and I remember Mr. Davitt said that it was the first good house he had spoken to— a result achieved by the ladies stepping forward in the cause. Though I did not tremble as I stood for the first time before so big an audience, and saw the sea of faces all looking at me, and though my voice sounded firm, yet I was greatly frightened, nevertheless. But I got through it all right and spoke for nearly half an hour, though I helped myself out by a number of extracts and quotations. You can imagine how apprehensive I was about this, my first really public appearance, when I tell you that I practised for it beforehand. I was staying at the New York Hotel with my daughter at the time, and I used to rehearse in my room. I remember we had a good deal of amusement on the effect of this on the boarders who heard me, for they thought I was giving my daughter some terrible scoldings. They listened in astonishment, never having heard such a thing before.

The first piece I read to the Irish in New York was one on Union. I thought it essential on my son Charles' platform, as I thought it to be solid and individual. From a literary standpoint I have

written hardly anything except about the Irish.
My life and my thoughts have been given to this
cause, and no doubt this has much to do with turning the mind of my son so strongly in this
direction. In 1846 I wrote a poem entitled "The
Irish Exiles," being an address by the Irish exile
to his country. It was elicited by the Irish emigration on account of the great famine. It began this
way:

> Dear home of my soul, my Erin, farewell,
> My fond heart now beats to thy sorrowing knell;
> Thy glory is fled and thy spirit lies low,
> And deep the despair where hope once shed a glow.

This poem was sent to my father. He had it
published and it was copied all over the Union.
My speeches were usually impromptu or on very
few notes which nobody could understand but
myself. A long speech of mine was printed in
the *Irish Nation* of New York, about the middle
of the eighties. In 1883 I furnished an article
entitled "Incidents in Ireland and The New Irish
Nation" to the *New York Daily News* of May
13, 1883. More of my public life, and my public
speeches and writing I deem it unnecessary to
refer to. John Ridpath, the historian, once referred in complimentary terms to some of my
speeches, especially one that I delivered at Albany,
N. Y. People used to want me at the close of my
speeches to "go on," but I am of a nervous tem-
perament and found it very hard to get through
what I had already said. I deem it unnecessary to

say more of myself. I have written thus fully to show more of the foundation of my son's character. I have been disposed to literary pursuits since I was six years of age. I used to print little stories. My mother kept them all and they were sewed up in little covers, which had printed on them, "Instructive and Improving Stories for Young Children."

As said above, nearly all my writings have been with reference to Ireland. Before I close I will copy a poem that I wrote on one occasion when I was very ill. It was written about three years ago, when I was alone with my friend, Mrs. Knoud, who was devoted to me during all my illness of many weeks, and came in one day after a consultation of three physicians and told me that I was dying. I remarked that I was not dying, but the instance left an impression on my mind, which resulted in the penning of the following lines :

MALADI DU PAYS.

I'm sick; I'm sick with absence, with loneliness and grief;
I'm sick; I'm sick with weakness—age brings me no relief.
My spirit, vainly turning, seeks for some fair form I love;
Oh, God! 'Tis worse than dying, for there is no hope above.

Mother! Thy warm and tender arms reach to me from the past.
Brother! Thine, strong and circling, were too great, too good to last.
Father! Tho' knowing little of thy grand old love and-truth,
My spirit's radiance answered thine e'en from my earliest youth.

Husband! whose simple vow formed an undercurrent strong,
Whereon my life could speed unharmed amid a happy throng.
Children! like loving flowers, voices like living songs.
Immortal music! still I crave your soft and gentle cheers,
But my heart grows faint with sobbing, my eyes dim with the tears.
Ah! what a goodly lot was mine! What sweetness was therein!

Sweet in the very roses—in Eden without sin—
I quench my thirst with bitterness—no light is in my cloud,
My only hope that time will make of grief my very shroud.

I'm crushed; I'm crushed and writhing, I lie so lone and low,
The idle wind that touches seems to smite me as a blow,
'Tis chilling to my soul—chill as an ice-bound breath,
Chill as that tyrant, that despair—chill as the words of Death !

Oh, the laughter, song and dance, when my spirit, like a bird,
Flew forth on friendship's greeting—flew forth on love's sweet word—
A denizen from heaven sent, above the world of care ;
Lightly it pressed the cloud, pressed light e'en the very air,
For it all things were pure and sweet, it was so true and fond ;
The present seemed a heaven, none more fair could seem beyond.

My habits have always been very studious since quite young, especially at night, being the quiet time ; my custom is to begin to write when everybody goes to bed, when only the ghosts and the rats are about. I frequently begin after midnight and write until the dawn of the morning. For years I have had a large correspondence with my friends, and I answer their letters at night. I rarely get more than three or four hours sleep out of the twenty-four. One thing remarkable about myself, is my eyesight. Though I am now nearly seventy-six years of age, I have never needed to wear glasses. This remarkable fact also applies to my mother and my grandmother. My grandmother died at ninety-two without ever having used spectacles, and my mother at seventy-five.

"OLD IRONSIDES," MY PRESENT HOME.

"Old Ironsides," occupying a prominent point overlooking the Delaware at Bordentown, N. J., is the same house which used to be called "Mont-pelier." The old mansion was bought in 1816 by my father. It was then an immense cottage, with a basement, parlor floor and garret. My father brought me here as an infant in 1817. This was his home from that time till his death. The nickname "Old Ironsides," given my father, came from the ship *Constitution*, which he commanded in the United States Navy. It afterwards attached itself to and still designates this place. The title was also given him because it was so applicable to himself, so strong and active, and living to such a great age. He died at the age of ninety-two years. When he was eighty-five years old he ran up a tree after a boy who was stealing his apples. The boy went out on a branch and my father followed him. The branch was not strong enough and both came to the ground without hurting either.

I am often asked why I remain on the old homestead—in this big lonesome house alone. My answer is, to take care of it for my family, hoping and believing it will be valuable for them when they want it. I desire to preserve it in the family from the fact that it is the home of my childhood and the birthplace of my only brother, Charles, now dead. Also, because of the fact that my father lived here for more than half a century, and around it cling all the fond recollections of my infancy and early childhood. Sitting at the window in my old age I look out upon the placid

waters of the majestic Delaware, flowing to the
sea with the same graceful curve around the
grounds, so beautiful and grand, looking almost as
they did when my brother and I in early childhood
played together here.   The old cherry tree which
we used to climb and pick the fruit from is still
standing—my eyes are looking upon it now.   These
ties are too sacred and too dear to my heart to
give up in my declining years.   These facts, aside
from the belief that the property will some day be
valuable to my impoverished descendants in
Europe, make it dearer to me.   I cannot leave it.

Times are growing to be worse and worse in
Europe, and this in after years may be their only
asylum.   For this reason only, I cling desperately
to the old home.   I have written this sketch for
the life of my idolized son, who came to his untimely death through over-exertion in behalf of
his idolized country.   I have written it at the
request of the publishers, who assure me that in
giving his life and public service to the country,
they are doing so with the idea of holding up his
virtues and beneficent deeds in a true light to the
world.   Whatever else I may have done in life in
giving such a son as this to the Irish poor, I feel
that I have contributed to humanity a blessing and
to Ireland a boon, that the lapse of coming years
can never efface.   If he has planted in the hearts
of the Irish people the ideas of liberty and of
union, which shall lead them finally from under the

thralldom which has cursed them for the centuries gone by, I shall only be happy and satisfied to have paid the cost which has wrung from my heart many bitter tears and taken from me the pride of my life in the prime and glory of his manhood. For many years I have lived alone, so far as the members of my immediate family are concerned. My daughter Fanny spent a few years with me here, but the rest of my children have been, by the hand of Providence, kept at a post of duty remote from me, or were removed by death.

To the friends of Liberty and the Irish people, I bequeath my life and the memory of the past.

CHAPTER VII.

ANNA AND FANNY PARNELL'S WORK.

IT was, I think, on or about January 1st, 1882, that Miss Anna Parnell was first brought in a prominent manner to public attention, here and elsewhere. The Gladstone Coercion Government had expressly forbidden the holding of Irish political or other meetings, threatening those who participated in them with arrest and imprisonment. In defiance of these threats she presided over a largely attended meeting of the central body of the Ladies' League, in Dublin, on the first day of the year. On the following day, as if to mark the citizens' approval of her intrepidity, the freedom of the city of Dublin was voted to John Dillon and her distinguished brother. Many of her literary efforts have been published in this country and in Ireland and England. It is due to her to say that her works were almost entirely, like those of her gifted and charming sister, Fanny, devoted to the Irish cause. In it their young lives were enlisted, and no danger was too great, no risks too perilous to swerve them in the least from what they felt to

70

be more than a duty. Their devotion to Ireland
manifested itself in every act. She died suddenly
at Bordentown, N. J., July 19th, 1882. Her
patriotic mother says of her: "While I was in
Ireland, Fanny went out but little in society, being
so young; but Lord Carlisle always said she was
the loveliest in the room whenever she appeared,
and the beauty of her complexion was such that
Henry Doyle, the brother of Richard Doyle, who
illustrated 'Punch,' said it fairly lit up the boxes
where she sat at the theatre. She went to reside
with her sister Delia, Mrs. Thompson, in Paris,
and there made an immense sensation. Accounts
of her wit and beauty appeared in the *Figaro* of
that day. Her aunt, Lady Howard, Belgrave
Square, London, invited her to stop with her.
One day, after Fanny's arrival, on returning from
riding in the park with her uncle, the footman
came down the steps and said that Lady Howard
was dead. After my establishment in Temple
Street was broken up, I took my three younger
daughters with me to my brother's in Paris.
Fanny studied painting in oils there and my brother
did all in his power by giving parties and having
receptions to render Fanny's stay with him
delightful. His carriage and horses were at our
service. People said Fanny was destined to be a
grande Dame, the wife of some great character,
taking an active part both in diplomatic and political life. Diplomatists surrounded her, entranced

by her flow of sparkling wit, her beautiful style,
'like that of a princess' they said. She had a
systematic routine of occupation and cultivated her
talents. She thought nothing of her dress, but
let me dress her as I liked. She took part in
tableaux with great effect. She appeared once
as the Angel at the Gates of Paradise. A wealthy
gentleman, afterwards made a Duke by the
Emperor Napoleon, persisted for two years in trying to get Fanny to accept him. My brother's
reception rooms were always full of visitors, and
the file of young Frenchmen was like that at a
regal drawing room. I took her out in London,
too, for a few months. Then my dear brother
became ill and died at Rome and I had to come
to this country to administer his property. My
son Charles, always so kind and careful, would
not let me come alone, but sent Fanny with me.
Our stay in America has, with few exceptions,
been terrible and heartrending, to none more a
detriment than to poor Fanny. Here she got
malaria. Here her nerves gave way. Here she
died of exhaustion and a weak heart after walking
through the hot sun to provide entertainment for
Mr. Michael Davitt and Mr. W. Redmond, whom
she had invited to Ironsides. She begged me not
to return here then as she wanted to have an undis-
turbed talk with Davitt. Her one continual
thought was her brother, her country, Ireland, and
the poor Irish, and the Irish movement. When I

came back she said to me with extreme distress and terror: 'O Mama, Davitt hates Charlie!' I said, 'Oh, no, my dear, you mistake.'"

A LOVELY HEROINE.

An accomplished writer in London *Truth* says of Miss Anna Parnell: " In snowy weather Miss Parnell used to wear out-of-door skirts of Bloomer shortness, and Wellington boots. She was a girl of a nervous, resolute disposition—wayward, a little snappish, and absolute mistress of the house; but she was liked by humble neighbors, with whom, in their trials, she often commiserated. Her mother and elder sisters were frequent absentees, and her brothers were away at school. The late Mr. Parnell read and thought a good deal, administered justice as a magistrate in a fair and benignant way. Had he been a person of active habits, Miss Anna's destiny would have taken another shape. From infancy she had been troubled with a good deal of febrile energy, which she took from the American side of the house. Unhappily for her, no outlet by which she could work it off was afforded to her. The rector of the parish and his wife were well-intentioned persons, but purse-proud, narrow-minded Philistines. Miss Anna thought them humbugs. They were unable to perceive that she had some fine qualities, and ascribed her marked individuality to bad American form. On the whole, she

appeared to them an undesirable young lady for
their son to fall in love with, and they were afraid
two pretty daughters of the wax-doll type would
not be improved by associating with her. They
might as well have feared the example of a
mountain goat upon sheep reared in a grassy
park. As the curate's wife was in the unfortunate
position of the little woman that lived in a shoe,
she did not venture to strike up a friendship with
a girl who was counted eccentric, self-willed and
ungenteel at the rectory. Miss Anna had no
intimate friendship to soften a nature in which
there was a good deal of steel, heated too often
by a brooding fancy. The persons of her age
and sex in the neighborhood who inspired her
with most sympathy were not on her social plane.
They were the daughters of one Commeford, a
rich miller and freeholder, whose picturesque
grounds were only separated from Avondale by
those of the glebe house."

The Misses Commeford were Roman Catholics,
which, in Ireland more than twenty years ago,
was a barrier to intimate acquaintance with
Protestant families. They were open-hearted
and winsome girls, who hunted daringly on clever
horses, and had all the accomplishments which
are to be acquired in a first-class conventional
school in Dublin. But they had bounded minds,
which were unable to take in Carlyle, or soar to
transcendental heights with Emerson. "The

Bride of Abydos" was not too old fashioned to excite their enthusiasm. Anna Parnell could not endure the meek heroine of that poem, after whom so many French dogs are called. She was a reader, even then, of New York and Boston journals, and had dipped into the lectures of American oratoresses who stood on the equal rights platform. The mental inferiority to which women were condemned by ecclesiastical authority was accepted as a matter of course by the miller's pleasant daughters, but it galled Miss Anna and chilled her sympathy for them. If they had revolted against St. Paul she would have been their close friend in spite of the castle prejudices that stood between her and them.

Mrs. Parnell denied the alleged perfection of the British Constitution, and the young Parnells imbibed Fourth-of-July ideas about George III., and other members of the royal family, with whose inherited infirmities they were made acquainted. Visits to the States, and intercourse with American relatives and friends, gave an un-English bias to their minds, and opened their eyes to see many things in their native land which might otherwise have remained unperceived. Miss Anna was old enough when Mrs. Beecher Stowe was being lionized in Europe to take an interest in the controversy aroused in America by a message on the slavery question from the Duchess of Sutherland and other noble ladies to

their sisters in the United States. There was
a fearful beam in the eye of Stafford House—the
Sutherland evictions, the memory of which was
still fresh in America. Miss Parnell, in different
harangues to Irish peasants, has charged the
late Lord Carlisle with having advised the landlords of the sister isle to imitate the Sutherland
example in clearing off tenants and converting
their estates into grazing farms. That amiable
nobleman had not witnessed the evictions and
had seen the sheep-runs on his brother-in-law's
North of Scotland estates. If he had known
what inhuman cruelty had been practised, he
would have been the last man in the world to
say to the Whig nobles who possess tracts of
land in Ireland: "Make this country the teeming
mother of innumerable flocks and herds." Charles
Stewart Parnell is bound to Ireland by the Avondale estate. Miss Anna's attachment to the
country and the people had hindered her from
settling in the United States, where she had a
brother and sister. The former owns in Alabama
the largest peach orchard in the world. Although "a woman of steel," the Home Ruleress
has poetic sensibilities. She loved the old trees
at Avondale, the river in the deep glen, the weeping sky with short sunbursts, and the whistling
wind, which to her ears is full of music. The
vale of Avoca is seen by her through a prism
colored by the national melodist. Since Moore's

time, great has been the deterioration of the
scenery there. "The purest of crystal" is sullied
by water pumped from lead and copper mines.
"The brightest of green" has been effaced by
the mounds of rubbish which the miners cast up.
Miss Parnell has the prompt intellect of a New
Englander. Her ideas rapidly generate actions;
but if her head is hard it is not cruel. Excitable
nerves dominate her. "She has the courage of
her opinion." "You surely don't think they
would dare to shoot him?" said an English
tourist, who had got by accident into a conversation with her about a fearless and almost ruthless
agent.

"I'm afraid not," was the terrible reply. "In
these parts anger evaporates in threats."

Her zeal in accomplishing her self-appointed
mission eats her up. There have been occasions
on which she has had reason to congratulate herself on her remarkable slenderness. However
tired a horse may be, he is always strong enough
to carry Miss Parnell. In the reign of Forster
she hid from constables supposed to be in pursuit of her by merely standing behind a poplar
tree. On one occasion she went to witness two
evictions and to harangue the martyrs of landlordism and their friends. The cottages from
which the tenants were to be ejected faced each
other, but were on opposite sides of a large river.
A bridge was at some distance below them.

After the first part of the sub-sheriff's task was got through, he instructed the policemen not to let Miss Anna Parnell nor any of her following over the bridge. This done, he proceeded to cross it himself. He was apprehensive that she might call upon the victims and those who came to sympathize with them to oblige him to beat a hasty retreat. But the excited lady was not to be baulked. She, for a moment, looked keenly at the strong-flowing river. No boat was visible. A notion flashed across her brain. "Is there any one here," she demanded, "who has ever waded in rainy weather like this to the other side?" A tall fellow, in knee-breeches and a patched-up coat, stepped forward to answer in the affirmative. "How deep is it in the deepest place?" asked Miss Anna. "Up to my arm-pit." "Do you know how to swim?" "I do, your ladyship." "So that if you lose your balance and fall you can still keep your head above water?" "That I can." "Well, put me sitting on your shoulder and wade over with me." The man was only too proud to obey. He gallantly descended into the river, assuring Miss Parnell that she weighed no heavier than a feather. She was at the second cottage before the sub-sheriff reached it. During her manifestly dangerous passage through the river nobody thought of the evictions. Her skirts were drenched, for the water was up in some parts to the man's chin. It seemed miraculous that both were not swept away. She was greeted on landing with cries of "Long life to your ladyship!" This action, much more than her orations, explains her influence with the common people. So long as the Avondale Home Ruleress keeps in the van of the Nationalist army, her brother will not be thrown over by the advanced section of the Land League, because she has numbers on her side.

"My son was just then out of prison. It was Fanny who induced me to help the Irish Land League in every way possible to me. She was one of those who begged her brother to come to this country. The last year of her life she said she would never forgive herself for having prevailed on her brother to come to America. She made a trip through New York and other States and Canada in the interest of the Ladies' Land League. She seemed then strong the autumn before her death. She spoke with great delight of the honesty, fervor and kindness of the Canadian Irish Land Leaguers, and thought them much more zealous and earnest than the American members of the order.

"Not being able to lecture much, she continued to write and to reply to all letters to her concerning the Irish Land League, a great task. She kept up a busy correspondence with her sister Anna, then in the Irish National League in Dublin. Certainly a great difference between her happy, peaceful time in Dublin, her brilliant time in Paris and London, and her time of devotion in aiding her brother's movement, often doing the work of her friends in addition to her own.

"She threw herself out of her social sphere, like her brother, just at the time when she might have made a great home, had loving ones about her, and chosen enjoyments, interests and occupations wherein her great talents, which amounted to genius, would have shown pre-eminent and gained celebrity for her; where her pen would have been useful, honorable and profitable in many ways. She was almost miraculously gifted with penetration, knowledge of character, wisdom, decision, strength of mind and a great, a generous spirit free from fault or weakness. Her unselfishness and benevolence were wonderful. Such perfect beings die young. Their path is one of undiminished lustre that can end only in Heaven and that soon."

Tributes to the memory of the young songstress, who was so suddenly cut off in the bloom of her youth, appeared in prose and verse in the daily newspapers and in the weekly and monthly periodicals and magazines published here, in Europe and in the Australian colonies. Branches of the Land League everywhere met and heard sympathetic speeches and passed resolutions, all in the same sentiment, regretful of her loss, grateful and appreciative of her continuous and unselfish services in the cause of Irish freedom. A few of the poetic effusions, humble violets on her grave, will give our readers a faint idea of the estimation in which she was held.

FANNY PARNELL.

Died July 20, 1882.

BY PATRICK SARSFIELD CASSIDY.

Dead? Oh, it can't be—it must not be so—
   No; the blurred print but mocks our dull eyes;
For our spirits refuse to acknowledge the blow,
   Or our minds to such loss realize.
Our hearts turn rebels to such a decree,
   E'en the hand that approved were Divine—
What! she, our young Priestess—but no, it can't be—
   Stricken down at the steps of the shrine.

Tell us not, tell us not, that the form we have loved,
   So instinct with young resolute life,
And the genius that lit up our cause, are removed
   From our side in the thick of the strife.
A warrior's heart in a maiden's frail form—
   Strength softened by womanly grace—
Was hers; and a spirit to ride on the storm
   When it broke on the foe of our race.

No thought in the limitless spaces of mind,
   No pain in the heart's widest zone,
Was farther away than that she who had twined
   Herself round our hearts as our own
Should sink in death's sleep in a moment like this,
   When the battle-wave swells at full tide,
And Liberty's dawn is ascending to kiss
   The land of her love and her pride.

Oh, it surely can't be that her spirit has pass'd
   From the struggle in hour so supreme,
When the glorious result that her prescience forecast
   In the future-deciphering dream

Of the poet, seems nearing a truth—
  When the transfiguration's at hand
Of a people, enslaved beyond mercy or ruth,
  Rising up as a free-born Land!

Has she, whose young soul was our battle's bright star,
  That flashed living light through the gloom,
That warmed us and thrilled us in righteousness' war,
  Has she gone to the gloom of the tomb?
Has the light-flashing banner she bore in the throng
  Of the conflict gone down in the dust?
Does the malice of fate that pursued us so long
  Seek to break the last chord of our trust?

It can't be, and my heart from its innermost core
  Refuses its faith to the tale;
Were it so I would hear from her Erin's far shore
  Every wave on the strand give a wail;
And the gloom that would shadow the face of her land
  Would in sympathy seek out my soul,
And plunge it in gloom beyond words' poor command,
  And grief beyond powers of control.

Ah, no, it can't be that her spirit, so rare,
  With liberty's lightnings aflame,
With courage that mocked the grim face of despair,
  And put cowardly doubtings to shame—
It can't be that it's gone ere her eyes had beheld
  The glory of Erin reborn—
That her requiem bell in our hearts should be knell'd
  'Mid the salvos of Liberty's morn.

The flash of her spirit, the sweep of her powers,
  The *verve* and fire of her song,
The lightnings she hurled against Tyranny's towers,
  The blows that she dealt unto wrong—
Are they lost to our cause when the beautiful face
  Of success flushes fair on our flag—
When the sun-blaze she yearned for bids fair to replace
  The cloud upon mountain and crag?

Have the lips—truly touched by celestial fire—
    That sung Erin's deep agony,
Been hushed when the poets, in jubilee choir,
    Are weaving the song of the free?
Is the ear stricken deaf that but loved Erin's praise
    In the days of her squalor and shame,
When the harpings and shoutings and banner's bright blaze
    Give welcome to freedom and fame?

Personified spirit of Erin! not dead
    Art thou unto us and thy land;
No grave 'mid the earth-damps, no vault's narrow bed,
    Could hold thee in mortal command.
Yes; your heart in its cere-clothes would quiver and toss
    Till it rent them apart, and you stood,
Transfigured and glorified, looking across
    The battle's wrong-whelming flood!

No, thou art not dead, beloved sister of song;
    Thy spirit and Erin's are one,
And active still must be thy war upon wrong
    'Till the centuried crimes are undone.
The brain that fed ours shall continue to feed—
    The genius that guided to guide—
Oh, passionate priestess of Liberty's creed,
    Such spirit as thine never died!

                —New York, *July*, 1882.

THE DEAD SINGER.

BY JOHN BOYLE O'REILLY, IN THE PILOT.

"She is dead!" they say; "she is robed for the grave; there are lilies
    upon her breast:
Her mother has kissed her clay-cold lips, and folded her hands to rest;
Her blue eyes show thro' the waxen lids: they have hidden her hair's
    golden crown;
Her grave is dug, and its heap of earth is waiting to press her down."

"She is dead!" they say to the people—her people for whom she sung,
Whose hearts she touched with sorrow and love, like a harp with life-
    chords strung.

And the people hear—but behind their tear they smile as though they
    heard
Another voice like a Mystery proclaim another word.

"She is not dead!" it says to their hearts; "true Singers can never
    die:
Their life is a voice of higher things unseen by the common eye;
The truths and the beauties are clear to them, God's right and the human
    wrong,
The heroes who die unknown, and the weak who are chained and scourged
    by the strong."
And the people smile at the death-word, for the mystic voice is clear:
"THE SINGER WHO LIVED IS ALWAYS ALIVE: WE HEARKEN AND
    ALWAYS HEAR."

And they raise her body with tender hands and bear her down to the
    main,
They lay her in state on the mourning ship, like the lily-maid Elaine;
And they sail to her isle across the sea, where the people wait on the
    shore
To lift her in silence with heads all bared to her home for evermore—
Her home in the heart of her country—Oh, a grave among our own
Is warmer and sweeter than living on in the stranger lands alone!

No need of a tomb for the Singer! Her fair hair's pillow now
Is the sacred clay of her country, and the sky above her brow
Is the same that smiled and wept on her youth, and the grass around is
    deep
With the clinging leaves of the shamrock that cover her peaceful sleep.
Undreaming there she will rest and wait, in the tomb her people make,
Till she hears men's hearts like the seeds in Spring all stirring to be
    awake,
Till she feels the motion of souls that strain till the bands that bind them
    break;
And then, I think, her dead lips will smile and her eyes be raised to see,
When the cry goes out to the Nations that the Singer's land is free!

CHAPTER VIII.

THE PATRIOT'S CAREER.

Of all his old-time friends and honored colleagues, few knew more of Charles Stewart Parnell's history and inner life than the Hon. T. P. O'Connor, who says of him:

Grip and grit: in these two words are told the secret of Mr. Parnell's marvellous success and marvellous hold over men. When once he has made up his mind to a thing he is inflexible; immovable by affection or fear or reasoning. He knows what he wants, and he is resolved to have it. Throughout his career he has often had to make bargains; he has never yet been known to make one in which he gave up a single iota which he could hold. But it takes time before one discovers these qualities. In ordinary circumstances Mr. Parnell is apparently the most easy-going of men. Though he is not emotional or effusive, he is genial and unaffected to a degree; listens to all comers with an air of real deference, especially if they be good talkers; and apparently allows himself to follow implicitly the guidance of those who are speaking to him. He is for this reason one of the most agreeable of companions, never raising any difficulties about trifles, ready to subject his will and his convenience to that of others; amiable, unpretending, a splendid listener, a delightful host. But all the softness and the pliancy disappear when the moment comes for decisive action. After days of apparent wavering, he suddenly becomes granite. His decision is taken, and once taken is irrevocable. He goes right on to the end, whatever it may be. In some respects, indeed, he bears a singular resemblance to General Grant; he has his council of war, and nobody could be a more patient or more respectful listener, and, ordinarily, nobody more ready to have his thinking done for him by others. But when affairs reach a great climax, it is his own judgment upon which he acts, and upon that alone.

Mr. Parnell has not a large gift of expression. He hates public speaking, and avoids a crowd with a nervousness that sometimes appears almost feminine. He likes to steal through crowded streets in a long, heavy Ulster and a small smoking-cap that effectually conceal his identity, and when he is in Ireland is only happy when the quietness of Avondale secludes him from all eyes but those of a few intimates. From his want of any love of expressing himself, it often happens that he leaves a poor impression on those who meet him casually. More than one man has thought that he was little better than a simpleton, and their mangled reputations strew the path over which the Juggernaut of Parnell's fortunes and genius has mercilessly passed. He is incapable

HON. T. P. O'CONNOR, M. P

of giving the secret of his power, or of explaining the reasons of his decisions.　He judges wisely, with instinctive wisdom, just as Millais paints; he is always politically right, because, so to speak, he cannot help it.　This want of any great power and any great desire to expose the line of reasoning by which he has reached his conclusions has often exposed Parnell to misunderstandings and strong differences of opinion even with those who respect and admire him.　The invariable result is that, when time has passed, those who have differed from him admit that they were wrong and he right, and once more have a fatalistic belief in his sagacity.　Often he does not speak for days to any of his friends, and is seldom even seen by them.　He knows the enormous advantage sometimes of pulling wires from an invisible point. During this absence his friends occasionally fret and fume and wonder whether he knows everything that is going on ; and, when their impatience has reached its climax, Parnell appears, and lo! a great combination has been successfully laid, and the Irish are within the citadel of some time-honored and apparently immortal wrong.　Similarly it is with Parnell's nerve.　In ordinary times he occasionally appears nervous and fretful and pessimistic; in the hour of crisis he is calm, gay, certain of victory, with the fanaticism of a Mussulman, unconscious of danger, with a blindness half boyish, half divine.

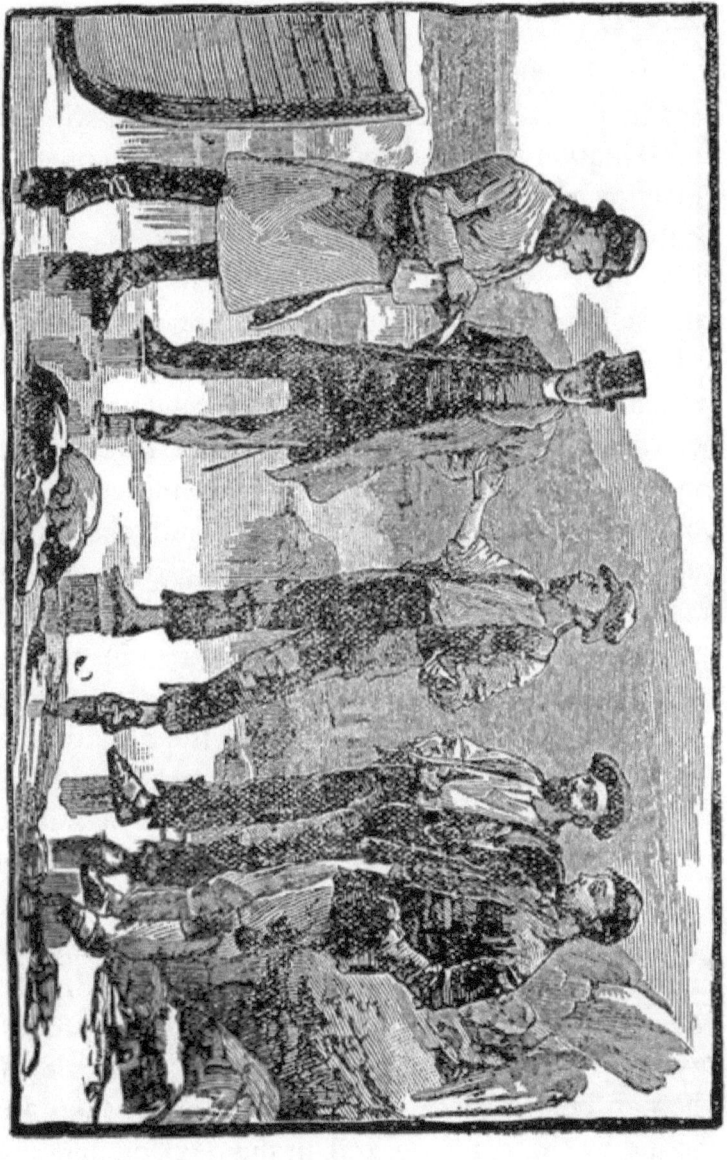

DESTITUTE FISHERMEN SOLICITING A LOAN.

Mr. Parnell is not a man of large literary reading, but he is a severe and constant student of scientific subjects, and is especially devoted to mechanics. It is one of his amusements to isolate himself from the enthusiastic crowds that meet him everywhere in Ireland, and, in a room by himself, to find delight in mathematical books. He is a constant reader of engineering and other mechanical papers, and he takes the keenest interest in machinery. It is characteristic of the modesty and, at the same time, scornfulness of his nature, that all through the many attacks made upon him by gentlemen who wear their hearts upon their sleeves, he has never once made allusion to his own strong love of animals; but to his friends he often expressed his disgust for the outrages that, during a portion of the agitation in Ireland, were occasionally committed upon them. He did not express these sentiments in public, for the good reason that he regarded the outcry raised by some of the Radicals as part of the gospel of cant for which that section of the Liberal party is especially distinguished. To hear a man like Mr. Forster refusing a word of sympathy, in one breath, for whole housefuls of human beings turned out by a felonious landlord to die by the roadside, and, in the next, demanding the suppression of the liberties of a nation because half-a-dozen of cattle had their tails cut off; to see the same men who howled in delight be-

EVICTED—HOMELESS.

cause the apostle of a great humane movement,
like Mr. Davitt, had been sent to the horrors of
penal servitude, shuddering over the ill-usage of
a horse, was quite enough to make even the most
humane man regard this professed love of animals as but another item in the grand total of
their hypocrisy. Mr. Parnell regards the lives of
human beings as more sacred than even those of
animals, and he is consistent in his hatred of op-
pression and cruelty wherever they may be found.
His sympathies are with the fights of freedom
everywhere, and he often spoke in the strongest
terms of his disgust for the butcheries in the
Soudan, which the Liberals, who wept over Irish
horses, and Irish cows, received with such Olym-
pian calm. In 1867 the ideas that had been sown
in his mind in childhood first began to mature.
His mother was then, as probably throughout her
life, a strong Nationalist, and so was at least one
of his sisters. Thus Mr. Parnell, in entering upon
political life, was reaching the natural sequel of
his own descent, of his early training, of the
strongest tendencies of his own nature. It is
not easy to describe the mental life of a man who
is neither expansive nor introspective. It is one
of the strongest and most curious peculiarities
of Mr. Parnell, not merely that he rarely, if ever,
speaks of himself, but that he rarely, if ever,
gives any indication of having studied himself.
His mind, if one may use the jargon of the

Germans, is purely objective. There are few
men who, after a certain length of acquaintance,
do not familiarize you with the state of their
hearts or their stomachs or their finances; with
their fears, their hopes, their aims. But no man
has ever been a confidant of Mr. Parnell. Any
allusion to himself by another, either in the exuberance of friendship or the design of flattery,
is passed by unheeded; and it is a joke among
his intimates that to Mr. Parnell the being
Parnell does not exist.

It is plain from the facts we have narrated
that Parnell's great strength is one which lies in
his character rather than in his attainments. Yet
his wonderful successes won in the face of numerous and most bitter opponents testify to
mental abilities of a very high order. Mr. Gladstone has said of him, "No man, as far as I can
judge, is more successful than the hon. member
in doing that which it is commonly supposed that
all speakers do, but which in my opinion few
really do—and I do not include myself among
those few—namely, in saying what he means to
say." Mr. Parnell is moreover very strong in
not saying the thing which should not be said.
Too many of his countrymen, it may be safely as-
serted, are of that hasty and impulsive tem-
perament which may betray, by a word prema-
turely spoken, some point which should have been
held from the enemy, and which might easily

have been made, at some later time, a stronghold
of defence in the parliamentary contest. Mr.
Parnell has few qualities which have hitherto
been associated with the idea of a successful Irish
leader. He has now become one of the most
potent of parliamentary debaters in the House of
Commons, through his thorough grasp of his
own ideas and through his exact knowledge of
the needs of his country. But Mr. Parnell has become this in spite of himself. He retains to this
day, as we have before stated, an almost invincible repugnance to public speaking; if he can,
through any excuse, be silent, he remains silent,
and the want of all training before his entrance
into political life made him, at first, a speaker
more than usually stumbling. His complete success in overcoming, not indeed his natural objection to public speaking, but the difficulty with
which his first speeches were marked, affords one
of the many proofs of his wonderful strength and
singleness of purpose. It is not a little remarkable that his first successful speech was criticised for its vehemence and bitterness of tone,
and for the shrillness and excessive effort of the
speaker's voice. It seems probable that the
embarrassing circumstances of his position while
addressing an unsympathizing body of legislators,
combined with a sense of his own inexperience,
may have produced the appearance of excessive
vehemence of manner.

Nature has stamped on the person of this remarkable man the qualities of his mind and tem-
perament. His face is singularly handsome, and
at a first glance might even appear too delicate
to be strong. The nose is long and thin and
carved, not moulded; the mouth is well cut; the
cheeks are pallid; the forehead perfectly round,
as round and as striking as the forehead of the
first Napoleon; and the eyes are dark and un-
fathomable. The passer-by in the streets, taking
a casual look at those beautifully chiselled
features and at the air of perfect tranquillity,
would be inclined to think that Mr. Parnell was a
very handsome young man, who probably had
graduated at West Point, and would in due time
die in a skirmish with the Indians. But a closer
look would show the great possibilities beneath
this face. The mouth, especially the under lip,
speaks of a grip that never loosens; the eye,
when it is fixed, tells of the inflexible will beneath; and the tranquillity of the expression is
the tranquillity of the nature that wills and wins.
Similarly with his figure. It looks slight almost
to frailty; but a glance will show that the bones
are large, the hips broad, and the walk firm; in
fact, Mr. Parnell tramps the ground rather than
walks. The hands are firm, and even the way
they grasp a pencil has a significance.

This picture of Parnell is very unlike the portraits which have been formed of him by the

imagination of those who have never met him.
When he was first in the storm and stress of the
era of obstruction, he used to be portrayed in the
truthful pages of English comic journalism with a
battered hat, a long upper lip, a shillelah in his
hand, a clay pipe in his caubeen. Even to this
day portraits after this fashion appear in the
lower-class journals that think the caricature of
the Irish face the best of all possible jokes. Parnell is passionately fond of Ireland; is happier
and healthier on its soil than in any other part of
the world, and is almost bigoted in the intensity
of his patriotism. But he might easily be taken
for a native of another country. Residence for
the first years of his life in English schools has
given him a strong English accent and an essentially English manner; and from his American
mother he has got, in all probability, the healthy
pallor, the delicate chiselling, the impassive look,
and the resolute eye that are typical of the children of the great Republic.

Such is the man in brief who to-day is perhaps
the most potent personality in all the many nations and many races of the earth. The Russian
Czar rules wider domains and more subjects; but
his sway has to be backed by more than a million
armed men, and he passes much of his time shiv-
ering before the prospect of a sudden and awful
death at the hands of the infuriated among his
own people. The German is a more multitudi-

nous race than the Irish and almost as widely
scattered; but Bismarck requires also the protection of a mighty army and of cruel coercion laws,
and the German who leaves the Fatherland regards with abhorrence the political ideas with
which Bismarck is proud to associate his name.
Gladstone exercises an almost unparalleled sway
over the minds, hearts, imaginations of Englishmen; but nearly one-half of his people regard
him as the incarnation of all evil; and shallow-
pated lieutenants, great only in self-conceit, dare
to beard and defy and flout him. But Parnell has
not one solitary soldier at his command; the jail
has opened for him and not for his enemies, and
except for a miserable minority he is adored by
all the Irish at home, and adored even more fervently by the Irish who will never see—in some
cases who have never seen—the shores of the
Green Isle again. In one way or another,
through intermixture with the blood of other
peoples, the Irish race can lay claim to some
twenty millions of the human race. Out of all
these twenty millions the people who do not regard Parnell as their leader may be counted by
the few hundreds of thousands. In cities separated from his home or place of nativity by oceans
and continents, men meet at his command, and
spill their money for the cause he recommends.
Meetings called under his auspices gather daily
in every one of the vast States of America, in

Canada, in Cape Colony; and the primeval woods
of Australia have echoed to the cheers for his
name.   But this is but a superficial view of his
power.   A nation, under his guidance, has shed
many of its traditional weaknesses; from being impulsive has grown cool and calculating ; from being
disunited and discordant has welded itself into
iron bands of discipline and solidarity. ˙ In a race
scattered over every variety of clime and soil and
government, and in every stratum of the social
scale from the lowest to the highest, there are
men of every variety of character and occupation
and opinion.   In other times the hatred of these
men over their differences of method was more
bitter than their hatred for the common enemy
who loathed alike their ends and their means.
Now they all alike sink into equality of agreement before the potent name of Parnell, high and
low, timid and daring, moderate and extreme.
Republics change their Presidents, colonies their
governors and ministers; in England now it is
Gladstone and now it is Salisbury that rules; but
Parnell remains stable and immovable, the apex
of a pyramid that stretches invisible over many
lands and seas, as resistless apparently as fate,
solid as granite, durable as time.

It was many years before the world had any
idea of this new and potent force that was coming
into its councils and affairs.   Charles Stewart
Parnell was born in June, 1846.   He is descended

THE LATE MR. HENRY GRATTAN, M. P.

GRATTAN'S PARLIAMENT.

Henry Grattan moving the declaration of Irish Rights, 1782.

from a family that had long been associated with
the political life of Ireland. The family came
originally from Congleton, in Cheshire; but like
so many others of English origin had in time
proved its right to the proud boast of being
Hibernior Hibernis ipsis. So far back as the
beginning of the last century a Parnell sat for an
Irish constituency in the Irish Parliament. At the
time of the Union a Parnell held high office, and
was one of those who gave the most substantial
proof of the reality of his love for the independence of his country. Sir John Parnell at the
time was Chancellor of the Exchequer and had
held the office for no less than seventeen years.
It was one of the vices of the old Irish Parliament
even in the days after Grattan had attained com-
parative freedom in 1782 that the Ministers were
creatures of the Crown and not responsible to and
removable by the Parliament of which they were
members. There was everything, then, in these
years of service as a representative of the Crown
to have transformed Sir John Parnell into a time-
serving and corrupt courtier. But Sir John Bar-
ington, the best known chronicler of the days of
the Irish Union, describes Sir John Parnell in his
list of contemporary Irishmen as "Incorruptible;"
and "Incorruptible" he proved; for he resigned
office and resisted the Act of Union to the bitter
end. A son of Sir John Parnell—Henry Parnell
—was afterwards for many years a prominent

member of the British Parliament, became a Cabinet Minister, and was ultimately raised to the
Peerage as the first Baron Congleton. John
Henry Parnell was a grandson of Sir John Parnell.
In his younger days he went on a tour through
America; there met Miss Stewart, the daughter
of Commodore Stewart, fell in love with her, and
was married in Broadway. It is unnecessary to
speak to Americans of the immortal "Old Ironsides." Suffice it to say that the bravery, calm-
ness, and strength of will which were characteristic of the brave commander of the "Constitution"
are inherited by his grandson, the bearer of his
name; for the full name of Mr. Parnell, as is
known, is "Charles Stewart Parnell." There was
also something significant in the fact that the man
who was destined to prove the most potent foe
of British misrule in Ireland should have drawn
his blood on the mother's side from a captain who
was one of the few men that ever brought humili-
ation on the proud mistress of the seas.

The young Parnell, chiefly because he was a
delicate child, was sent to various schools in
England during his boyhood, and finally went to
Cambridge University—the university of his
father. Here he stayed for a couple of years, and
for a considerable time thought of becoming a
lawyer. But he changed his purpose, with a
regret that sometimes even in these days of
supreme political glory finds wistful expression.

Almost immediately after his years at Cambridge he went abroad for a tour; and like his
father he chose America as the first place to visit.
While travelling through Georgia—where his
brother has now a great peach-orchard—he met
with a railway accident.   He escaped unhurt;
but John, his elder brother, was injured; and
John says to this day that he never had so good
a nurse as "Charley."   Then Mr. Parnell came
back to his home in Avondale, County Wicklow,
and gave himself up to the occupations and
amusements of a country gentleman.   At this time
he was known as a reticent and rather retiring
young man.   He must have had his opinions
though; for he was brought up in a strongly
political environment.   Probably owing to her
father's blood Mrs. Parnell had always a lively
sympathy with the rebels against British oppres-
sion in Ireland.   She had a house in Dublin at
the time when the ranks of Fenianism had been
descended upon by the government; and when
in Green Street Court-house, with the aid of informers, packed juries, and partisan judges, the
desperate soldiers of Ireland's cause were being
consigned in quick and regular succession to the
living death of penal servitude.   There were in
various parts of the city fugitives from what was
called in these days justice; and among the places
where most of these fugitives found a temporary
asylum and ultimately a safe flight to freer lands

7

and till better days was the house of Mrs. Parnell.
Fanny Parnell is also one of the family figures
that played a large part in the creation of the
opinions of her brother. At an early age she
showed her poetic talents; and from the first
these talents were devoted to the description of
the sufferings of Ireland and to appeals to her
sons to rise against Ireland's wrongs. When the
Fenian movement was in its full strength it had
an organ in Dublin called *The Irish People;* and
into the office of *The Irish People* Fanny Parnell
stole often with a patriotic poem.

In the midst of these surroundings came the
news of the execution of the Manchester Martyrs.
The effect of that event upon the people of Ireland was extraordinary. The three men hanged
had taken part in the rescue of two prominent
Fenian soldiers. In the scrimmage a policeman,
Sergeant Brett, had been accidentally killed, and
for this accidental death several men were put on
their trial for murder. The trial took place in
one of the periodical outbursts of fury which unhappily used to take place between England and
Ireland. The juries were prejudiced, the judges
not too calm, and the evidence far from trust-
worthy. Three men—Allen, Larkin, and O'Brien
—were sentenced to death. Though many humane Englishmen pleaded for mercy, the law was
allowed to take its course, and Allen, Larkin, and
O'Brien were executed. A wild cry of hate and

sorrow rose from Ireland. In every town multi-
tudes of men walked in funeral procession, and to
this day the poem of "God Save Ireland," which
commemorates the memory of Allen, Larkin, and
O'Brien, is the most popular of Irish songs.

CHAPTER IX.

To anybody acquainted with the nature of Mr. Parnell it will be easy to understand the effect which such a tragedy would have upon his mind. If there be one quality more developed than another in his nature it is a hatred of cruelty. When he was a magistrate he had brought before him a man charged with cruelty to a donkey. Fanny Parnell was the person who had the man rendered up to justice, and her brother strongly sympathized with her efforts. The man was convicted, and was sentenced to pay a fine of thirty shillings. The miscreant might as well have been asked to pay the national debt, and the fine was a sentence of prolonged imprisonment. The sequel of the story is characteristic of the family. Miss Parnell herself paid the fine and released the ruffian. It was his strong sympathy with suffering and his hatred of cruelty that first impelled Mr. Parnell to lead the crusade against the use of the odious lash in the British army and navy. So deep, indeed, is his abhorrence of cruelty and even of bloodshed, that he is strongly opposed to capital punishment; and once, when one of his colleagues voted against a motion condemnatory of capital punishment in the House of Commons, he expressed the hope, half joke, whole earnest, that some day that colleague might be taught a lesson by being himself hanged as a rebel. The Manchester tragedy then touched Parnell in his most tender point, and from that time forward he was an enemy of English domination in Ireland.

But he seemed to be in no hurry to put his convictions into action. He is not a man of exuberant enjoyment of life. He has too little imagination and too much equability for ecstasies, but he enjoys the hour, has many and varied interests in life, and could never, by any possibility, sink to a slothful or a melancholy dreamer. His proud and self-respecting nature, too, saved him from any tendency towards that wretched and squalid viciousness which is the characteristic of so many landlords' lives in Ireland. He is essentially temperate; eats but plainly, and drinks nothing but a small quantity of claret. Nor could he descend to the pure horsiness which makes so many country gentlemen regard the stableman's as the highest of arts and pursuits.

One of the reasons why Mr. Parnell delayed his entrance into public life was the state of Irish politics at that moment. There was little movement in the country of a constitutional character. The representation was in the hands of knavish office-holders or office-seekers. The professions of political faith were so many lies, and the constituencies distrustful of all chance of relief from the Legislature, allowed themselves to be bought, that they might afterwards be sold. All that was earnest and energetic and honest in Ireland sought relief for her misery in desperate enterprises, or stood aside until better days and more auspicious stars. Then the landlords of the country remained entirely, or almost entirely, aloof from the popular movements. With the single exception of the late Mr. George Henry Moore, the representation of Ireland was abandoned by the country gentlemen, who in other times had occasionally rushed out of their own ranks and taken up the side of the people. It is a curious fact, but the man who, perhaps, had more influence than almost any other in bringing Mr. Parnell into the arena of Irish nationality, has himself proved a recreant to the cause.

In 1871 was fought the Kerry election. This election marked one of the turning-points in the modern history of Ireland. During the Fenian trials Isaac Butt was the most prominent figure in defending the prisoners. He was a man who had started life with great expectations and supreme talents. Before he was many years in Trinity College, Ireland's oldest university, he was a professor; he had been only six years at the bar when he was made a Queen's counsel. He was the son of a Protestant rector of the North of Ireland, and adhered for some years to the prejudices in which he had been reared. In his early days

THE LATE ISAAC BUTT, M.P.

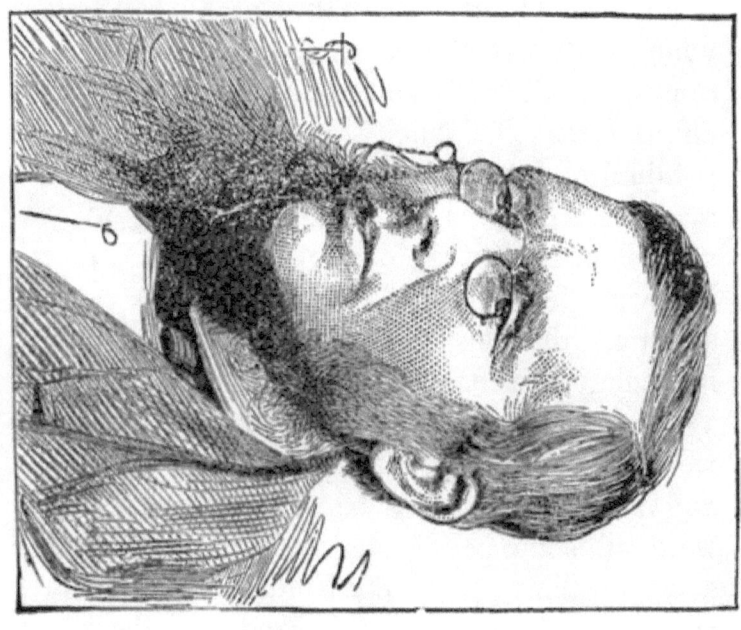

MR. JOSEPH GILLIS BIGGAR, M.P.

every good thing in Ireland belonged to the
Protestants. The Catholics were an outlawed
and alien race in their own country. O'Connell,
not many years before, had carried Catholic
emancipation, but Catholic emancipation was alive
only in the letter. The offices—the judgeships,
the fellowships in Trinity College, the shrievalties,
everything of value or power—were still exclusive·
ly in the hands of the Protestants. O'Connell, in
1843, was so thoroughly sick and tired of vain appeals to the English Legislature that he resolved
to start once again a demand for a native Irish
Legislature. He opened the agitation by a debate in the Dublin Corporation, and Butt, who was
a member of that body, though he was but a
young man, was chosen by the Conservatives to
oppose O'Connell, and delivered a speech so
effective that O'Connell himself complimented his
youthful opponent, and foretold the advent of a
time when Butt himself would be among the advocates instead of the opponents of an Irish Legislature. It was not till a quarter of a century
afterward that this prophecy was realized. Butt,
immediately after the Fenian trials, began an
agitation for amnesty, and in this way gradually
went forward to a primary place in the confidence
and in the affections of his countrymen. There
were still some people who believed in the power
and the willingness of the English Parliament to
redress all the wrongs of Ireland, and there was

JOSEPH CHAMBERLAIN, M.P.

T. BRENNAN.

some justification for this faith in the fact that
William Ewart Gladstone was then at the head of
the English state, and was passing the Disestablishment of the Irish Church, the Land Act of
1870, and the Ballot Act, three measures which
mark the renaissance of Irish nationality. But
one of these very measures Isaac Butt was able
to show was the very strongest proof of the necessity for an Irish Legislature. The Land Act of
1870 is an act the defects of which have passed
from the region of controversy. Mr. Gladstone
himself offered the strongest proof of its break-
down by proposing in 1881 an entirely different
Land Act. In fact it would not be impossible to
show that in some respects the Land Act of 1870
aggravated instead of mitigated the evils of Irish
land tenure. It put no restraint on the raising of
rents, and rents were raised more mercilessly than
ever; it impeded, but it did not arrest eviction; it
caused as much emigration from Ireland as ever.
Yet all Ireland had unanimously demanded a different bill. Mass-meetings all over the country
had demonstrated the wish of the people, and expectation had been wrought to a high point. The
fruit of it all had been the halting and miserable
measure of 1870.

It was this fact that gave the farmers into the
hands of Butt. The population of the towns was
always ready to receive and to support any National leader who advocated an Irish Parliament;

indeed there is scarcely a year since the Act of
Union in 1800 when the overwhelming majority
of the Irish people were not in favor of the restoration of an Irish Parliament.   At that moment,
too, another force was working in favor of a renewed agitation for Home Rule.   The Protestants
were bitterly exasperated by the Disestablishment
of the Irish Church.   Some of the more extreme
Orangemen had made the same threats then as
they are making now, and, while professing the
strongest loyalty to the Queen, had used language of vehement disloyalty.   For instance, one
Orange clergyman had declared that if the Queen
should consent to the Disestablishment, the
Orangemen would throw her crown into the
Boyne.   To the Irish Protestants Butt could appeal with more force than any other man.   He
was an Irish Protestant himself, brought up in
their religious creed and in their political prejudices.   He made the appeal with success, and it
was Irish Protestants that took the largest share
in starting the great Irish movement of to-day.
The Home Rule movement received definite form
for the first time at a meeting in the Bilton Hotel
on May 19, 1870.   It was held in the Bilton
Hotel in Sackville (now O'Connell) street, and
among those who were present and took a prominent part were Isaac Butt, a Protestant; the Rev.
Joseph Galbraith, a Protestant clergyman and a
Fellow of Trinity College; Mr. Purdon, a Prot-

estant, and then Conservative Lord Mayor of
Dublin; Mr. Kinahan, a Protestant, who had been
High Sheriff of Dublin; Major Knox, a Protestant, and the proprietor of the *Irish Times*, the
chief Conservative organ of Dublin, and finally
Colonel King Harman, a Protestant, who has
since gone over to the enemy and become one of
the bitterest opponents of the movement which he
was largely responsible in starting.

It was a Protestant, too, that won a victory that
was decisive. In 1871 there was a vacancy in the
representation of the County of Kerry. At once
the new movement resolved to make an appeal
to the constituency in the name of the revived demand for the restoration of an Irish Parliament.
The friends of Whiggery, on the other hand,
were just as resolved that the old bad system
should be defended vigorously. And this election at Kerry deserves to be gravely dwelt on by
those who regard the present movement as a sec-
tarian and a distinctly Catholic movement. The
Whig candidate was a Catholic—Mr. James Arthur Dease, a man of property, of great intellectual powers, and of a stainless character; and Mr.
Dease was supported vehemently and passionately by Dr. Moriarty, the Catholic Bishop of the
Diocese of Kerry. The Home Rule candidate on
the other hand was a Protestant—Mr. Rowland
Ponsonby Blennerhassett; and he had but few ad-
herents among the Catholic clergy of the diocese;

and the clergy who did support him fell under the displeasure of their bishop. The struggle was fought out with terrible energy and much bitterness; the end was that the feeling of Nationality triumphed over all the influence of the British authorities and of the Catholic bishop, and Blennerhassett, the Protestant Home Rule candidate, was returned.

Blennerhassett belonged to the same class as Mr. Parnell. He was a landlord, a Protestant, and a Home Ruler. Mr. Parnell was a landlord, a Protestant, and a Home Ruler. The time had apparently come when constitutional agitation had a fair chance; and when men of property who sympathized with the people would be welcomed into the National ranks. A few years after this came the general election of 1874; and Mr. Parnell thought that his time of self-distrust and hesitation had passed; and that he might put himself forward as a National candidate. But his chance was destroyed by a small technicality of which the government took advantage. It is the custom in Ireland to appoint young men of station and property to the position of high sheriffs of the counties in which they live. The high sheriff cannot stand for the constituency in which he holds office unless he be permitted by the Crown to resign his office. Mr. Parnell applied for this permission and was refused. And thus in all probability he was unable to represent his native county in Parliament. But he had not long to wait. When a member of Parliament accepts office he has to resign his seat in the British Parliament and submit himself once more to the votes of his constituency. A Colonel Taylor, a veteran and rather stupid hack of the Tory party, was promoted by Mr. Disraeli to the position of Chancellor of the Duchy of Lancaster—a well-paid sinecure—after many years' service as one of the whips of the party. Colonel Taylor was member for County Dublin. He had to seek re-election on his appointment to the chancellorship; and Mr. Parnell resolved to oppose him.

Mr. Parnell was beaten, of course, by a huge majority; for in those days, though the majority of the people of County Dublin were, as they are now, energetic Nationalists, the franchise suffrage was so restricted that a small minority was able to always win the seat. But Mr. Parnell had borne himself well in the struggle; and though he was held to be absolutely devoid of speaking power, yet he made many friends and admirers by the pluck with which he fought a forlorn hope. The next year the man who had been chiefly instrumental in bringing him into public life died—honest John Martin. At the time of his death John Martin was member for County Meath. The county, always strongly National, looked for a man capable of stepping into the place of a noble patriot. Parnell was selected.

Parnell was now at last embarked on the career of an Irish politician. He had not been long in the House when he discovered that things were not as they should be, and that the movement, though it appeared powerful to the outside public, was internally weak and to some extent even rotten. Butt, the leader of the Irish party, was a man of great intellectual powers, and was honestly devoted to the success of the cause. He was ready also to work very hard himself, and he drafted all the bills that were brought in on various subjects by his followers. But he was old, had lived an exhausting life, was steeped in debt, an1 had to divide his time and energies between the calls of his profession as a lawyer and his duties as a legislator. Such double calls are especially harassing in the case of a man who is at once an Irish lawyer and an Irish politician. The law courts are in Dublin, the imperial Parliament is in London; the journey between the two cities, part by sea and part by land, is fatiguing even to a young man, and thus it was quite impossible that Butt could attend to his duties as a lawyer in Dublin and as a politician in London without damage to both. This seriously interfered with his efficiency, and was partly accountable for the break-down of himself and his party.

But he had, besides, personal defects that made him unfit for difficult and stormy times. He was a soft-tempered, easy-going man who was without

much moral courage, incapable of saying No, and
with a thousand amiable weaknesses which leaned
to virtue's side as a man, but were far from vir-
tuous in the politician. As a speaker he was the
most persuasive of men. He discussed with such
candor, with such logic, with temper so beautiful,
that even his bitterest opponents had to listen to
him with respect. But the House of Commons
has respect only for men who have votes behind
them, and can turn divisions, and Butt was unable
to turn divisions.

This brings us to the second defect in the Home
Rule party of Butt. Most of his followers were
rotten office-seekers. When in 1874 Butt had an
opportunity of getting a party elected he was
beset by the great weakness of all Irish movements—the want of money. The electoral insti-
tutions of England were, and to a certain extent
still are, such as to make political careers impossible to any but the rich or the fairly rich. The
costs of election are large, members of Parliament
have no salary, and living in London is dear; and
thus as a rule nobody has any chance of entering
into political life unless he has a pretty full purse.
The result was that when the contest came Butt
was in a painful dilemma. The constituencies
were all right, and were willing to return an honest Nationalist, but there were no honest candidates, for there was no prospect but starvation to
anybody who entered into political life without

considerable means. Butt himself was terribly pressed for money at that very moment. He had to fly from a warrant for debt on the very morning when Mr. Gladstone's manifesto was issued, and John Barry, now one of the members for County Wexford, tells an amusing tale of how he received the then Irish leader in the early morn at Manchester, where Barry lived. It was from England that Mr. Butt had to direct the electoral campaign, and his resources for the whole thing amounted to a few hundred pounds. To American readers these facts ought especially to be told, for they serve two objects: First, they show how it is that though the feeling of Ireland has always been strongly National, representatives of these opinions have not found a place in Parliament until a comparatively recent period; and secondly, because they bring out clearly the enormous influence which America has exercised in the later phases of Irish policy by her generous subscriptions to the combatants for human rights and human liberty in Ireland.

The result of all these circumstances was that Butt was compelled to fight constituencies with such men as turned up, and in the majority of cases to be satisfied with the old men under new pledges. Of course, these old representatives were quite as ready to adopt the new principles of Home Rule as they would have adopted any other principles that secured them re-election,

and through re-election the opportunity of selling
themselves for office.   Many of the members of
the Home Rule party of 1874 were men, accordingly, who had been twenty or thirty years engaged
in the ignoble work of seeking pay or pensions
from the British authorities, and as ready as ever
to sell themselves.   Of course, such a spirit was
entirely destructive of any chance of getting real
good from Parliament.   The English ministers
felt that they were dealing with a set of men
whose votes they could buy, and were not going
to take any steps for the redress of the grievances
of a country that was thus represented.

It was no wonder, then, that when Mr. Parnell
entered Parliament he at once began to meet with
painful disillusions.   Mr. Butt's plan of action was
to bring forward measures, to have them skilfully
and temperately discussed, and then to submit to
the vote when it went against him.   The Home
Rule question was opened every year.   Mr. Butt
himself introduced the subject in a speech of great
constitutional knowledge, of intense closeness of
reasoning, and of a statesmanship the sagacity of
which is now proved by the adoption of Butt's
views by the leading statesmen of England.   Then
the leaders of both the English parties got up;
each in turn condemned the proposal with equal
emphasis; the division was called; Whig and
Tory went into the same lobby; the poor Irish
party was borne down by hundreds of English

votes, and Home Rule was dead for another year.
Parnell's mind is eminently practical.   Great
speeches, splendid meetings, imposing proces-
sions—all these things are as nothing to him
unless they bring material results. He was as
great an admirer as anybody else of the genius
of Isaac Butt, but he could see no good whatever
in great speeches and full-dress debates that left
the Irish question exactly where it was before.
He saw, too, that Isaac Butt was the victim of one
great illusion.   Butt founded his whole policy on
appeals to and faith in the reason of the House
of Commons.   Parnell saw very clearly that at
that period the keeper of the conscience in the
House of Commons on the Irish question was the
division lobby. "Appeal to the good sense and
good feeling of the House of Commons," said
Butt; and the House of Commons replied by
quietly but effectually telling him that it didn't
care a pin about his feelings or his opinions—its
resolution was fixed never to grant Home Rule
to Ireland.   Parnell naturally began to think of
an opposite policy.   "Attack the House through
its own interests and convenience," said he to
Butt, "and then you need not beg it—you can
force it to listen."

In relating the history of Mr. Parnell's career,
it is eminently proper for me to introduce to the
reader some of the distinguished men who stood
so nobly by that illustrious Irishman in his battles
for the autonomy of his native land.   Notable
among them was Joseph Gillis Biggar.

He was born in Belfast, County Antrim, on August 1, 1828. He was educated at the Belfast Academy, where he remained from 1832 to 1844. The record of his school-days is far from satisfactory. He was very indolent—at least he says so himself—he showed no great love of reading— he was poor at composition, and, of course, abjectly hopeless at elocution. The one talent he did exhibit was a talent for figures. It was, perhaps, this want of any particular success in learning, as well as delicacy of health, which made Mr. Biggar's parents conclude that he had better be removed from school and placed at business. He was taken into his father's office in the provision trade, and he continued as assistant until 1861, when he became head of the firm.

Mr. Biggar's first attempt to enter Parliament was made at Londonderry in 1872. He had not the least idea of being successful; but he had at this time mentally formulated the policy which he has since carried out with inflexible purpose—he preferred the triumph of an open enemy to that of a half-hearted friend. The candidates were Mr. Lewis, Mr. (afterwards Chief Baron) Palles, and Mr. Biggar. At that moment Mr. Palles, as Attorney-General, was prosecuting Dr. Duggan and other Catholic bishops for the part they had taken in the famous Galway election of Colonel Nolan—and Mr. Biggar made it a first and indispensable condition of his withdrawing from the

4

contest that these prosecutions should be dropped.
Mr. Palles refused; Mr. Biggar received only 89
votes, but the Whig was defeated, and he was
satisfied.   The bold fight he had made marked
out Mr. Biggar as the man to lead one of the as-
saults which at this time the rising Home Rule
party was beginning to make on the seats of
Whig and Tory.   He himself was in favor of trying his hand on some place where the fighting
would be really serious, and he had an idea of
contesting Monaghan.   When the general election of 1874, however, came, it was represented
to Mr. Biggar that he would better serve the
cause by standing for Cavan.   He was nominated,
and returned, and member for Cavan he has since
remained.   Finally, let the record of the purely
personal part of Mr. Biggar's history conclude
with mention of the fact that, in the January of
1877, he was received into the Catholic Church.
The change of creed for a time produced a slight
estrangement between himself and the other
members of his family, who were staunch Ulster
Presbyterians, and there were not wanting mali-
cious intruders who sought to widen the breach.
But this unpleasantness soon passed away, and
Mr. Biggar is now on the very best of terms with
his relatives.

Not long after the night of Mr. Biggar's celebrated four hours' speech, a young Irish member
took his seat for the first time.   This was Mr.

Parnell, elected for the county of Meath in succession to John Martin. The veteran and incorruptible patriot had died a few days before the opening of this new chapter in Irish struggle. There was a strange fitness in his end. John Mitchel had been returned for the county of Tipperary in 1875. After twenty-six years of exile he had paid a brief visit to his native country in the previous year. He had triumphed at last over an unjust sentence, penal servitude, and the weary waiting of all these hapless years, and had been selected as its representative by the premier constituency of Ireland. But the victory came too late. When he reached Ireland to fight the election he was a dying man. A couple of weeks after his return to his native land he was seized with his last illness, and after a few days succumbed, in the home of his early youth and surrounded by some of his earliest friends. John Martin had been brought by Mitchel into the national faith when they were both young men. They had been sentenced to transportation about the same time; they had married two sisters; they had both remained inflexibly attached to the same national faith throughout the long years of disaster that followed the breakdown of their attempted revolution. Martin, though very ill, and in spite of the most earnest remonstrances of friends, went over to be present at the death-bed of his life-long leader and friend.

At the funeral he caught cold, sickened, and in a few days died. He was buried close to Mitchel's grave.

After Mr. Parnell's first election to Parliament, he, in common with his associate, Mr. Biggar, was deeply impressed by considering the impotence that had fallen upon the Irish party. Both were men eager for practical results, and debates, however ornate and eloquent, which resulted in no benefit, appeared to them the sheerest waste of time, and a mockery of their country's hopes and demands. Probably they drifted into the policy of "obstruction," so called, rather than pursued it in accordance with a definite plan originally thought out. There was in the Irish party at this time a man who had formulated the idea from close reflection on the methods of Parliament. This was Mr. Joseph Ronayne, who had been an enthusiastic Young Irelander, and though, amid the disillusions that followed the breakdown of 1848, he had probably bidden farewell forever to armed insurrection as a method for redressing Irish grievances, he still held by an old and stern gospel of Irish nationality, and thought that political ends were to be gained not by soft words, but by stern and relentless acts. He, if anybody, deserves the credit of having pointed out, first to Mr. Biggar and then to Mr. Parnell, the methods of action which have since proved so effective in the cause of Ireland.

When one now looks back upon the task which these two men set themselves, it will appear one of the boldest, most difficult, and most hopeless that two individuals ever proposed to themselves to work out.

They set out, two of them, to do battle against 650; they had before them enemies who, in the ferocity of a common hate and a common terror, forgot old quarrels and obliterated old party lines; while among their own party there were false men who hated their honesty and many true men who doubted their sagacity. In this work of theirs they had to meet a perfect hurricane of hate and abuse; they had to stand face to face with the practical omnipotence of the mightiest of modern empires; they were accused of seeking to trample on the power of the English House of Commons, and six centuries of parliamentary government looked down upon them in menace and in reproach. In carrying their mighty enterprise, Mr. Parnell and Mr. Biggar had to undergo labors and sacrifices that only those acquainted with the inside life of Parliament can fully appreciate. Those who undertook to conquer the House of Commons had first to conquer much of the natural man in themselves. The House of Commons is the arena which gives the choicest food to the intellectual vanity of the British subject, and the House of Commons loves and respects only those who love and respect it. But the first principle of the active policy was that there should be absolute indifference to the opinion of the House of Commons, and so vanity had first to be crushed out. Then the active policy demanded incessant attendance in the House, and incessant attendance in the House amounts almost to a punishment. And the active policy required, in addition to incessant attendance, considerable preparation; and so the idleness, which is the most potent of all human passions, had to be gripped and strangled with a merciless hand. And finally, there was to be no shrinking from speech or act because it disobliged one man or offended another; and therefore, kindliness of feeling was to be watched and guarded by remorseless purpose. The three years of fierce conflict, of labor by day and by night, and of iron resistance to menace, or entreaty, or blandishment, must have left many a deep mark in mind and in body. "Parnell," remarked one of his followers in the House of Commons one day, as the Irish leader entered with pallid and worn face, "Parnell has done mighty things, but he had to go through fire and water to do them."

Mr. Biggar was heard of before Mr. Parnell had made himself known; and to estimate his character—and it is a character worth study—one must read carefully, and by the light of the present day, the events of the period at which he first started on his enterprise. In the session of

LIFE IN IRELAND.

LIFE IN IRELAND—CELEBRATING MASS IN A CABIN.

1875 he was constantly heard of; on April 27 in that session he "espied strangers;" and, in accordance with the then existing rules of the House of Commons, all the occupants of the different galleries, excepting those of the ladies' gallery, had to retire. The Prince of Wales was among the distinguished visitors to the assembly on this particular evening, a fact which added considerable effect to the proceeding of the member for Cavan. At once a storm burst upon him, beneath which even a very strong man might have bent. Mr. Disraeli, the Prime Minister, got up, amid cheers from all parts of the House, to denounce this outrage upon its dignity; and to mark the complete union of the two parties against the daring offender, Lord Hartington rose immediately afterwards. Nor were these the only quarters from which attack came. Members of his own party joined in the general assault upon the audacious violator of the tone of the House. Mr. Biggar was, above all other things, held to be wanting in the instincts of a gentleman. "I think," said the late Mr. George Bryan, another member of Mr. Butt's party, "that a man should be a gentleman first and a patriot afterwards," a statement which was, of course, received with wild cheers. Finally, the case was summed up by Mr. Chaplin. "The honorable member for Cavan," said he, "appears to forget that he is now admitted to the society of gentlemen." This was

one of the many allusions, fashionable at the
time—among genteel journalists especially—to
Mr. Biggar's occupation. It was his heinous offence to have made his money in the wholesale
pork trade. Caste among business men and
their families is regulated, both in England and
Ireland, not only by the distinction between
wholesale and retail, but by the particular article
in which the trader is interested. It was not,
therefore, surprising that an assembly which tol-
erated the more aristocratic cotton should turn up
its indignant nose at the dealer in the humbler
pork. But much as the House of Commons was
shocked at the nature of Mr. Biggar's pursuits,
the horror of the journalist was still more extreme and outspoken. "Heaven knows" (said a
writer in the *World*), "that I do not scorn a man
because his path in life has led him amongst provisions. But though I may unaffectedly honor a
provision dealer who is a Member of Parliament,
it is with quite another feeling that I behold a
Member of Parliament who is a provision dealer.
Mr. Biggar brings the manner of his store into
this illustrious assembly, and his manner, even for
a Belfast store, is very bad. When he rises to
address the House, which he did at least ten
times to-night, a whiff of salt pork seems to float
upon the gale, and the air is heavy with the odor
of the kippered herring. One unacquainted with
the actual condition of affairs might be forgiven if

he thought there had been a large failure in the bacon trade, and that the House of Commons was a meeting of creditors, and the right honorable gentlemen sitting on the Treasury Bench were members of the defaulting firm, who, having confessed their inability to pay ninepence in the pound, were suitable and safe subjects for the abuse of an ungenerous creditor."

These words are here quoted by way of illustrating the symptoms of the times through which Mr. Biggar had to live, rather than because of any influence they had upon him. On this self-reliant, firm, and masculine nature a world of enemies could make no impress. He did not even take the trouble to read the attacks upon him. The newspapers of the day were full of sarcasm against Mr. Biggar, the chief points made against him being directed at his alleged "grotesque appearance" and "absurdity." Indeed, the impression made upon such Americans as have derived their information regarding Irish affairs chiefly from the London periodicals has been that Mr. Biggar was a man of no sort of intelligence, and of no possible weight in Parliamentary counsels, but that he was simply a hornet who was always ready to sting John Bull's leathern sides. That this hornet was a sore annoyance it was very evident. That he was fearless and persistent was equally plain. No man was more ready to assert Biggar's lack of scholastic acquirements than he himself was prompt to admit the fact. And few were more apt, at the same time, to denounce those pretended patriots who were only looking out for the opportunity to don the English livery.

CHAPTER X.

And here, perhaps, it would be as well to pause for a moment and explain to an American reader what are the means which a British government has at its disposal for corrupting political opponents. Few Americans realize the splendor of the prizes that are at the disposal of the British authorities. Americans know that members of Parliament are paid no salary; they hear the boasts of the enormous and immaculate purity of public life in England; and they, many of them, infer that political life in England is preceded by the vows of purity and poverty. As a matter of fact, there is no country in the world in which politics has prizes so splendid to offer. The salaries reach proportions unexampled in ancient or modern times. The Lord Chancellor of England, for instance, has a salary of fifty thousand dollars a year as long as he is in office, and once he has held office—if it be only for an hour—he has a pension of twenty-five thousand dollars a year for the remainder of his days. The Lord Chancellor, besides, has extraordinary privileges. He is the head of the judiciary of the country; he is Speaker of the House of Lords; he is a peer with right of succession to his children; he is a member of the cabinet. The Speaker of the House of Commons has a salary of twenty-five thousand dollars a year, a splendid house in the Parliament buildings; fire and light and coal free; and when he retires he gets a pension of twenty thousand dollars a year for life and a peerage. Several of the cabinet ministers receive salaries of twenty-five thousand dollars a year. The Lord Chief-Justice of the Queen's Bench gets a salary of forty thousand dollars a year, and the puisne judges get a salary each of twenty-five thousand dollars a year.

In Ireland—one of the poorest countries in the world—the official salaries are on almost an equal scale of extravagance. The Lord-Lieutenant receives a salary of one hundred thousand dollars a year and many allowances. The Chief Secretary for Ireland receives a salary of twenty-five thousand dollars a year, with many allowances. The Lord Chancellor has a salary of forty thousand dollars a year during office, and, as in the case of the Lord Chancellor of England, has a pension for life even if he have held the office for but an hour; the pension is twenty thousand dollars a year. The Chief-Justice of the Queen's Bench Court has a salary of twenty-five thousand dollars a year; and the puisne judges, who, as in England, hold their offices for life, have a salary of nineteen thousand dollars a year. The Attorney-General in Ireland has a nominal salary of

$12,895, but he has fees besides for every case in which he prosecutes; and, as times of disturbance bring many prosecutions, he thrives on the unhappiness of the country. Frequently the salary of the Irish Attorney-General, in times of disquiet, has run up to fifty thousand dollars in the year, or even more. Then, as everybody knows, England has innumerable colonies, and in all her colonies there are richly paid offices. The average salary of a governor of a colony is twenty-five thousand dollars, and there are chief-justiceships, and puisne judgeships, and lieutenant-governorships, and a thousand and one other things which can always be placed at the disposal of an obedient and useful friend of the administration.

The difficulty of the Irish struggle will be understood when it is recollected that, in antagonism to all this, the Irish people have nothing to offer their faithful servants. In Ireland there are, practically speaking, no offices in the gift of the people. From the judgeships down to a place in the lowest rank of the police, everything is in the gift of the British government. Nor is this all. The Irish patriot has, you know, always ran the risk of collision with the authorities, and, in consequence, faced the chances of imprisonment. Mr. Parnell has been in prison; Mr. Dillon has been thrice in prison; Mr. O'Kelly has been in prison; Mr. Sexton has been in prison; Mr. William O'Brien has been in prison; Mr. Healy has been

K. O'DOHERTY.

in prison; Mr. Timothy Harrington has been three times in prison; Mr. Edward Harrington has been in prison; Dr. O'Doherty was sent to penal servitude in '48; Mr. J. F. X. O'Brien was sent to penal servitude in 1867, having first been sentenced to be hanged, drawn, and quartered. Out of the eighty-six Irish members of the present Irish party no less than twenty-five have been, on one excuse or other, and for longer or shorter terms, imprisoned by the British authorities. The choice, then, of the Irish politician lay between wealth, dignity, honors, ease, which were offered for traitorous service by the British government, and the poverty and hardship and lowliness, with a fair prospect of the workhouse and the gaol, which were the only rewards of the faithful servant of the Irish people. Isaac Butt himself was a signal and terrible example of what Irish patriotism entails. We have already described how hard he had to work in his closing days to meet the strain of professional and political duties When he was wrestling with the growing disease that ultimately killed him, he was beset by duns and bailiffs, and his mind was overshadowed with the dread thought that he had left his children unprovided for. And to-day, in poverty—perhaps in misery—they are paying the penalty of having been begotten by a great and a true Irishman. Any man of political experience or reading will know how easy it is for a government to rule a

MR. THOMAS SEXTON, M.P.

MR. W. H. O'SULLIVAN, M.P.

JUSTIN McCARTHY. M.P.

MR. T. M. HEALY. M.P.

country if it have the gift of wealth to bestow, or the curse of poverty to entail. In our own days we have seen France ruled for twenty years by an autocrat through bayonets and offices; and the offices were just as important an element in the governing as the bayonets. The fears of the timid, the hopes of the corrupt, are the foundations of unjust government in all ages. If Americans be sometimes impatient at the duration of British domination and the helplessness of Irish efforts to overthrow it, they must always take into account the vast influence which an extremely wealthy country has been able to exercise over an extremely poor country by the gift of richly-dowered office.

HOW SHAW WAS DEPOSED.

It was not until the end of 1879, or rather the beginning of 1880, that the Irish members of the Imperial Parliament of Great Britain and Ireland chose Charles Stewart Parnell as their leader, or, as they styled it in those days, "Chairman of the Party." Those of them who were elected in the early campaign of 1880 who believed that "the Tories could be brought around to a reasonable way of thinking by soothing talk and amiableness of action," favored the retention of Mr. Shaw as leader. The others, who favored the election of Mr. Parnell, were manly and outspoken in their assertions that the time was at hand when Ireland was either to fall back into landlordism, rack-rent, eviction and starvation, or to go forth to a future of independence, prosperity, and tranquil labor. It is a strange fact, yet nevertheless

true, that at this vital juncture the easy
going Mr. Shaw was very near being appointed
leader.   The different men who had been elected
were at the time personally unknown to each
other.   When they entered the Council Chamber
of the city of Dublin, where this great gathering was taking place, they had had no opportunity whatever of meeting in consultation and
of exchanging ideas and preparing a united line
of action.   Some of them, indeed, who were most
favorable to the claims of Mr. Parnell were supposed to be hostile.

Nor had Mr. Parnell himself taken any trouble
to put forward his claims.   It is the singular
fortune of this extraordinary man to have obtained all his power and position without effort
on his part, and apparently without gaining any
particular pleasure from his success.   He had
been down in the country on the night before the
meeting, and did not reach Dublin until morning.
Up to that time, Mr. Parnell had not seen any of
even his own friends.   But some of them had
met on their own hook; had talked over the
situation; and had in a general way adopted a
line of action.   This was to put forward, and if
possible to carry, Mr. Parnell as leader.   The
gentlemen who formed this nucleus for the meeting of the following day were: Messrs. John
Barry, Comins McCoan, Richard Lalor, James
O'Kelly, Mr. Biggar and T. P. O'Connor.   Mr.

Healy was not then a member of Parliament; but he was Mr. Parnell's Secretary; and he was present at the meeting. Some of these gentlemen met Mr. Parnell the next morning in the street, as he was on his way to the city hall. He did not receive the proposal that he should be elected very cordially. His own idea was, and remained till an advanced period of the meeting, that Mr. Justin McCarthy should be elected; as being a man extreme enough in opinion for the Parnellites, and moderate enough in counsel for the followers of Mr. Shaw.

A debate of some length took place, with the final result that twenty-three voted for Mr. Parnell, and eighteen for Mr. Shaw. The Lord Mayor of Dublin, Mr. Edmund Dwyer Grey, presided over the meeting at its start. When the election was over there was an interval. After this Mr. Parnell quietly took the chair. Thus simply Mr. Parnell was installed in the great position of Leader of the Irish people.

The English papers did not take much notice of the election at the moment; but it was felt that the Imperial Parliament would be met in a spirit of uncompromising demand that might lead to great events and to stormy times. Before the meeting the Irish members had concluded to discuss the land question; and at once it became apparent that there were differences of opinion that might lead to an ultimate split between the two sections. Mr. Shaw could not get beyond the old demand for the "Three F's;" and insisted that this should be the battle-cry of the new party. But some of the followers and friends of Mr. Parnell insisted that the time had past for dealing with the Irish question on these lines, and that a bold move should be at once made towards the proprietorship of the soil by the peasantry of Ireland, as by the peasantry of France and Belgium.

When the party came to London, another, though not at first sight a very serious, difference of opinion arose. As the result of the general election, Mr. Gladstone had come back with a splendid majority. The fight had taken place on the foreign policy of England—and especially on its policy in the East and in Asia. Ireland was not mentioned often, though Lord Beaconsfield, with · characteristic unscrupulousness, had attempted to get a majority on an anti-Irish cry. The Liberals were uncommitted so far as Ireland was concerned, but there was a general understanding that a Ministry which contained such a man as Mr. Gladstone would be inclined to view the demands of Ireland with favor. However, the Parnellites knew that a Liberal Ministry has dangers as well as advantages. The tribe of Irish office-seekers was already on the watch, and it was quite possible that before very long it would be offering its mercenary service to the

Ministers. In that way the party would be demoralized; and Ireland once more would be hopeless because betrayed.

These and other considerations underlay the question which now came to be discussed between the different sections of the Irish party; that question was where the Irish members should take their seats. It should be explained to the American reader that in the House of Commons the rule is for the party in power to take its place on the right of the Speaker's chair. When the Liberals are in power they are on the right of the Speaker. When the Tories come in they pass over to the opposite side, and sit on the left of the Speaker's chair. The right is the Ministerial, the left the Opposition side of the House. The benches on each side are divided about half down by a passage; this passage is known in Parliamentary phraseology as the gangway. Hitherto the Irish members had sat on the benches below the gangway on the opposition side of the House. There could be no objection to this course as long as the Liberals were out of power; then the Irish were naturally a part of the general opposition to the Tory Ministers. But the Liberals were now in office; they were sympathetic; and the question rose whether the Irish members should, by remaining on the opposition side of the House, make open declaration of opposition to them as to the Tories. The

Parnellites gave "Yes" as the answer to this question; the section led by Mr. Shaw answered "No."

An American reader at first sight will perhaps be inclined to smile at the importance attached to this apparently trivial point; but there were important issues underneath the question of the seats. The Government was friendly to Ireland, and no Minister had kindlier intentions than Mr. Gladstone. But the Ministry and Mr. Gladstone were the creatures of the political forces around them; and in 1880, as in every year since the Union, the wishes of Ireland were on one side and the political forces of England pretty solid on the other. Ireland wanted a radical, almost a revolutionary change in the Land laws; she wanted equally a radical if not a revolutionary change in the relations of the two countries; and to these changes the majority of Mr. Gladstone's supporters were just as inimical as the bitterest Tory. If Ireland, then, were to pursue Radical ends she must come into collision with Mr. Gladstone and the Liberal Ministry, painful as that might be. If, on the other hand, the interests of English parties and not those of Ireland were to be considered supreme, the Irish would be justified in taking their places among the Liberals. The Parnellites thought — and events proved the justice of their views — that it was impossible to serve the God of Irish rights and the Mammon of English parties. Mr. Parnell and his friends resolved to remain in opposition; Mr. Shaw and his followers sat among the Liberals like good Ministerialists. One of the consequences foretold by Mr. Parnell of this action soon came about. Before long Mr. Shaw found place after place become vacant beside him; his friends had sold themselves for place and pay.

Another and more important of the prophecies of Parnell was also realized before long. His contention was that between the demands of an Irish Nationalist party and the will of an English Liberal Ministry there would come irreconcileable differences that must lead to hostile collision. The very opening day of the session proved this. It will be remembered that the Land question had reached a very acute stage in Ireland. The farmers once more were demanding the protection of their lives and property from the destruction brought upon them by plundering landlords, and the country had just narrowly escaped from the jaws of famine. At the very moment, indeed, when Parliament met there were still 800,000 men and women in the receipt of relief from the various funds raised by charitable organizations throughout the world. But, nevertheless, all this tragedy had not come to the knowledge of the English authorities; and the Imperial Parliament were as ignorant of it all as if it had never existed. The knowledge in England on the question was confined to a vague impression that there was some distress in Ireland, but then that odious and tiresome country was always more or less in distress; and there was a strong impression that Mr. Parnell had made very violent and wholly unjustifiable speeches. Of course all this simply meant that the farmers were once again putting forward claims that no British Ministry could possibly consent to; that wicked agitators were stirring up the people to impossible demands; that murder was walking abroad through the country; and that if anything were wanted in Ireland it was a new Coercion Bill by which the Irish people could be brought to a condition of good sense and good temper.

Meantime it may be as well to pause here for a moment and hear from the Irish people themselves what it was that they demanded. In April of 1880 there had taken place a convention in Dublin of the Land League, and there the following platform of Land reform had been laid down:

To carry out the permanent reform of land tenure we propose the creation of a Department or Commission of Land Administration for Ireland. This Department would be invested with ample powers to deal with all questions relating to land in Ireland. (1) Where the landlord and tenant of any holding had agreed for the sale to the tenant of the said holding, the Department would

19

execute the necessary conveyance to the tenant
and advance him the whole or part of the purchase-money; and upon such advance being made
by the Department such holding would be deemed
to be charged with an annuity of £5 for every
£100 of such advance, and so in proportion for
any less sum, such annuity to be limited in favor
of the Department, and to be declared to be re-
payable in the term of thirty-five years.

(2) When a tenant tendered to the landlord
for the purchase of his holding a sum equal to
twenty years of the Poor Law valuation thereof
the Department would execute the conveyance
of the said holding to the tenant, and would be
empowered to advance to the tenant the whole
or any part of the purchase-money, the repayment of which would be secured as set forth in
the case of voluntary sales.

(3) The Department would be empowered to
acquire the ownership of any estate upon tender-
ing to the owner thereof a sum equal to twenty
years of the Poor Law valuation of such estate,
and to let said estate to the tenants at a rent
equal to 3½ per cent. of the purchase-money
thereof.

(4) The Department or the Court having juris-
diction in this matter would be empowered to de-
termine the rights and priorities of the several
persons entitled to, or having charges upon, or
otherwise interested in any holding conveyed as

SIR W. V. HARCOURT, M.P.,
Chancellor of the Exchequer.

HON. JOHN MORLEY, M.P.,
Chief Secretary for Ireland.

above mentioned, and would distribute the purchase-money in accordance with such rights and
priorities; and when any moneys arising from a
sale were not immediately distributed the Department would have a right to invest the said moneys
for the benefit of the parties entitled thereto. Provision would be made whereby the Treasury could
from time to time advance to the Department such
sums of money as would be required for the pur-
chases above mentioned.

The doctrines laid down in this programme
were afterwards in the main adopted by the Imperial Parliament, but not until there had been a
vast amount of fierce struggling and bitter suffering.

This platform formulated demands for the permanent settlement of the land problem. Meantime there was a point which demanded attention
and immediate legislation. What was to be done
with the people whom the disastrous failure of the
crops made incapable of paying the rents? It was
now that the defects of the Land Act of 1870
came out more clearly than ever before. A vast
proportion of the Irish tenants were at the mercy
of the landlords, and the landlords were merciless.
Evictions were going on all over the country.
The mass of poverty and hopeless misery was
being daily increased, and if the landlords were
allowed to go on at the present rate, there was
fair chance of a national disaster. To all these

things the reply of the Government was absolutely nothing. The Queen's speech contained paragraphs upon all possible subjects, and with regard to almost every nation in the Queen's dominions, but of Ireland not one word.

It was discovered that upon the Irish Land question the Queen's speech was a perfect reflex of the state of mind among the Queen's ministers. On the question of Ireland the ministerial mind was a blank. Mr. Gladstone is too frank a man not to reveal to the public at some time or other the workings of his mind. Speaking four years afterwards to his constituents in Midlothian, he used the following remarkable words:

"I must say one word more upon, I might say, a still more important subject—the subject of Ireland. It did not enter into my address to you, for what reason I know not; but the Government that was then in power, rather, I think, kept back from Parliament, certainly were not forward to lay before Parliament, what was going on in Ireland until the day of the dissolution came and the address of Lord Beaconsfield was published in undoubtedly very imposing terms. . . . I frankly admit that I had much upon my hands connected with the doings of that Government in almost every quarter of the world, and I did not know— no one knew—the severity of the crisis that was already swelling upon the horizon, and that shortly after rushed upon us like a flood."

This certainly is one of the most astonishing confessions that were ever made by a Minister, and it throws as much light as any other speech of Mr. Gladstone upon the vexed question as to whether the union of the Legislatures is good for England or for Ireland.   Of all the Ministers that ever reigned in England, there has never been one of more voracious reading or more restless activity or who more nearly approached to omniscience than Mr. Gladstone.   He could speak of a passage in Homer, a poem of Dante, a conceit of Voltaire; of a forgotten passage in the history of Greece or in the discoveries of Sir Robert Peel; he can discourse upon the deepest secrets of theology and the highest problems of statesmanship or the smallest points of detail, such as railway fares and freight rates, with equal ease and with equal command.   Yet here was a great national tragedy taking place in Ireland, with all the attendant horrors of a mighty national convulsion, and Mr. Gladstone, the Prime Minister of England, within three hours' reach of Ireland by steam, was absolutely ignorant of everything going on there.   That one fact alone was one of the most potent arguments that could be used in favor of removing Irish affairs from the mercy of English incapacity.

'The Irish members immediately after they heard the Queen's speech found themselves face to face with a question of dispute about the seats in the House of Commons. Were they to be patient with the Ministry, to consult its ease and its interests and to postpone the pressing demands of Ireland until such time as ministers might consider opportune and convenient? It was held that such a course would be a betrayal of the interests and the hopes of Ireland. In the face of a tragedy so terrible, of sufferings so keen, as were racking Ireland it was decided that delay was death, and that it was their duty as Irish representatives to press forward the claims of Ireland without the least regard for anything save Ireland's supreme agony and mighty need. Accordingly they at once proposed an amendment to the Queen's speech insisting that the Land question of Ireland required immediate dealing with. Their demands were regarded either as wicked or ridiculous. Here was a Ministry just come into office scarcely warm in its place and with difficulties to encounter and errors to amend in all parts of the world! But the reply of the Irish members was that if there were an Irish Parliament the voice of Ireland would demand and would receive immediate attention; and that it was not the fault of Ireland that an overworked Ministry and a Parliament with all the world to survey had the sole control of Irish interests and Irish fortunes. . . . Mr. Shaw joined the Government in its policy; and so the division between the two sections of the Irish party widened to an impassable chasm, and from this time forward they rarely if ever kept together.

The amendment to the Queen's speech was of course lost, but the Irish party were not yet done with the question. They immediately brought in a bill the object of which was to suspend evictions for a certain period until Ireland was able to recover from the stunning blow of the ruined harvest. The bill by some miracle was allowed to escape blocking and came before the House of Commons at two o'clock one morning. Mr. Gladstone saw now that the question could no longer be avoided, asked for a postponement of the Irish Bill, and in a few days afterwards announced that the Government themselves were prepared to deal with the question which this bill raised. And thus within a few days after the opening of Parliament the Parnell party had gained an important victory; and instead of Ireland being without attention or without relief it was placed in the forefront of the Ministerial programme.

This was the way in which the measure known as the Disturbance Bill was brought into being. This bill gave the power to County Court Judges to suspend evictions in cases where, owing to the distress, the tenant was unable to pay the existing rent. The bill led to fierce discussions—the landlord party on both sides of the House opposing it vehemently. In the end it passed through

the House of Commons; but when it got to the
House of Lords it was rejected by an overwhelming majority. It had not gone through the House
of Commons, however, without extorting from
Mr. Gladstone some very remarkable words with
regard to the state of Ireland. Thus he brought
out clearly the relentless cruelty of the landlords.
"If," he said on this subject, "we look to the total
numbers we find that in 1878 there were 1,749
evictions; in 1879 2,607; and, as was shown by
my right honorable and learned friend, 1,690 in
the five and a half months of this year—showing
a further increase upon the enormous increase
of last year, and showing in fact unless it be
checked that 15,000 individuals will be ejected
from their homes without hope, without remedy
in the course of the present year." "By the failure of the crops during the year 1879 the act
of God had replaced the Irish occupier in the
condition in which he stood before the Land Act.
Because what had he to contemplate? He had
to contemplate eviction for his non-payment of
rent; and, as a consequence of eviction, starvation; and it is no exaggeration to say, in a country where the agricultural pursuit is the only pursuit, and where the means of the payment of rent
are entirely destroyed for a time by the visitation
of Providence, that the poor occupier may under
these circumstances regard a sentence of eviction
as coming, for him, very near a sentence of
death."

DANIEL O'CONNELL, THE GREAT IRISH AGITATOR.

Very remarkable consequences followed from the rejection of the Disturbance Bill by the House of Lords. There were 15,000 people about to be evicted from their homes—about to have decreed against them by the landlords sentences of death. The tenant was left, therefore, to use Mr. Gladstone's words again, "without hope, without remedy."

CHAPTER XI.

COERCION IN FULL SWING.

In January, 1881, Parliament was called together, nearly a month earlier than usual, in order to give "the Forster Government" time to pass its subsequent measures of Coercion. After their passage there began a fierce and merciless war between the Irish people and the British authorities.

One of the first acts of the detestable Forster was the employment of retired or dismissed military and civil officers to put down all free expression of opinion. One of these ruffians, Clifford Lloyd, may be taken as a fair sample of his fellows. It is related of him by gentlemen whose honor and veracity have never been impugned that in carrying out his despotic instructions "he arrested a village, almost to the last man; he insulted women in the grossest manner. Men or women who stood in the streets to exchange salutations were accused of 'obstructing the pathway,' and the latter, especially, were on the most frivo-

lous pretexts brought before a stipendiary magistrate and subjected to indignities reserved only
for the abandoned.   He had the audacity to have
imprisoned in solitary confinement for periods
often of six months, some of the most refined
women of Ireland, on charges of vagrancy. Children of the most tender years were repeatedly
put in the docks charged with 'endangering the
peace of the Queen.'"   What these poor babes
did to endanger the physical or mental peace of
the old lady no man could find out, and no other
reason could be assigned than that Lloyd wished
to strike terrorism into the hearts of the people.

Newspapers were proceeded against for daring
to mention these villainies.   The prisons were
crowded, evictions were ruthlessly carried on in
almost every quarter of the island, and the dastardly work of the evicting bailiffs was protected
by a force of 13,000 policemen, armed with rifles
and swords or bayonets, supplemented by foot
soldiers, cavalry, artillery and blue jackets. All
of these were on hand to assist the landlords, non-
resident and otherwise, in driving starving tenants
from their homes. The Irish people, driven to
desperation, were at last at bay. The British
Government capped the climax of their audacity
by the arrest on the morning of Thursday, October 13, 1881, of Charles Stewart Parnell, "under
the Coercion Act." John Dillon, Thomas Sexton,
J. J. O'Kelly and William O'Brien, the fearless

THE OBNOXIOUS PROCESS-SERVER.

editor of *United Ireland*, and about 600 prominent
Land Leaguers, were also placed in prison, as
"suspects." The Irish Land League, which had
been organized in Dublin, on October 21, 1879,
with Mr. Parnell as its President, was suppressed,
and the famous "No Rent" manifesto was issued
by its leaders in retaliation. The manifesto and
the antecedent events, fraught as they were with
so much of suffering and misery among the Irish
peasantry, that elicited the indignation not alone of
this country, but also that of the civilized world,
require separate chapters to themselves.

THE FAMINE OF 1879.

In my boyhood days, I read, with the hot tears
blinding my eyes, the pitiful story of the Irish
famine of 1847-49. The potato crop, which was
almost the sole support of the population, was
struck with blight in the fall or autumn of 1846,
and rotted in the ground. Then, as in the later
and disastrous famine of 1879-80, the action of
the British Government was slow, blundering and
impotent. The unfortunate peasantry died in
hundreds of thousands, "amid scenes," says
David Power Conyngham, "of anguish and horror beyond human power adequately to portray."
From the day on which, in 1877, Mr. Parnell was
elected a member of Parliament for Meath until
he sailed for this country in December of 1879,
famine brooded over the land. The wholesale

EVICTED—DRIVEN FROM THE HOUSE WE BUILT.

evictions of 1877 were immediately followed by a
general failure of the crops.   A subsequent wet
season and general failure of the crops marked
the year 1878.   The peasantry, especially in the
far north, the west and parts of the south of
Ireland were suffering from want, and but few
efforts, save those of Mr. Parnell, his associates
of the Irish Land League, and the devoted and
patriotic Roman Catholic clergymen were then
exerted to relieve them.

As the big circle of the country covered in
what was then known as "the famine districts"
gradually grew larger, until it almost seemed
as if the entire country would be involved
in the famine, so the news of the sad state
of affairs became noised abroad, and helping
hands and generous hearts on this side of the
broad Atlantic gave freely and liberally in aid of
the distressed.   James Gordon Bennett, of the
New York Herald, George W. Childs, the philan-
thropist, whose good deeds in aid of suffering humanity and whose charity and generosity are
known the wide world over, Anthony J. Drexel,
the eminent head of the great banking-house of
Drexel & Co., and, indeed, all of the leading men
and good women of the United States vied with
each other, not alone in the number and volume of
their individual donations of money, provisions,
clothing, etc., but in forming citizens' committees,
in every section, whose sole object it was to help

in swelling the general fund for the relief of Ireland. I was the Secretary of the Philadelphia Relief Committee and gladly bear testimony to the good work so well done in those trying days by John Wanamaker, who is now the Postmaster-General of the United States, Thomas Dolan, Thomas Martindale, the gallant and accomplished Dr. William Carroll, William F. Roantree, the noble-hearted Irish patriot, the flower of whose early life was spent in British dungeons, where he was consigned on charges of "treason-felony," Charles A. Hardy, of the Catholic *Standard*, and other members of the Committee. The working classes in every State in the Union were as earnest in the work of relief as the wealthy. The delvers in the coal regions of Pennsylvania, the toilers in the mills, factories, and work-shops of Philadelphia, Boston, Providence, Baltimore, New York, Chicago, San Francisco, St. Louis, New Orleans, Cincinnati, Charleston, aye, and of every city, town and village, however small, gave of their earnings gladly and freely. Many instances came to my knowledge of poor factory girls giving an entire week's work to the sacred cause. How was it in Ireland at this time? What was the condition of affairs that brought forth this bountiful measure of substantial sympathy from the American heart?

The landlords, absentees and residents as well, through their agents, were on all sides exacting

LIFE IN IRELAND—A FARMER'S CABIN.

the last penny of their rack-rents from the distressed people. The crops of all kinds were rotten in the ground. A blight, bitter and accursed, overspread the land like a pall. The people had no money to buy food and no means of procuring any. James Redpath, who made a personal tour of inspection to report on the state of the farmers, wrote that "from every county came official announcements that the destitution is increasing." A geographical allocution of the distress gives to the County Leitrim (in round numbers) 47,000, Roscommon 46,000, Sligo 48,000, Galway 124,-000, Mayo 143,000.

These "round numbers" are 3750 under the exact figures, and they do not do anything like conveying a full or adequate idea of the extent of the distress, for they do not include the North, where in the County Donegal, for example, as in the County Antrim, the condition of the poor was appalling. A few quotations, however, from some of the parishes of these counties on the west coast will tell their own story: "privation beyond description," "their famine-stricken appearance would make the stoniest heart feel for them," "no food," "no clothing," "no fuel," "destitution appalling." Each one of these phrases, says Mr. Redpath, is a literal quotation from the businesslike reports of the local committees of the Mansion House.

The bodies organized for helping the distressed were known as The Mansion House Relief

Committee, The Bennett Relief Committee, The Duchess of Marlborough Committee, The Philadelphia Citizens' Committee, and The Land League Relief Committee.   Each of them had its own way or method of relief, and it was fortunate, indeed, for the sufferers when that frightful scourge, which has gone down into history under the name of "The Famine Fever," began its awful ravages among the already sadly-stricken people, that their ramifications extended so far that they absolutely had every county and town-land on their relief books.

And what do these books tell? A story sickening in its details, teeming with instances of shocking barbarity and heartless brutality on the part of the landlords, and of sorrow, want, and abject misery on the part of the tenantry. Let me call a few of these instances. The Rev. James Stephens, of Killybegs, reports of one family in his parish, thus: "Thomas Gallagher, of Correan; eleven of a family, five of them with bass-mats tied around them for clothing, no fire, no bed but a small heap of straw." Take another report, that of the Rev. J. Maguire, of Cloumany, who tells that "I was called to attend a man who the doctor declared was dying from a disease brought on from want of nourishment. The man was rolled up in what had once been a shawl. This and an old sheet were the only covering he had on him. The house was destitute of every kind of furniture.   The children were literally naked and gathered around a few smouldering sods."

And these were not by any means isolated cases, for precisely similar was the condition of things in the six counties of Munster, where the Mansion House. Committee was represented by two hundred and fifty local committees.   Their reports showed that 232,759 persons were "in terrible distress" in that province.   Here are the reports in round numbers: County Waterford 8,100, Tipperary 17,000, Limerick 17,000, Clare 43,000, Cork 70,000, Kerry 75,000.

Mr. James Redpath, in one of his soul-stirring lectures, says: "I have been in several villages where every man, woman and child in them would have died from hunger within one month, or perhaps one week, from the hour in which the relief that they now solely rely on should be refused, because the men have neither a mouthful of food nor any chance of earning a shilling, nor any other way of getting provisions for their families until the ripening of the crops in autumn. I have entered hundreds of Irish cabins in districts where the relief is distributed.   These cabins are more wretched than the cabins of the negroes were in the

DARKEST DAYS OF SLAVERY.

"The Irish peasant can neither dress as well, nor is he fed as well as the southern slave was fed, and dressed, and lodged.   Donkeys, and cows, and

RENT DAY (As it was before Coercion)—DRINKING HIS HONOR'S HEALTH.

pigs, and hens live in the same wretched room with the family. Many of these cabins had not a single article of bed-clothing, except guano sacks or potato bags, and when the old folks had a blanket it was tattered and filthy. I saw only one woman in all these cabins whose face did not look sad and care-racked, and she was dumb and idiotic."

" The Irish have been described by novelists and travelers as a light-hearted and rollicking people—full of fun and quick in repartee—equally ready to dance or to fight. I did not find them so. I found them in the west of Ireland a sad and despondent people, care-worn, broken-hearted, and shrouded in gloom. Never once in the hundreds of cabins that I entered—never once, even—did I catch the thrill of a merry voice nor the light of a joyous eye. Old men and boys, old women and girls, young men and maidens—all of them, without a solitary exception—were grave or haggard, and every househould looked as if the plague of the first-born had smitten them that hour."

CHAPTER XII.

SPREADING THE LIGHT.

Immediately after his arrival in this country on January 2, 1880, Mr. Parnell, who was accompanied by John Dillon, delivered addresses in many of the large cities of the Union, and wherever they went his cool, argumentative and dispassionate discourses gained hosts of influential American friends, who contributed freely and liberally to the Irish cause. The first contribution to the Land League funds was $1,000 from Mr. George W. Childs. On the second of February, 1880, Mr. Parnell had the honor of a formal reception by the United States Congress, and his address to the United States Senators and Representatives on that occasion really solidified the interest which since then has remained, deep and abiding in the breasts of the American people. Through the united efforts of Mr. Parnell and Mr. Dillon over £70,000 were sent from America to Patrick Egan, the Land League's treasurer in Dublin.

172

This is the Patrick Egan whom the rancor of
the British Government drove to a hasty flight to
Paris, France, to escape incarceration in the
Kilmainham Jail for alleged participation in the
work of the Irish Invincibles.   He is the same
Patrick Egan who, but a few short years after he
landed on our shores, was elected President of
the Irish National League of America.   He is the
same Hon. Patrick Egan whom the President of
the United States, the Hon. Benjamin F. Harrison,
has appointed United States Minister to Chi

Before leaving New York for his home in Ireland, Mr. Parnell held a conference with several
prominent men from various parts of the Union.
The result of their deliberations was a conference,
lasting two days, which was held in Trenor Hall,
New York, on May 18 and 19, 1880, at which
the Hon. Patrick A. Collins, of Boston, presided.
Appropriate resolutions were there drawn up and
agreed to, a provisional constitution adopted and
the following elected as national officers: J. J.
McCafferty, President; Rev. Lawrence Walsh,
Treasurer; Michael Davitt, Secretary.

Almost immediately after the meeting the President resigned, and the patriot, Michael Davitt,
went home to Ireland to face threatened imprisonment.   The conduct of the entire executive
business of the Land League was thus thrown
upon Father Walsh.

Feeling the necessity for prompt and energetic
work, that patriot priest used every exertion to

further the success of the movement. Branches were formed in New York, Philadelphia, Boston, Chicago, and other great cities and centres of population, and contributions to the League funds were transmitted to Ireland through the *Irish World, Boston Pilot*, and other journals, as well as through the regular treasurer.

Father Walsh found, after laboring incessantly and unwearyingly for several months, that more concerted action and a more effective organization were absolutely necessary. Hence, he issued a call to the delegates of the various branches to meet in convention at Buffalo, N. Y., on the 12th and 13th of January, 1881.

This was really the first Land League Convention held in the United States of America. Its results were as great as they were far-reaching, both in the number of Land League branches that were organized throughout the country and in the amount of money contributed by and through its members. In their ranks were to be found, standing shoulder to shoulder, Jew and Gentile, Protestant and Roman Catholic, Presbyterian and Methodist, Baptist and Unitarian, all of them actuated by a common sentiment, the love of freedom. At their head was a Central Council, composed of the Hon. Patrick A. Collins, Boston, Mass., President; Rev. Lawrence Walsh, Waterbury, Conn., Treasurer; Thomas Flatley, Esq., Boston, Mass., Secretary.

RENT DAY (As it is under Coercion)—NO RENT.

The work of stirring up the people to do their whole duty by the home leaders of the movement, received a fresh impetus in October, 1881, when the cable flashed the news across the Atlantic Ocean of the determination of William Ewart Gladstone's government to put down the Irish National League by force. The first step in that direction was sufficient of itself to set aflame the hearts of Irishmen all over the civilized world. Mr. Parnell, the President of the League, was arrested on the 13th of that month, and within two days afterwards Thomas Sexton, John Dillon, J. J. O'Kelly, William O'Brien, and others were imprisoned as "suspects." The Executive of the League now felt the necessity to take some strong steps to thwart the Irish landlords, and to show the British Government by absolute proofs that the Irish people would not tamely submit to this unjustifiable incarceration of their representatives. As a last resource the Irish Executive called on the tenants to "pay no rent." They did so in the following document, which, as will be seen by its date, was issued on the 18th of October, 1881. Many enemies of the Home Rule movement, in America and elsewhere, in their attempts to justify the arrest of Mr. Parnell, assert that "he was imprisoned because he issued the No-Rent Manifesto." The exact converse is the truth. The manifesto was issued because the leaders of the national organization were deprived of their liberty. As a historic interest is attached to the document, and, as its alleged contents have been the cause of, at times, bitter contention, I append it, *verbatim*, as it was issued from the patriots' prison :

" *To the Irish People.*

"FELLOW COUNTRYMEN : The hour has come to test whether the great organization, built up during years of patient labor and sacrifice, and consecrated by the allegiance of the whole Irish race the world over, is to disappear at the summons of a brutal tyranny. The crisis with which we are face to face is not of our making. It has been deliberately forced upon the country, while the Land Act is, as yet, untested, in order to strike down the only power which might have extorted any solid benefits for the tenant-farmers of Ireland from that Act, and to leave them once more helplessly at the mercy of a law invented to save landlordism and administered by landlord minions.

"The Executive of the Irish National Land League, acting in the spirit of the resolutions of the National Convention—the most freely elected body ever assembled in Ireland—was advancing steadily in the work of testing how far the administration of the Land Act might be trusted to eradicate from the rents of the Irish tenant-farmers the entire value of their own improvements, and to reduce these rents to such a figure as should forever place our country beyond the peril of periodical famine. At the same time they took measures to secure, in the event of the Land Act proving to be a mere paltry mitigation of the horrors of landlordism in order to fasten it the more securely on the necks of the people, that the tenant-farmers should not be delivered blindfolded into the hands of hostile law courts, but should be able to fall back upon the magnificent organization which was crushing landlordism out of existence when Mr. Gladstone stepped in to its rescue. In either event the Irish tenant-farmers would have been in a position to exact the uttermost farthing of their just demand.

"It was this attitude of perfect self-command—impregnable while there remained a shadow of respect for law, and supported with unparalleled enthusiasm by the whole Irish race—that moved the rage of the disappointed English Minister. Upon the monstrous pretext that the National Land League was forcing upon the Irish tenant-farmers an organization which made them all-powerful, and was keeping them, by intimidation, from embracing an Act which offered them nothing except helplessness and uncertainty, the English Government has cast to the winds every shred of law and justice, and has plunged into an open reign of terror, in order to destroy by the foulest means an organization which was confessedly too strong for it within the limits of its own English constitution.

" Blow after blow has been struck at the Land
League, in the mere wantonness of brute force.
In the face of provocation which has turned men's
blood to flame, the Executive of the Land League
adhered calmly and steadily to the course traced
out for them by the National Convention. Test
cases of a varied and searching character were,
with great labor, put in train for adjudication in
the Land Courts. Even the arrest of our President, Mr. Charles Stewart Parnell, and the excited
state of popular feeling which it evoked, did not
induce the executive to swerve in the slightest
from that course; for Mr. Parnell's arrest might
have been accounted for by motives of personal
malice, and his removal did not altogether derange
the machinery for the preparation of the test
cases which he has been at much pains to perfect. But the events which have since occurred—
the seizure, or attempted seizure, of almost all the
members of the executive and of the chief officials
of the League, upon wild and preposterous pre-
tences, and the violent suppression of free speech
—put it beyond any possibility of doubt that the
English Government—unable to declare the Land
League an illegal association, defeated in the
attempt to break its unity, and afraid to abide the
result of test cases, watched over by a powerful
popular organization—has deliberately resolved
to destroy the whole machinery of the Central
League, with a view to rendering an experi-

mental trial of the Act impossible, and forcing it
upon the Irish tenant-farmers on the Government's
own terms.

"The brutal and arbitrary dispersion of the
Central Executive has so far succeeded that we
are obliged to announce to our countrymen that
we no longer possess the machinery for adequately presenting the test cases in court according to the policy prescribed by the National Convention.   Mr. Gladstone has, by a series of
furious and wanton acts of despotism, driven the
Irish farmers to choose between their own organization and the mercy of his lawyers—between
the power which has reduced landlordism to
almost its last gasp and the power which strives
with all the ferocity of despotism to restore the
detestable ascendency from which the Land
League has delivered the Irish people.

"One constitutional weapon alone now remains
in the hands of the Irish National League.   It is
the strongest, the swiftest, the most irresistible of
all.   We hesitated to advise our fellow-countrymen to employ it until the savage lawlessness of
the English Government provoked a crisis in
which we must either consent to see the Irish
tenant-farmers disarmed of their organization and
laid once more prostrate at the feet of the landlords, and every murmur of Irish public opinion
suppressed with an armed hand, or appeal to our
countrymen to at once resort to the only means

now left in their hands of bringing this false and brutal Government to its senses.

"Fellow-countrymen, the hour to try your souls and redeem your pledges has arrived. The Executive of the National Land League, forced to abandon the policy of testing the Land Act, feels bound to advise the tenant-farmers of Ireland from this forth to pay no rent under any circumstances to their landlords until the Government relinquishes the existing system of terrorism and restores the constitutional rights of the people. Do not be daunted by the removal of your leaders. Your fathers abolished tithes by the same method without any leaders at all, and with scarcely a shadow of the magnificent organization that covers every portion of Ireland to-day.

"Do not suffer yourselves to be intimidated by threats of military violence. It is as lawful to refuse to pay rents as it is to receive them. Against the passive resistance of an entire population, military power has no weapons. Do not be wheedled into compromise of any sort by the dread of eviction. If you only act together in the spirit to which in the last two years you have countless times solemnly pledged your vows, they can no more evict a whole nation than they can imprison them. The funds of the National Land League will be poured out unstintedly for the support of all who may endure eviction in the course of the struggle. Our exiled brothers in

America may be relied upon to contribute, if
necessary, as many millions of money as they have
contributed thousands, to starve out landlordism
and bring English tyranny to its knees. You
have only to show that you are not unworthy of
their boundless sacrifices in your cause. No
power on earth except faint-heartedness on our
own part can defeat you. Landlordism is already
staggering under the blows which you have dealt
it, amidst the applause of the world.

"One more crowning struggle for your land,
your homes, your lives—a struggle in which you
have all the memories of your race, all the hopes
of your children, all the sacrifices of your imprisoned brothers, all your cravings for rent-enfran-
chised land, for happy homes and national freedom,
to inspire you—one more heroic effort to destroy
landlordism at the very source and fountain of its
existence—and the system which was, and is, the
curse of your race and of your existence, will
have disappeared for ever. The world is watching to see whether all your splendid hopes and
noble courage will crumble away at the first threat
of a cowardly tyranny. You have to choose
between throwing yourself upon the mercy of
England and taking your stand by the organization which has once before proved too strong for
English despotism; you have to choose between
all-powerful unity and impotent disorganization;
between the land for the landlords and the land

for the people! We cannot doubt your choice. Every tenant-farmer of Ireland is to-day the standard-bearer of the flag unfurled at Irishtown, and can bear it to a glorious victory.

"Stand together in the face of the brutal and cowardly enemies of your race; pay no rents under any pretext; stand passively, firmly, fearlessly by while the armies of England may be engaged in their hopeless struggle against a spirit which their weapons cannot touch; act for yourselves if you are deprived of the counsels of those who have shown you how to act; no power of legalized violence can extort one penny from your purses against your will; if you are evicted, you will not suffer; the landlord who evicts you will be a ruined pauper, and the Government which supports him with its bayonets will learn in a single winter how powerless is armed force against the will of a united, determined and self-reliant nation.

"Signed: Charles S. Parnell, President, Kilmainham Jail; A. J. Kettle, Honorary Secretary, Kilmainham Jail; Michael Davitt, Honorary Secretary, Portland Prison; Thomas Brennan, Honorary Secretary, Kilmainham Jail; John Dillon, Head Organizer, Kilmainham Jail; Patrick Egan, Treasurer, Paris.

"18th October, 1881."

CHAPTER XIII.

PUSHING ON THE WORK.

DAILY the ranks of the Land Leaguers received fresh accessions, and the recruits were not confined either to what has often in Ireland been contemptuously styled "the lower orders" or to any particular sect. The farmer and the physician, the lawyer and the mechanic, the clergyman and the shopkeeper, the "retired gentleman" and the clerk, the titled owner of big estates and the sturdy laborer joined hands in the movement that now, thanks to the unceasing efforts and untiring energy of Parnell, Dillon, Davitt, O'Brien, O'Connor, Biggar and the other members of the Irish Parliamentary Party, promised to sweep all opposition before it, like a whirlwind. Meetings were held in every townland night after night, branches of the League were organized everywhere, and the women, old and young, took as deep and as active an interest in building up and increasing the strength and resources of the movement as the men. I am satisfied that in many cases their fiery energy and burning eloquence shamed the weak-kneed and

184

the lukewarm into vigorous co-operation with their more worthy countrymen.   There were not wanting humorous incidents to enliven the campaign.   One of the most noteworthy was a "People's Hunt," which took place on January 7, 1882, near Maryborough, Queen's County, and was established under the high-sounding name of The National Hunting Association.   Nearly two hundred ladies and gentlemen on horseback participated in the "Hunt," and were accompanied by a large pack of dogs, which bore on their collars such significant names as "Rack-rent," "Revolver," "Buckshot," and "Dynamite!"   Five days afterwards the Royal Irish Constabulary, as the police in Ireland are termed, were present in force at the Newcastle West Petty Sessions, where the members of the Drumcollogher Ladies' Land League were sentenced to one month's imprisonment for the crime of daring to belong to such an organization.   The authorities felt that this action was not enough to mark their displeasure at the temerity of the people in holding such a "Hunt."   So, two weeks later, they instructed the police to arrest a number of children, whose ages ranged from seven to ten years old, for whistling the tune of "Harvey Duff,"* at Cappamore, County Limerick.   On February 14, 1882, they went still further and "proclaimed"

---

* "Harvey Duff" was a satire of a rather harmless character directed against the police.

five baronies of the County Roscommon and twelve baronies of the County Waterford. These severities so weighed down the spirits and dampened the courage of Parnell's followers that they felt it a duty that they owed to themselves as well as to the authorities to give some notable and public expression of their sentiments. To the number therefore of over two thousand, the tenant farmers were sent as representative delegates from the various counties in Ireland to Avondale, Mr. Parnell's country-seat, where they performed all of the agricultural work that was necessary. That was on the 16th of February, 1882, and on the 25th of that month the men of Meath elected Michael Davitt, who was then in prison, to succeed the lamented A. M. Sullivan, who had resigned his seat in Parliament. On April 9th Mr. Parnell was released from Kilmainham jail on parole, to attend the funeral of a nephew in Paris. He returned to his cell on the 24th, remaining there until his release with Dillon and O'Kelly, on the 2d of May, 1882, two days after which Michael Davitt was released from Portland prison. It was about this time that "Buckshot Forster" refused the Chief Secretaryship of Ireland, and was succeeded by Lord Frederick Cavendish, who, with Thomas Henry Burke, the Under-Secretary, was assassinated while walking towards the Vice-regal Lodge, in Phœnix Park, Dublin. That murderous deed was

MICHAEL DAVITT.

one of the deadliest blows that was dealt to the Irish cause for many years. Again the evil fortune that has so often blighted the Irish cause on the threshold of victory intervened, and in one day the hopes of Ireland were blasted, and the cause of Irish liberty was thrown back for years. Lord Frederick Cavendish had gone over to Ireland as the new Chief Secretary, and as the bearer of the new message of peace to the Irish people. He was a man of amiable temper, and of high purpose, and well fitted in every way to be the medium of reconciliation. On the very day of his arrival in Dublin, he and Mr. Burke, the Under Secretary, were assassinated in the Phœnix Park. This was on May 6th. It turned out afterwards he was unknown to those who killed him, and that his death was due to the accidental circumstance of his being alone with Mr. Burke. The tragedy created terrible excitement and anger in England. A cry for vengeance was raised, and the Ministry had to bow before the storm, and, having dropped coercion, were obliged once more to introduce it. Mr. Parnell was assailed with special bitterness; and Mr. Forster was once more elevated to the position and eminence which he had forfeited. In a remarkable passage of his evidence by James Carey, a man who played a prominent part in the conspiracy, and afterwards betrayed his companions, here is an extract from his evidence in cross-examination by Mr. Walsh:

Q. When you became a member of the Order of Invincibles, was it for the object of serving your country that you joined?   A. Well, yes.

Q. And at the time when you joined with the object of serving your country, in what state was Ireland?   A. In a very bad state.

Q. A famine, I think, was just passing over her?   A. Yes.

Q. The Coercion Bill was in force, and the popular leaders were in prison?   A. Yes.

Q. And was it because you despaired of any constitutional means of serving Ireland that you joined the Society of Invincibles?   A. I believe so.

However, England was not in a humor to listen, and the Crimes Act was passed in the House of Commons after a vain resistance by the Irish members. This act enabled juries to be packed and other methods to be adopted by which in despotic countries prisoners are cajoled or terrorized into giving evidence true or false. A number of men were put upon their trial before juries consisting entirely of landlords exasperated by the loss of power and by the crimes committed. A number of men were in this way convicted and were hanged. A sickening doubt afterwards arose as to whether these men were innocent or guilty, and this was especially the case with regard to a man named Myles Joyce. His case was debated over and over again in the House of

Commons, and it is still a question of doubt as to whether he was condemned justly. A man named Bryan Kilmartin was sent to penal servitude on a charge of having shot a man with intent to murder. The judge declared emphatically that the man was guilty beyond all doubt. Attempt after attempt to have his case investigated failed; but finally the matter was brought before the House of Commons. It was proved that a man who had gone to America immediately after the crime, and who had on his death-bed confessed to the offence, was the real culprit, and Bryan Kilmartin, proved innocent, had to be released

CHAPTER XIV.

JUSTICE to the memory of Charles Stewart Parnell demands that his biographer place on record that honorable man's hearty detestation of the murders of Lord Cavendish and Mr. Burke, and his sincere and eloquent denunciation of the murderers. While men's minds were still aflame with anger over the dastardly deed and many of Ireland's best friends in America and the British colonies read with horror its foul details, Charles Stewart Parnell, John Dillon, and Michael Davitt issued the following address:

"To the People of Ireland:

"On the eve of what seemed a bright future for our country, that evil destiny which has apparently pursued us for centuries, has struck at our hopes another blow which cannot be exaggerated in its disastrous consequences. In this hour of sorrowful gloom we venture to give expression to our profoundest sympathy with the people of Ireland in the calamity that has befallen our cause through this horrible deed, and with those who determined at the last hour, that a policy of con-

191

ciliation should supplant that of terrorism and
national distrust.   We earnestly hope that the attitude and action of the Irish people will show to
the world that an assassination such as has
startled us almost to the abandonment of hope
of our country's future, is deeply and religiously
abhorrent to their every feeling and instinct.   We
appeal to you, to show by every manner of expression that, amid the universal feeling of horror
which the assassination has excited, no people feel
so deep a detestation of its atrocity, or so deep a
sympathy with those whose hearts must be seared
by it, as the nation upon whose prosperity and re-
viving hopes it may entail consequences more
ruinous than those that have fallen to the lot of
unhappy Ireland during the present generation.
We feel that no act that has ever been perpetrated
in our country during the exciting struggles of
the past fifty years has so stained the name of
hospitable Ireland as this cowardly and unpro-
voked assassination of a friendly stranger, and
that until the murderers of Cavendish and Burke
are brought to justice that stain will sully our
country's name."

Usually a reticent man Mr. Parnell was on this
occasion outspoken and vehement.   His whole
soul was aroused.   To a number of friends he
said :

"I am horrified more than I can express.   This
is one of the most atrocious crimes ever committed.

Its effect must certainly be most damaging to the interests of the Irish people. I have always found Lord Frederick Cavendish a most amiable gentleman, painstaking and strictly conscientious in the fulfilment of his official duties. I did not share the disappointment expressed in Liberal Irish circles regarding his appointment, as I anticipated that the principal reforms during the present session, such as the amendment of the Land Act, would be under Mr. Gladstone's personal supervision, and I believed that administrative reforms would be somewhat postponed. I cannot conceive that any section of the people of Ireland could have plotted deliberately against the life of Lord Frederick, and I am surprised that the Dublin police, who had been able to protect Mr. Forster, should apparently not have taken any steps to watch over his successor during the few hours of his official life in Ireland. There seems to be an unhappy destiny presiding over Ireland, which always comes at a moment when there seems some chance for the country, to destroy the hopes of her best friends. I hope the people of Ireland will take immediate and practical steps to express their sympathy with Mr. Gladstone in his most painful position."

Mr. Dillon and Mr. Sexton fully concurred with Mr. Parnell in his opinion of the outrage, and Mr. Sexton, to an interviewer on the subject, said:

"I am bewildered and horrified. I regard Lord

Frederick Cavendish as an amiable and painstaking gentleman. He was certainly considered a capable administrator. The first feeling on the appointment of Lord Frederick was undoubtedly one of disappointment, but it began to be gradually understood that Mr. Gladstone sent him to Ireland to have the advantage of the service of one with whom he had long worked, thereby enabling him to apply his own will more freely to the Irish difficulties. There is no reason to believe that there was the slightest personal feeling against Lord Frederick in any political quarter of Ireland. I cannot help surmising that he must have been mistaken by the murderers for some one else. Mr. Burke had been connected with the castle for many years. Public feeling from time to time identified him with many harsh measures, but well-informed persons have always held that he confined himself vigorously to his duties. He was rather averse than otherwise to concerning himself with political matters. He was very little known to the Dublin populace. He was present unrecognized at a great political meeting in Phœnix Park last summer. He belonged to a land-owning family. Many people have for a long time believed him to be the real governor of Ireland. The crime is the more inexplicable when one considers the good temper of the crowds at the rejoicing over the release of the suspects."

Michael Davitt also spoke in no uncertain tones of the crime. He said:

" No language I can command can express the horror with which I regard the murders or my despair at their consequences. When I heard of them on Saturday night I could not credit the news. I grieve to think that when the government had just run a risk in introducing a new policy—when everything seemed bright and hopeful, when all expected the outrages to cease—this terrible event should dash our hopes. I wish to God that I had never left Portland. The crime was without motive. It is not only the most fatal blow that has ever been struck at the Land League, but one of the most disastrous blows which has been sustained by the national cause during the last century. Its occurrence at this particular juncture seems like a terrible destiny. My only hope is that the assassins may be discovered and punished as they deserve. It is wonderful how the outrage could occur within a few hundred yards of the constabulary depot."

As I have already stated this tragedy swept away for a time the power of Mr. Parnell and of Mr. Gladstone for good for Ireland. The Kilmainham Treaty, the terms of which the great Irish leader dictated from his cell in that celebrated prison, had brought the Gladstone government to its knees in its unreserved and frank acknowledgment of the failure of Coercion.

This confession in its completeness involved the sacrifice of the men who were chiefly responsible for Coercion, and accordingly " Buckshot Forster" and Lord Cowper resigned from the ministry. Coercion was renewed and carried out with extraordinary severity until the defeat of the government on the 8th of June, 1885, when Lord Salisbury became Prime Minister, and Lord Carnarvon, Viceroy of Ireland, and the Tory Party struck an alliance with Mr. Parnell. The general election of 1885 took place, and then came the startling announcement that Mr. Gladstone had become a Home Ruler, and the introduction of the Home Rule Bill. The defeat of the bill and the defeat of the liberals at the polls followed in 1886, and the Tory *régime* of the past five years was imposed upon Ireland. The share that Mr. Parnell took in the work of the general election is so well known that there is no need to recount it. When the Coercion Act was introduced a thunderbolt fell on the political world. On the 18th of April, 1886, a vote was to be taken in the House of Commons on the second reading of Mr. Balfour's Coercion Bill. It was not by an accident—as we now know—but by set purpose, that on that very day the *Times* published the letter attributed to Mr. Parnell. The letter was in these words—

5, 15, 1882.

DEAR SIR—I am not surprised at your friend's

anger, but he and you should know that to denounce the murders was the only course open to us. To do that promptly was plainly our best policy.

But you can tell him, and all others concerned, that though I regret the accident of Lord F. Cavendish's death, I cannot refuse to admit that Burke got no more than his deserts.

You are at liberty to show him this, and others whom you can trust also; but let not my address be known. He can write to House of Commons.

Yours very truly,
CHAS. S. PARNELL.

The *London Times* took care to set forth this extraordinary document with every form of display which is at the disposal of a printing office. The letter was given in *fac-simile*, and was spread over several columns; the first leading article was devoted to it, and, in fact, no method of concentrating public opinion upon it was neglected. A series of articles were published, all of them directed against Mr. Parnell and his associations, under the startling head-line of "Parnellism and Crime."

Some other forged letters followed, and arising out of them Mr. F. H. O'Donnell, ex-M. P. for Dungarvan, brought an action for libel against the *Times*. After the collapse of that action Mr.

Parnell demanded a Parliamentary inquiry, which was refused by the government, who ultimately, however, appointed a special commission, consisting of Sir James Hannen, Mr. Justice Smith, and Mr. Justice Day. At the opening of that famous investigation there was a memorable scene presented. The enemies of Mr. Parnell were ranged against him in the court, and looked assured of coming triumph. The same calm, inscrutable aspect characterized the Irish leader. He attended day by day at the court until the Pigott forgeries were exposed, and on April 30, 1890, he entered the witness box and went through the ordeal of several days' examination and cross-examination. This was the most memorable trial of modern times, and for that reason I give in detail its most striking and prominent scenes and incidents.

13

CHAPTER XV.

THE first sitting of the Special Commission appointed by the Special Commission Act, 1888, was held on the 22d of October, 1888, in No. 1 Probate Court of the Royal Courts of Justice in London.

The Special Commission Act, which was passed during the first part of the present Session, is as follows:

An Act to constitute a Special Commission to inquire into the charges and allegations made against certain members of Parliament and other persons by the defendants in the recent trial of an action entitled "O'Donnell versus Walter and another." (13th of August, 1888.)

Whereas charges and allegations have been made against certain members of Parliament and other persons by the defendants in the course of the proceedings in an action entitled "O Donnell versus Walter and another," and it is expedient that a Special Commission should be appointed to inquire into the truth of those charges and allegations, and should have such powers as may be necessary for the effectual conducting of the inquiry :

Be it, therefore, enacted by the Queen's most Excellent Majesty, by and with the advice and consent of the Lords Spiritual and Temporal and Commons, in this present Parliament assembled, and by the authority of the same, as follows :

1.—(1) The three persons hereinafter mentioned —namely, the Right Honorable Sir James Hannen, the Honorable Sir John Charles Day, and the Honorable Sir Archibald Levin Smith, are hereby appointed Commissioners for the purposes of this Act, and are in this Act referred to as the Commissioners.

(2) The Commissioners shall inquire into and report upon the charges and allegations made against certain members of Parliament and other persons in the course of the proceedings in an action entitled " O'Donnell versus Walter and another."

2.—(1) The Commissioners shall, for the purpose of the inquiry under this Act, have in addition to the special powers hereinafter provided, all such powers, rights and privileges as are vested in Her Majesty's High Court of Justice, or in any Judge thereof, of the occasion of any action including all powers, rights and privileges in respect to the following matters :

(i) The enforcing the attendance of witnesses and examining them on oath, affirmation, or

promise and declaration ; and (ii) the compelling
the production of documents and (iii) the punishing persons guilty of contempt and (iv) the issue
of a commission or request to examine witnesses
abroad ; and a summons signed by one or more
of the Commissioners may be substituted for, and
shall be equivalent to, any form of process capable of being issued in any action for enforcing
the attendance of witnesses or compelling the
production of documents.

(2) A warrant of committal to prison issued
for the purpose of enforcing the powers conferred
by this section shall be signed by one or more of
the Commissioners, and shall specify the prison
to which the offender is to be committed.

(3) The Commissioners may, if they think fit,
order that any document or documents in the
possession of any party appearing at the inquiry
shall be produced for the inspection of any other
such party.

3. If any person, having been served with a
summons under this Act, shall fail to appear according to the tenor of such summons, the Commissioners shall have power to issue a warrant
for the arrest of such persons.

4. If any person summoned to attend before
the said Commissioners who shall refuse, neglect,
or fail to attend in pursuance of any summons,
shall, notwithstanding the dissolution of the Commission, be liable to punishment for contempt of

the High Court of Justice, on the motion of any person who has appeared at the inquiry before such Commissioners.

5. A warrant or order for the arrest, detention, or imprisonment of a person for contempt of the Commissioners shall, notwithstanding the Special Commission is dissolved or otherwise determined, be and remain as valid and effectual in all respects as if the Special Commission were not so dissolved or otherwise determined, and upon such dissolution or determination all the powers, rights, and privileges of the Commissioners with respect to such warrant or order, and to a person arrested, detained, or imprisoned, or to be arrested, detained, or imprisoned by virtue thereof, shall devolve upon and be exercised by the Queen's Bench Division of the High Court of Justice or a Judge thereof; and such contempt, and a proceeding with respect thereto, shall not be in any wise affected by such dissolution or determination of the Special Commission.

6. The persons implicated in the said charges and allegations, the party to the said action, and any person authorized by the Commissioners may appear at the inquiry, and any person so appearing may be represented by counsel or solicitor practising in Great Britain or Ireland. Where it shall appear to the Commissioners that any person affected by any of the said charges or allegations is at any time during the holding of

the said inquiry detained or imprisoned, the Commissioners may order the attendance of such persons at such inquiry in such manner, for such time, and subject to such conditions as regards bail, or otherwise, as to the Commissioners may seem fit.

7. The Commissioners shall have power, if they think fit, to make reports from time to time.

8. Every person who, on examination of oath, affirmation, or promise and declaration under this Act, wilfully gives false evidence, shall be liable to the penalties for perjury.

9. Any person examined as a witness under this Act before the Commissioners, or under a commission to examine witnesses abroad, may be cross-examined on behalf of any other person appearing before the Commissioners. A witness examined under this Act shall not be excused from answering any question put to him on the ground of any privilege, or on the ground that the answer thereto may criminate or tend to criminate himself; provided that no evidence taken under this Act shall be admissible against any person in any civil or criminal proceeding except in case of a witness accused of having given false evidence in an inquiry under this Act, or of a person accused of having procured, or attempted or conspired to procure the giving of such evidence.

10.—(1) Every person examined as a witness

under this Act who, in the opinion of the Commissioners, makes a full and true disclosure touching all the matters in respect of which he is examined, shall be entitled to receive a certificate signed by the Commissioners stating that the witness has, on his examination, made a full and true disclosure as aforesaid.

(2) If any civil or criminal proceeding is at any time thereafter instituted against any such witness in respect of any matter touching which he has been so examined, the court having cognizance of the case shall, on proof of the certificate, stay the proceeding, and may in its discretion award to the witness such costs as he may be put to in or by reason of the proceeding ; provided that nothing in this section shall be deemed to apply in the case of proceedings for having given false evidence at an inquiry held under this Act, or of having procured, or attempted, or conspired to procure, the giving of such evidence.

11. This Act may be cited as the Special Commission Act, 1888.

The following are the particulars of the charges or allegations made by the defendants in the action of "O'Donnell versus Walter," delivered pursuant to the order of the Special Commission, dated the 17th day of September, 1888.

THE "LONDON TIMES" CHARGES.

The names of the members of Parliament

against whom the charges and allegations were made are set out in the schedule hereto.

The members of Parliament mentioned in the schedule were members of the conspiracy and organization hereinafter described, and took part in the work and operations thereof with knowledge of its character, objects and mode of action.

From and including the year 1879 there have existed societies known as the Irish Land League, the Irish National Land League, and Labor and Industrial Union, the Ladies' Land League, the Ladies' Irish Land League and Labor and Industrial Union, the National League and the affiliated societies in Great Britain and America, all forming one connected and continuous organization.

The ultimate object of the organization was to establish the absolute independence of Ireland as a separate nation. With a view to effect this one of the immediate objects of the said conspiracy or organization was to promote an agrarian agitation against the payment of agricultural rents, thereby securing the co-operation of the tenant farmers of Ireland, and at the same time the impoverishment and ultimate expulsion from the country of the Irish landlords, who were styled the "English Garrison."

The mode of action was to organize a system of coercion and intimidation in Ireland, which was sustained and enforced by boycotting, and the commission of crimes and outrages.

The organization was actively engaged in the following matters :—

1. The promotion of and inciting to the commission of crimes, outrages, boycotting, and intimidation.

2. The collection and providing of funds to be used, or which it was known was used for the promotion of and the payment of persons engaged in the commission of crimes, outrages, boycotting and intimidation.

3. The payment of persons who assisted in, were affected by, or accidentally or otherwise injured in the commission of such crimes, outrages, and acts of boycotting and intimidation.

4. Holding meetings and procuring to be made speeches inciting to the commission of crimes, outrages, boycotting and intimidation. Some of the meetings referred to which were attended by members of Parliament with the approximate dates and place of meeting, are given in the schedule hereto.

5. The publication and dissemination of newspaper and other literature inciting to and approving of sedition and the commission of crimes, outrages, boycotting and intimidation, particularly the *Irish World*, the *Chicago Citizen*, the *Boston Pilot*, the *Freeman's Journal, United Ireland, The Irishman, The Nation*, the *Weekly News, Cork Daily Herald*, the *Kerry Sentinel*, the *Evening Telegraph*, the *Sligo Champion*.

6. Advocating resistance to law and the constituted authorities and impeding the detection and punishment of crime.

7. Making payments to or for persons who were guilty, or supposed to be guilty, of the commission of crimes, outrages and acts of boycotting and intimidation for their defence, or to enable them to escape from justice, and for the maintenance of such persons and their families.

8. It is charged and alleged that the members of Parliament mentioned in the schedule approved, and by their acts and conduct lead people to believe that they approved of resistance to the law and the commission of crimes, outrages and acts of boycotting and intimidation when committed in furtherance of the objects and resolutions of the said societies, and that persons who engaged in the commission of such crimes, outrages and acts would receive the support and protection of the said societies and of their organization and influence.

The acts and conduct specially referred to are as follows:

9. They attended meetings of the said societies and other meetings at various places and made speeches, and caused and procured speeches to be made, inciting to the commission of crimes, outrages, boycotting and intimidation.

10. They were parties to, and cognizant of, the payment of moneys for the purpose above men-

tioned, and as testimonials or rewards to persons
who had been convicted, or were notoriously
guilty of crimes or outrages, or to their families.

11. With knowledge that crimes, outrages and
acts of boycotting and intimidation had followed
the delivery of speeches at the meetings, they expressed no *bonâ fide* disapproval or public condemnation, but, on the contrary, continued to be
leading and active members of the said societies
and to subscribe to their funds.   .

12. With such knowledge as aforesaid they
continued to be intimately associated with the
officers of the same societies (many of whom fled
from justice), and with notorious criminals and
the agents and instruments of murder and con-
spiracies, and with the planners and paymasters
of outrage, and with the advocates of sedition,
violence and the use of dynamite.

13. They and the said societies, with such
knowledge as aforesaid, received large sums of
money which were collected in America and elsewhere by criminals and persons who were known
to advocate sedition, assassination, the use of
dynamite and the commission of crimes and outrages.

14. When on certain occasions they considered
it politic to denounce, and did denounce, certain
crimes in public, they afterwards made communications to their associates and others with the
intention of leading them to believe that such

denunciation was not sincere. One instance of this, of which the said defendants propose to give evidence, is the following letters :—

Letter from C. S. Parnell, dated the 15th of May, 1882.

Letter from the same, the 16th of June, 1882.

Another letter from the same of the same date.

The following are persons who are guilty of crime or advocates of treason, sedition, assassination, and violence with whom it is alleged the said members of Parliament continued to associate :—

Frank Byrne, who admitted his connection with the Phœnix Park murders, and who was supplied with money by Mr. C. S. Parnell, which enabled him to escape to America.

Patrick Egan, the treasurer of the Land League, who, during the years 1881 and 1882, organized and procured the commission of crimes and outrages in various parts of Ireland.

Patrick Ford, the editor of the *Irish World*, who remitted large sums of moneys to the said association, and for the purposes aforesaid.

James Carey, the Phœnix Park informer.

Captain M'Cafferty, implicated in Phœnix Park murder.

Tynan, who organized the Phœnix Park murders.

J. Mullett, convict.

T. Brennan, who was secretary of the Land

League, and paid some of the perpetrators of the Phœnix Park and other murders and outrages.

Edward M'Caffery, convict.

Patrick J. Sheridan, who was an organizer of the Land League, who organized outrages and acts of violence, and was implicated in the Phœnix Park murders.

M. J. Boyton, organizer of the Land League and instigator of crime.

J. W. Nally, convicted of crime.

John Walsh, of Middlesbrough, organizer of the Invincible conspiracy in Ireland.

Thos. F. Bourke, who was convicted of high treason on the 24th of April, 1866.

James Stephens, chief of the Fenian organization.

J. J. Breslin, Hospital Superintendent of Richmond Gaol, a member of the Irish Republican Brotherhood, who aided Stephens' escape.

Hamilton Williams, the partner of Gallagher, the convicted dynamitard, and himself a dynamitard.

Alexander Sullivan, a member of the Clan-na-Gael.

Transatlantic (Mooney).

Augustine Ford.

Ellen Ford.

Maria Doherty.

Father Eugene Sheehy.

Dr. William Carrol.

P. A. Collins.

C. O'M. Condon, sentenced to death for the murder of Sergeant Brett.

John Devoy, convicted of Fenianism, and a trustee of the Skirmishing Fund raised by the *Irish World*.

O'Brien, M'Carty, and Chambers, convicted Fenians.

John Finerty, dynamitard.

John Daly, dynamitard.

General Millen, dynamitard.

W. F. Mackay-Lomasney, a convicted Fenian.

Stephen Joseph Meaney, a convicted Fenian.

James Redpath, advocate of crime.

Jeremiah O'Donovan Rossa.

John O'Leary, convicted of Fenianism.

P. J. Gordon, Francis Tully, Father Egan, Father Coen, John Roche, of Woodford, P. N. Fitzgerald, Laurence Egan, J. Riordan, J. Connel, Timothy Horan, Jeremiah Riordan, J. Dowling, Patrick Nally, M. M. O'Sullivan, M. J. Kelly, Thomas Fitzpatrick, Maurice Murphy, Martin Egan, J. M. Wall, A. M. Forrester, J. P. Quinn, W. F. Moloney, Pearson Reddington, members of the Land League and implicated in crime.

Anna Parnell, H. Reynolds, H. Lynch, Mrs. Moloney, Clara Stritch, Mrs. Moore, members of the Ladies' Land League who paid for the commission of crime.

MR. GEO. J. GOSCHEN, M.P.

MR. JOHN DILLON, M.P

Names of Members of Parliament against whom it is proposed to give evidence of Charges and Allegations:— ·

Thomas Sexton, Joseph Gillis Biggar, Joseph Richard Cox, Jeremiah Jordan, James Christopher Flynn, William O'Brien, Dr. Charles K. D. Tanner, William J. Lane, James Gilhooly, Joseph E. Kenny, John Hooper, Charles Stewart Parnell, Maurice Healy, James Edward O'Doherty, Patrick O'Hea, Arthur O'Connor, Michael McCartan, John J. Clancy, Sir G. H. Grattan Esmonde, Bt., Timothy D. Sullivan, Timothy Harrington, William H. K. Redmond, Henry Campbell, Patrick J. Foley, Matthew Harris, David Sheehy, John Stack, Edward Harrington, Denis Kilbride, Jeremiah D. Sheehan, James Leahy, Patrick A. Chance, Thomas Quinn, Dr. Joseph Francis Fox, Michael Conway, Luke Patrick Hayden, William Abraham, John Finucane, Francis A. O'Keefe, Justin McCarthy, Timothy M. Healy, Joseph Nolan, Thomas P. Gill, Daniel Crilly, John Deasy, John Dillon, James F. O'Brien, Patrick O'Brien, Richard Lalor, James J. O'Kelly, Andrew Commins, LL.D., Edmund Leamy, ʽP. J. O'Brien, Thomas Mayne, John O'Connor, Matthew J. Kenny, Jasper D. Pyne, Patrick Joseph Power, James Tuite, Donal Sullivan, Thomas Joseph Condon, John E. Redmond, John Barry, Garrett Mich. Byrne, Thomas P. O'Connor.

The meetings at which the particular Members of Parliament made speeches:—

PLACE.	COUNTY.	DATE OF MEETING.	MEMBER.
Ballycastle..........	Antrim........	30 Nov., 1880.	J. G. Biggar.
Cork	Cork...........	5 Oct., 1879...	C. S. Parnell.
Cork	Cork...........	3 Oct., 1880...	C. S. Parnell.
Cork	Cork...... ...	3 Oct., 1880...	A. O'Connor.
Cork	Cork...........	3 Oct., 1880...	T. D. Sullivan.
Cork	Cork:.........	26 June, 1881...	John O'Connor.
Cork	Cork...........	2 Oct., 1881...	C. S. Parnell.
Cork	Cork...... ...	2 Oct., 1881...	T. M. Healy.
Ovens..............	Cork...........	15 Feb., 1885...	J. C. Flynn.
Kanturk.........	Cork...........	12 April, 1885...	W. O'Brien.
Cork	Cork...........	12 April, 1885..	J. Deasy.
Clonakilty.........	Cork...........	29 June, 1885...	J. Deasy.
Innishannon.........	Cork	22 July, 1885..	J. Deasy.
Kealkil.............	Cork...... ...	23 July, 1885..	Dr. Tanner.
Macroom...........	Cork...........	6 Sept., 1885..	John O'Connor.
Durrus.............	Cork...........	18 Oct., 1885	J. Deasy.
Coachford	Cork...........	8 Nov., 1885..	Dr. Tanner.
Middleton	Cork...........	15 Nov., 1885..	W. J. Lane.
Drimoleague.......	Cork...........	22 Nov., 1885..	Dr. Kenny.
Molly McCarthy's Bridge...........	Cork...........	23 Jan., 1887..	Dr. Kenny.
Bantry..............	Cork...........	17 Sept., 1880..	T. M. Healy.
Castletown	Cork...........	24 Oct., 1880..	T. M. Healy.
Middleton	Cork...........	13 April, 1884..	W. H. Redmond.
Boherbue	Cork...........	16 Nov., 1884..	John O'Connor.
Banteer............	Cork...........	20 Nov., 1884..	John O'Connor.
Kitsboro	Cork...........	6 Sept., 1885..	J. C. Flynn.
Queenstown	Cork...........	20 Sept., 1885..	J. Deasy.
Blackstaffs Cross....	Cork...........	4 Oct., 1885...	J. Deasy.
Ballydehob.........	Cork...........	4 Oct., 1885...	Dr. Tanner.
Millstreet..........	Cork...........	15 Dec., 1885...	Dr. Tanner.
Ballyvourmey.......	Cork...........	3 Jan., 1886..	Dr. Tanner.
Ballyvourmey...... .	Cork...........	3 Jan., 1886....	John O'Connor.
Kealkd............	Cork...... ...	22 Aug., 1886..	J. Gilhooly.
Youghal............	Cork...........	7 Nov., 1886..	W. J. Lane.
Youghal............	Cork...........	7 Nov., 1886..	J. C. Flynn.
Inchiquin	Cork...........	5 Dec., 1886...	Dr. Tanner.
Inchiquin	Cork...........	6 Dec., 1886...	W. O'Brien.
Ennis.....	Clare..........	19 Sept., 1880.	C. S. Parnell.
Ennis.....	Clare..........	19 Sept., 1880.	T. D. Sullivan.
Ennis.............	Clare..........	9 Nov., 1885...	T. M. Healy.
Ennis.............	Clare..........	12 Nov., 1882..	— Redmond.
Ennis.............	Clare..........	12 Nov., 1882..	W. J. Kenny.
Kilrush...	Clare..	16 Dec., 1882...	W. J. Kenny.

PLACE.	COUNTY.	DATE OF MEETING.	MEMBER.
Tulla	Clare	24 May, 1885	W. O'Brien.
Newmarket on Fergus.	Clare	23 Jan., 1887	J. R. Cox.
Belturbet	Clare	29 Nov., 1880	J. G. Biggar.
Kingscourt	Cavan	6 Jan., 1886	Mat. Harris.
Cardonagh	Donegal	25 March, 1881	T. M. Healy.
Donegal	Donegal	18 April, 1881	J. Dillon.
Letterkenny	Donegal	13 Feb., 1885	W. O'Brien.
Ballyshannon	Donegal	9 Nov., 1880	J. J. O'Kelly.
Lucan	Dublin	25 Jan., 1885	J. J. Clancy.
Lucan	Dublin	25 Jan., 1885	W. O'Brien.
Skerries	Dublin	1 Feb., 1885	Daniel Crilly.
Clondalkin	Dublin	22 Feb., 1885	T. Harrington.
Staggart	Dublin	29 March, 1885	J. J. Clancy.
Durdown	Dublin	12 April, 1885	T. D. Sullivan.
St. Margarets	Dublin	8 Nov., 1885	J. J. Clancy.
Tempo	Fermanagh	1 Jan., 1881	J. J. O'Kelly.
Loughrea	Galway	6 Jan., 1880	Mat. Harris.
Riversville	Galway	19 Sept., 1880	Mat. Harris.
Killeenadeema	Galway	26 Sept., 1880	T. P. O'Connor.
Killeenadeema	Galway	26 Sept., 1880	Mat. Harris.
Kilconnelly	Galway	5 Dec., 1880	Mat. Harris.
Ahascragh	Galway	19 Dec., 1880	Mat. Harris.
Ballymacward	Galway	26 Dec., 1880	Mat. Harris.
Loughrea	Galway	17 March, 1881	John Dillon.
Mountbellew	Galway	17 March, 1881	Mat. Harris.
Galway	Galway	20 March, 1881	Mat. Harris.
Killimore	Galway	25 March, 1881	Mat. Harris.
Clifden	Galway	3 April, 1881	Mat. Harris.
Carna	Galway	7 April, 1881	Mat. Harris.
Dunmore	Galway	22 May, 1881	Mat. Harris.
Kilkerrin	Galway	12 May, 1885	Daniel Crilly.
Kilreech	Galway	19 May, 1885	Mat. Harris.
Galway	Galway	30 Aug., 1885	J. Redmond.
Loughrea	Galway	10 Sept., 1885	A. O'Connor.
Loughrea	Galway	10 Sept., 1885	Mat. Harris.
Ballinasloe	Galway	18 Oct., 1885	Mat. Harris.
Athenry	Galway	26 Oct., 1885	Mat. Harris.
Athenry	Galway	26 Oct., 1885	J. Dillon.
Gurteen	Galway	29 Nov., 1885	D. Sheehy.
Gurteen	Galway	29 Nov., 1885	M. Harris.
Loughrea	Galway	16 Oct., 1886	J. Dillon.
Portumna	Galway	26 Sept., 1886	Mat. Harris.
Killimore	Galway	21 Nov., 1886	D. Sheehy.
Headford	Galway	27 June, 1880	Mat. Harris.
Eyre Court	Galway	27 Sept., 1885	Mat. Harris.
Ballinasloe	Galway	27 Sept., 1881	T. P. O'Connor.
Galway	Galway	30 Aug., 1885	J. Redmond.
Woodford	Galway	20 March, 1881	J. Dillon.
Loughrea	Galway	6 March, 1884	M. Harris.

14

PATRICK EGAN,

President of the Irish National League of America.

Place.	County.	Date of Meeting.	Member.
Beaufort	Kerry	16 May, 1880	C. S. Parnell.
Castleisland	Kerry	10 Oct., 1880	A. O'Connor.
Castleisland	Kerry	10 Oct., 1880	J. G. Biggar.
Brosna	Kerry	24 Oct., 1880	T. Harrington.
Killorglin	Kerry	31 May, 1885	E. Harrington.
Killarney	Kerry	30 Aug., 1885	J. D. Sheehan.
Killarney	Kerry	30 Aug., 1885	W. O'Brien.
Killarney	Kerry	30 Aug., 1885	T. M. Healy.
Listowel	Kerry	18 Oct., 1885	W. O'Brien.
Listowel	Kerry	18 Oct., 1885	T. Harrington.
Killarney	Kerry	15 May, 1881	T. Harrington.
Tralee	Kerry	6 March, 1881	T. Harrington.
Dingle	Kerry	20 Feb., 1881	T. Harrington.
Killorglin	Kerry	4 March, 1881	T. Harrington.
Kenmare	Kerry	20 Sept., 1885	E. Harrington.
Knocknagoshill	Kerry	6 Jan., 1886	E. Harrington.
Kiltoom	Roscommon	17 Oct., 1880	M. Harris.
French Park	Roscommon	19 June, 1881	J. R. Cox.
Ballinagare	Roscommon	18 Sept., 1881	Dr. Commins.
Boyle	Roscommon	29 Jan., 1884	W. O'Brien.
Roscommon	Roscommon	17 Aug., 1884	W. O'Brien.
Athlone	Roscommon	5 Oct., 1884	W. Redmond.
Boyle	Roscommon	21 Dec., 1884	W. Redmond.
Strokestown	Roscommon	28 Dec., 1884	J. J. O'Kelly.
Strokestown	Roscommon	25 Oct., 1885	J. G. Biggar.
Strokestown	Roscommon	25 Oct., 1885	J. O'Kelly.
Breedogne	Roscommon	30 Aug., 1885	J. J. O'Kelly.
Mount Irvine	Sligo	6 June, 1880	Mat. Harris.
Pomeroy	Tyrone	10 Dec., 1880	John Dillon.
Gortin	Tyrone	6 April, 1881	J. R. Cox.
Gortin	Tyrone	6 April, 1881	T. Sexton.
Carrick-on-Suir	Tipperary	7 Sept., 1880	Dr. Kenny.
Templemore	Tipperary	10 Oct., 1880	J. Dillon.
Holyford	Tipperary	17 Oct., 1880	J. Dillon.
Ormond Stile	Tipperary	11 April, 1881	J. Dillon.
Carrick-on-Suir	Tipperary	7 Sept., 1884	W. O'Brien.
Bansha	Tipperary	8 Feb., 1885	John O'Connor
Bansha	Tipperary	8 Feb., 1885	W. O'Brien.
Fethard	Tipperary	12 April, 1885	T. Mayne.
Holycross	Tipperary	12 April, 1885	John O'Connor
Holycross	Tipperary	5 July, 1885	D. Sheehy.
Newport	Tipperary	30 Aug., 1885	J. O'Connor.
Cahir	Tipperary	20 Sept., 1885	J. O'Connor.
Cahir	Tipperary	20 Sept., 1885	T. Mayne.
Ballingarry	Tipperary	4 Oct., 1885	T. Mayne.
Roscrea	Tipperary	11 Oct., 1885	T. Mayne.
Enniscorthy	Wexford	26 Oct., 1879	W. Redmond
Rosemount	Wexford	13 Sept., 1885	W. Redmond.
Rosemount	Wexford	13 Sept., 1885	J. G. Biggar.

PLACE.	COUNTY.	DATE OF MEETING.	MEMBER.
Wexford	Wexford	9 Oct., 1881	C. S. Parnell.
Wexford	Wexford	9 Oct., 1881	J. J. O'Kelly.
New Ross	Wexford	26 Sept., 1880	C. S. Parnell.
Killinick	Wexford	18 Sept., 1881	Redmond.
Killinick	Wexford	18 Sept., 1881	G. M. Byrne.
New Ross	Wexford	22 June, 1884	J. Redmond.
Cushenstown	Wexford	31 Aug., 1884	E. Leamy.
Cushenstown	Wexford	31 Aug., 1884	W. O'Brien.
Newtownbarry	Wexford	1 Feb., 1885	W. Redmond.
Taghmon	Wexford	24 May, 1885	W. Redmond.
Gorey	Wexford	23 Aug., 1885	W. Redmond.
Gorey	Wexford	23 Aug., 1885	W. O'Brien.
Knocknagoshill	Kerry	6 Jan., 1886	E. Harrington.
Knocknagoshill	Kerry	6 Jan., 1886	J. D. Sheehan.
Knocknagoshill	Kerry	6 Jan., 1886	J. Stack.
Newton Sandes	Kerry	25 Oct., 1886	J. Dillon.
Clonmacnoise	King's County	5 Sept., 1880	M. Harris.
Phillipstown	King's County	18 Oct., 1885	James Leahy.
Edinderry	King's County	10 Jan., 1880	Dr. Fox.
Kildare	Kildare	15 Aug., 1880	John Dillon.
Athy	Kildare	10 Oct., 1880	James Leahy.
Kildare	Kildare	24 April, 1881	John Dillon.
Nurney	Kildare	15 Feb., 1885	W. H. Redmond.
Kilkenny	Kilkenny	2 Oct., 1880	C. S. Parnell.
Clough	Kilkenny	3 April, 1881	John Dillon.
Ballyragget	Kilkenny	9 Oct., 1881	A. O'Connor.
Mullinavat	Kilkenny	14 April, 1884	P. J. Power.
Shanagolden	Limerick	5 June, 1881	J. R. Cox.
Murroe	Limerick	31 July, 1881	W. Abraham.
Abbeyfeale	Limerick	8 March, 1885	E. Harrington.
Killinallock	Limerick	12 April, 1885	T. Harrington.
New Castle	Limerick	31 May, 1885	W. Redmond.
Cappermore	Limerick	2 Sept., 1885	W. O'Brien.
Longford	Longford	17 Oct., 1880	C. S. Parnell.
Longford	Longford	18 March, 1881	Justin M'Carthy.
Edgeworthstown	Longford	27 March, 1881	Mat. Harris.
Longford	Longford	27 March, 1881	T. M. Healy.
Longford	Longford	27 March, 1881	J. M'Carthy.
Lanesboro	Longford	16 Aug., 1885	W. Redmond.
Dundalk	Louth	12 April, 1885	W. Redmond.
Navan	Meath	12 Oct., 1879	C. S. Parnell.
Broomfield	Monaghan	9 Aug., 1885	W. Redmond.
Irishtown	Mayo	2 May, 1880	C. S. Parnell.
Cong	Mayo	11 July, 1880	Mat. Harris.
Ballyhaunis	Mayo	10 Oct., 1880	Mat. Harris.
Castlebar	Mayo	3 Nov., 1885	John Dillon.
Castlebar	Mayo	3 Nov., 1885	C. S. Parnell.
Knockaroo	Queen's County	22 Feb., 1880	Richard Lalor.
Woolfhill	Queen's County	28 Sept., 1884	A. O'Connor.

PLACE.	COUNTY.	DATE OF MEETING.	MEMBER.
Maryborough	Queen's County	5 Oct., 1884.	A. O'Connor.
Maryborough	Queen's County	5 Oct., 1884....	J. Deasy.
Maryborough	Queen's County	5 Oct., 1884. ...	D. Kilbride.
Ballickmoyler.........	Queen's County	5 April, 1885..	W. Redmond.
Ballickmoyler........	Queen's County	5 April, 1885. .	A. O'Connor.
Mayo..............	Queen's County	20 Sept., 1885..	D. Crilly.
French Park.........	Roscommon....	1 Aug., 1880..	M. Harris.
Waterford............	Waterford.....	18 Dec., 1882...	J. G. Biggar.
Lismore	Waterford.....	24 May, 1884..	T. M. Healy.
Portlaw.............	Waterford.....	13 Sept., 1885..	E. Leamy.
Kilrossenty	Waterford.....	6 Dec., 1885...	G. M. Byrne.
Bray...............	Wicklow.......	31 Dec., 1882...	R. Lalor.
Ballinglass	Wicklow.......	21 Oct., 1883..	J. J. O'Kelly.
Kilbrennan	Westmeath....	10 Oct., 1880..	T. D. Sullivan.
Ballymore..........	Westmeath....	8 May, 1881....	T. Harrington.
Kilrush	Clare	29 May, 1887..	D. Sheehy.
Kilrush	Clare	29 May, 1887..	J. R. Cox.
Bandon.............	Cork	18 Sept., 1887..	J. Hooper.
Carrigrohane........	Cork	18 Sept., 1887..	J. Deasy.
Carrigrohane........	Cork	18 Sept., 1887..	Dr. Tanner.
Carrigrohane........	Cork	18 Sept., 1887..	O'Hea.
Shanbally..........	Cork	23 Oct., 1887..	J. Hooper.
Ballinadee..........	Cork	30 Oct., 1887..	J. Hooper.
Kanturk............	Cork	30 Oct., 1887..	J. C. Flynn.
Kanturk............	Cork	30 Oct., 1887..	W. O'Brien.
Carrigadrohid........	Cork	6 Nov., 1887..	Dr. Tanner.
Farnanes............	Cork	16 Nov., 1887..	J. C. Flynn.
Farnanes............	Cork	16 Nov., 1887..	J. Gilhooly.
Newry.............	Down	25 Sept., 1887..	M. M'Cartan.
Dromore	Down	1 Nov., 1887..	W. K. Redmond.
Killesher............	Fermanagh....	27 Oct., 1887..	W. K. Redmond.
Killesher............	Fermanagh....	27 Oct., 1887..	J. Jordan.
Loughrea............	Galway........	18 Oct., 1887..	D. Sheehy.
Abbey (Woodford)...	Galway........	21 Oct., 1887..	D. Sheehy.
Milltown...........	Galway........	13. Nov., 1887..	W. K. Redmond.
Milltown...........	Galway........	13 Nov., 1887..	L. P. Hayden.
Mohill.............	Leitrim........	16 Oct., 1887..	M. Conway.
Mohill.............	Leitrim........	16 Oct., 1887..	L. P. Hayden.
Longford...........	Longford	9 Oct., 1887...	T. M. Healy.
Longford...........	Longford	9 Oct., 1887...	L. P. Hayden.
Edgeworthstown......	Longford	20 Nov., 1887..	E. Harrington.
Edgeworthstown......	Longford	20 Nov., 1887..	T. M. Healy.
Ballyhaunis	Mayo.........	30 Sept., 1887..	J. F. X. O'Brien.
Kells	Meath.........	4 Dec., 1887...	P. O'Brien.
Kells	Meath.........	4 Dec., 1887...	W. K. Redmond.
Mountmellick........	Queen's County	18 Sept., 1887..	— M'Donald.
Castlerea	Roscommon....	29 Sept., 1887..	J. R. Cox.
Boyle..............	Roscommon....	1 Oct., 1887...	J. R. Cox.
Athlone.............	Roscommon....	6 Nov., 1887..	D. Sullivan.

PLACE.	COUNTY.	DATE OF MEETING.	MEMBER.
Athlone............	Roscommon....	6 Nov., 1887..	T. D. Sullivan.
Clonmel............	Tipperary......	6 Nov., 1887..	D. Sheehy.
Clonmel............	Tipperary......	6 Nov., 1887..	T. Mayne.
Tallow............	Waterford.....	25 Sept., 1887..	J. D. Pyne.
Tallow............	Waterford.....	25 Sept., 1887..	J. Deasy.
Tallow............	Waterford.....	25 Sept., 1887..	T. M. Healy.
Tallow............	Waterford.....	25 Sept., 1887..	P. J. Power.
Tang	Westmeath....	2 Oct., 1887...	J. Tuite.
Tang	Westmeath....	2 Oct., 1887...	D. Sullivan.
Arklow...........	Wicklow.......	24 Sept., 1887..	W. K. Redmond.
Kilfenora..........	Clare..........	15 Dec., 1886...	— Kenny.
Kilfenora..........	Clare..........	15 Dec., 1886...	J. Jordan.
Kilfenora..........	Clare..........	4 Dec., 1887...	— Flynn, M. P.
Ennis.............	Clare..........	3 Sept., 1887..	J. Dillon.
Cork.............	Cork	21 March, 1880	J. G. Biggar.
Carrigaline........	Cork	9 Jan., 1887....	W. J. Lane.
Coolderriby........	Cork	25 Jan., 1887..	Dr. Tanner.
Bantry............	Cork	29 May, 1887..	J. Deasy.
Bantry............	Cork	29 May, 1887..	J. Gilhooly.
Ballyrushin	Cork	12 June, 1887...	J. C. Flynn.
Mitchelstown	Cork	10 July, 1887..	W. O'Brien.
Mitchelstown	Cork	10 July, 1887..	J. C. Flynn.
Mitchelstown	Cork	10 July, 1887..	T. Condon.
Mitchelstown	Cork	9 Aug., 1887..	W. O'Brien.
Mitchelstown	Cork	11 Aug., 1887...	W. O'Brien.
Meelin	Cork	14 Aug., 1887...	J. C. Flynn.
Queenstown........	Cork	6 Sept., 1887..	P. O'Hea.
Queenstown........	Cork	6 Sept., 1887..	W. J. Lane.
Goleen............	Cork	11 Sept., 1887..	J. Deasy.
Goleen	Cork	11 Sept., 1887..	J. Gilhooly.
Letterkenny........	Donegal.......	4 Sept., 1887..	A. O'Connor.
Caroudough........	Donegal.......	12 Sept., 1887..	J. Doherty.
Loughrea..........	Galway........	7 July, 1887....	D. Sheehy.
Abbeyfeale.........	Limerick.......	9 June, 1887...	D. Sheehy.
Collon............	Louth	29 May, 1887..	D. Crilly.
Drogheda..........	Louth	17 July, 1887..	W. O'Brien.
Drogheda..........	Louth	17 July, 1887..	W. K. Redmond.
Carrickmacross......	Monaghan.....	17 April, 1887..	D. Sheehy.
Claremorris........	Mayo.........	19 Jan., 1887..	J. E. Redmond.
Ballincostello	Mayo.........	31 Jan., 1887..	J. Deasy.
Ballinrobe	Mayo.........	21 March, 1887	D. Crilly.
Newport	Mayo.........	5 June, 1887...	D. Crilly.
Newport	Mayo.........	5 June, 1887...	J. Deasy.
Lewisburg	Mayo.........	19 June, 1887..	J. Deasy.
Luggacurren........	Queen's County	24 July, 1887..	W. O'Brien.
Hillstreet	Roscommon....	19 Jan., 1887..	J. R. Cox.
Boyle.............	Roscommon....	28 Aug., 1887...	J. J. O'Kelly.
Ballina...........	Tipperary......	21 June, 1887..	D. Sheehy.
Ballieborough	Cavan........	21 Oct., 1880..	J. G. Biggar.

Place.	County.	Date of Meeting.	Member.
Bawnboy	Cavan	30 Oct., 1880	J. G. Biggar.
Bantry	Cork	17 Oct., 1880	T. M. Healy.
Millstreet	Cork	15 Dec., 1885	Dr. Tanner.
Millstreet	Cork	15 Aug., 1886	Dr. Tanner.
Dublin	Dublin	22 Nov., 1883	T. Sexton.
Dublin	Dublin	23 Nov., 1883	C. S. Parnell.
Kyhbeg	Galway	21 Nov., 1886	D. Sheehy.
Portumna	Galway	15 Nov., 1885	M. Harris.
Woodford	Galway	17 Oct., 1886	J. Dillon.
Gurteen	Galway	10 Oct., 1886	W. O'Brien.
Athy	Kildare	10 Oct., 1886	R. Lalor.
Tullyallen	Louth	8 April, 1888	J. Dillon.
Castleblayney	Monaghan	30 Nov., 1886	W. K. Redmond.
Kellystown	Meath	22 April, 1888	J. Dillon.
Kiltoom	Roscommon	17 Oct., 1880	M. Harris.
Boyle	Roscommon	20 Jan., 1884	W. O'Brien.
Berrisokane	Tipperary	27 Feb., 1881	J. Dillon.
Finea	Westmeath and Cavan	4 Nov., 1880	J. G. Biggar.
Gorey	Wexford	23 Aug., 1885	W. H. K. Redmond.
Dungarvan	Waterford	5 Oct., 1881	T. M. Healy.
Dungarvan	Waterford	5 Oct., 1881	J. Leathy.
Dungarvan	Waterford	5 Oct., 1881	C. Parnell.

CHAPTER XVI.

IN view of the numerous applications for admission that had been received, the idea had been entertained at one time of fitting up a part of the great hall of the Royal Courts of Justice for the purposes of the inquiry, but in consequence of the great difficulties and inconvenience that had to be met the proposal was not carried out, and it was decided that the inquiry should be conducted in Sir James Hannen's Court.

The body of the court was reserved for the parties concerned, their counsel and solicitors, and the representatives of the Press. A new and strong temporary gallery had been constructed in front of the permanent one, and two small side galleries had been placed over the corridors which form the entrances of the court. Each gallery had two rows of benches, giving room for sixty people, and the seats in them were reserved mainly for members of Parliament who were directly interested in the case. A new witness box had been provided on a lower level than the old one, and projecting almost into the centre of the court. Outside the court doors strong barriers had been erected. As on the former occasions, no person was admitted into the court without a ticket. The arrangements made by Mr. H. Cunynghame, Secretary to the Commission, were adequate and satisfactory.

Shortly after 10 o'clock those holding tickets began to arrive, and long before 11 o'clock, the hour fixed for the commencement of the sitting, all the allocated seats were occupied. Mr. Parnell and many other Irish Home Rule members were present.

The counsel representing *The Times* were the Attorney-General (Sir R. Webster, Q. C.), Sir H. James, Q. C., Mr. Murphy, Q. C., and Mr. W. Graham, of the English Bar, and Mr. Atkinson, Q. C., and Mr. Roman, of the Irish Bar.

Mr. Parnell was represented by Sir C. Russell, Q. C., and Mr. Asquith ; and the other members of Parliament against whom charges and allegations have been brought by Mr. R. T. Reid, Q. C., Mr. F. Lockwood, Q. C., Mr. Lionel Hart, Mr. A. O'Connor, and Mr. A. Russell, of the English Bar, and Mr. T. Harrington, of the Irish Bar.

The Commissioners having taken their seats upon the Bench,

SIR C. RUSSELL said,—My Lords, I have an application to make to your Lordships before the order of proceedings is discussed—an application

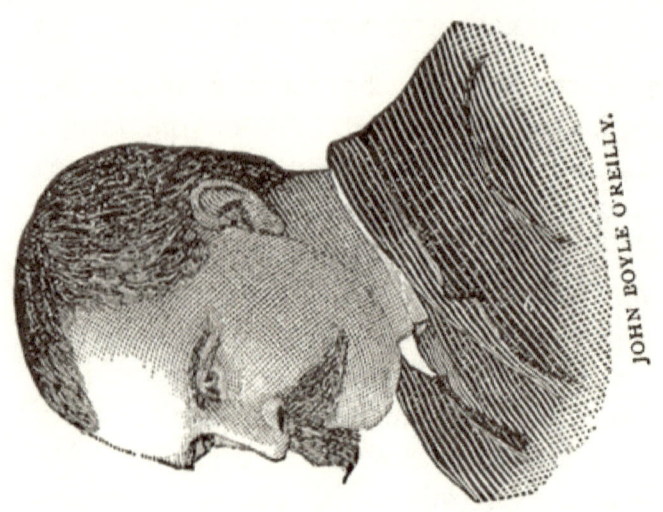

JOHN BOYLE O'REILLY.

JAMES REYNOLDS.

in which my learned friends are not interested.
It is an application under section 6 of the Special
Commission Act for the release of Mr. William
Redmond, a member of Parliament, against whom
certain particulars have been delivered. I have
to ask for an order for his release, in order that
he may attend this inquiry, on such substantial
bail as your Lordships may think fit.

The PRESIDENT.—When was he convicted?

SIR C. RUSSELL.—My Lords, the affidavit on
which I move shows that he is now confined in
Wexford Prison, that he is a material witness on
behalf of his colleagues, and is a person against
whom charges have been made. He is now under
sentence of three months' imprisonment in Wexford Prison. The affidavit does not say when
he was convicted, but I believe about a month
ago.

The PRESIDENT.—When did he commit the
offence for which he was convicted?

SIR C. RUSSELL.—I believe it was on the occasion of certain evictions when certain tenants
were resisting the process of eviction. I am informed it was on the 14th of August.

The PRESIDENT (after consulting his colleagues).
—We have already had a similar application in
the case of Mr. Dillon, which we granted under
certain conditions which I think I may say were
easy. We were anxious that these proceedings
should be commenced in such a way that all feel-

ing of irritation should, as far as possible, be allayed. My brothers and I propose to follow the same course now in regard to Mr. Redmond that we pursued in regard to Mr. Dillon, but I think it right to point out that this power given to us to release prisoners must not be construed into immunity from imprisonment for all those against whom convictions have been obtained. Without giving any expression of opinion I desire to point out that in future applications will be made under totally different circumstances. However, in order that our action may be prompt, we will give you an order for Mr. Redmond's immediate release until further order, but he will be required to enter into his own recognizances in £1000 that he will take no part in any public proceedings whatever during the time of his temporary release or while this inquiry is proceeding, and that he will surrender himself when the period arrives to undergo the remainder of his sentence.

SIR C. RUSSELL.—I would point out that Parliament meets on the 6th of November.

The PRESIDENT.—I did not mean that.

SIR C. RUSSELL.—Would your Lordships make the order merely subject to any further order, so that he might be re-committed if he took part in any proceedings of which your Lordships disapproved?

The PRESIDENT.—We are of opinion that we

must adhere to the terms which we laid down in the case of Mr. Dillon.

SIR C. RUSSELL.—Mr. Dillon was not released under your Lordships' order, but by the Government.

The PRESIDENT.—Yes; but we laid down certain conditions in his case, and to those conditions we must adhere.

SIR C. RUSSELL.—Would the conditions allow him (Mr. Redmond) to take part in public proceedings out of Ireland?

The PRESIDENT.—No.

SIR C. RUSSELL.—Then my application is unavailing, for Mr. Redmond would not comply with the conditions.

The PRESIDENT.—Oh, very well, then.

The ATTORNEY-GENERAL.—Perhaps it would be convenient now for my learned friends to state for whom they appear. I appear, with my learned friends, Sir Henry James, Mr. Murphy, Mr. Atkinson, Mr. Graham and Mr. Ronan, for the proprietors of *The Times*.

SIR C. RUSSELL.—I appear, with my friend, Mr. Asquith, for Mr. Parnell.

Mr. REID.—I appear, with Mr. T. Harrington and Mr. Arthur Russell, for Mr. Dillon, Mr. Healy and others whose names I shall hand in.

Mr. LOCKWOOD.—I appear, with Mr. Lionel Hart and Mr. A. O'Connor, for certain other gentlemen, the rest of the members of Parliament charged, a list of whom I shall hand in.

Mr. HAMMOND (solicitor).—I appear for Mr. P. A. Chance.

The ATTORNEY-GENERAL.—Might I be allowed to ask whether your Lordships have arrived at any determination as to how many days a week your Lordships intend to sit? I hope not every day.

The PRESIDENT (after consulting his colleagues). —We shall be ready to hear what counsel have to say, but our present view is to sit every day except Saturday.

The ATTORNEY-GENERAL.—I confess I had hoped that, having regard to the burden and gravity of the case, your Lordships would have thought four days a week sufficient. Your Lordships will have considerable matter to digest.

The PRESIDENT.—We shall be happy to hear what counsel have to say on the subject, and if we find there is a general concurrence of opinion on the matter we shall be anxious to meet their wishes.

SIR C. RUSSELL.—So far as I can gather there is not only a general concurrence but a unanimous feeling.

The PRESIDENT.—We have already intimated our own feeling. It will, we think, be better to go on every day this week except Saturday, and

THE LATE MR. A. M. SULLIVAN, M.P.

MR. T. D. SULLIVAN, M.P.

we shall be ready to listen to any further application on the subject.

SIR C. RUSSELL.—As to Wednesday next, my Lords?

The PRESIDENT.—With regard to Wednesday I have taken on myself to excuse our attendance at the proceedings connected with the opening of the Courts.

SIR C. RUSSELL.—I have some applications to make to your Lordships in regard to the particulars and discovery that were ordered.

The ATTORNEY-GENERAL.—We have had no notice of any application, and the particulars were delivered on Monday.

The PRESIDENT.—It would certainly have been according to practice to have given notice of your application.

SIR C. RUSSELL.—The first application I have to make is in relation to discovery.

The PRESIDENT.—Is it based on affidavit?

SIR C. RUSSELL.—Yes.

The ATTORNEY-GENERAL.—Which was sworn this morning.

SIR C. RUSSELL.—Yes; only a few moments ago.

The PRESIDENT.—Would it not be more convenient to let the applications stand over till to-morrow morning? I do not think that will make any material difference.

SIR C. RUSSELL.—I do not think it will. There

is, however, another matter which I may mention by way of giving notice to my learned friends. No particulars have been delivered as to the "other persons" against whom allegations have been made and are intended to be made here. We know that there is in the particulars the omission of the name of a gentleman who has taken a prominent part in the politics of Ireland—Mr. Michael Davitt. He was not a party to the application for particulars, and that may be the reason why his name is omitted. But one part of the application which I shall press upon your Lordships to-morrow morning is that particulars be given of any other persons than those enumerated against whom it is intended to substantiate any charges.

The ATTORNEY-GENERAL.—I shall make my observations on that matter when the application is made.

The PRESIDENT.—Very well.

·The Attorney-General then rose to open the case, which he did in a tiresome, labored argument, which pretended to be a summary of what he expected to prove, but in which he introduced letters and other matters which the laws governing the rules of evidence, I am told, almost absolutely prevented his doing in what lawyers claim to be "the regular way."

O'SHEA'S EVIDENCE.

The seventh sitting of the Commission, held on October 31st, saw the famous O'Shea on the witness stand. The proceedings that day are interesting in many ways. After the Commissioners had taken their seats the Attorney-General said: "With your Lordships' permission I propose to call a witness who is obliged to leave England—namely, Captain O'Shea. He has only with difficulty, I believe, remained until to-day, and as he has to leave for Spain, I would ask your Lordships to allow me to call him now.

SIR C. RUSSELL.—My learned friend was good enough yesterday evening to intimate to me that he intended calling Captain O'Shea this morning. But I have to tell your Lordships that it will be impossible for me at this stage of the case to cross-examine him on the part of those I represent. Therefore, if Captain O'Shea has to go to Spain he must come back again. I shall have to ask your Lordships to allow me to postpone my cross-examination, and under these circumstances I would put it to my learned friend whether he still thinks it necessary to proceed with the examination to-day.

The ATTORNEY-GENERAL.—I cannot understand any reason why Captain O'Shea should not be examined, and cross-examined as well, to-day. He has been subpœnaed by both sides, and I do not see why he should not be examined and cross-examined in the ordinary course. Whatever course my learned friend sees fit to take, I opened the points on which Captain O'Shea would give material evidence, and I must lay that evidence before this Commission.

SIR C. RUSSELL.—The only thing I intimated was that Captain O'Shea will have to attend again at a later stage.

The ATTORNEY-GENERAL.—That will rest with your Lordships. Your Lordships will form a judgment as to whether he ought to be cross-examined when your Lordships have heard his evidence.

SIR C. RUSSELL.—No.

The ATTORNEY-GENERAL.—You are not a judge, Sir Charles.

SIR C. RUSSELL.—Nor are you.

The ATTORNEY-GENERAL.—I am submitting this point, that no case has been made out as yet for postponing the cross-examination, and the application will have to be made in ordinary course at the close of the examination in chief.

SIR C. RUSSELL.—I am making that application now.

The PRESIDENT.—I think it is, of course, very desirable that we should hear the evidence of this witness. But I should be disposed to say that, when counsel states that he is not prepared to cross-examine, cross-examination should be reserved. Therefore it is for you, Mr. Attorney, to say whether, after the intimation you have received, you should persevere in the examination.

The ATTORNEY-GENERAL.—Yes; I think I should wish to take his examination in chief now. I hope when my learned friend's application for the postponement of the cross-examination is made, your Lordships will require it to be supported by some grounds other than the statement of my learned friend that he is not prepared. As Sir C. Russell has himself stated, I intimated to him last night that it was our intention to call Captain O'Shea to-day. But your Lordships will, no doubt, deal with the matter when it arises.

CHAPTER XVII.

CAPTAIN W. H. O'SHEA was then sworn and examined by the Attorney-General.

Were you formerly member of Parliament for county Clare?—Yes.

During what years were you in Parliament?—I was a member for Clare from 1880 to 1885.

Have you been in Parliament since?—Yes. I stood for a division of Liverpool at the dissolution of 1885, and was beaten, and then I became member for Galway.

Until the dissolution of 1886?—No; I resigned my seat.

The PRESIDENT.—When?

Witness.—I think the 9th of June.

The ATTORNEY-GENERAL.—From the year 1880 up to 1883 and 1884 were you on friendly terms with Mr. Parnell?—Yes.

I should have said till 1885?—Yes; until June, 1886. May or June, 1886.

In the earlier part of 1881 had you frequent private communications with Mr. Parnell on political matters?—Yes.

235

And, without going into details for the present, did you communicate, at Mr. Parnell's request, with any official personages?—I communicated, at Mr. Parnell's request, with Mr. Gladstone in June, 1881.

Certain matters passed between you and Mr. Gladstone, at Mr. Parnell's request, in 1881?—Yes.

Did you know from Mr. Parnell whether the 1881 negotiations were made with the knowledge of his other colleagues or not?—No; they were made without the knowledge of his other colleagues, according to the information given to me.

Whom do you mean by "Mr. Parnell's other colleagues?"—I mean his colleagues in Parliament—those who formed his party.

Did you have at that time any communications with Mr. Parnell in reference to Mr. Egan?—No.

Did you know at that time from Mr. Parnell whether the communications were known to Mr. Egan?—No. I ascertained afterwards they were not known to him.

From whom did you afterwards ascertain that?—From Mr. Parnell.

Did you know Mr. Egan yourself?—No.

Did you know in 1881 what Mr. Egan was doing or where he was?—I do not remember.

When did you learn that the 1881 negotiations were not known to Mr. Egan?—After Mr. Glad-

stone's speech in the House of Commons on the
16th of May, 1882.

What was it that Mr. Parnell said to you that
led you to the opinion that the 1881 negotiations
were not known to Mr. Egan?—Subsequently to
the speech I have referred to Mr. Parnell expressed regret at the awkwardness of Mr. Gladstone in introducing the matter, and he said that
that speech annoyed Mr. Egan and, I believe,
others.

Did he say who the others were?—Not to my
knowledge.

After the negotiations or communications of
1881 did the matter drop until the beginning of
1882?—The matter was brought before the Cabinet in 1881 and rejected.

SIR C. RUSSELL.—How can you say that? You
were not in the Cabinet? (Laughter.)

The ATTORNEY-GENERAL.—This is not a laugh-
ing matter. The matter, as far as you were concerned, dropped until the early part of 1882?—
The matter was dropped, but I recommenced it
in 1882.

In April, 1882, where was Mr. Parnell?—He
was on parole, being released from Kilmainham.

Who were his colleagues in Kilmainham—Mr.
Dillon and Mr. O'Kelly.

Did you know where Mr. Egan was then?—I
have no doubt he was in Paris.

Did you in the early part of 1882 enter into

certain communications with members of the Government?—Yes.

Were those communications in 1882 without the direct authority of Mr. Parnell?—Without any authority whatever from Mr. Parnell, direct or indirect.

Please answer this question—Yes or no. Did you receive certain communications from certain members of the Government in the course of these communications?—Yes.

Had you any communications from Mr. Parnell until his release on parole?—No.

When was he released on parole? Do you know?—I cannot remember the date.

How did you first know of it?—Mr. Parnell called on me.

Where?—I was at No. 1, Albert-mansions.

Had you any other house?—Yes; I had a house at Eltham. I had an attack of gout from which I was recovering. Mr. Parnell went first to Eltham to see me, and then came to Albert-mansions.

SIR C. RUSSELL.—The exact date of Mr. Parnell's release on parole is the 10th of April.

The ATTORNEY-GENERAL.—Will you tell us what passed at that interview with regard to the communications you had been engaged in up to that time with certain representatives of the Government?—I mentioned to him what I had done. I

W REDMOND, M. P.

J. E. REDMOND, M. P

mentioned that I had written to Mr. Gladstone, and he expressed himself pleased at the fact.

Do you remember anything else being referred to at that meeting with regard to the communication to Mr. Gladstone?—No, because that was just after my communication with Mr. Gladstone, and I promised that as soon as I got an answer I would communicate it to him.

Do you remember on that occasion anything being said about his release?—We spoke about his release, but it was arranged that it should not be a conditional matter in any way.

I think you said if you got an answer you would communicate with him in Paris?—I did.

Did he leave before you received any answer? —Yes. He dined with me and went off by the London, Chatham, and Dover Railway that night.

Did you subsequently, shortly after, receive a reply from Mr. Gladstone?—Yes.

Did you receive any letter from Mr. Parnell while in Paris?—Yes.

Have you got that?—Yes. Here it is.

It is dated 16th of April?—Yes.

The letter was then read:

"Grand Hotel, 12, Boulevard des Capucines, Paris,   APRIL 16, 1882.

" MY DEAR O'SHEA:—Your letter with enclosure, which I now return, has duly reached me, and is very interesting. I trust that something may come out of the correspondence, and certainly the prospect looks favorable. You were right to accentuate the difference between a gift and a loan. If you read Fottrell's evidence before the Lord's Committee you will see what I mean. The latter will only benefit the lawyers, who are making far too much out of the Irish land question as it is. I think Fottrell's estimate of the amount requisite very near the mark. I cannot at all see how the ownership of land in Ireland in the occupation of tenants can ever again fetch the prices of the interval between '70 and '77. A permanent settlement is most desirable for everybody's sake, and this can only be done by extending the term of repayment. According to my calculation about eight millions of pounds sterling would enable three-fourths of the tenants (those at or under £30 valuation) to become owners at fairly remunerative prices to the landlords. The larger class of tenants can do well enough with the Law Courts if Mr. Healy's clause be fairly amended. I am very much obliged for your kind inquiries regarding my sister. She was very much cut up, but is somewhat better now. My presence here has been a great help to her in every way. I shall probably be returning through London Sunday next, and will look you up if I have time. "Yours very truly,

"CHAS. S. PARNELL."

Now, on receipt of that letter from Mr. Parnell, did you make certain communications, continue making communications, with certain members of the government?—Yes.

Did Mr. Parnell return from Paris before you expected him or not?—He returned from Paris sooner than I expected him.

On what date did you see him again?—I cannot remember perfectly the date; but I should think it was on the Wednesday.

That is April 19, I think; it would probably be April 19. Did he telegraph to you that he was coming?—Yes.

Where to?—To Eltham.

Did you know whether any of Mr. Parnell's immediate followers, other than those who were in Kilmainham, were in London at the same time? —Yes, a good many of them.

Did you see Mr. Parnell alone?—Oh, yes, I saw Mr. Parnell alone; I never had anything to do with any one but Mr. Parnell.

Do you remember on the Wednesday a conversation with Mr. Parnell about Mr. Davitt?— I have no doubt that there was a conversation respecting Mr. Davitt; but I cannot remember the exact date.

Never mind about the date. Do you remember on the occasion of Mr. Parnell being out of Kilmainham whether he said anything about Mr. Davitt?—Yes. I was particularly anxious that

Davitt should be released, and I exerted myself to that purpose.

Will you tell us what passed between you and Mr. Parnell with reference to Davitt's release?—At that time nothing more than that. We spoke about it; he agreed that it would be very advantageous indeed if Mr. Davitt were to be released. I felt strongly myself, and spoke to him strongly on the point also.

Did he say anything about negotiations with Mr. Davitt, or about any difficulty?—Not at that time.

On that occasion, at Eltham, do you remember his referring to the release of others of his colleagues?—He remained several days before he returned to Kilmainham—

How many times did you see him?—Oh, constantly.

Did he say anything about the release of any other of his colleagues?—Yes; he saw an objection to the release of certain of his colleagues.

Explain what you mean by an objection.—He thought it would be inexpedient to release certain prisoners.

Why?—Because they would not. He did not think that they could be released at that time with advantage to the policy which was being pursued.

Do you remember whether on that occasion at Eltham he mentioned any names?—Yes; there were some names which I was to mention to Mr. Chamberlain, and which I did mention to Mr. Chamberlain.

As persons not to be released?—Yes; as persons not to be released; but neither Mr. Chamberlain nor myself approved of it.

Can you tell me the names of any you remember?—Yes; Brennan.

Was Mr. Brennan in Kilmainham at that time? —I rather think he was in another gaol.

Did you know what Mr. Brennan was—what his occupation had been?—I know he was an agitator.

Did you know he was connected with the League?—Oh, yes. I think I must have known that.

Did you know he was secretary, or treasurer, or what?—I knew he was an official of the Land League.

Now, on that occasion, Mr. O'Shea—I am speaking of the visit to Eltham—were the outrages discussed?—Oh, yes; largely discussed.

Will you tell us what was said, the substance of what was said, between you and Mr. Parnell on that occasion, when he was on that visit, before he went back to Kilmainham?—Communications were being carried on by the government at that time, and in the course of those communications naturally the question of the release of prisoners came up. It is only fair to

Mr. Parnell to say that he never made any conditions himself in the discussion of these matters
as to the conduct he should adopt—

SIR C. RUSSELL.—Oh, no, no; your communications—

The ATTORNEY-GENERAL.—No, Mr. Parnell's
future conduct.

The Witness.—He authorized me to say that
he would do his utmost to do what he afterwards
said in the Kilmainham letter.

The ATTORNEY-GENERAL.—Well, we are not
going into the Kilmainham letter at present.
What did he authorize you to say he would do ?—
Put down outrages.

Did he say anything in regard to rent?—Yes.

What did he say?—That a No-rent Manifesto
should be drawn up.

Did he say anything about advice to tenants as
to payment of rent?—I take it that that was
included in the drawing up of a No-rent Manifesto.

Do you remember whether he referred at all to
intimidation or boycotting?—Yes.

What did he say?—He had always thought
that if the question of arrears were settled it
would be a matter of material benefit; that outrages would be put down and boycotting also;
and he would endeavor to do that by the aid of
his friends.

SIR C. RUSSELL.—Would your Lordship allow the shorthand writer to read that answer?

The PRESIDENT.—Certainly.

The shorthand writer having done so,

The ATTORNEY-GENERAL, resuming the examination of the witness, asked, Did you embody the result of your conversation with Mr. Parnell in a written memorandum?—Hardly, but—

Did you at the time embody it in a memorandum?—Yes.

Which you handed, I think, to a member of the government?—It was by myself or a member of the government.

The PRESIDENT.—" Or " or " for? "—With a member of the government.

The ATTORNEY-GENERAL.—Have you got that? The witness produced a document which was handed to the Attorney-General.

The ATTORNEY-GENERAL.—Whose handwriting is this in?—Mr. Chamberlain's.

The document was handed back to the witness.

The ATTORNEY-GENERAL.—What I want to ask you, looking at that, is, Did it at any rate truthfully represent the substance of what Mr. Parnell had said to you? Up to that time I mean?—Yes.

The ATTORNEY-GENERAL.—I put that in, my Lords.

SIR C. RUSSELL.—Well, I have not seen it, and

do not know whether it is evidence; but I do not object.

The PRESIDENT.—I understand you do not object, Sir Charles?

SIR C. RUSSELL.—No, my Lord; I would rather the document was read.

The PRESIDENT.—Will you look at it, Sir Charles?

SIR C. RUSSELL.—If your Lordship pleases.

The document was handed to Sir C. Russell and then to the Secretary of the Commission, who proceeded to read it:—" 22d April, 1882,"—That is in pencil on the top left-hand corner—" 72, Prince's-gate, S. W. If the government announce a satisfactory plan of dealing with arrears, Mr. Parnell will advise all tenants to pay rents, and will denounce outrages and resistance to law and all processes of intimidation, whether by boycotting or in any other way. No plan of dealing with arrears will be satisfactory which does not wipe them off compulsorily by composition, one-third payable by tenant, one-third by the State from the Church Fund or some other public source, and one-third remitted by the landlord, so that the contribution by the tenant and the State shall not exceed one year's rent; the balance, if any, to be remitted by the landlord. Arrears to be defined as arrears accruing up to 1881."

The ATTORNEY-GENERAL.—Now, Mr. O'Shea, did you, on April 23—only answer my question, yes or no—write a letter to Mr. Chamberlain?—Yes.

Of which I think you have a copy? You need not trouble to read it, only answer my question. I think it is April 23, 1882?—Yes.

In substance, on the question of outrages, payment of rent, boycotting, and intimidation, do you remember, prior to Mr. Parnell's returning to Kilmainham, anything more passing between him and you—I am speaking of that period prior to your going to Kilmainham?—I do not remember anything else.

Mr. Parnell went back to Kilmainham—just answer my question, yes or no—did you continue the negotiations which had been commenced before and continued while Mr. Parnell was in London, after he went back to Kilmainham?—Yes.

On April 27, 1882, did you consider it desirable to go to Kilmainham to see Mr. Parnell yourself?—Yes.

Did you know, Mr. O'Shea, with reference to what passed before and while you were at Kilmainham, whether the fact of your negotiations was known to the other members of the party?

SIR C. RUSSELL.—My Lord, I object to that question.

The ATTORNEY-GENERAL.—I think my learned

friend does not quite understand my question, I meant from Mr. Parnell.

The ATTORNEY-GENERAL having repeated his question, the witness said—During my interview in Kilmainham I was told they were not.

The ATTORNEY-GENERAL.—Had anything passed between you and Mr. Parnell prior to your going to Kilmainham as to your going there?—Yes, a letter.

Had anything passed in conversation as to your going to Kilmainham?—I do not remember.

Have you the letter—had you received a letter?—Yes, I received a letter.

Upon this particular matter with reference to your going to Kilmainham?—Yes.   Do you want the letter?

I want it if you have it there.   Witness handed a letter to the learned counsel, and it was read by the secretary as follows:

"APRIL 27, 1882.

"MY DEAR O'SHEA:—Wednesday's proceedings were very promising so far as they went. I think it would be well now to wait and see what proposals are made, as an appearance of over-anxiety on your part might be injurious. The journey from London was very fair and quiet, and I got as far as Holyhead without being recognized. If you come to Ireland I think you had best not see me, for reasons I will explain hereafter.

"Yours very truly,
"C. S. PARNELL."

The ATTORNEY-GENERAL.—Do you know what Wednesday's proceedings were?—Yes, a Wednesday's debate in the House of Commons on a Bill brought in by one of Mr. Parnell's colleagues.

Which of his colleagues? Do you remember? —Mr. Redmond, I think. I am not quite certain, but I am almost certain.

Did you receive a telegram from Mr. Parnell about the same time?—Yes; but I do not think I received it until I returned from Kilmainham.

That period does not come till afterwards. You had left London before the telegram arrived. Did anything pass between you and Mr. Parnell while at Kilmainham with reference to what he referred to in that letter as to the desirability of your not seeing him?—Yes; but arising out of that he told me he should, on my leaving, immediately inform Mr. Dillon and Mr. O'Kelly that some one had been to see him.

Anything more?—Not that I remember.

I do not want to anticipate or come to the interview, but I want to know whether or not Mr. Parnell referred to the reasons he mentions in his letter for not seeing you. He says, you know, in his letter, "if you come to Ireland I think you had best not see me, for reasons I will explain hereafter." Did he refer to those reasons when you met?—As far as I remember he did not. He thought it was injudicious that I should see him at that time at Kilmainham among all the others there.

You had an order to see him?—Yes, Mr. Forster gave me an order, so that I might make it clear to the Cabinet how everything was going on.

You went to Kilmainham, I think, in a four-wheeled cab?—Yes, with the Deputy Chairman of the Irish Prisons Board.

Was a letter written by you in Kilmainham and signed by Mr. Parnell?—No, the letter was written by Mr. Parnell.

Written while you were there?—Yes, written while I was there.

The whole of that letter was written by Mr. Parnell?—Yes, the whole of it was written by him.

Before that letter was written, will you tell us what conversation passed between you and Mr. Parnell on the subject of outrages, intimidation, and payment of rent?—Yes; I explained to him that this was a very important matter to several members of the Cabinet, and must be clearly set out, and we had a long conversation, the outcome of which was the letter, in which, I think, he stated exactly what he wanted.

I will read the letter, of course, presently, but was only a hurried reference made to the question of outrages?—Oh, no; much more than that. There was an earnest conversation respecting the No-rent Manifesto and outrages. Apart from my official character, I asked Mr. Parnell privately if he was sure he would be able to carry out the guarantee he had given with the aid of his colleagues, and to put down boycotting, outrages, and the no-rent movement? He gave me that assurance, saying that the outrages were largely committed by the sons of tenants in arrear. The Arrears Bill, he said, would, of course, have a good effect on them, and that he had every confidence that his authority and that of his colleagues was so great that I might assure the Ministry that he would be able to do what they wanted.

Do you remember whether this particular part of the conversation occurred before or after the letter was written?—I should think both before and after.

The ATTORNEY-GENERAL.—My Lords, I think it is best to try and get the whole of the conversation before I read the letter. Inasmuch as I understand that the conversation took place before the letter was written, I will not divide it.

(To witness) Did Mr. Parnell refer to any particular men or names?—Yes.

To whom?—He spoke of what ought to be done in the case of my success in getting his release, and carrying the negotiations through, on which his release would, of course, immediately take place. It is due to Mr. Parnell to say that his condition of release was never put forward as an absolute condition.

No; that is not suggested. What I want to know is this—do you remember his referring to anybody else in connection with the putting down of outrages?—Yes; we had a long conversation about it. He was anxious that certain men should be released.

Who were they?—Boyton and Sheridan.

Will you tell me what he said about Sheridan?—He said that he had been an organizer in the west, that he knew everybody, and that Mr. Parnell believed that, if he were released and he could see him, he would be able to use him for the purpose of putting down outrages. I am not quite sure, however, that it was a question of release in Sheridan's case. I think there was merely a warrant out against him.

Did Mr. Parnell tell you anything you were to do or to say with regard to Sheridan?—Yes; I was to repeat what he had said to Mr. Forster, and I did repeat it to him.

Just give us as a collected statement, if you can,

of what you were to repeat to the government with regard to Sheridan.—That he had been an organizer in the west of Ireland; that he had made many acquaintances in the district, and that he would be a most useful man to use for the purpose of putting down outrage and boycotting if Mr. Parnell saw him.

The ATTORNEY-GENERAL.—" If Mr. Parnell saw him." I do not know whether your Lordships heard the end of the sentence.

The PRESIDENT.—Yes, we did.

The ATTORNEY-GENERAL.—Now, did he say anything more as to the necessity of his seeing Sheridan?—Yes, he said that he was very anxious to see him in the case of his own release.

You mentioned a short time ago something about Boyton. What did Mr. Parnell say about Boyton?—Very much the same thing, only he had been an organizer, not in the west, but in another province.

Did he name the province?—Yes, I rather think that it was Leinster; but I am not at all certain.

In this conversation was Egan's name mentioned at all?—Yes.

What did he say about Egan?—He said he was anxious to see him, and that I ought to get Egan back also.

Did he say why you should try and get Egan back?—I have no doubt he knew——

SIR C. RUSSELL.—No, no.   Tell us, please, what he said.

The ATTORNEY-GENERAL.—As far as you recollect tell us what Mr. Parnell said about Egan? —He said he should be anxious to see him, as then he should be able to show him the advantages of the policy he was adopting.

Now, do you remember asking him anything about these three men collectively as to his power over them—that is to say, over Egan, Sheridan, and Boyton?—Yes.

What did he say?—In the course of conversation he told me several times that he was confident that if he saw them first he should be able to induce them to do what he wanted.

Do you remember the actual expression he used when he said if he saw them first?—Yes. He said if he got the first run at them.

Had you yourself any knowledge of the working of the Land League?—No, no private knowledge; none except what was in the general knowledge of the public. I had no private knowledge of its affairs, and I was never connected with its affairs.

Had you ever been connected with it?—No.

Now, in the course of this conversation, was Mr. Davitt's name referred to?—Yes.

What passed at Kilmainham with reference to Mr. Davitt?—Very much the same conversation passed with reference to him as to the others.

He was in a different position, as he was in penal servitude. Mr. Parnell said he was very anxious to see Mr. Davitt released, and he was anxious that the release of the other men should include Mr. Davitt.

Do you remember anything being said at Kilmainham as to when Mr. Davitt should be released?—No, because nothing was arranged at that time about his release.

Did anything pass on that occasion about Mr. Parnell seeing Mr. Davitt or not?—All I can say is that Mr. Parnell said that he was anxious that the release should include Mr. Davitt.

Now you have referred to these three men—do you recollect any conversation taking place about keeping these persons in prison?—That subject was not referred to then.

Did you bring away a letter signed by Mr. Parnell?—Yes.

What did you do with it?—I took it the next morning — Sunday — to Mr. Forster, at his house.

Have you a copy of it?—No; but it has been published.

You have not got the letter itself?—No; it was handed to the Cabinet.

SIR C. RUSSELL.—How can you know that?

The PRESIDENT.—You ought to leave out the reference to the Cabinet. Of course you ought not to know what was done there. (Laughter.)

The ATTORNEY-GENERAL.—Was that letter read by Mr. Parnell on the 15th of May in your hearing in the House of Commons?—Yes; but it was read by Mr. Parnell with certain omissions.

The ATTORNEY-GENERAL.—I will read the whole letter as it was signed by Mr. Parnell. The actual print of it is to be found in "Hansard," vol. 269, p. 672, as it was read by Mr. Parnell himself in the House of Commons. It is dated from Kilmainham, April 28, 1882, and it is in the following terms:—

17

CHAPTER XVIII.

MY DEAR MR. O'SHEA.

" I was very sorry that you had left Albert-mansions before I reached London from Eltham, as I had wished to tell you that, after our conversation, I had made up my mind that it would be proper for me to put Mr. M'Carthy in possession of the views which I had previously communicated to you. I desire to impress upon you the absolute necessity of a settlement of the arrears question, which will leave no recurring sore connected with it behind, and which will enable us to show the smaller tenantry that they have been treated with justice and some generosity. The proposal you have described to me, as suggested in some quarters, of making a loan, over however many years the payment might be spread, should be absolutely rejected, for reasons which I have already explained to you. If the arrears question be settled upon the lines indicated by us, I have every confidence—a confidence shared by my colleagues—that the exertions which we should be able to make, strenuously and unremittingly, would be effective in stopping outrages and intimidation of all kinds. As regards permanent legislation of an ameliorating character, I may say that the views which you always shared with me, as to the admission of leaseholders to the fair-rent clauses of the Act, are more confirmed than ever. So long as the flower of the Irish peasantry are kept outside the Act there cannot be the permanent settlement of the Land Act which we all so much desire. I should also strongly hope that some compromise might be arrived at this Session with regard to the amendment of the tenure clauses of the Land Act. It is unnecessary for me to dwell upon the enormous advantage to be derived from the full extension of the purchase clauses, which now seem practically to have been adopted by all parties. The accomplishment of the programme I have sketched out to you would, in my judgment, be regarded by the country as a practical settlement of the land question, and would, I am sure, enable us to co-operate cordially for the future with the Liberal party in forwarding Liberal principles ; and I believe that the Government at the end of the Session would, from the state of the country, feel themselves thoroughly justified in dispensing with further coercive measures.

> " Yours, truly,
> "CHAS. S. PARNELL."

The PRESIDENT.—To whom is that letter addressed?

The ATTORNEY-GENERAL.—It is addressed to "My dear Mr. O'Shea."

The PRESIDENT.—The witness says that the whole of the letter was not read by Mr. Parnell.

The ATTORNEY-GENERAL.—The letter is dated from Kilmainham on the 28th of April, 1882. It was in Mr. Parnell's handwriting, and is signed by him, and is addressed to Mr. O'Shea. When the letter was first read in the House of Commons by Mr. Parnell some words were left out, were they not?—Yes.

Do you recollect which words they were that were left out?—Yes, they were these:—"And would, I am sure, enable us to co-operate cordially for the future with the Liberal party in forwarding Liberal principles" in measures connected with Ireland. Mr. Parnell read from a copy I gave him. A few minutes afterwards the omission was challenged by Mr. Forster, and I read the omitted passage.

The ATTORNEY-GENERAL.—However, were the omitted words contained in the letter which was signed by Mr. Parnell?—Yes.

And within a few minutes after the first part of the letter was read in the House of Commons the omitted portions were read also?—Yes.

In fact, they together appear on the same page of "Hansard"?—Yes.

I am afraid I must go back to one matter that has escaped my recollection. Do you recollect Mr. Parnell mentioning any names of persons to whom he would, after your departure, make a communication?—Yes; he said he would make a communication to Mr. Dillon and Mr. O'Kelly. He said that he would let them know as much as was good for them.

Do you recollect any other references which he made to his fellow-prisoners at that time?—No.

When you came back to London did you give a letter to Mr. Forster on the 30th?—Yes; on Sunday morning, which I believe was the 30th.

Did you continue negotiations on the basis of what had passed between you and Mr. Parnell on your return to London?—Yes.

Do you remember it being determined to release Mr. Parnell and some of his fellow-prisoners, such as Mr. Dillon and Mr. O'Kelly? —Yes.

They were released on the night of Tuesday, the 2d of May?—Yes.

Had you any communication between your interview at Kilmainham and the 6th of April with regard to Mr. Davitt's release?—With Mr. Parnell when he returned to London.

How soon after his return to London did you communicate with him?—Very soon after; I think on the Thursday morning.

When he returned to London, did he come and see you?—Yes.

What did he say to you?—I told him that Mr. Davitt was to be released, and he said to me that it would be inexpedient that he should be released until he saw him, and asked me to see the proper authority on the subject.

As to what?—As to Mr. Davitt's release being postponed until he should be able to go down and see him personally.

Did you do so?—Yes.

Did Mr. Parnell on the same occasion when he came and saw you say anything further about Sheridan?—Yes.

What did he ask you to do as regards Sheridan? —He asked me, when I saw the proper authority on the subject of deferring Mr. Davitt's release, at the same time to get the warrant which was out against Sheridan cancelled.

The two matters which Mr. Parnell spoke to you about when he came to see you were, first, the deferring the release of Mr. Davitt until he had seen him, and, secondly, the cancelling of the warrant which was out against Sheridan?— Yes.

Did anything more of importance occur on that occasion?—I cannot remember now.

Now, answer this question, yes or no. Did you make a communication to the authorities as to Mr. Davitt's release being delayed?—Yes.

Do you remember the date fixed until when his release was to be delayed?—Yes; it was Saturday, the 6th.

Did you communicate to Mr. Parnell the result of your interview with the authorities?— Yes, with respect to Mr. Davitt and Sheridan.

Did Mr. Parnell subsequently go down to Portland?—Yes.

With whom?—I think with Mr. Dillon.

On the morning of Saturday, the 6th?—Yes.

Did anything else of importance pass between you and Mr. Parnell after that, prior to the Phœnix Park murders?—I do not recollect.

Did Mr. Parnell come to you on the Sunday morning?—Yes; at No. 1, Albert-mansions.

At what time on the Sunday morning did Mr. Parnell come to you?—It was early in the day; I do not recollect the exact hour.

Do you recollect that day a manifesto being referred to?—Yes.

How many interviews did you have with Mr. Parnell on that day?—Several.

Do you recollect going to see Mr. Hamilton at Mr. Parnell's request?—Yes.

Who was Mr. Hamilton?—He was secretary to Mr. Gladstone.

Did Mr. Parnell say whom he had seen about the manifesto?—Yes; he told me all about the matter.

Tell us what he said.—He said the manifesto had been drawn up. I do not know that I saw it before he showed it to me at Mr. Chamberlain's house.

LORD HARTINGTON, M. P

LORD R. CHURCHILL, M. P.

At what time of the day was that?—In the afternoon.

Did he say by whom it had been drawn up?— Yes; by Mr. Davitt, and that it was a mistake for me to suppose that he was not in favor, of the manifesto, as he was in favor of it, as it was necessary to pander to Mr. Davitt's vanity; but he added that I must draft it.

Oh, I see; he objected to the English of it. It was the bombast of the document he objected to?—Yes.

Do you recollect on one of these occasions on that day Mr. Parnell saying anything about himself?—Yes, he spoke of the danger in which he was.

When was that?—That was in a cab on the way back from Mr. Chamberlain's house.

Do you remember what he said?—Yes, he said he was in personal danger, and asked me to get police protection for him.

Did you do anything for him?—Yes.

What?—When I returned to Albert-mansions I found there a request that I should go to Sir William Harcourt immediately, and I went.

Did you make any communication to Sir William Harcourt in reference to police protection?—Yes.

Do you know whether it was granted?—Yes.

Was any one else present besides Sir William Harcourt when you made that request?—I do not recollect, but I rather think his son was.

Just answer this question, yes or no—Was a communication made to you by Sir William Harcourt the same day with reference to the withdrawal of the warrant against Sheridan?—Yes; that was what he had sent for me for. He told me—

You must not tell me what he told you. Just answer the question, yes or no, because I am supposed to know what you can say and what you cannot say. Did you have an interview with Mr. Parnell afterwards?—Yes.

Did you say anything to him about the Sheridan difficulty?—Yes.

What did you say?—I told him that I had been informed that Sheridan, whose warrant was cancelled on the previous Thursday at my request, was a murderer and a concocter of murder, that the police had informed the Home Secretary of the fact that he could not be allowed to remain in this country without arrest, but that, having been informed of that, I—having been the cause of his warrant being cancelled—had begged that he should be given at least "short law." I said that he must be communicated with immediately. Mr. Parnell told me that he had no communication with him directly, but knew a person who could communicate with him, and he went out for the purpose of seeing that person.

Did he say who it was? Did he mention the name of the person?—No.

How long was he gone?—He was gone for some time.

What did he say when he came back?—He said that he thought that it was all right.

Did you learn from Mr. Parnell who was the person who could communicate with Sheridan?—I do not remember. I do not think so.

Now will you look at the signature to that letter dated the 15th of May, 1882?

SIR C. RUSSELL.—Is that the alleged Parnell letter?

The ATTORNEY-GENERAL.—Yes. In whose handwriting do you say that signature is?—I know nothing about signatures.

I know you are not an expert. But as far as you can say—in whose handwriting do you believe that signature to be?—It appears to be Mr. Parnell's signature.

Now just look at the two letters of the 16th of June, 1882. Whose signatures do you believe these to be?—I believe them to be Mr. Parnell's.

Can you tell me, did the occurrence of the Phœnix Park murders appear to affect Mr. Parnell's health?—Yes, I think they did. They certainly affected his spirits.

What was the condition of his nerves and health about this time and for a month or five weeks afterwards?—I can only say that he was very much dispirited by what had occurred.

Now just look at this document of the 9th of January, 1882.

The PRESIDENT.—What is this document and the letters of the 16th of June? I do not carry their nature in my mind.

The letters were then handed up to the President. Subsequently, the witness's attention was again called to the letter of January 9, 1882, and he said,—I believe the signature to be that of Mr. Parnell.

The ATTORNEY-GENERAL.—Just look at these other three documents. Their contents, my Lord, are not material. They are put in merely for the sake of the handwriting. (To witness.) Now take those three letters in your hand and tell us whose handwriting you believe them to be? —I believe them to be Mr. Parnell's.

Where are you now engaged, Mr. O'Shea—in what business or place?—I am not engaged in business, but I am engaged on business in Madrid.

Are you obliged to leave England?—Yes, it would be very inconvenient if I were detained here, or if I had to come back for the purpose of attending the Commission.

Is your business in Madrid pressing?—Yes.

The PRESIDENT.—Now, Sir Charles.

SIR C. RUSSELL.—The latter part of the witness's evidence, my Lords, has come upon me by surprise—namely, that part which relates to the opinion of this witness as to the signatures to the letters. I would suggest whether it would not be convenient to go at once into the whole case of the letters. It will be possible for me in a day or two to cross-examine this witness and thus save the necessity of his returning from Madrid.

The PRESIDENT.—I understand your difficulty is due to the evidence as to the handwriting.

SIR C. RUSSELL.—Not wholly, my Lord. I own I could not ask Mr. O'Shea to come back to be cross-examined as to that part only.

The ATTORNEY-GENERAL.—May I make one observation in reference to this application? I shall not for one moment oppose any suggestion in this matter that your Lordships think reasonable, but I do respectfully submit that to postpone the cross-examination of this witness without some ground being shown is very inconvenient. My statement as to Mr. O'Shea's evidence was made on Tuesday or Wednesday last, and I submit that no adequate ground has been shown for postponing this cross-examination.

SIR C. RUSSELL.—I have not made the application to your Lordships idly or without a full recognition of my responsibility in making it.

The PRESIDENT.—I think it right to state that, so far as the examination has proceeded, we are unable to see any reason why the cross-examination should be postponed. In a matter of this kind, however, we are obliged, and we are usually justified, to rely on the statement made by counsel. If Sir Charles Russell says that he is not in a position to cross-examine now, we feel bound to grant his application, but it is right that I should point out that if, from any unforeseen causes, we should not have the advantage of this witness's attendance again, his evidence must be taken without the cross-examination.

SIR C. RUSSELL.—There can scarcely be a question as to obtaining this gentleman's presence except under circumstances beyond human control.   He lives and is a resident in London.

The PRESIDENT.—It is not necessary to enter into any discussion.   I have stated the view of the Court on this point.

SIR C. RUSSELL.—I feel that we should have a clear understanding.   Am I to understand that the power of the Court will not be used to compel the attendance of Mr. O'Shea at a later stage?

The PRESIDENT.—We, of course, would use the powers of the Court to compel the attendance of a witness if necessary.   But I must repeat that if, from any unforeseen cause, his attendance cannot be procured, his evidence already given must be taken as un-cross-examined.

SIR C. RUSSELL.—I hope I am not unduly pressing the Court in asking for an assurance that the ordinary powers of the Court will be used to enforce the attendance, if necessary, of Captain O'Shea for cross-examination.

The PRESIDENT.—I have already said so.   The

Court will exercise its powers to enforce the attendance of any witness it deems necessary.

Witness.—Might I make a statement, my Lords?

The PRESIDENT.—With regard to your attendance?

Witness.—Yes. I would ask that no unreasonable delay should take place. It would be very hard on me to be kept here.

SIR C. RUSSELL.—I have already made a proposition which I thought might be considered by my learned friend. I did not know this witness was to give evidence on the genuineness of the letters.

The PRESIDENT.—You say that this evidence has surprised you, Sir Charles Russell; but your application for the postponement of the cross-examination was made before that evidence was given.

SIR C. RUSSELL.—That is so. But——

The PRESIDENT.—I cannot see why, because some unexpected evidence has been given, you cannot cross-examine.

SIR C. RUSSELL.—If the whole case with regard to the letters was gone into, then in two or three days I would be ready to cross-examine the witness. Perhaps my learned friend could say when he proposes to take that part of the case.

The ATTORNEY-GENERAL.—I cannot make any statement on that point. We will lay the evidence before your Lordships as far as we can in proper order. I have applied to your Lordships to take this witness out of the proper order because he is obliged to leave England. It is altogether unreasonable of my learned friend to ask me to enter into any arrangement or bargain.

SIR C. RUSSELL.—I ask for no bargain.

The PRESIDENT (to witness).—When do you propose to leave London?

Witness.—That depends on your Lordships. I did propose to leave to-morrow.

The PRESIDENT.—When do you propose to return?

Witness.—I would return when your Lordships wish—at your Lordships' convenience. But I should prefer to wait here until after my cross-examination.

The PRESIDENT.—It appears to me, Sir Charles, that you should prepare yourself within the next few days to cross-examine this witness.

SIR C. RUSSELL.—I should be in no better position then than now unless the Attorney-General is prepared to accede to my suggestion. I am afraid your Lordships do not fully appreciate my difficulty.

The PRESIDENT.—You have something in reserve that you do not feel at liberty to disclose now?

SIR C. RUSSELL.—I do not say that exactly, my Lord.

The PRESIDENT.—I can do no more than repeat what I have said. We shall, of course, insist upon Mr. O'Shea's return if it appear necessary to do so. But if from any accident whatever he is not here when we desire his presence, we shall deal with the evidence he has already given.

SIR C. RUSSELL.—Does your Lordship say that it will be a matter within your Lordship's discretion whether Captain O'Shea shall be required to return?

The PRESIDENT.—Certainly, certainly.

SIR C. RUSSELL.—Then, my Lords, under those circumstances I must go on.

The PRESIDENT.—Very well.

SIR C. RUSSELL then proceeded to cross-examine the witness :—

When, Mr. O'Shea, were you first applied to by *The Times* to be a witness in this case?—On the 3d of August.

What are you reading?—Merely certain extracts from my diary.

Let me see them. Was it by letter that you were applied to?—Indirectly. I was asked whether I had any objection to give information to *The Times.*

By whom were you asked?—A letter was written by Mr. Buckle.

Have you got it?—No. It was not to me; it was to Mr. Chamberlain.

Did Mr. Chamberlain see you?—Yes; but I do

18

not think he was asked to see me. I went to see him on another matter.

Where?—To his house.

On what business?—To talk over the attack made by Mr. Parnell on Mr. Chamberlain and myself in the House of Commons.

What was the date of that attack?—The 31st of July, I think.

In the present year?—Yes.

And you went to consult with Mr. Chamberlain as to what course he ought to take?—Yes.

- To talk over matters and consider whether you ought to make some answer in the public Press or he in the House of Commons?—No; I had already written to *The Times*, and my letter appeared on the 2d of August.

And in the course of talking over the matter of Mr. Parnell's attack on you and Mr. Chamberlain he introduced Mr. Buckle's letter?—Yes; he told me he had received a letter from Mr. Buckle.

Did he show you the letter?—I am not quiet sure.

Will you swear he did not?—I do not think he did. I am not sure whether he showed it to me to read or not.

What was in the letter?—Whether I should mind giving evidence in the case.

What date do you give for that?—The first days of August. I should think the 3d.

Was it in reference to this Commission or to

" O'Donnell v. Walter " ?—Oh, in reference to this Commission. " O'Donnell v. Walter " had been over for a long time.

Did you agree to give that evidence ?   No.

When did you agree to give evidence ?   After I had been subpœnaed by Mr. Parnell.

When were you subpœnaed by Mr. Parnell ?—. On Thursday, the 23d of August.

Then did you see Mr. Chamberlain after that ? No ; Mr. Chamberlain had left town.

Did you communicate with him ?—Certainly.

You professed your readiness to give evidence for *The Times?*—Yes, on the 24th of August.   I said I would do so in order to have an opportunity of refuting the slanders circulated about me by Mr. Parnell and his friends in regard to these letters.

Then you volunteered to give evidence in order to have an opportunity of refuting these slanders, you say ?—Certainly.

It was a matter of personal concern to yourself ?—Yes, of great personal concern.

To whom did you make that communication ? —To Mr. Buckle.

Direct ?—No.

Through whom ?—Through Mr. Houston.

Who is Mr. Houston ?—He is a journalist.

Connected with any paper ?—I do not know.

Where does he live ?—In Cork-street, London.

Are his initials E. C. ?—I think so.

LORD SPENCER,

HON, G. O. TREVELYAN.

Former Chief Secretary for Ireland

Is he secretary to the Loyal and Patriotic Union ?—I do not really know.

Have you not heard that he is ?—I do not know that I have. I have an idea that he is.

Is not this the union that is supported by a combination of Irish landlords—I will not call it a landlords' land league—but is it not something of that nature ?—I know nothing about it. I have seen its pamphlets, but I do not know how it is supported.

How did you come to be in communication with Mr. Houston ?—Mr. Houston called on me on Sunday, the 12th of August.

In the present year ?—Yes.

Was that your first acquaintance with him ?—I had known him before.

Did he tell you his connection with this matter ? —Yes; he told me that he was very anxious that I should give information on the political part of the question to himself or Mr. Buckle.

Did he tell you how he came to speak to you in the matter ?—No.

Did you ask him ?—He said he called on the part of Mr. Buckle.

Did you ask him in what character or capacity ? No. I knew he was interested in the case of *The Times*.

Did you ask him whether he had anything to do with the publication or with the letters ?—I did not.

Have you seen him since that interview?—Yes,
I have seen him several times since.

In reference to this matter?—Yes.

Did you make a statement to him of your evidence?—Yes. It was he who took down the
statement of my evidence for Mr. Buckle.

Was that taken down at one interview or several?—I think it was taken down at one interview.

Can you give me the date of that?—I think it
was the day on which I asked *The Times* to sub-
poena me—the 24th of August last.

You gave that statement to Mr. Houston, and
he took it down?—Yes, in shorthand.

Did you speak to Mr. Houston about the case?
Yes, in a cursory way.

Did he produce the letters to you?—No.

Or speak to you about the letters?—I should
say he must have spoken about the letters.

Did he speak about the letters more than once?
—I have no doubt he did.

Did he tell you what part he had to do with the
letters?—No.

Did you ask him how the letters had been obtained?—Yes. He told me it was a State secret
in *The Times* office. I would ask you to allow me
to turn back and give a fuller answer to a question you put to me a few moments ago. You
asked me what he told me about the letters. He
told me that he had heard that Mr. Parnell and
his friends had stated that I was engaged in a con-

spiracy to get these letters, and that it was through me that they were got. As I have never stabbed a man in the back, I was naturally very anxious to come here and state on my oath that this statement was not true.

Then Mr. Houston told you there were rumors about you?—Yes.

Not only about you, but others?—Yes.

When did he tell you that?—He spoke about the matter several times.

18

CHAPTER XIX.

WHEN O'SHEA HEARD THE SLANDERS.

BUT he told you this at the first interview?—
I told him that I knew that these slanders
were being circulated.

Did he refer to this at the first interview?—
Most probably.

Did you learn from him whether *The Times*
had got the letters all in one batch or separately?
—No.

Did you ask him?—No.

When did you first hear of these slanders?—I
returned home in July, and heard the matter
spoken about then. I think I heard first of the
matter as an absolute certainty on August 1, when
Mr. Chamberlain told me that Mr. John Morley
had informed him of it.

What did Mr. Chamberlain say?—That Mr. Parnell believed that I had had something to do with
procuring what is generally called the fac-simile
letters. I am not perfectly certain whether this

occurred on the 1st, 2d, or 3d of August, but it was on one of those days.

Whom else have you seen from *The Times* in addition to Mr. Houston since this question arose?—I have met Mr. Buckle at dinner. It was on August 22d at the Hôtel Previtali.

Who were there beside yourself and Mr. Buckle?—Sir Roland Blennerhasset.

Who else?—No one else.

Were you the host or the guest?—I was the guest; Sir R. Blennerhasset was the host.

He was, I believe, formerly member of Parliament for Kerry, and one of Mr. Butt's Home Rule party?—Yes.

He has not been in Parliament since 1885 I believe?—I think that is so.

Did you discuss at all on that occasion the question where these letters had come from?—No, I do not remember that they were mentioned; but if so, there was no discussion.

Do you know the name of Pigott?—Yes, I know the name.

What is the Christian name?—I do not know.

You know the person to whom I allude?—I suppose you allude to a former editor of a newspaper in Dublin.

Quite so. I am told his Christian name is Richard. Is that so?—Yes, I believe it is.

Did you hear his name mentioned in connection with these letters?—Yes.

Did you learn from Mr. Houston that he had obtained them from Pigott?—No. What I heard was that it was said that I had entered into some combination or conspiracy to get these letters with Pigott. No; I am not quite certain of that, I think he was one of those who were named, but I am not certain.

What did he say about Pigott?—I do not remember anything particular that he said besides what I have just told you.

What did he say about Pigott in relation to the letters?—He said, if he mentioned Pigott's name —of which I am not certain—that the report spread about was that I was connected with some men, of whom Pigott was one, to obtain these letters.

Was any other name mentioned?—Yes; Mr. Philip Callan, whom I have not spoken to for four years.

Did he say anything *pro* or *con* as to Pigott's connection with the matter?—Not that I remember.

Then the suggestion was that there were rumors that you and Pigott and Mr. Callan and another person had to do with the letters?—Wait a moment; you are going too far with the name of Pigott. I do not remember for certain that Pigott's name was mentioned, that he was mentioned as being one of the confederates who obtained the letters.

You personally do not know Pigott? To the best of my belief I have never seen him. I certainly do not know him.

The other gentleman—Mr. Callan—you have not spoken to for several years? Not for five or six years.

Did Mr. Houston tell you that he had taken Pigott to the solicitor for *The Times?* No.

Do you know that he did? No.

Do you say that Mr. Houston's communication to you with respect to the letters amounted to nothing beyond what you have told us? Nothing more.

He made no statement about the origin of the letters or as to who was the medium in their passage to *The Times?* .No.

He made no statement as to who took the letters to *The Times?* I am sure he did not.

At no time? To the best of my belief he did not.

Do you know who took them? No.

Have you been told who brought them? No.

Now, having had this letter, was that before or after the date when you made your statement? it was before I made the statement. On the 15th, the Wednesday before, I had seen Houston again, and I told him that I might tell Mr. Buckle the political matter. But even then I withdrew the offer on the 17th.

When finally did you come to an agreement? On Friday, August 24th.

Where?   I went to Houston's room, at 3 Cork
Street, and he took down from me in shorthand
the accounts of the Kilmainham Treaty.

When, if at all, did you go to Mr. Soames?
On Wednesday last for the first time, to ask when
I should be called.

Did you hand the documents to which you have
referred to-day to Houston?   Yes; but they never
left my possession.

You mean that you showed them to him, keeping possession of them?   I do not think I showed
all of them.   I showed those to which the Attorney-General has referred to-day.

You told my learned friend in your examina-
tion-in-chief that you were in Parliament in 1884
and 1885 as member for Clare.   At the last election for Clare you were not supported by Mr.
Parnell?   No.

Did you complain that he had treated you un-
fairly?   Yes.

Broken faith with you?   Yes.

In not supporting you?   Yes.

Can you tell me when the members of the Irish
party agreed to the arrangement which, I believe,
is generally called the pledge—the arrangement
as to sitting and acting together?   No, I do not
remember.

Was it not in October, 1885, just before the
election?   I should say that was very probable.

You declined, I think, to take that pledge? Certainly.

I am told it was not in October, but it was before the election. You declined to accede to the arrangements, and in November, 1885, you stood for the Exchange Division of Liverpool? Yes.

Were you supported at your election by Mr. Parnell? Yes.

As we know, that was a short Parliament? Yes; it was dissolved after the rejection of Mr. Gladstone's Home Rule scheme.

In the spring of 1886 you stood for Galway? Yes.

And you were supported by Mr. Parnell? Yes.

Against the wishes of some of his colleagues? Yes.

You gave an assurance that you would act with the Irish members? I agreed with Mr. Parnell without giving any pledge. It was arranged that I should contest Galway as a Liberal, that I should go there and receive his support, and that I should not sit with his party for a short time. During the heat of the contest he telegraphed to Colonel Nolan, asking——

Oh, we cannot have that. ' But you asked me. He telegraphed to ask whether, if he came to Galway, I would allow him to say that I would sit on the same side of the House as one of the party.

And you were returned for Galway by means of his assistance? Yes, and immediately wished to resign on account of that pledge.

When did you resign? I resigned on the day after the division on the Home Rule Bill.

Had you made an application for the Chiltern Hundreds? Yes, at that time.

Do you recollect when the Home Rule Bill went to a division on the second reading? No; but I should think on June 8th.

You did not vote on that occasion? No.

You walked out? Of course I did, as I did not vote.

I mean you had not paired? No, I had not.

As you have told us, you committed suicide to save yourself from slaughter; you resigned? That is your comment upon my action.

But it is a fact, is it not? I do not know. I resigned because I thought it my duty to resign. Nobody knew for certain that there would be a dissolution

CHAPTER XX.

Give me the date of your resignation. The day of the division on the second reading of Mr. Gladstone's Home Rule Bill, or the day before. The date of the notice as to the Chiltern Hundreds was the day after the division.

Did you, in the beginning of 1886, state that certain persons knew that Mr. Parnell had paid for the escape of the Phœnix Park murderers? No, I do not think I said that. I said that it had been stated not of the Phœnix Park murders, but of one Byrne.

You stated that people had said so. On what date? I do not remember the date.

Who stated it? It was told me, I believe, in the first instance by a man called Mulqueeny, and I inquired into the statement. The statement had reference to a letter acknowledging a check which has since come out. I caused inquiries to be made as to whether the statement was correct, and I understood that it was not. I understood that the authorities had had no such letter.

287

Who is Mulqueeny? He is an Irishman resident in London, who assisted me greatly when I was canvassing an East-end constituency for a friend of mine. I met him at a meeting in Whitechapel.

What is he? I think he is employed as a clerk by one of the dock companies.

He told you this, then? I think he told me first. I am not sure as to the date.

Who else told you? I do not remember.

Am I to understand that any one else told you, or that you do not remember whether any one did? I think you must take it that I do not remember.

It is a very serious statement. Yes; but I investigated it and found that the authorities knew nothing about it.

Who were the other persons besides Mulqueeny? I do not remember anybody else.

Was there anybody else? I may have made inquiries of others, but I cannot remember.

I want to get to the bottom of this matter. I want to know from whom you heard this statement besides Mulqueeny, if from anybody. I cannot say that I heard it from anybody else, although I have the idea that I did.

Can you say when you first heard it? I have just told you that I cannot fix the date.

Was it before you heard the story from Mulqueeny? I have said that I have no recollection of hearing it from anybody else. I cannot go further than that.

Was the first statement from Mulqueeny? I should say so.

You say you investigated the matter ; to whom did you apply? I asked Mr. Chamberlain.

Any one else? Through him the Minister of the department which had to do with the matter.

Did you yourself apply? I do not remember. I heard that nothing was known of the letter.

When Mulqueeny made this statement, what did he say? He said that a letter had been taken from the Land League rooms in Palace-chambers —a letter from Byrne acknowledging the receipt of money from Mr. Parnell.

Taken by whom? He believed that it had been taken by the police. It was on that account that I asked for information.

Mulqueeny told you nothing more? I do not remember.

Then he told you that the police had taken a letter from the Land League chambers in London, which purported to be a letter from Byrne acknowledging the receipt of money? Not quite that. He said that a letter had been taken by the police acknowledging the receipt of money.

I do not desire to press you unduly upon this point, but I may have to press you upon it later on. Try and fix as nearly as you can the date

when that communication was made to you.   I do
not think I shall be able to fix the date.

Try and fix the time of year.   I do not think I
can go any further.

Surely you can tell us what the year was?   No,
I really cannot.

How long ago?   I cannot say.   You see the
matter did not impress itself much upon my mind
when I heard that the authorities had not got the
letter.

Do you know Mulqueeny's address?   No.   He
called upon me recently and told me that he had
left his house.

When did he call?   Within the last few days.
I think on Saturday last.

Did you believe the information to be correct as
to the payment to Byrne?   As I have intimated,
when we inquired into the matter and found that
the letter was not supposed to be in the hands of
the authorities, I did not, I presume, pay much
more attention to it.

Did you ever see that letter from Byrne?   No,
except in the newspapers.

Yes, but not the original letter?   No.

It was after that statement by Mulqueeny that
you became a candidate for Galway?   I should say
that was so, certainly.

Well, of course, you could not have believed
this statement about Mr. Parnell at that time?
Oh, no, certainly not.

You had come to the conclusion that it was not true? I have no doubt of it.

I believe Mr. Parnell did go to Galway to speak for you? He did.

After your inquiry whether such a letter had been obtained, did you tell Mulqueeny the result of your investigation? I certainly did.

How did you make appointments with Mulqueeny? He used sometimes to call upon me.

Casually or by appointment? Generally, I should think, casually, if I had not some electioneering for him to do.

Electioneering, where? In the East-end of London. Mr. S. Montagu, member for Whitechapel, is a personal friend of mine, and I was anxious to secure his return. It was at one of his meetings that I first heard of Mulqueeny.

You are not able to charge your recollection with having heard about the Byrne letter from anybody besides Mulqueeny? No, I am not able.

Did you ever hear from Mulqueeny how the Byrne letter was supposed to have been got from the office? Yes, how he supposed it had been got.

You found that the statement was not correct? I inquired whether the letter was in the hands of the authorities, and the person applied to replied that he had no knowledge of the document.

If it had been taken by the police the fact of its existence would have been known in the

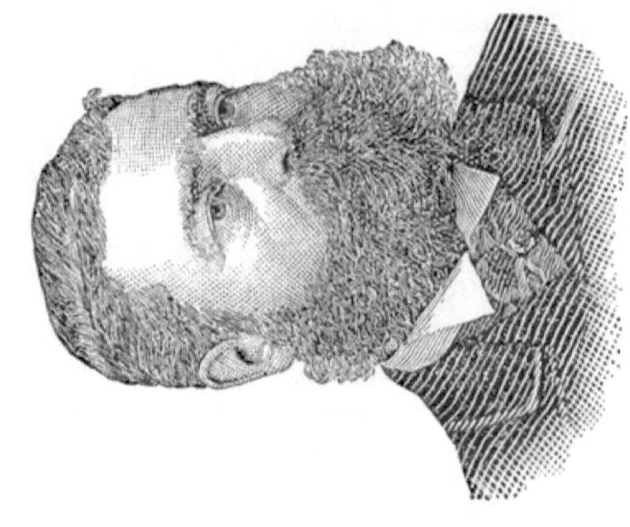

MILES M. O'BRIEN.

MICHAEL J. REDDING.

department where you applied? I suppose so; I
do not know.

You told Mulqueeny that it was not known in
that department? Yes.

Did you discuss at all how it could have been
obtained? I have heard.

Is Mulqueeny a member of any secret society?
I do not know. He is a Nationalist. Whether
he is a member of a secret society of course I
cannot tell. He has told me that he was an
advanced Nationalist.

Did he ever tell you that he was a member of
a secret society? He never told me that he was.

He conveyed it to you, then? He told me that
he was an advanced Nationalist and at one time a
member of the Land League.

Did you see him anywhere else than in your
own place? Yes, at meetings when canvassing
the constituency in the East-end.

Only there? Only there.

Do you know the house of a Mrs. Lynch in
Wardour Street? It is very likely that I have
been there once.

I ask you, do you know the house? I am not
certain that the woman's name is Lynch; but I
was once in a house in Wardour Street.

What is the house remarkable for? In what
way?

In any way? I do not know what it is remarkable for.

How did you come to go there? I went there because a number of advanced Nationalists had signed a declaration protesting against my exclusion from Irish politics, and I was told that I should meet some of them there.

The PRESIDENT.—I understand that this house is a public house?

WITNESS.—Yes, my Lord.

SIR C. RUSSELL.—When you use the phrase "advanced Nationalists," do you mean to convey to the Court that these persons were Fenians? I mean to convey that they were members of the old Nationalist party.

Do you mean to convey that they were Fenians? They never told me that they were.

Is that the impression in your own mind? I was never told that they were Fenians.

You believe they were? I do not know whether they were or not.

You say they signed a testimonial to you? No, a declaration protesting against my exclusion from politics. Mulqueeny brought the declaration to me, and it was with him that I went to this house.

Were you there only once? Only once.

Whom did you meet there? I cannot remember.

These persons who made the presentation complained of your exclusion from politics? Yes.

Were they all residents in this country? I do

not know.   The men of their party in the county of Clare were always great supporters of mine and very much devoted to me.   They were the old Nationalists.   I always told them how foolish I thought their adventures were, but they hated outrages as much as I do myself.

Surely these men were ex-Fenians.   Was that society pretty strong in Clare?   I do not know.

Can you form any opinion?   No; I have no means of forming an opinion.

Were there any signatures of persons residing in Paris to that document?   I do not know.   I am sorry I did not bring the parchment to court with me.

Were there any signatures from foreign parts? I cannot say; I have not seen the parchment for some time.

Was the signature of a man called Patrick Casey among them?   I do not remember; but you will have the document.

. The ATTORNEY-GENERAL.—Bring it with you to-morrow, please.

SIR C. RUSSELL.—Do you recognize the name? I do not remember whether or not the name is on the document.

Do you know who Patrick Casey is?   No, I do not.

Do you mean to say that you have never heard of him?   No, I do not mean to say that; but I have no knowledge of him.   I have never seen him.

19

Do you know that he is a professed dynamitard? No, I do not.

Do you not know that Mulqueeny went to Paris to get the signature of that man—aye or no? Well, now that you mention it, I think it is possible. I do not remember it, but it is possible.

Did you send him for that purpose? No, I did not.

Have you given Mulqueeny money? I have often given him money.

Did you pay the expenses of his journey to Paris? I should think not.

Do you say "No?" It is very likely if he asked me for the money afterwards that I paid it.

Do you recollect that he asked you? No.

What did you give Mulqueeny money for? I took a liking to the man. He was extremely useful to me at the time of the election and I liked him and his father, and when they wanted money I gave it to them. I have very often given money to Irishmen.

Did you meet at the house of Mrs. Lynch any persons besides those who signed this paper? I cannot recollect any names, but I remember what occurred. I explained my views upon politics and dwelt on the advantages to be derived from supporting the Liberal party.

Is this address framed and glazed? No; it is on parchment.

Did Mulqueeny tell you whether he had seen

Casey or not when he came back from Paris? I do not remember the name of Casey.

Did he tell you he had been over? I have no doubt he did; but I do not remember.

What did he tell you he had been over for? It was not the only time he went to Paris.

He went to Paris for a definite purpose, after which you paid his expenses? That I paid his expenses is not so likely as that I gave him a lump sum of money.

Now I have asked you about one statement, the statement made to you by Mulqueeny with reference to the Byrne letter. Did you in the winter of 1885–86 make any other statement, or was any other statement made to you? Of what nature?

Was any statement made to you by any one in the winter of 1885 suggesting that there were letters compromising Mr. Parnell? I do not remember.

Did you hear any one state at any time in the winter of 1885–86 that there were some American Fenians in London who were hostile to Mr. Parnell, and who held documents supposed to compromise him? Do not answer without thinking. I have not the slightest intention of doing so. I remember perfectly telling Mr. Parnell that I had heard there were Irish-Americans in London at one time, but I have no recollection whatever of saying that they were hostile to him, or that they held compromising documents. I may have said that they were hostile to him, because I believe they were hostile to him ; but I do not remember the other matter.

You believed that the Fenian body were opposed to his policy? Well, I mean the men who might come here for the purpose of promoting outrages. I believed Mr. Parnell to be absolutely free from any connivance at outrage.

You believed these men to be opposed to his policy? Of course, if his policy was not dynamite, and they came over with dynamite, they were opposed to his policy.

You believe he was opposed to dynamite? Most certainly, I believe Mr Parnell was opposed to the policy of dynamite and of outrage. Up to the end of June, 1886, I was perfectly confident that Mr. Parnell was a man of the highest honor.

And were perfectly confident that he had a sincere desire to follow out his agitation on constitutional lines? Certainly. I was a member of his party myself. It is only within the last two or three months that I saw a correspondence between Mr. Herbert Gladstone and Mr. Arnold Forster, in which Mr. Forster stated that Mr. Parnell had been in constant communication with Sheridan at the time that Sheridan was organizing crime. I was so astounded at the statement that I wrote to Mr. Arnold Forster to ask him about it. I did not believe that he had had anything to do

with Sheridan. He told me so often, and I believed it, even after I believed nothing else. I am
now speaking, of course, with regard to Sheridan
only.

Now, I wish to know what altered your opinion
in July, 1886? Negotiations took place at that
time, previous to the division on the second reading of the Home Rule Bill, and certain things
came to my knowledge at that time which absolutely destroyed the good opinion I had hitherto
held of Mr. Parnell.

Tell us anything whatever with regard to Sheridan which came to your knowledge. Mr. Parnell
wishes you to state fully anything ; you said you
changed the opinion which you had held of Mr.
Parnell up to June and July, 1886, in reference to
Sheridan. No, no; I changed it owing to something which came out during these negotiations ;
but I did not say it was on account of anything
connected with Sheridan.

I beg your pardon. You said you had told him
that there were American Fenians in London who
were hostile to him.

The PRESIDENT.—He has never used the word
Fenians. I noticed that what he spoke of was
American-Irish.

CHAPTER XXI.

ABOUT ADVANCED NATIONALISTS.

Sir C. Russell.—When you talk of advanced Nationalists do you not mean to convey the Fenians? Not necessarily, because there are other organizations—the Clan-na-Gael and others.

When you talk of the old Nationalists do you mean the old Fenians? Yes; a very different class of men from the dynamitards and Invincibles.

Who gave you the information that there were American-Irish who were in London and were hostile to Mr. Parnell? I did not say there were American-Irish here who were hostile to him. I did not qualify it in that way; I am sure I should not have done so. I do not know who told me.

Do not know who told you? Try and remember. It is a very long time ago, and I do not suppose that I attached much importance to it.

But we do. Who told you? Very likely Mulqueeny told me something about it. It might have been in conversation. I believed they were hostile.

Did he tell you where they were, or where they were staying? No; but he told me he had been threatened by one.

Did you make any further inquiries?. No.

I must press you ; did you not tell Mr. Parnell at the time I refer to—namely, in the winter of 1885–86, that American-Irish were in London and had letters compromising Mr. Parnell? I will swear that I did not say anything about letters relating to Mr. Parnell ; that is, with as great certainty as a man can swear to anything so long ago. To the very best of my belief, I did not say anything about letters.

You say that Mulqueeny told you that one of these men threatened him? Yes.

Did he give you the man's name? Yes.

Go on. I am not quite sure whether he told me it was one of those men, or another man who had threatened him.

What was the name? I think he mentioned the name of a General Carroll Thalis, or some such name.

As being one of the men in London? No, as being one of the men who threatened him.

Who was the other? Not an American.

What was his name? I do not know, but I think he was a civil engineer.

Was his name Hayes? I think it was.

And did you know him, sir? Yes.

Why did you not tell us at once? Because it had gone out of my head; I was not certain.

What is Hayes? I am told he was a civil engineer.

Is he an American? I do not know anything about him.

What did Mulqueeny report to you about him? He reported to me that he had seen him, had gone to see him at an hotel, and had been threatened by him, chiefly about the testimonial made to me. Mulqueeny got a letter telling him to go and see him.

Where? I think in Covent Garden.

The Bedford Hotel, perhaps? I do not know.

And he went? Yes; and saw this man or men, and they threatened him, if I remember rightly, on account of this testimonial or declaration of mine.

Is Hayes an Irish-American or not? I know nothing about him except that I have been told he is a civil engineer.

Did Mulqueeny tell you what he was? He told me that he was a civil engineer.

Well, when he came to tell you this story, you asked him who Hayes was? He told me that Hayes was a civil engineer, and, I believe, established in London.

Well, what had a civil engineer established in London to do with any testimonial presented to you? I do not know. I presume it was owing to some action taken by some of my enemies who prevailed on these people to act in this way.

I am asking you, did you not inquire from Mulqueeny what he was? He told me he was a civil engineer.

Did you not ask him what party in politics he belonged to? He told me he was a very violent man.

Did he tell you that Hayes was an emissary from New York? No; I think he told me that Hayes lived in London.

Did you see Hayes? No.

Are you certain? Yes, I am certain I did not.

Did you know he was supposed to be implicated in the attack on London Bridge? Yes, I had heard that.

You had no doubt, I suppose, what his character was? He was evidently very much opposed to me, for one thing.

Did he mention any other name to you? Yes, this General Carroll Thalis, or whatever his name was.

Any other name? I do not recollect.

Do you recollect the name of Cassidy? No.

Do you know anybody of that name? No.

Did you visit the hotel in Covent Garden? No, I did not.

Are you certain? Yes, I am certain I did not.

You say you are certain that you did not visit any hotel in Covent Garden at that time? I am certain—that is, with regard to these people. I may have gone to an hotel in Covent Garden in the whole of that year.

In reference to seeing any persons whom Mulqueeny had mentioned to you? Never.

What hotel do you suggest that you went to ? I did not suggest that I went to any hotel. I say that in the whole year I may possibly have called at an hotel in Covent Garden. The reason I stopped to guard myself in this matter was that I remember going to call on Mr. Edward Dwyer Gray and Mr. Daniel Gabbett also, at an hotel in Covent Garden.

And with that exception you did not call at an hotel in Covent Garden? I swear it.

After you had heard from Mulqueeny of the presence of this General Carroll Thalis, or some such name, and of Hayes, civil engineer, did you send Mulqueeny to Paris? I have not the slightest recollection of doing so.

Did you send him there to give a warning to Casey? No; I never had any intention of warning Casey.

Did you send Mulqueeny to give a warning to Casey? No, certainly not.

Did you send him to Paris after you became aware of the presence of the American-Irish in Covent Garden? I cannot remember that I did anything of the kind. To the best of my belief I did not.

That is a thing you would recollect. You are positive you did not, are you? Yes, I am positive ; I have no recollection of doing so whatever.

Are you able to say positively you did not? Yes, I say positively I did not.

It is not an event that occurs every day, to send Mr. Mulqueeny to Paris ; you are able to say positively you did not? Oh, yes, I am sure I did not.

Have you kept up your intimacy with Mulqueeny? Not exactly an intimacy ; I had not seen him for a long time, until some months ago, and had just come back from abroad and met him in Cannon Street, and he told me of his father's death, and I think I have seen him since then— once in July and twice since.

Since the political events of 1885–86, Captain O'Shea, when you tell us that you were badly treated by Mr. Parnell, have you threatened him ? How do you mean, threatened him—threatened Mr. Parnell ?

I am not talking about personal violence. Do you mean have I threatened him with retribution?

Threatened. Answer my question. No, I do not know that I have. I may have been angry ; certainly I was angry with him when I turned him out of my room in the Shelbourne Hotel in Dublin ; but I did nothing that could be called a threat. That incident occurred either at the end of October or the beginning of November, 1885.

Will you just explain how you turned Mr. Parnell out of your room ? I told him the sooner he went, the better I should be pleased, and that I did not want to see him again. I did not use any force.

Have you said you would be revenged on Mr. Parnell? I do not remember the expression.

Will you swear you did not? No; because one says so many things when one is angry; but I do not remember saying anything about revenge; I never have been revenged, at all events.

Have you said that you had a shell, charged with dynamite, to blow him up? I should say not. What kind of shell?

I do not know. I am not suggesting it was really dynamite. Oh, no.

When did you first hear of the letter which is called the fac-simile letter? When I saw it in *The Times* on the day it was published. I saw the letter itself for the first time last Wednesday.

I presume it was at Mr. Soames' office? Yes.

And you had not heard from any one, until that letter appeared, a suggestion made (excluding the Frank Byrne letter) that there were any letters in existence compromising Mr. Parnell? No, I was astounded when I saw it.

At this point the Court adjourned for luncheon. On its reassembling Sir Charles Russell continued his cross-examination of Captain O'Shea.

You were understood to say that except the statement made to you by Mulqueeny, which related to the Byrne letter, you had heard no statement from any one and made no statement yourself as to any other compromising letters and documents? Then I was not distinctly

understood.   I never said that I had not spoken
about them.

Am I to understand you that, though you cannot recollect the persons or person, you did hear
that there were in existence compromising documents or a compromising document?   Are you
talking about the Byrne letter?

No; you have told us you did hear of that letter. I am not troubling any more about that. My
question was, first of all, did you hear from any
one and at any time before the publication of the
fac-simile letter that there were in existence any
letters or documents of a compromising character?   That is what I answered you before I left
the Court, that I do not think I did so.

Is it that you do not recollect, or do not think,
or are you in a position to say positively that you
did not?   I am as positive as possible that I never
spoke about compromising documents.   Nor do I
remember any one speaking to me of there being
in existence compromising documents.   In fact,
in other words, I know nothing about these
letters.

I am not talking about these letters particularly.
There are many more.   Oh, yes.

Any letters?   I have had nothing to do with
any letters.

You do not appreciate my point. Did you until
the publication of the fac-simile letter have it
suggested to you by any one that there were in

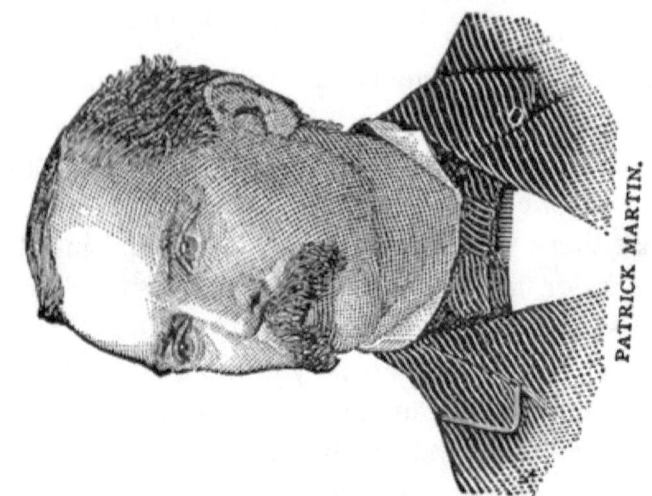

PATRICK MARTIN.

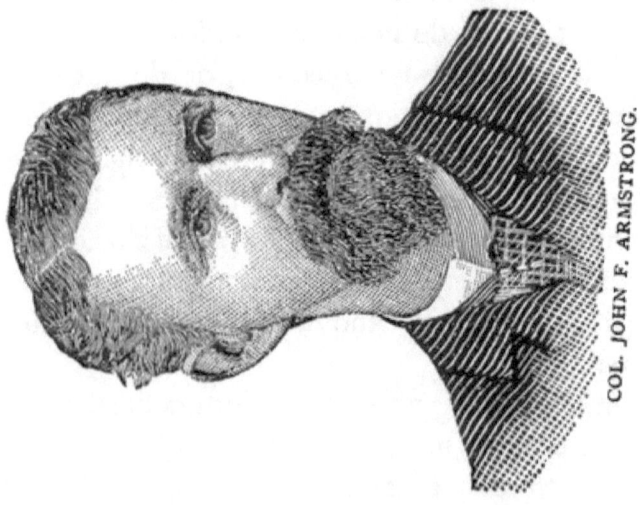

COL. JOHN F. ARMSTRONG.

existence compromising letters? To the best of my belief, no.

Very well, you are pretty positive about that? Yes.

You have spoken about your acquaintance with the advanced Nationalists. You say they are the old Nationalist party, who are opposed to outrage? Certainly.

The Physical Force party? The men who considered that they could fight their country's battle on the hillside against the British forces.

They were not persons who went in, or professed to go in, for assassination? On the contrary, they always spoke of it to me with the greatest abhorrence.

Some names have been mentioned here, among others, John O'Leary. Was he an advocate of assassination? On the contrary, as far as I am aware.

Was not, in point of fact, the policy, if it can be so called, of that Physical Force, or Hillside party, opposed to the constitutional party altogether? I mean up to a certain point? Most decidedly.

And you are aware, are you not, that for years after, in fact, up to the present time, the Fenians have been among the most strenuous opponents of Mr. Parnell's party? Certainly; I kept them apart as long as I could in county Clare.

How do you mean, "Kept them apart in county Clare?" I pointed out the folly of their ideas, and always considered it well that they should not join the Land League.

Among your reasons was one that the Land League was hostile to yourself? Certainly.

You have not made any concealment of your influence with that party? I do not, in the least, say here, or ascribe to myself, any influence with that party. What I do say is that there are a number of men in county Clare who have not only given me cordial support, but have shown me the greatest personal devotion. I am always proud of the support of those honest, honorable men.

You have expressed those opinions to Mr. Chamberlain? I expressed those opinions everywhere.

Then probably to him? Probably. I may have expressed them to you. It is a matter of such common conversation.

Up to May-June, 1886, you told us you believed in Mr. Parnell's honor, and that you knew he was opposed to outrage? Certainly.

And you stated that you knew he was opposed, and always had been supposed to be opposed to outrages. You continued of that opinion until a much later date? Yes.

And I think you fixed the date of the change of opinion upon the question of outrage at the appearance of Mr. Arnold Forster's letter? No; I await the judgment of the Commission. I have quite an open mind upon the subject.

Then, so far as concerns yourself, you have not, so far as Mr. Parnell's attitude towards outrage is concerned, altered your opinion? I have altered my opinion regarding Mr. Parnell, and, of course, that must affect a man's mind.

20

CHAPTER XXII.

CHAMBERLAIN'S LOCAL GOVERNMENT SCHEME.

Was it the fact, also, that in the Home Rule discussion you were very anxious to get Mr. Parnell's support for the modified or local government scheme of Mr. Chamberlain? The what?

The Home Rule scheme of Mr. Chamberlain? No; that was not at all the scope of any negotiations at the time.

SIR C. RUSSELL.—I am not talking of any negotiation. Witness.—The Home Rule Bill had nothing to do with local government.

SIR C. RUSSELL.—Were you or were you not in favor of Mr. Chamberlain's local government scheme? The local government scheme had nothing to do with the question.

The PRESIDENT.—Are the witness's opinions on such a subject material to our inquiry?

· SIR C. RUSSELL.—As a matter of opinion, certainly; as a matter of conduct, no.

MR. JUSTICE A. L. SMITH.—Why, as a matter of opinion, certainly?

SIR C. RUSSELL.—Because it explains the position he took up ; but I do not think I should be asked to give my reasons for a question asked in cross-examination at this stage.

The PRESIDENT.—The object of my interposition was to see the relevancy of the question.

SIR C. RUSSELL.—I do not think it irrelevant ; but it is not a first-class matter, and I must ask pardon if I was a little brusque in an observation I made just now. All I want to do is to explain that the question put to the witness was one I was justified in putting. To witness—You took Mr. Chamberlain's side in the discussion. You declined to vote for the Home Rule Bill. That is a fact, is it not? That is a fact; but not for the reason you have just stated.

SIR C. RUSSELL.—I have not given any reason.

WITNESS—You suggested the matter of local government.

SIR C. RUSSELL.—Well, were not Mr. Chamberlain's opinions in the direction of a Local Government Bill? Certainly not.

Very well, we differ about that. It was after the incident of May-June, 1886, that you altered your opinion of Mr. Parnell? Yes.

You have told us quite candidly you are awaiting the judgment of the Commission. Am I wrong in saying that you made a reference to Mr. Arnold Forster's letter? I spoke to you about it in the course of my cross-examination.

In which you stated you were astonished at it?
Yes. So much so, that I had an interview with him
about it.

In relation to your negotiations with the Government—when did those begin? In the year 1881.

I would like to remind you, my Lords, who may
not recollect it, the state of things was that there
was the Coercion Act of 1881 in operation.

The ATTORNEY-GENERAL.—You mean Mr.
Forster's Act?

SIR C. RUSSELL.—Certainly.

The ATTORNEY-GENERAL.—The suspension of
the Habeas Corpus Act.

SIR C. RUSSELL.—It was not generally called
that. It was called the Protection of Life and
Property Act. Was that so? Witness.—Yes.

The Land Bill that afterwards passed was under
discussion? Yes.

You are aware that there were some three or
four very important points for which the Irish
members were contending in relation to the Land
Bill. First of all, a comprehensive scheme for
arrears; next, that the improvement, or Healy
clauses, as they were subsequently to be called,
should be framed so as to prevent the possibility
of the tenants' improvements being taxed; and,
next, the inclusion of leaseholders. Those were
three important points, were they not? Yes, the
last I considered very important, indeed, and I
supported it to the utmost in my power.

However, the Bill was passed without any of those points being dealt with? The Healy clause was there.

Without being dealt with in the way the Irish members wished? Yes.

There was another point they were anxious about—the strengthening of the Bright clauses of the Act of 1870, so as to enable the tenants to more easily acquire their own holdings? Yes.

When you entered into communication, as you call it, with the government, was that with Mr. Parnell's knowledge in the first instance? At his request.

In the first instance? Or was it after you had written?

WITNESS.—In 1881?

SIR C. RUSSELL.—Yes.

WITNESS.—What I offered to Mr. Parnell was that if the Land League were broken up——

Those words were put forward? I am not quite sure.

What were the words then? The chief condition was that the Land League should be broken up on condition of the Irish landlords reducing their rents within a certain time, and that they should get compensation from the Exchequer.

Well? That was the principal proposal.

The whole proposal at that time? Certainly.

By letter, was it not? Certainly.

At all events, you communicated Mr. Parnell's principal point by letter? Yes, by letter, the principal part of which was that point. I do not say other points may not have been mentioned.

That was a letter to Mr. Gladstone? Yes.

Do you suggest the phrase was used of "breaking up the Land League"? I certainly used it to Mr. Gladstone—dissolve the Land League.

In your letter? The letter was written after my conversation with Mr. Gladstone. He said, "It is a very serious matter, and must be put before my colleagues." He said, "Put it down," and I put it down.

In that letter? I cannot say.

That was the only communication you had with Mr. Gladstone? At what time?

At that time. Yes.

All the rest was the communications which resulted in the release of certain persons from Kilmainham and which passed through yourself, and your principal medium of communication was Mr. Chamberlain? Oh, yes, but Mr. Chamberlain did not come in until the communications were put on foot by Mr. Gladstone, when I re-opened the communications with Mr. Gladstone in 1882; and it was subsequent to this, when the communications were entertained, that Mr. Gladstone delegated to Mr. Chamberlain, who knew nothing about the matter before, the business with me. I use the words "communications" and "business" because

I believe Mr. Gladstone objects to the word "negotiations."

SIR C. RUSSELL.—That is rather what I put to you—that after the re-introduction of the matter, the renewed negotiation was with Mr. Chamberlain? Yes, that is after the matter was taken up again.

What date do you fix as the beginning of the renewal of these negotiations? An early date in April.

Was that renewal without any communication with Mr. Parnell? Yes.

Or without any communication with any of his colleagues? Yes.

Entirely upon your own motion? Yes.

And the first intimation, as I understand, was made to Mr. Parnell on the occasion of his being allowed out on parole to attend the funeral of his relation? Yes.

Now, as regards the conversation, I think you say you had, I wish to make this clear. Is it not true that, when you mentioned the question of release, Mr. Parnell said that that must not even be discussed, or in any shape or way made a condition? Certainly, that was the case, and on the other side there was no bargain. Of course, one takes those things with a grain of salt, but that was the declaration on both sides.

Did not you understand that Mr. Parnell was most anxious as to the peace of the country, and that, among other things, the Arrears Bill should be settled?   Certainly.

Is it not the fact that in every reference that he made to the attempts to put down outrages he referred to the proposed measure of the Government as one which would help to tranquillize the country?   Certainly.

And you agreed with him?   Yes, having no knowledge as to what the Land League was myself.

Do you see any reason to differ from him now? No, and I have had codsiderable experience of Irish tenants myself.

What was the date at which the memorandum in Mr. Chamberlain's handwriting was written out; is the date on it in pencil correct? I cannot say.

When was that date put upon it? I have no doubt at the time.

The ATTORNEY-GENERAL.—What is the date?

WITNESS.—April 22, 1882.   It must have been either the 22d or 23d.

SIR C. RUSSELL.—Was that document left with you? Yes.

Did you interchange any copy of it with Mr. Chamberlain?   No; I wrote a note in reply to it.

Repeating it? Yes.   There may have been a little alteration in the words, but substantially the same.

Now, with reference to the discussion at Eltham, was anything discussed between you except the

Arrears Bill? Oh, yes; there must have been a great deal more.

Are you able to say there was? Certainly.

Was that the principal subject of discussion? The Arrears Bill, the general arrangement, and what would come out of it.

You were aware that Mr. Parnell had drafted in Kilmainham a Bill dealing with that question? Yes.

That was the Bill which was introduced on a Wednesday? Yes.

When he, in his letter of April, refers to Wednesday's proceedings being satisfactory so far as they went, he refers to that Bill? It certainly meant that.

Did it mean anything else than that? I mean you shook your head as if there was something more. Yes. The Arrears Bill was not the only matter of discussion, and although the Bill was brought in on the Wednesday everything was going on very satisfactorily.

No, no. He says "Wednesday's proceedings were very satisfactory so far as they went." That referred to the Bill introduced on the Wednesday? Well, not only. That referred to the way in which it had, by arrangement, been received.

Now, whatever the discussions between you and Mr. Parnell were, they were ultimately embodied in that letter which was afterwards read in the House of Commons? Yes.

That is the document, is it not, which you yourself gave to Mr. Parnell? (The document was
handed to the witness.) I do not know that it is.
It is in my handwriting.

SIR C. RUSSELL.—Your Lordships will recollect
a portion of the letter was not read. It is headed
"private and confidential," Kilmainham. It stops
at the words "outrages and intimidation of all
kinds."

The PRESIDENT.—Without the reference to the
Liberal party?

SIR C. RUSSELL.—Yes.

Sir C. Russell then read the letter as it is set
out above down to the words "outrages and intimidation of all kinds."

SIR C. RUSSELL.—At that discussion do you
recollect Mr. Parnell suggesting it would be far
better to allow him and his colleagues to remain
where they were for a few months more till the
Arrears Bill was passed? No.

Did he say it? I should think certainly not.

Do you say that he did not? No. I do not
recollect it.

Did not Mr. Parnell tell you, and did not you
know apart from his telling you, that the "No-rent"
manifesto had been in point of fact a dead letter
for some time?—No. It was not satisfactory to
myself or to others that no statement had been
made on that point.

Did Mr. Parnell state to you that in point of

fact the "No-rent" manifesto had been for a month at least a dead letter?—I do not remember his saying so to me then.

Did he say so to you in Kilmainham?—Yes, certainly.

You have said that Mr. Parnell especially stipulated, or desired to stipulate, that Mr. Davitt's release should be delayed until he saw him?—Certainly.

Did he tell you why?—Yes, because he wanted to see him before anybody else did.

Yes, but did he tell you why?—He wanted to see Mr. Davitt before anybody else did in order to explain to him the situation and policy.

Did he express any fear that Mr. Davitt might refuse to accept his release on a ticket-of-leave? I should think that that must have been afterwards.

I ask you whether that was not so at the time? —Certainly nothing of the kind. The statement he made was what I have just said—that he wanted to see Mr. Davitt before anybody else did in order to talk politics over with him.

I am asking you was it not mentioned by him whether Mr. Davitt would accept release on ticket-of-leave?—No.

You are clear about that?—Certainly.

In discussing the release of other persons who were prisoners, do you recollect him saying anything about the desirability of his being able to communicate with all of the executive of the Land League together?—I cannot remember any such broad statement as that.

I mean those men of whom he was speaking? —I do not remember him saying he wanted to see the whole of the executive of the Land League.

I mean persoñs more or less in authority in the League?—I presume they were not all in gaol.

I am speaking of those who are in gaol.—He wanted Egan to return to England before the release of Boyton and Sheridan.

And Brennan?—No.

What did he say about Brennan?—He said there were some men it would be advisable not to let out.

And Brennan was one of them?—Yes.

Who else?—I do not know.

Did you ask him who they were?—Certainly I did.

What did he say?—He said there were some men it would be injurious to let out.

Did you ask him who they were?—One was Brennan, but I do not remember the others.

Were there more than one?—I cannot remember the name of anybody except Brennan. I cannot remember how many there were, but there were more than one.

Very well. I think you stated that you discussed this matter with Mr. Chamberlain. Have you any memoranda?—The bulk of the memoranda relating to the matter were destroyed in 1883, at a time when there was a danger of a Select Committee of the House of Commons having to be appointed to inquire into the Kilmainham Treaty.

Was that done at Mr. Parnell's suggestion?—No.

Or Mr. Chamberlain's?—No.

Or yours?—No. It was suggested to me that it was politically expedient that the utmost reticence should be kept upon the subject.

By whom?—By Sir William Harcourt. (Loud laughter.) He stated that it was the opinion of another person—Mr. Gladstone.

The PRESIDENT.—This is the first occasion on which there has been any manifestation of feeling, and I take the opportunity of stating that I must request that everybody will refrain from any exhibition of the sort in the future.

SIR C. RUSSELL.—Was it then that you destroyed the memoranda?—Yes.

How is it that you have the memoranda which passed between you and Mr. Chamberlain?—A certain number of the memoranda were in a box, and I did not find them until afterwards.

Perhaps the most important lot?—Certainly not the most important to me.

SIR C. RUSSELL, to the Secretary.—Will you give me the letters put to the witness on the

question of handwriting? (To witness.) Would
you repeat the statement about Sir William Harcourt? My learned friend behind me desires it.

Witness.—There was a danger impending that
the government would have to agree to appoint a
Select Committee of the House of Commons to
inquire into the circumstances of the Kilmainham
Treaty, and I was informed by Sir William Harcourt that it was Mr. Gladstone's wish that I
should be as reticent as possible on the matter, as
it was expedient politically to be so.

Is that the whole of the matter?—Yes, that is
the whole of the matter.

And upon that you destroyed the documents in
your possession?—Yes, and other documents
were destroyed also.

Had you the name of being a gabbler or a bab-
bler that you had to be warned to be reticent?
Why did Sir William Harcourt come to warn you
to be reticent?—That you had better ask of Sir
William Harcourt himself. (To the Commissioners.) My Lords, I have a correction I should
like to make. On thinking over some of the
questions of Sir Charles Russell, I think I spoke
rather too positively, because it has come back to
my mind that Mr. Parnell did speak of the
possible refusal of Mr. Davitt to accept a ticket-
of-leave. On the Thursday I went to Sir William
Harcourt in reference to Mr. Davitt's release
standing over till the Saturday.

What was the reason given for postponing Mr. Davitt's release?—The reason given for that was that Mr. Parnell should have an opportunity of going down to Dartmoor.

Was that with a view to meet the possible objection on the part of Mr. Davitt that you have mentioned?—It is possible that that was one of the reasons. I believe the real reason was that Mr. Parnell wanted to see Mr. Davitt before he was released.

Was that the reason given by Mr. Parnell for his journey to Dartmoor?—I am not certain that he did not mention that as a reason. It was not the only one.

Did he give any other?—Yes, that he wanted to see him first.

Have you ever stated with reference to these negotiations that you were led to expect that you would be made Chief Secretary for Ireland?—No.

Did Mr. Chamberlain ever promise you that you would be made Chief Secretary?—No.

Nor intimate it to you?—That if the local government scheme had been adopted, he would have thought of it.

I believe a baronetcy was spoken of?—Never. I have never heard of such a notion before, except from some scurrilous speakers in Galway during the Galway election. I never made any reference to such a thing myself.

You have corrected one serious misstatement— namely, the statement made by the Attorney- General that Mr. Parnell was opposed to signing the manifesto with reference to the Phœnix Park murders. That is not true?—It is an absolute mistake, as I have stated just now.

On the contrary, did you not know that Mr. Parnell was so stunned and shocked by that crime that he was actually contemplating retiring from public life?—Yes, I took his letter to Mr. Gladstone that morning offering to retire from public life.

You knew enough of the political situation of the moment to know that a more cruel blow at Mr. Parnell's policy and the interests of the people you were both representing in Parlia- ment, could not have been struck?—So I con- sidered it.

And consider it so still?—Certainly.

How many letters have you received from Mr. Parnell altogether? About a dozen?—Oh, a great many.

How many would you say?—I really cannot say. A great many.

Have you received a dozen?—Yes, certainly, and a great many more.

Have you got them?—No. I very seldom keep letters.

Have you half a dozen of them?—No.

Have you any?—Yes, I have.

How many?—I do not know. I cannot tell you.

Two or three?—Yes, more.

You say you have received a dozen letters from Mr. Parnell?—Certainly, and an immense deal more, but I really cannot tell how many. I was on intimate terms with Mr. Parnell for several years, and to talk of only a dozen letters passing between us is absolute folly. The number must have been largely in excess of that.

When were you first asked your opinion about the handwriting of these letters?—On Wednesday.

By whom?—I went to Mr. Soames's office, and they were there shown to me.

With whom did you go?—By myself. The letters were shown to me by a gentleman in the office—probably Mr. Soames's managing clerk.

You had not seen the originals before?—Never. Of none of them.

Did you perceive any sign of any attempt at dissimulation in the character of the handwriting? —No.

Did all the letters occur to your mind as being natural and genuine?—Yes. I have a very strong opinion on that.

That they are?—Yes.

Do you feel equally strongly as to all of them? —I observed differences.

21

Will you take them in your hand and select those of the batch which you think are different? —I may say that I had no intention of giving evidence with regard to these letters at all.

My question was this—Does the signature in any one of these letters strike you as being more clearly in Mr. Parnell's handwriting than the others? Or is your evidence equally strong as to all?—I believe they have all been written by Mr. Parnell. If these letters had come to me I should have said they were written by Mr. Parnell; but I am really no judge in the matter.

I am not asking you as a expert. Does it strike you that there are any of these letters as to which you would have a stronger opinion than as to the others?—I think they are written by Mr. Parnell, and I cannot say any more than that.

My question is—Are there any of these letters, or signatures, which appear to you more strongly like Mr. Parnell's handwriting than others? If you cannot answer the question say so, and I will proceed—

The PRESIDENT.—May I be allowed, Sir Charles, to suggest another form of putting the question? Are there any of the signatures as to which he has any doubt?

SIR C. RUSSELL.—Yes, my Lord, but I should prefer to have an answer to the question as I put it.

The PRESIDENT.—You are referring him to an imaginary standard.

SIR C. RUSSELL.—Quite so, my Lord; but it is a standard which each man forms in his mind. (To the witness.) What do you say?—I do not know. As I have said, I am not an expert.

No, and I am not going to trouble you to enter into a minute criticism of the writing. I want to know whether your opinion is equally strong upon every one of the letters?—Yes, I understand the question, but my difficulty is in answering it. I think the handwriting is Mr. Parnell's, and I cannot say more than that.

I will repeat the question once more. Do all the letters seem to you to be equally unmistakably in the handwriting of Mr. Parnell, or are there any that strike you as less likely to be so than others?—I cannot answer the question. They all seem to me to be in his handwriting.

Very well. Now, you recollect the appearance of the fac-simile letter in *The Times?*—Yes.

Have you ever discussed with any one the question of how *The Times* got it?—I have often spoken about it, but I have never discussed with any one how *The Times* got it, because I do not know.

Not even how they might have got it?—I have heard various statements made about it in conversation.

Just tell us what they were?—I cannot, really. It is impossible.

Tell us, in substance, what where the suggestions you discussed and made as to how *The Times* got the letter.—I have seen various theories started about it in the newspapers.

What were they?—I do not know now.

Have you ever made any suggestion on the subject yourself?—No.

Did you hear any suggestion made as to whom it was addressed to?—There is one which commences "Dear E."

Do you take that to mean Mr. Egan?—Yes.

I am now talking about the fac-simile letter?—I have never heard any suggestion as to whom that might be addressed.

Nor formed an opinion yourself?—No. At first when I saw the letter I did not think it was genuine. My idea was that if you told a correspondent to show a letter to a man, and at the same time told him not to let him know your address, it would be rather insulting to him.

Did you suppose that the signature had been first obtained and the letter written above it?—No, I did not think anything about it.

Why did you believe the letter not to be genuine?—I could not understand why a man should say, "You can show him this letter, but do not tell him my address."

Is that the only reason why you thought it was not genuine?—That was the only reason.

Although you had no doubt about the handwriting?—I had no doubt about the signature.

Can you suggest anybody as the writer of the body of the letter or letters?—No.

Do you know the handwriting of Mr. Campbell, Mr. Parnell's secretary?—I have often received letters from him about the meetings of a company of which he and I were directors.

A land company was it not?—Yes, but I have not got any of the letters.

An emigration land company was it not?—Well, you ought to know as you were a director. (Laughter.)

Take these letters in your hand and tell me whether the body of any of them is in Mr. Campbell's handwriting?—I do not know, I cannot tell.

Just turn them over and look at them?—I have looked at them.

Are you speaking of all the letters?—Any of them.

Is there any one in Mr. Campbell's handwriting? —As well as I know Mr. Campbell's handwriting, I cannot say anything of the kind.

As to that you will express no opinion?—I know nothing about them.

There are only two other points I want to ask you anything about. You say Mr. Parnell asked you to have police protection for himself?—Yes.

Are you certain of that?—Absolutely certain.

Did you not get police protection for your own house?—Yes.

Did you not get police protection for your own rooms at Albert-mansions?—Yes.

Do you suggest that beyond watching your house where Mr. Parnell was staying, that Mr. Parnell was watched or followed by police?— Certainly, that is to say, Sir William Harcourt told me he should have them.

Police in uniform or detectives?—I do not know. I asked for police protection.

Did you at the same time ask for police protection for Albert-mansions?—Yes.

Where you lived? Mr. Parnell did not stay there?—No.

Then I understand you asked for three things —you asked for police protection for your house, for personal protection for Mr. Parnell, and police protection for your rooms in Albert-mansions?— I do not know whether it was for Albert-mansions. I was promised that I should be looked after.

Do you recollect a discussion in the House of Commons as to certain interviews you had with Mr. Forster?—Yes.

It is suggested to me that you had police protection in 1886 at Albert-mansions. Is that so? —Not that I know of, but one does not always know what the police do.

I believe you wrote a letter to *The Times* news-paper on May 18, 1882?—Yes.

Sir C. Russell.—I will read the letter from the *Freeman's Journal*, where it also appeared.

"Sir—Lest there should linger in the public mind the slightest misconception as to my repudia-tion of Mr. Forster's public version of my private conversation, I beg that you will insert the follow-ing statement:

"My assertion that I had been in frequent com-munication with him, Mr. Forster has had the coolness to describe as incorrect. I retort that, besides previous communications, I talked the whole situation over while walking with him from the House of Commons to the Irish Office, and while standing outside the latter building on Wednesday, the 26th of April. On Friday, the 28th, I walked with him from the Irish Office through the Park to Downing street, stopping several times on the way, as men often do when in earnest conversation. Among the matters of our discussion was a foolish answer which he had drafted to Mr. Cowen's question respecting the imprisoned members, and which he was fortunately not allowed to give in the House of Commons. I had another conversation—a short one—with him later in the day, at the Irish Office, and a third interview of some length in his room in the House of Commons, to which I was invited by him through the Irish Solicitor-General. During

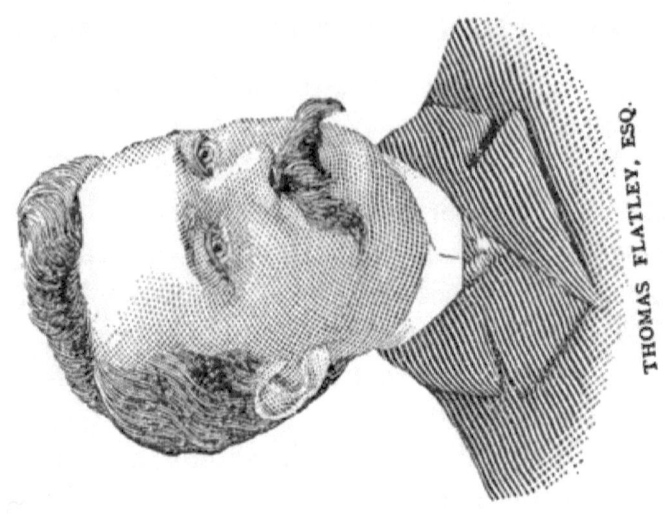

THOMAS FLATLEY, ESQ.

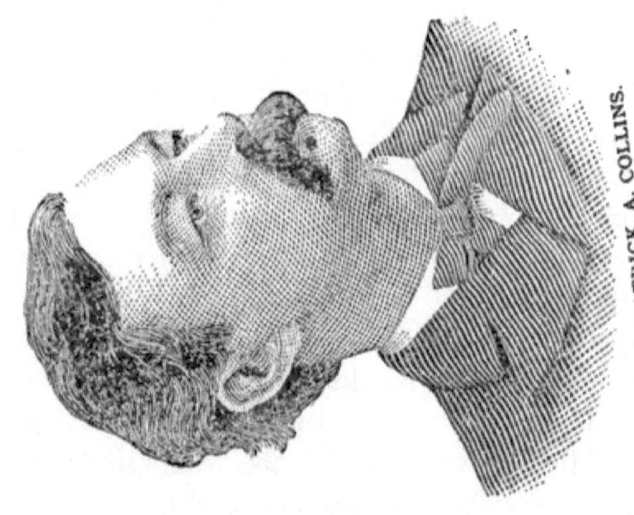

HON. PATRICK A. COLLINS.

this last one he suggested the best plan for visiting Kilmainham unostentatiously. But I confess he appeared nervous and demoralized, and I was obliged to point out and make him correct 'an extraordinary error in the letter which he handed me, addressed to Captain Barlow, deputy chairman of the Irish Prisons' Board. That error was nothing less than the substitution of another name for mine in the order for special facilities which he had just written. The order must be in Captain Barlow's possession. Let it be produced, for Mr. Forster's worst enemy cannot suggest its being concocted.'

"Now, as to the memorandum alleged by Mr. Forster to represent my conversation with him on April 30. In it he informed the Cabinet that I had used the following words :—'The conspiracy which has been used to get up boycotting and outrages will now be used to put them down.' The following are the facts :—I myself know nothing about the organization of the Land League. But I told Mr. Forster that I had been informed by Mr. Parnell the day before that if the arrears question were settled, that organization would explain the boon to the people and tell them that they ought to assist the operation of the remedial measure in the tranquillization of the country. I added that Mr. Parnell had expressed his belief that Messrs. Davitt, Egan Sheridan, and Boyton would use all their exertions,

if placed in a position to do so, to advance the
pacification, and that Mr. Sheridan's influence was
of special importance in the west, owing to the
fact that he had been the chief organizer of the
Land League in Connaught before his arrest,
while Mr. Boyton had held a similar appointment
in the province of Leinster.   On these points I had
heard no more, I knew no more, and I said no
more.   " Your obedient servant,
                    " WILLIAM HENRY O'SHEA.
"House of Commons."

SIR. C. RUSSELL.—That is correct?—Perfectly
correct.

You will bring the testimonial to which we
have referred into court to-morrow morning?—
Yes.

The ATTORNEY-GENERAL then asked whether
any of the other parties desired to cross-examine
the witness, and negative replies being given, he
left the box.

Mr. HEALY then rose and said,—I wish to put
a question to Mr. O'Shea.

The witness having been recalled,

Mr. HEALY said,—You were opposed at Galway by some members of the Irish party, and
you went there on a Saturday?—Yes.

Do you remember a paragraph in the *Freeman's
Journal* announcing your candidature?—Yes.

By the next train you were followed by certain Irish members?—Yes.

Who were they?—Yourself and Mr. Biggar.

We immediately addressed meetings against you, and attacked and denounced you by every means in our power?—Yes.

Mr. HEALY.—Quite so; that is all I want.

There was no re-examination of the witness.

CHAPTER XXIII.

THE INFAMOUS LE CARON.

And now, passing by days consumed in tedious wranglings and the reading of the public speeches of the accused by the Attorney-General, as well as the evidence of small-fry informers, I come to the 5th of February, when the infamous spy, Le Caron, gave his testimony. On this side of the Atlantic, at least, his career, as he told it on the witness-stand, will be read with deep interest.

Major Le Caron, who wore the badge of the Federal Army, was called and examined by the Attorney-General.

What is your name? My baptismal name is Thomas Willis Beach.

Where were you born? I was born in Colchester.

Under what name have you passed during the last number of years? I have been known for the last twenty-eight years as Henri Le Caron.

What is your age? I am forty-eight years of age.

I gather that you have been to the United States. When did you go? Soon after the breaking out of the war of rebellion in 1861.

Did you enlist in the army? I did.

The American army? The Northern army.

Did you attain any rank in the American army?
I did. I entered as a private at the commencement of the war, and after serving two years as a
private and non-commissioned officer, I became
second lieutenant, first lieutenant——

The PRESIDENT.—What did you ultimately become?

WITNESS.—I was regimental adjutant with the
rank of major. I was known as Major Le Caron.

The ATTORNEY-GENERAL.—Did you pass con-
tinually under that name during the twenty-eight
years you were in America? I did altogether.

Were you not known by any other name?
Never.

Now, you must please answer these questions
I am about to put to you directly, either yes or no.
In the year 1864 did you become acquainted with
a person named John O'Neill? I did.

Captain John O'Neill? Yes.

Did he make any communication to you respecting the Fenian organization? He did.

In the year 1865 did O'Neill make a communication to you with reference to the invasion of
Canada? He did.

Did you communicate with your father? I did.

Now, just answer, yes or no, please. Do you
know whether communication was made to a
member of Parliament?

SIR C. RUSSELL.—Really, my Lords, I must object to that question.

The PRESIDENT.—Of course, we must not get behind that phrase "does he know."

The ATTORNEY-GENERAL.—Did you yourself communicate with a member of Parliament? I did not.

In consequence of a communication made to you did you communicate with the Government? No.

Did you take any part in the expedition against Canada? I allied myself——

SIR C. RUSSELL.—I must ask, my Lords, whether this is evidence?

The PRESIDENT.—Of course, at present it is not.

The ATTORNEY-GENERAL.—It is necessary to lead up to subsequent matters.

The PRESIDENT.—I do not think that what took place in 1865 can throw much light on the inquiry.

The ATTORNEY-GENERAL.—Very well, my Lord. (To witness.) Did you at any time join the Fenian organization? I did.

In what year? In 1865 or the beginning of 1866.

Tell us where you joined it? At Nashville, Tennessee.

Had you any office or position in that organization? Not at that time.

Had you at any time? Yes.

When? Would it be permitted to me to state that part of my story?

You had better simply answer my question at present. When did you obtain any office in the Fenian organization? In the spring of 1868.

What was the office? Military organizer.

Where? All over the United States.

What was the name of the office in the organization? I was called on the pay-roll of the organization military organizer. I was commissioned with the rank of major in the Irish Republican army.

Now, just answer yes or no, please. When you were holding that office, was there a convention at Philadelphia—in 1868? In 1869.

What work was being carried out by the organization in 1869? It was contemplating the invasion of Canada.

Did you take any part in the preparations for that? I did.

What? I acted as inspector-general and afterwards as adjutant-general for the Fenian Brotherhood. I was intrusted with the laying of arms and ammunition and war material along the Canadian line of territory. I attended every council of war that was held in the organization.

Did you communicate what was going on to the Canadian Government? I communicated every detail to the Canadian Government.

Was any descent made on Canada? There were two—on May 30, 1866, and June 12, 1870.

One was attempted following upon your efforts to deposit arms along the border? Yes.

Was that the one in June, 1870? Yes.

Was that a failure? Both were lamentable failures.

Did you at that time know J. J. O'Kelly? No.

When did you first know Mr. J. J. O'Kelly?

SIR C. RUSSELL.—He has not said that he ever knew him.

The ATTORNEY-GENERAL.—Did you at any time know Mr. J. J. O'Kelly? Personally or by reputation?

Personally? I first met him personally in the House of Commons in the month of March, 1881.

Now, only just give me the date, please. When did you first know him by name? I first heard of him in the year 1875.

You say you met Mr. O'Kelly in the House of Commons; you mean Mr. J. J. O'Kelly, member of Parliament? I do.

What did you do after the invasion? I returned to the West, completed my studies, and graduated as a doctor of medicine.

Did you hear something in connection with the Fenian organization? Only answer yes or no, please. Yes.

Where were you at that time? At that time I was practicing medicine in Braidwood, near Chicago.

How far is Braidwood from Chicago? About fifty miles.

CHARLES STEWART PARNELL.   343

Who first made a communication to you about any organization in connection with the old Fenian body? I first heard of it in New York city, but not in an official way.

From whom? In 1875 I became acquainted with the fact.

I only want to know from whom? Colonel Clingen.

Where did he reside? At Chicago.

On hearing of this did you communicate with London? Yes.

With whom? Did you communicate with the Government or with whom? With the Government.

Did you receive any instructions? Yes.

Did you join the organization? Yes.

Who proposed you? Alexander Sullivan, of Chicago.

The name of this man your Lordships will find connected with a number of things in this case. He is one of the persons charged.

SIR C. RUSSELL.—No, no. He is charged as one with whom the members associated.

CHAPTER XXIV.

LE CARON JOINS THE "V. C."

The ATTORNEY-GENERAL.—Very well, an associate and not a member ; that is the distinction, my Lords. (To witness.) Just tell us who Alexander Sullivan was ? At that date he was a member of the executive body of the United Brotherhood, a body known as the V. C.

I want to ask you, first, had Alexander Sullivan any business ? He was clerk to the Board of Public Works in Chicago.

Had you known him before he proposed you ? Yes.

How long ? About eleven years.

Had he been connected with the Fenian organization or not ? Yes.

Do you know whether, prior to 1875, he had been connected with the Fenian organization ? I do.

SIR C. RUSSELL.—Does he know of his own knowledge ?

The ATTORNEY-GENERAL.—Do you know of your own knowledge ? Yes.

What was the name of the organization for which you were proposed ? The United Brotherhood.

Was it spoken of as the United Brotherhood of the V. C., or in any other way ? Always as the V. C. .

Just explain this –V. C. were taken as U. B.? Yes.

That is the letter following the letter which was intended was used? Yes.

So that U would become V, and B would become C ? Yes.

Do you know the name Clan-na-Gael ? Yes.
What was that ?

SIR C. RUSSELL.—Does he know what it was?

The ATTORNEY-GENERAL.—Do you know of your own knowledge what it was ? Yes. It was a secret organization known as the V. C.

The V. C. was the same as the Clan-na-Gael, then ? Yes.

Now, just tell me a little more about the cipher, please. What would Ireland be? Jsjti.

No, that is " Irish ;" I want to know what Ireland is ? Jsfmboe.

What was the governing authority called? The F. C.

I do not quite know how that was obtained ? From the words Executive Body.

That is to say, the E of the Executive became the F, and the B of Body became the C ? Yes, sir.

JOHN J. HYNES.

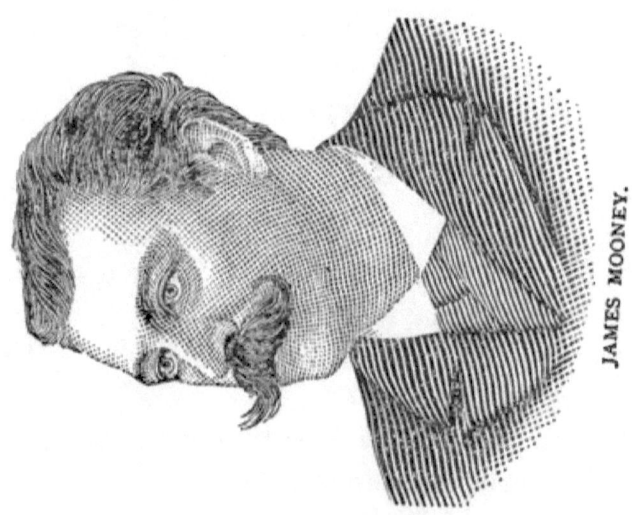

JAMES MOONEY.

Was there any sign for the secretary? He was known as Y.

Treasurer?—Z.

Chairman?—X.

Now, you have said that you were proposed by Sullivan. Do you know whether Alexander Sullivan was a member of the Executive Body? On that exact date, no.

Was the country divided into districts at all for the purposes of this body? Yes, sir.

How were these districts named or known? By letters of the alphabet, from A to N.

Was there any directory? Yes, sir.

How nominated? The directory or Executive Body at that time consisted of district members, one in each district, in connection with the chairman, secretary, and treasurer.

How was the district member known; had he any symbol? Yes, sir.

What? A cross.

Was a cipher used for him or not? No, none. D. M. and E. N. at another time.

CHAPTER XXV

OBJECTS OF THE "V. C."

And what was the object of this U. B. (United Brotherhood)? It was to bring about the establishment of an Irish Republic, of an independent Irish Republic in Ireland, and the independence of that nation ; and it was believed that the only method whereby that could be accomplished was by the force of arms.

The wretched informer here identified copies of the "Constitution" and by-laws, etc., of the V. C., and under the skillful lead of the Attorney-General brought to the attention of the Royal Commission a large number of documents, copies of which had been sent to him as Senior Guardian of the Camp to which he belonged. His story throughout was a most exciting one to the hundreds of thousands of Irishmen here and elsewhere who were identified with the "United Brotherhood," either directly or indirectly. He told of the secretly arranged plans of "the Executive Body" to raise funds, to keep alive the enthusiasm of the rank and file, and of his own

348

election as Senior Guardian of Camp 463, Illinois.

Attempting to connect Mr. Parnell with the " U. B.," the Attorney-General asked:

Do you remember the visit of Mr. Parnell and Mr. Dillon to America in 1880?—I remember it by public report.

Do you know whether any other members of Parliament went over with Mr. Parnell and Mr. Dillon in that year?—I do not know.

Did Mr. Healy come at that time?—I believe he was there at the same time.

Did you know, as an officer of the body about which you have told us, who arranged the meetings attended by Mr. Parnell, Mr. Dillon, and Mr. Healy?—Invariably, without exception, during both the western and the eastern tours, the arrangements were exclusively in the hands of the leaders of the revolutionary organization.

In the hands of the leaders of the United Brotherhood, or Clan-na-Gael?—Yes.

Tell us whom you mean?—I mean such men as Alexander Sullivan, J. F. Finerty, Judge Prendergast, Judge Moran, W. J. Hynes, J. M. Smythe, John Devoy, J. D. Breslin, Martin Pigane, James Callagher, J. D. Carroll, W. D. Carroll, James Tracey, and Fitzgerald.

After reading circulars issued by the patriot John Devoy, the Attorney-General continued:

Tell us what passed between you and Devoy?—I spent four days with him and had a series of conversations with him. He informed me that it was contemplated by the organization to inaugurate a new system of warfare—cold-blooded murder and destruction of property.

The President.—What organization?

Witness.—Our organization, that to which he and I belonged?

The Attorney-General.—Go on with the conversation, please.—It was to be a warfare characterized by all the rigors of Nihilism.

Anything further?—He spoke of the condition of the organization in Ireland. While the executive of the I. R. B. (Irish Republican Brotherhood) were not in favor of inaugurating a movement of this kind, yet it was a very difficult matter to rerestrain the fire-eating element which would be very likely, when evictions commenced, to attack some of the flying columns in portions of the country where the organization was powerful, mentioning particularly the county of Mayo, where he said the organization was more powerful than in any other part of Ireland. This would result disastrously to those engaged. He also stated that the movement then being inaugurated by O'Donovan Rossa was alienating from our organization some good men whom it was desirable to keep, but who could not be kept unless active operations were commenced.

The President.—This is your summary of a

conversation which passed between you and Devoy during several days?

Witness.—Yes, my Lord.

The President.—It is his opinion of what was likely to occur?—Yes, my Lord.

The President.—If that is a correct summary of it, I am of opinion that it is inadmissible.

The Attorney - General. — The summary scarcely included the first part.

The President.—Very well; I cannot exactly follow all he said.

The Attorney-General.—I will bring out the point in another way, my Lord. (To Witness.) In 1880 or the beginning of 1881, had you a conversation with Alexander Sullivan?—Yes; I repeatedly saw him in the beginning of 1881.

Do you remember seeing Sullivan with Patrick Meleady?—No; I saw Patrick Meleady with John Devoy.

Was Alexander Sullivan a member of the executive?—He was.

Was Patrick Meleady?—He was a prominent member of the United Brotherhood.

Did you have any conversation with Sullivan as to any plan of warfare?—Yes; in the beginning of 1881.

What was it?—I ascertained——

The President.—No, no; what did he say?

Witness.—Alexander Sullivan told me that there was an intention to reorganize the organization, to inaugurate a species of active warfare on this side of the water, and attack the enemy secretly and silently whenever an opportunity might present itself. He said that the organization on this side of the water, from some lack of courage of the leaders, could not be depended upon.

Sir C. Russell.—Is England or Ireland referred to?

The President.—He means this side of the water with regard to the Atlantic.

Witness (continuing).—He said that operations would be directed from the United States side; the matter was in good hands, but it would take time to complete.

Did you have any conversation with Meleady? —Yes.

Do you remember a man named Whelan being mentioned?—Yes; he was mentioned by Patrick Meleady in company with Colonel Flynn and John Devoy. It was said he had invented and submitted to the New York organization for use a new hand grenade and torpedo, composed of something more explosive than anything at that time known. It was made in a very compact and portable form, so that at least a dozen could be carried in a hand-satchel. By means of a system of time-fuse they could be located in a number of places by the same man, who could be well out of the way before any of them exploded. Patrick

Meleady also said that he was well acquainted with this side of the water, and he volunteered his services to come over and engage in that part of the work.

What part?—Locating and planning matters relating to destruction by dynamite, torpedoes, and hand-grenades.

Where did this conversation with Meleady in Devoy's presence take place?—It took place in my office, in New York, in the fall of 1880.

When you refer to the revolutionary organization, do you mean the same that you have previously alluded to?—Yes.

You have spoken of a circular which Devoy sent to you; did he lecture in your neighborhood?—Yes. I presided over one of the demonstrations and introduced him. The lecture was given at Braidwood, Ill., about the beginning of April, 1881.

Do you know whether any of Devoy's lectures at which you were present were reported in any papers?—I could not say. If I looked over a file of the *Irish World* I could find them if they were there.

How long did Devoy stay with you at Braidwood?—I saw him at intervals extending over three weeks, and continuously for four days.

Do you remember his saying anything about a rising in Ireland?—Yes; he said he anticipated that if there should be a rising in Ireland it would result disastrously.

Did he fear it or expect it?—He feared that a premature movement would take place.

Did he say anything about O'Donovan Rossa? —Yes. He considered that something should be done to prevent some of the more rabid, who were demanding that "something should be done," from flocking to the standard of Rossa. He said that it would be necessary for us to do something to keep them in the organization.

What do you mean by the "standard of Rossa"? —After the Convention of 1879 Rossa was expelled from the organization for malfeasance in office—for misappropriating some $13,000 of the Skirmishing Fund.

I understood you to say that he was expelled after the Convention of 1879.—He was a delegate at that Convention, and was expelled some year or so after. He then formed an organization bitterly opposed to the leaders of the V. C. (United Brotherhood), desiring to be one himself.

He was not a leader of the V. C. (United Brotherhood) after 1879?—No; but he was a member of the United Brotherhood.

Following these questions were many which introduced and sought to implicate in the movement the Hon. Patrick Egan, U. S. Minister to Chile, the Hon. Thomas Sexton, Lord-Mayor of Dublin, Dr. Kenny, Mr. O'Kelly, T. P. Brennan,

REV. CHARLES O'REILLY

REV. THOMAS J. CONATY.

and other prominent men. The arrival of Patrick
Egan was dwelt on repeatedly, and the fact that
he was the guest of Alexander Sullivan after
which Le Caron presented to the Commissioners
the following extracts from the Revolutionary
Directory to the Senior Guardians :

" These instructions are for the exclusive use of
S. G.'s (Senior Guardians) only, and are not·to
be read or mentioned as being received by any
one else under any circumstances whatever, but
are to be enforced as coming from the Constitution or laws, when they are prohibitory or man-
datory.   When, however, the suggestions contained herein require that some one take the
initiative, or when they require organization or
action, the S. G. is looked to to put the suggestions into operation both by counsel, action,
and example.

"1. It shall be the duty of the S. G.'s to dili-
gently inquire, without informing the parties or
any one else, the names and address of the men
best fitted for private work of a confidential and
dangerous character, and report the same in a list
made out or furnished for that purpose to Y (the
Secretary), and this list shall be made out at such
stated periods as they may be demanded.

" 2. S. G. will prohibit any and all argument,
discussion, or reply to any and all statements or
charges, from any source, affecting the welfare of

the organization of which he is to be the judge, either in writing or interview or in any manner whatever by any member of the organization.

"3. It shall be the duty of S. G's. to urge or organize military companies, rifle clubs, signal corps, or schools of skirmishers, such as may be best adapted to the locality and the tastes of the men, and they shall report in writing the character, number, and resources of the same.

"4. In cities and towns accessible to navigation it is deemed important to ascertain all the persons skilled in navigation available to the purposes of the organization, and report their names, experience, and character to the foregoing address.

*   *   *   *   *   *

"6. S. G.'s are instructed to make their places of meeting so far as possible their own property by lease or ownership. Where the same is possible several clubs should be established, the profits to revert to the order.

"7. As the successful working, increase in members, and the resources, is always largely due to the personal exertions of S. G.'s, it is urged that every S. G. be active and energetic in increasing the strength and resources of the organization. D.'s (camps) of instruction for officers and D.'s should be held as often as possible, and every man drilled to perfection in his place in the work of meetings. D.'s should be opened promptly, and the work of the order carried out rigidly in order to inculcate fully the spirit and habit of obedience.

*　　*　　*　　*　　*　　*

" 9. S. G.'s are requested to take such steps as may be practical without increasing expenses to the organization to fully organize every locality within their reach, where there is at present no D., and put the same in complete working order. To fully carry out the spirit of this suggestion the contingent funds of D.'s or private subscriptions is suggested as the best means of furnishing any necessary funds.

" Where possible and practical S. G.'s and other officers and the D.'s in a body are requested as often as possible to interchange visits and social reunions.

*　　*　　*　　*　　*　　*

" 12. Where it is deemed important that some able or distinguished brother might do good by visiting or addressing the D., the S. G. will make the same known to Y. (the Secretary), and where practical or possible their wants will be supplied.

" 13. When possible and practical, and the same can be done without interfering with the work of the organization, it is urged that the open organization (National League) be aided as far as possible.

" 14. The complete development and training

of all branches, military, naval, and civic, likely to be useful in a struggle such as we are waging is deemed of the very highest importance, and it is made the duty of the S. G.'s to spare no effort to make their local organization of whatever nature as effective as possible in some particular branch and art of warfare.

" 15. All communications must be carefully destroyed or returned to Y. if so desired, after being read at successive meetings as often as directed.

" 16. The following suggestions are made with a view of indicating locations best adapted to particular branches of the art of war, but in every instance S. G.'s will use their own judgment or follow the instincts of their men in adopting the art or branch of war to be cultivated.

" The seaports and coast lines for navigation—torpedoes and artillery.

" The Western Territories—calvary.

" The mining regions—engineering, explosives, and sharpshooting.

" The Western States—infantry and artillery.

" The Southern States—infantry, cavalry, and artillery.

"Where there are more than one D., and less than three they should take each different branches of warfare for study.

" In the cities of New York, Brooklyn, Chicago, Boston, and Philadelphia D.'s might by a mutual understanding each select some of the technical higher branches—one for telegraphy, one for signals, one for arsenal and repair work, one for commissairies' work, one for scouts and spies, one for general instruction in the art of war.

"In all cases the very youngest members should be selected for the schools, as they are more sensitive to new ideas, and more easily learned. When the work is once commenced a thousand suggestions and improvements will occur to the S. G.'s of D.'s, all of which they are earnestly requested to push forward as rapidly as possible.

" Respectfully and fraternally,

"The R. D. (Revolutionary Directory) and

F. C. (Executive Body)."

CHAPTER XXVIII.

Le Caron's testimony about the sad death of Mr. Lomasney is of interest. He was asked:

You were saying, in connection with the Mackey Lomasney incident, that the matter was mentioned at the meeting of the Convention in 1888; who were present there?—At that meeting? By name?

Yes.—Luke Dillon, Patrick Egan, Samuel Morrice, John Devoy, O'Meagher Condon—

That is sufficient for my purpose. Now, what passed, only with reference to this Lomasney incident; what was said about anything being done for his family? Was any resolution come to?— Yes, it appears in the official report of the proceedings of that meeting. The discussion was brought up by the delegate from Detroit, Michigan. He cited the amount appropriated soon after the supposed death of Lomasney for his old father and his wife and children.

The Attorney-General.—Will your Lordships permit me to postpone putting in this document

361

in order of date? It is necessary on account of the Lomasney incident being finished in 1888. I try to be chronological. Now I will just read the resolution this gentleman has referred to :—

"The case of Mr. Lomasney, whose two sons were sacrificed in the cause of ——, was then brought to the attention of the Convention. It was ordered unanimously that the executive body be instructed to look after the welfare of the family."

On his cross-examination the spy, Le Caron, was asked :

Had you any business in America besides the patriotic business?—Yes, sir.

What was it?—I have "run"—I practiced medicine soon after graduating. I graduated in the spring session of 1872 as doctor of medicine, and I have practiced medicine at intervals from that time to this. I have also been the proprietor at times of three different chemists' shops, and have also been president of a pharmaceutical association.

Did you make your living at that or was it a pretence?—I made a very large amount of money at that time. More than sufficient to live on.

Now about this U. B. or V. C. (United Brotherhood). You told us yesterday that you were high up in the military branch of the organization? —Yes.

But as regards the Civil Council, the Executive

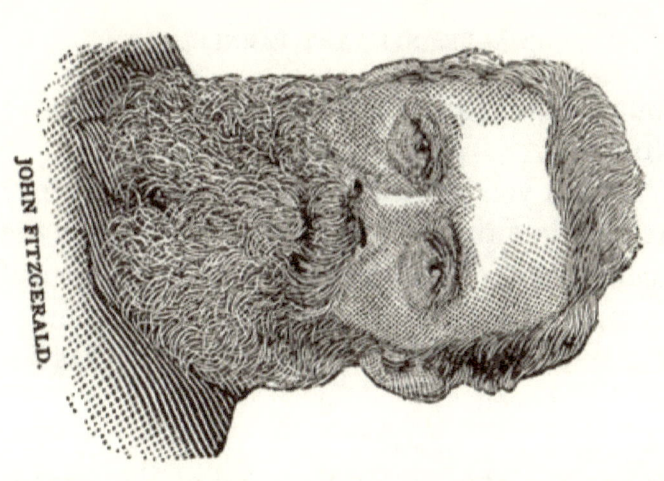

JOHN FITZGERALD.

JOHN P. SUTTON.

—you were not a member of the Executive Body?
—No.

What did you call the head of the organization?
—At one time the district members composed the
Executive Body. At another time the number of
six composed the Executive Body. At another
time the triangle. At another time it was increased to seven.

You have not answered my question. Was
there any designation for the head of this organization?—Yes, sir, the Executive Body.

No, no, that would consist of several.—That
was the name given to the leaders.

Was there no one person who corresponded to
the Fenian centre or head centre, or something of
that kind?—They acted collectively. They chose
a chairman or presiding officer of the Executive
Body from time to time.

Then there was no one who would correspond
to what we have heard described in reference to
Fenianism as head centre?—We had no such
name as head centre.

Or any corresponding name?—The Executive
Body, sir, the council.

Can you tell me who is supposed to be at the
head of the organization now?—Yes.

Who?—I submitted the official list yesterday.

CHAPTER XXIX.

Who?—Bradley, of Philadelphia. Patrick Egan is the first name on the executive.

You know that of your own knowledge?—Yes, sir. I voted for him and saw him elected. O'Meagher Condon and Luke Dillon are members of the executive.

You do not follow me. Who is the head, the present head?—I think they elected Bradley as chairman of the Executive Body.

You say you think. You do not seem to have a personal knowledge.—I have a personal knowledge of that. If you will allow me to refresh my memory with a list I could tell you. My own knowledge is that I voted for Mr. Bradley.

You mean you did; you know you did?—I do not like to swear; I might commit myself.

Now you mentioned yesterday, I think, the numbers of this V. C. or U. B. at some period. What was the number you mentioned yesterday? —At an early date it averaged from 11,000 to 13,000.

365

In 1877 about 11,500?—Yes, sir; and it got as high as 23,000.

When was that? Was that in the end of 1881?—Oh! a little later than that.

The beginning of 1882?—Yes, sir; 22,000 in 1882.

Do you recollect the suppression of the Land League and the arrest of the Irish leaders?—Yes.

That gave a great impetus, did it not, to the organization in America?—The first arrest in 1881?

Yes, toward the end of 1881?—Yes, it did, sir.

Did not the highest point of your membership occur at the end of 1881 and beginning of 1882?—No, sir.

When do you say it was?—To-day; it always increased.

You think the numbers are greater to-day than before?—Yes; and I can prove it by reports I can submit to you.

You have reports that will show that?—Yes.

Which you can give to the Court?—I can, sir.

Reports sent over from time to time to Anderson?—Yes.

Mr. Cunynghame, will you kindly give me those two bundles of documents? (The Secretary handed the documents to Sir Charles Russell.)

Sir C. Russell.—The first document which I have here is the constitution of the V. C. (United

Brotherhood) No. 1, in 1877. It was then a secret society?—Yes.

Bound by a secret oath?—It was.

And except the members of the society, who, I presume, had certain signs and passwords, the ordinary world would know nothing about it?— Excepting the public name which they had, and meeting as a public society by a public name at a public hall.

You mean in the districts where they were strong they belonged to some club, or something of. that kind?—Either strong or weak, every district, every camp was compelled to be known by a public name only.

Ay, ay; but what I mean is the outside public would know them—take your own illustration— at Braidwood by the name of the Emmett Club? —Yes.

Would any person who was not prepared to take, or had not taken, the oaths of the secret society be eligible for the Emmett Club?—I would like to hear that question again.

Would anybody except a sworn member be eligible for membership in the Emmett Club?— He became a sworn member as soon as he became a member.

You mean that when he joined the Emmett Club he was obliged to take the oath?—Yes.

Then no persons were eligible for the Emmett Club unless they became members?—The Emmett Club was the secret organization and nothing else.

Yes, I understand now, the public name of the secret organization. You have handed in a document, John Devoy's report in 1880, as envoy?—Yes.

Is John Devoy a member of the United Brotherhood, or V. C., or whatever name it is known by now?—Yes.

Have you known him as such?—For years, sir.

Recently?—Yes, sir; I met him as a brother delegate of my own at the last Convention in the month of June, 1888.

What is John Devoy?—He has been a journalist.

What paper?—Years ago he was telegraph editor of the *New York Herald*. After that, in company with others, he was editing a paper known as the *Irish Nation*.

After that?—He was lecturing through the country, subsisting in part upon that.

Upon the proceeds of lectures?—Yes. He has been actively engaged in politics. He is what I would term an Irish professional politician.

In America, you mean?—Yes.

Is he connected with journalism now or not?—I could not say.

Were there many of these printed documents which you produce here—this report of the pro-

ceedings of the ninth general Convention of the
V. C. (United Brotherhood)—were there many of
these printed ?—I have no means of ascertaining
the exact number.

Who had charge of that ?—The Executive Body,
with the assistance of their paid secretary, probably.

You have suggested rather than stated in your
evidence that you had to do with Gallagher and
Lomasney. Did you take part in any deliberation
at which either of these wicked plots was devised ?
—Yes, sir.

You yourself took part?—Yes, sir.

And advised in them ?—I did not deem myself
of sufficient importance to make suggestions and
put myself too forward in these matters.

You appeared to advise ?—I offered no objection.

And gave information at once ?—Immediately.
On the first opportunity that presented itself.

And did you suggest that you knew that Gallagher was the agent in the one case and Lomasney in the other ; did you suggest that you knew
at the time that either of these was selected ?—
Before they were suggested?

Did you know when they were selected ?—The
actual time, no, sir.

Did you know that they had been selected ?—
—Yes.

You knew that they had been selected ; you

24

knew the persons ?—I did, sir, and was able to describe the persons.

And knew when they left the country ?—The exact date, no ; approximately.

I suppose you had persons in your pay helping you in this business ?—Not in my pay.

In your service ?—I had friends.

When did O'Donovan Rossa, according to your opinion, cease to be an important factor in this wretched movement ?—He commenced to be a bone of contention immediately following the Convention of 1879.

And after that did his power wane away ?—It did in that organization.

Do you suggest that he set up another ?—I say that he did.

At what date ?—I cannot give you the exact date, as I did not belong to it.

Can you fix the date at which O'Donovan Rossa was expelled from your organization ?—At this moment, no. It was after the circular of April 19.

Are you clear it was after ?—It was after the Convention of 1881, in fact.

In this same circular of yours it is stated that at a regular meeting of the V. C. (United Brotherhood) a resolution was adopted expelling Rossa from the V. C. on account of this same action. How do you reconcile that with your statement? —Kindly give me the date of that.

ROGER WALSH.

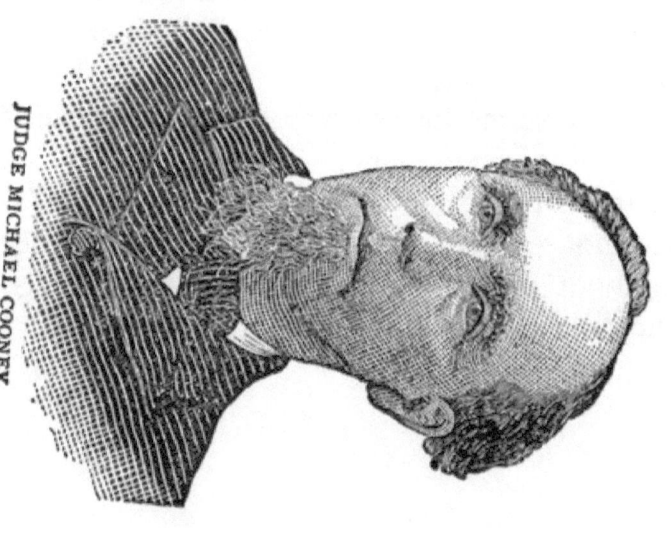

JUDGE MICHAEL COONEY.

April 19, 1880.—That is the truth if it so states. My recollection is that I received notice of his expulsion either in the beginning of 1882 or the end of 1881.

Now, during the period from 1880 to January, 1882, what names would you give to their Lordships as those of the most influential and most leading men in your organization?—W. J. Hynes, Alexander Sullivan, J. F. Finerty, Dr. Guirey, Judge Prendergast, Judge Moran, John Devoy, D. Cronin, J. D. Breslin, Judge Fitzgerald, Fitzpatrick, J. F. Armstrong, of Georgia; Luke Dillon, Dr. Carroll, J. E. Fox, Reynolds, J. D. Carroll, D. K. Walsh.

You have mentioned the names I wanted, but if you wish to add any I do not wish to stop you. —No.

Now, give me four or five of the most considerable—the most influential—men in the U. B. (United Brotherhood) from 1880 to 1882?—I could not give you the names of any four; there would not always be the same four; it changed hands in 1881.

CHAPTER XXX.

THE INFLUENTIAL MEN.

Well, from August, 1881, to the end of 1882?
—Alexander Sullivan, W. J. Hynes, Michael Boland, John Devoy.

Now, I think that of these four names, you have mentioned two as those of persons you saw with a view of bringing about what you describe as an understanding?—Yes, a better understanding.

Those two, I think, were Sullivan and Devoy? —And Hynes.

Now, I want to ask you about some of these men whose names you have enumerated. What is Sullivan?—He is a lawyer in Chicago, Ill.

What is his position?—As a lawyer or in society?

As a lawyer.—Very good, as a lawyer.

He does not move among the aristocracy of Chicago?—By no means.

Have you partaken of his hospitality? Were you intimate with him socially?—Yes.

Then he was not unworthy of your society?— No; he was very useful. (Laughter.)

373

Finerty I think you mentioned?—Yes.

What was he—I mean as the world knew him, not as a dynamiter?—He was first oil inspector for the city of Chicago.

Petroleum, I suppose?—Yes. It is a political office.

Was he a member of Congress?—Yes; he has been for one term.

As far as America is concerned, would you say that these men were respectable American citizens, speaking of their general repute?—As far as America is concerned, yes.

Was Sullivan born in America?—He was born in Canada, the son of a British soldier and pensioner.

Finerty?—Born in Tipperary.

Judge Moran?—He was Judge of the Appellate Court of Illinois.

Is that the Supreme Court?—An intermediate court between the Circuit and Supreme Court.

Is he Irish-born?—I could not tell.

Is he a man who holds a respectable position as far as America is concerned?—He is very much respected.

As a Judge?—Yes, and as a man, I believe, in that community.

Judge Prendergast; is his reputation good?—As a lawyer and as a judge, among a certain party very good; with the other party very bad. He is a Democratic judge, and is biased in favor of his own party, and unpopular with the other party in consequence.

What is Agnew?—He is now a builder and contractor.

Is he a respectable man?—Personally, yes,

I think you mentioned Smyth; what is he?—One of the largest furniture merchants in Chicago.

Michael Boland; what was he?—By profession a practicing lawyer.

Did he serve in the army during the war?—Yes.

Is his position good as a lawyer?—No.

Not as good as Sullivan's?—He has not practiced law for some years; he practices spasmodically.

What is his private character?—Bad. He has been expelled from the organization for misappropriation of funds, and has a very bad name.

From the U. B. (United Brotherhood) organization?—Yes.

Dr. Carroll, of Philadelphia; what do know of him?—As far as I know, a very fine gentleman, and a man of education.

General Collins, Boston?—As a politician, very high.

Did he also serve in the war?—Yes.

Did you mention him as a member of the U. B. (United Brotherhood)?—I did not.

He was President of the Land League, was he not?—He was one of the original presidents.

Well, now, is his a position of undoubted respectability?—As far as I know, yes.

As far as his political position is concerned he was chairman, was he not, of the Democratic Convention in St. Louis which nominated President Cleveland?—Yes; at the last Convention.

Was it not in 1881 that General Collins was President of the Land League?—Yes.

I think you said that at the Philadelphia Convention in 1883 he was again proposed?—Yes, his name was mentioned there.

You know, do you not, that the members of the V. C. (United Brotherhood) objected to him because he had spoken in very strong condemnation of the murders in the Phœnix Park?—Yes, it was generally mentioned.

Do you suggest that General Collins was in any way in sympathy with any except constitutional movements?—At this date you are now speaking of?

Yes.—I do not suggest that at this date he was. Well, 1882.—Not in 1882.

In 1883?—Nor in 1883, nor even afterward to my knowledge. I can only speak of him since 1881.

You are speaking as far as you know him?—Yes.

Boyle O'Reilly; was he a member of the U. B.? —Not to my knowledge.

What is he?—Editor of the *Boston Pilot*.

Is he, or not, a respectable man ?—He is.

In good position ?—Among a certain class, yes.

What is he in politics ?—A Democrat.

Is he in that set a man of good position and respected ?—Yes.

Hynes you spoke of; what is he ?—A practicing attorney in Chicago.

Has he a large practice ?—Now, a very good one.

Judge Fitzgerald; he is a Cincinnati gentleman, is he not ?—Yes.

What is he ?—He has been admitted to the Bar, and has been a police magistrate and alderman.

James Reynolds; what was he ?—Engaged in mercantile business, I believe.

Where ?—New Haven, Connecticut.

What is his position ?—I could not pass an opinion.

Then may I take it that as far as the American world is concerned the men I have mentioned, with the exception of Boland, were men of respectable position ?—In a certain class, certainly.

When you talk of a certain class, do you mean with regard to politics ?—Not altogether.

What distinction do you draw ?—Politics constitute one thing, respectability and morality another. A man pointed out as charged with murder could not move in respectable society.

I am asking, as far as the world is concerned,

and not with regard to any felonious designs which they may or may not have in concert with yourself?—Not all good.

A great many of them—Most of them. I think the majority.

Am I not right in saying that if by any means the control of the nomination of the permanent chairman of the Land League Convention had been lost, with him rested the appointment of the executive?—Not always. That was done by vote of the Convention. The majority in the Convention decided that matter always.

In reply to Sir Charles Russell's cross-questions, Le Caron considerably modified a part of his previous testimony. For instance, he swore that "it was perfectly true that the Parnell League meetings in every State were honored with the presence of hundreds of governors and mayors of States and ex-governors and mayors of States, the judges of the State Supreme Court, of literary men of eminence, of clergymen of every denomination, and men of distinction in every walk of life—Americans, not merely Irish."

Le Caron's attempts to make the Commission believe that the League officers were almost *all* U. B. men were upset by Sir Charles Russell's sharp fire of incisive questions. Thus the latter reading aloud this list: The Hon. P. A. Collins, president; Patrick Cronin, vice-president; T. V. Powderly, second vice-president; Lawrence

M. J. RYAN.

E. JOHNSON.

Walsh, of Waterbury, and T. Flaherty, treasurers, asked Le Caron, Do you suggest that any of these were members of the United Brotherhood?—Powderly.

The Mayor of Scranton?—Yes, he was a district member.

Of the U. B.?—At that time V. C.

Anybody else?—That is the only one I recollect.

What was Powderly?—District member.

I do not mean with regard to organization, what was his position in the world?—He was mayor of Scranton, in Pennsylvania.

But being mayor was not his business. What business had he?—As long as I have known him he has had no business. He might have had at one time. He is one of the originators of the organization and has supreme command of the Knights of Labor.

Do you suggest that Powderly was a man in favor of a villainous policy of dynamite outrage?—In 1880? I would not judge the man.

Here is another failure in the same direction:

Was General Jones a member of the United Brotherhood?—He was not a member of the U. B., but he took a very important part in the work of the organization.

Was he a member of the U. B. or not?—No. I will explain. He was always an active worker in connection with the U. B. or the V. C. (United

Brotherhood) men, and was the negotiator between the Russian Minister at Washington and
the Revolutionary Directory, to form an alliance
to make war upon a Power then at peace with
Russia. The first negotiations commenced—

The President.—Do you want to follow this up,
Sir Charles?

Sir C. Russell.—No, my Lord. (To witness.)
Did you make a report upon that to your em-
ployers?—I did.

CHAPTER XXXI.

HOW LE CARON WAS PAID.

The best way in which I can tell my readers the inside facts about the payment of blood-money to Le Caron by the British Government and its representative on American shores—the Canadian Government—is to quote the fellow's own sworn testimony.

Cross-examined by Mr. Reid.—Who first introduced you to the U. B. in America?—I introduced myself.

When was that?—In 1865.

Did you not become a member of that association on the invitation of anybody?—My particular friends were J. D. O'Reilly and General John O'Neill.

Who introduced you to the U. B. or V. C., or whatever it is called?—Alexander Sullivan, personally.

You told us that for the first three years you received no pay from the government?—Not one cent.

382

During that time were you communicating with the government to the same extent and with the same frequency as afterward ?—Oh ! dear, no.

You only occasionally communicated with the government, then, during those three years ?— My communications only extended over some six months altogether at that time.

In the first three years ?—Yes.

When was it that you first became in the regular pay of the government ?—In February, 1868.

What was the arrangement about your pay ?— That I should have sent to me from time to time no specific sum but ample funds.

And that arrangement, I suppose, was acted upon until the present date ; until quite recently ? —No.

When did that arrangement terminate ?—It terminated in the month of August, 1870—that is, the specific arrangement.

During that period did you receive large sums ? —During the whole of that period I received £50 a month.

Was any part of that money spent by you on your own expenditure ?—During that time it did not cover my expenses.

You spent more than £50 a month ?—I did.

Do you mean in paying other persons ?—No.

How did you spend the money then ?—in what way ?—In traveling about the country and in supporting my family.

In anything else? My general expenses were very high.

Of course, supporting a family is what we all have to do, whether we receive money from the Government or not. (Laughter.) But I am speaking of your expenditure in reference to your commission from, or duty to, the Home Government. What was your expenditure during that period?—I received during that period far more than the sums I have mentioned for expenses, but not from the Home Government.

Do you mean from private persons?—No; I am now referring to the Canadian authorities.

How much money in all did you receive from the Home Government, or from the Colonial Government?—Altogether, I should put it at about £2,000.

During the three years?—Yes. About that. That includes expenses for men who were in daily communication with me.

Men who were in your pay?—No; their salaries were paid by either the Home or the Canadian Governments. I merely paid their expenses.

How much of this £2,000 do you say you spent for public purposes, apart from what you expended for your private requirements?—Every cent.

What was it that you spent it in? I do not want the names of persons, but the class of expenditure.—Well, sir, I can produce one important item. I lent Mr. John O'Neill $365.40 to save his reputation and to secure a strong hold of him. He was in default, and that gave me an immense control over the man.

I think you told me that it included the expediture for the support of your family ?—I did. My family lived upon a portion of the sum.

You say that the arrangement was altered after 1870. Was some new arrangement made ?—It was.

Have you been receiving sums of money since ? —Yes.

Very considerable sums of money ?—In the aggregate, yes.

And I suppose you lived upon it as well as spent it for the purposes in which you were engaged ?—Yes, I spent it in many ways.

CHAPTER XXXII.

THE FORGED LETTERS.

It was on Thursday, February 14th, that the London *Times* people put their solicitor, Soames, on the stand, to talk about the alleged Parnell letters, fac-similes of which had been printed in the *Times*. He swore that the *Times* obtained all of those letters from Pigott, and that the price paid for all of them, including the famous letter of May 25th, was less than $25,000. Soames produced five letters, and the Attorney-General said they had been photographed, at the same time handing photographs to Chief Justice Hannan. Soames said the letters were submitted to an expert in April, 1887, but before that genuine specimens of Parnell's writing were collected, and other specimens were since gathered. He submitted genuine specimens of Mr. Parnell's signature, which he had obtained since the fac-similes were published, including letters and summonses, which Parnell signed as magistrate, orders of admission to the House of Commons, a paragraph written for a newspaper, and the Kilmainham Jail book, one containing nine signa-

tures, the first written in December, 1881, and
the last in May, 1882. Soames said he believed
that the body of the famous letter was written by
Mr. Campbell, Parnell's private secretary, and
the signature by Mr. Parnell. He spoke of other
letters written by Egan, O'Kelly and Davitt,
which were found in informer Carey's house and
elsewhere. The first payment for alleged letters
to Pigott was £1,000; the successive payments,
which were all made by Houston, Secretary of
the Loyal Orange Patriotic League, were £200,
£30, £40, £12, £180, £550, £342 and £100.
In all Pigott turned over twelve of Parnell's letters up to January, 1888, and these, with the
later letters of Egan and others, made a total of
seventeen.

On the following day, Parnell and his friends
were put in high glee by the result of evidence
given before the Commission by Soames' attorney and MacDonald, the manager of the *Times*.
It was generally acknowledged that such an exposure of imbecility and recklessness on the part
of men controlling the greatest newspaper was
rarely before seen. MacDonald confessed that
when he published the forged letter he had taken
no means whatever to examine its authenticity
beyond a reference to one handwriting expert.
He had never asked for information, had not
even asked the name of the recipient of the letter.
He did not know, and did not ask for months

M. D. GALLAGHER

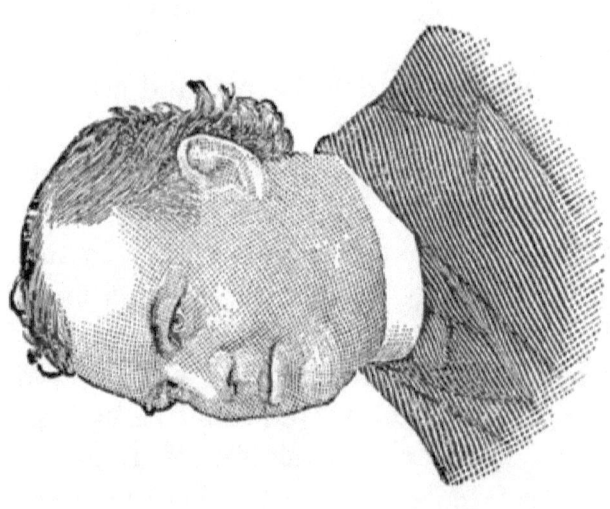

REV. MAURICE J. DORNEY

afterwards, from whom the letters had been obtained by the *Times* agent, and did not know till this day whom they were supposed to be directed to. The people in the Court almost stood aghast at this open confession of the incredible recklessness with which the charge of incitement to assassination was made by the greatest paper in England. A part of the examination revealed a nice little counterplot going on for weeks. Parnell knew months ago that Pigott had forged the letters. Labouchere, who is warm in favor of the Irish party, and who has great love for amateur detective work, got into communication with Pigott, and from his own lips received a confession of forgery. The forgery was not by tracing over, but by imitating the handwriting for a long time. The exposure of the signature to a microscope reveals that it was broken at several points, showing trepidation and slowness. Forger Pigott carefully considered a long time whether it was better to make a clean breast, in hopes of reward, to Labouchere, or to stick to the *Times*.

And now I come to the memorable day that brought Pigott on the stand, and it is necessary for a thorough understanding of this aged ruffian's testimony and perfidy that I should quote Secretary Houston's evidence on cross-examination.

He said he destroyed Pigott's letter to him, in accordance with an agreement made between them, that they were intended for the witness'

eye alone, and were not to be used publicly.   Up
to the time the witness went to Paris, Pigott had
not given him the names of any of the persons
connected with the letters secured by the *Times.*
He did not consider that a knowledge of the men
from whom the letters were obtained was important in connection with the question of their
genuineness.   Witness said his part was done
when the letters were obtained.   He accepted
them without securing any means of testing
Pigott's statement in the event of their genuineness being questioned, because he understood
that it was useless to attempt to make a complete
case, and further inquiry would only handicap
himself.

He had no means whatever of testing any part
of Pigott's story, which he regarded as probable,
especially as the newspaper reports of the dispute
between Mr. Parnell and the American extremist,
to some extent, confirmed Pigott's story that the
letters were left in a bag found in a room in Paris.
Witness showed the letters to Lord Hartington
and asked his advice as to their disposition, but
his Lordship refused to advise him.   He did not
offer the letters to the *Pall Mall Gazette.* He saw
Mr. Stead, editor of the *Gazette*, before he obtained possession of the letters, and asked him to
make up matter that would lead to the disclosure.
Mr. Stead said he had lost £3,000 by the publication of the "Modern Babylon" articles, and he

would not like to touch anything else unless he knew it would be successful.

When witness visited Paris he had no genuine specimens of either Mr. Parnell's or Mr. Egan's writing. He accepted the letters solely on Pigott's words.

"If," said the witness, "Pigott had been needy or fraudulent enough to attempt to commit perjury, my actions would have assisted him, but I do not admit that he was either. Pigott's interviews with Mr. Labouchere shook my faith in him, and, therefore, my mind was not easy until he had signed the sworn declaration."

Witness further said that he might have told Mr. Stead that Messrs. Sexton and Dillon were implicated in the Phœnix Park murders, but if he did so, it was on the authority of a statement made by Eugene Davis to Pigott, a copy of which was produced by the witness. He did not know where the original was. Two days before the commission opened, Pigott wrote him an abusive letter, demanding that after giving testimony before the commission he should be given £5,000.

Mr. Houston said that Pigott told him to whom several of the letters were addressed. He did not think that Pigott's statements were very accurate, because Pigott only repeated what other persons said. Between October, 1886, and January, 1888, he had paid Pigott £200, but the *Times* paid the bill from May, 1887. He understood

25

that Pigott obtained the second batch of letters from the same friends that supplied the first
batch, but he did not inquire about the matter.
He did not think it strange that the second batch
was not obtained earlier. Prior to November,
Pigott informed witness that Mr. Welehan, a
Tullamore solicitor, had called upon him and informed him that a gentleman from America wanted
to have an interview with him in London. He did
not say that the man came from Egan. Welehan
asked Pigott if he had any of Egan's letters, as
he was prepared to purchase them at a high price.
Pigott, when he wrote to witness, demanding
£5,000, said he had been coerced in Mr. Soames'
office, into making a statement under false pre-
tenses. Witness did not answer the letter.

Attorney-General Webster read a copy of the
notes made by Pigott of the latter's conversation
with Eugene Davis. According to these notes,
Davis stated that Egan took him into his confidence. Davis knew that the I. R. B. and the T.
B. were connected with the League one working
openly and the other secretly the "B. S." finding
men and the League finding money. Egan was
in Paris with Parnell, O'Kelly, Dillon, Brennan
and Harris, in 1881. He told Davis that he had had
long conferences with those gentlemen, and that
all had agreed that the situation rendered reprisals
against England imperative, and that England's
power could be neutralized only by removing as

many of her leading men as possible. Walsh, Sheridan and others were to be sent to Ireland to plan the murders. Immediately after Parnell's arrest, Egan appealed to the Fenian leaders to execute the work more energetically. Walsh went to Dublin and appointed Carey, Mullett and Curley as chief men. Tynan, Byrne, Colbert and Sheridan were also associated with him. Egan was invariably consulted regarding projected outrages and murders. Egan strongly reproved Tynan for failing to appear at Kingbridge in time to give the signal for Mr. Forster's murder. Davis was present in a cafe in Paris when Tynan related the whole history of the Phœnix Park murders. Tynan took pride in having given the signal for the attack. Egan professed to be highly delighted, but regretted that Tynan had not commenced work earlier. Egan gave Byrne a letter, a fac-simile of which was published by the *Times*. There was a plot to murder the Prince of Wales and Mr. Gladstone, during the carnival at Cannes. Byrne and Tynan were under the instructions, but did not attempt to carry out the plan. Houston, under cross-examination, said he did not regard all of the statements as accurate. This reply was greeted with laughter. Houston said that the suggestion that he destroyed Pigott's letters because they cast doubt upon the genuineness of the letters published by the *Times*, was without foundation. He destroyed them because he believed that, if they were allowed to exist and were published, the lives of certain persons would be placed at the mercy of certain assassins. Replying to Sir Charles Russell, Houston said that Davis was in England and that Soames subpœnaed him.

PIGOTT, THE PERJURER.

Richard Pigott, a well-dressed and benevolent-looking man, apparently about sixty years of age, was then called. He testified that he was proprietor of the Fenian organ, the *Irishman*, in 1865. He belonged to the Supreme Council, F. B. All the members of the Amnesty Association in 1870 were Fenians. Parnell belonged, and about 1871 Biggar, Barry, Harris, Nearey, Mullett and Murphy belonged to the Supreme Council of the I. R. B. Witness belonged to the R. B. until August, 1881. He was not an active member.

He detailed the negotiations in 1879, by which the *Irishman* and the *Flag of Ireland* were sold to a company in which Parnell and Egan were shareholders. He did not doubt that the Leagues provided the money. Later Egan said he proposed to render the lives of the English officials in England not worth an hour's purchase, and, replying to a question, said that of course Parnell was aware of this proposal.

The witness continued slightly in touch with the I. R. B. after the sale of his papers. Directly after Egan's flight to Paris, Pigott received a letter in which Egan asked for the address of Davis, who was a writer for the *Irishman*, and who had gone to Paris to prepare for the priesthood. Pigott corroborated Mr. Houston's testimony with reference to the preliminary negotiations regarding the search for documents. It was understood that the affair should be kept absolutely secret. He did not know Davis then, except as a contributor to the *Irishman*. Davis signed his articles, " Owen Roe."

CHAPTER XXXI.

THE END OF "DIRTY DICK."

THE sensation of the next day's proceedings was the production at the opening of the court, by Sir Charles Russell, of two letters which "Dirty Dick Pigott" wrote to Archbishop Walsh, of Dublin. The first of them is worthy of publication, inasmuch as it was written only three days before *The Times* published the forged Parnell letters. It read as follows:

"PRIVATE AND CONFIDENTIAL: My Lord—The importance of the matter about which I write will doubtless excuse this intrusion on your attention. I briefly wish to say that I have been made aware of the details of certain proceedings, which are in preparation, with the object of destroying the influence of the Parnellite party in Parliament. I cannot enter more fully into details than to state that the proceedings referred to consist in the publication of certain statements purporting to prove the complicity of Parnell himself and some of his supporters in murders and outrages in Ireland, to be followed, in all probability, by the

(396)

institution of criminal proceedings against those
parties by the Government. Your grace may be
assured that what I speak is with full knowledge,
and I am in a position to prove beyond all doubt
or question the truth of what I say; and I will
further assure your grace that I am also able to
point out how these designs may be successfully
combated and finally defeated. I assure your
grace that I have no other motive except to respectfully suggest that your grace would communicate the substance of what I state to some one
or other of the parties concerned [on, however, the
specific understanding that my name be kept
secret] to whom I could furnish details and exhibit proofs and suggest how the coming blow may
be effectively met. For reasons which, no doubt,
your grace will have no difficulty in discovering, I
could not apply to any of the parties direct, and that
is why I venture to ask your grace's interference.
At the same time I know that in adopting this
course I run the risk of incurring your grace's
displeasure, but perhaps the deep interest which
your grace is known to take in the preservation
of the integrity of the party that is so seriously
threatened will plead my excuse. Moreover, I
am forced to beg your grace's assistance from a
strong conviction in my own mind, founded on
what I have learned and the evidence relied on,
which is *prima facie* serious, that the proceedings,
unless met in the way I can suggest, will succeed

in their object. In any case, therefore, I trust your grace will regard this letter as private and confidential, except that it may be referred to in furtherance of the motives with which it was sent.

"P. S.—I need hardly add that did I consider the parties really guilty of the things charged against them I should not dream of suggesting that your grace should take part in an effort to shield them. I only wish to impress upon your grace that the evidence is apparently convincing and probably would ensure conviction if submitted to an English jury.

"RICHARD PIGOTT."

One other incident was very significant. Before asking a single question in cross-examination, Sir Charles Russell directed Pigott to write the following words on a sheet of paper: "Likelihood, livelihood, proselytism, Patrick Egan, hesitancy." Pigott spelled the latter "ency" instead of "ancy," and the same mistake was made in the forged Parnell letter.

On being closely pressed on the witness stand, Pigott voluntarily exclaimed: "I may say at once that the statements I made to Archbishop Walsh were unfounded." This, of course, produced a sensation, which was intensified when Sir Charles Russell said to him, "You deliberately wrote lies."

He admitted having written to Patrick Egan, attempting to blackmail him for the sum of £500, and having also on June 2, 1881, offered the late William E. Forster, then Chief Secretary for Ireland, papers which he said would break up the league for £1500 or £1000. Forster then loaned Pigott £150 as a "private loan." Sir Charles Russell produced letter after letter until the witness became dazed and forgot everything, or pretended to, declaring that while the letters were his, he "had no recollection of them." He denied hotly having "fabricated the forged letters."

On the morning of Saturday, February 23, 1889, Pigott went to the residence of Mr. Henry Labouchere, and in the presence of Mr. George Augustus Sala, signed a confession stating that the letters upon which the *Times* based its charges against the Irish members of the House of Commons were forgeries. He said that he had forged all the letters secured by the *Times*, which purported to have been written by Patrick Egan, Charles Stewart Parnell, Michael Davitt and Mr. O'Kelly. That statement or confession was presented to the Commission on the following Wednesday amid the greatest excitement. Pigott was called to again take the stand, but he did not appear. It was found that he had fled, and warrants were issued for his arrest. It is due to my good friend, the Hon. Patrick Egan, that I should

JOHN GROVES.

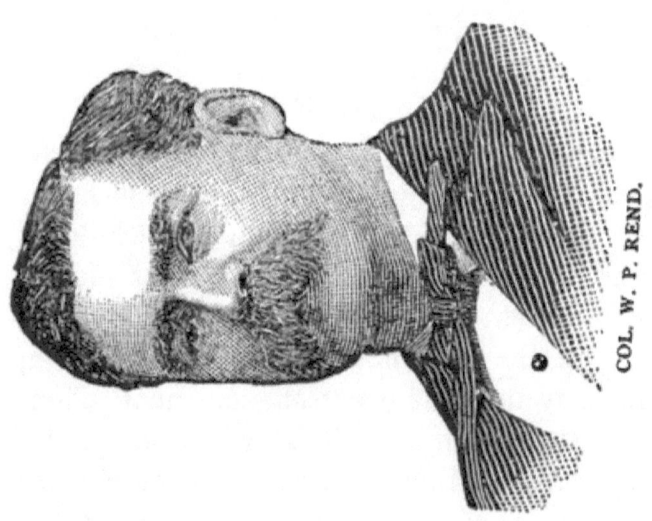

COL. W. P. REND.

state here and now that he was the man who discovered Pigott's vile plots, unearthed his forgeries and sent such complete information on those subjects from America to Parnell that the latter was able through Labouchere to wring a confession of his guilt from " Dirty Dick."

On the 1st of March, 1889, Pigott was arrested at the Hotel Des Ambassadeurs, in Madrid, Spain, where he had registered under the name of Ronald Ponsonby. When he was arrested he apparently took the situation calmly, and thus threw the officers off the scent. With the excuse that he wished to get his overcoat he retired to an alcove and there shot himself in the mouth with a revolver. He died instantly.

Attorney-General Webster tendered an apology on behalf of the *Times* for the publication of the forged letters, and the *Times* editorially, while endorsing that apology, said: "We deem it right to express our regret most fully and sincerely that having been induced to publish the letters as Mr. Parnell's or to use them in evidence against him."

That really ended the *Times* case and vindicated Mr. Parnell triumphantly before the world. Mr. Parnell, finding it impossible to respond to the multitude of letters he received from both Europe and America, congratulating him upon the collapse of the *Times'* case against him, thanked the writers through the press, which nobly stood by him in every quarter of the globe. The communications received by Mr. Parnell comprised letters from unexpected quarters and from persons in the highest ranks of art, literature, and science.

THE O'SHEA DIVORCE CASE.

The trial of the O'Shea divorce case began in the Divorce Court, in London, on Monday morning, November 17, 1890, before Justice Butt and a special jury. A few days before that Mr. Parnell inspired his followers with courage and set at rest the hopes of the Tories and the fears of the Liberals *pro tempore existente* by the following letter which he sent to the Irish members:

"DEAR SIRS—You will permit me, in accordance with my usual custom, to remind the members of the Irish Parliamentary Party that the session will open on Tuesday, the 25th inst., when it is most desirable that our full strength should be available.

"I wish to lay stress upon the necessity for the attendance of every man upon the opening day, as it is unquestionable that the coming session will be one of combat from the first to the last, and that great issues depend upon its course. I am, dear sirs,

"Yours truly,
"CHARLES STEWART PARNELL."

Contrary to public expectation neither Mrs.

O'Shea nor Mr. Parnell were represented by counsel at the hearing of the divorce suit. As neither the respondent nor co-respondent made any defense, the case was given to the jury on the morning of the day on which it was opened, and they returned a verdict that adultery had been committed by Mrs. O'Shea and Parnell, and that there had been no connivance on the part of Captain O'Shea. The court granted a decree in divorce, with costs to the petitioner, and also awarded him the custody of the younger children. This trial marked the beginning of the end of Parnell's career as an Irish statesman.

It is but simple justice to Mrs. O'Shea and to our departed friend and leader to say that there are grave doubts among well-informed parties as to their guilt. Both of them proud, high-strung, and, to a large extent, imperious in their natures, disdained to go before a divorce court, either to explain or palliate the alleged questionable transactions in which Captain O'Shea declared they were guilty participants. As Mrs. Delia T. S. Parnell says of Mrs. Kate O'Shea, "She comes of illustrious ancestry, not one of whom have at any time been even suspected of being guilty of anything dishonorable. Her immediate family were on terms of the closest intimacy with Queen Victoria and the members of the royal family, and all of them were proud to recognize her as her friend. Her ardent love for Ireland, although differing in race, her deep and earnest sympathies for the suffering and down-trodden peasantry, naturally attracted Mr. Parnell to her. They moved in the same social circle, and being a woman of great influence he naturally sought her presence to gain that influence for his people.

It is difficult to describe—in an adequate way —the tremendous excitement that the issue of the trial raised in every part of the civilized world. Calls were heard on all sides, imperiously demanding that Parnell should "retire" from the leadership of his party. Calls equally loud and equally as imperious were made upon him to "stand firm," and unfortunately, indeed, for the success of the Irish cause the members of the Irish Parliamentary Party became divided. Frequent meetings of the party were held in caucus and fiery speeches made by his friends and opponents, resulting finally in a split and the formation of opposing clans who have now gone down to history under the titles of "Parnellites" and "Anti-Parnellites." The minority stood by him and the majority, largely through the influence of Healy, Dillon, Davitt and O'Brien, named Justin McCarthy as their leader. At this time John Dillon and William O'Brien were in this country, having escaped the detectives who held warrants for their arrest. They were accompanied by Ex-Mayor O'Sullivan, of Dublin, T. P. O'Connor, T. P. Gill, and Timothy Harrington. They had come for the purpose of raising money for the Irish Parliamentary Fund, and had addressed immense mass meetings in Philadelphia, New York and Chicago. They had already raised almost $100,000 in a brief stay of but a few days, when the news was flashed over the cable of the grave situation in Irish affairs.

Numerous conferences were held by them with leading Irish-Americans. I participated in a number of those conferences, and am free to say that at all of them the most kindly feeling was invariably exhibited on their part towards Mr. Parnell. They finally decided, after a letter had been published from Mr. Gladstone, demanding Mr. Parnell's retirement, that for the sake of the cause which they represented he should at least retire temporarily.

On Friday, November 28, 1890, Mr. Parnell issued a manifesto to the Irish people, and set forth why, in his opinion, it would be disastrous to the best interests of the party for him to withdraw at that time. He defied his political opponents and appealed to the people of Ireland to sustain him in the stand he had taken. A canvass made that same day among the members of the Irish Parliamentary Party disclosed the fact that fifty-three of its members were opposed to his retention of the party leadership. On the same day, a meeting of Scotch Liberal members of Parliament was held, at which a resolution was adopted, declaring that "Mr. Parnell ought to retire." Two days afterwards he heard from the American visitors, John Dillon, William O'Brien, T. P. O'Connor, T. P. Sullivan and Thomas P. Gill. They declared against his continued leadership and condemned his manifesto for its attitude towards Mr. Gladstone and the English people. On the previous Saturday he had called a meeting of the Irish members at the Westminster Palace Hotel, London, and only twenty-four of them attended. The Catholic Hierarchy, without exception, and all of the Irish clergy had now declared against him. On November 30th Mr. Gladstone said: "Mr. Parnell's manifesto has widened the gulf made by recent disclosures and separated him from the Liberal party, who have now to consider the great and noble cause of justice for Ireland apart from any individual name. But I am glad to think, so far as appears, there will not be a severance between us and the Nationalist party, for Mr. Parnell throws over his colleagues. He acknowledges in them no right or authority, and goes past a constitutional representative of his country in his fanciful appeal to the nation which had chosen him to speak its wants and wishes."

On Saturday morning, December 6, 1890, Messrs. Redmond, Sexton, Healy, Leamy, and the two Parliamentary whips, Power and Dersey, a committee appointed at the previous day's

meeting of the Irish members of Parliament to
confer with Mr. Gladstone, drove to the residence
of the Liberal leader. Their deliberations lasted
an hour. At Mr. Gladstone's instance, no reference was made directly or indirectly to the question of Mr. Parnell's leadership. Mr. Gladstone
gave no definite promise, but Messrs. Healy and
Sexton reported that he said sufficient, in their
opinion, to justify the Irish party in considering
his assurances satisfactory. These were that he
would make a genuine attempt to deal with the
constabulary and Land Questions to the satisfaction of the Irish people. The strife of the
opposing clans continued to increase, and Parnell
announced his intention of "Re-organizing the
League." Messrs. O'Brien and Gill sailed for
France from this country, and whilst they were
on the ocean, Mr. Parnell and a party of his
friends seized O'Brien's newspaper, the *United Ire
land.* A conference was finally arranged at
Boulogne between William O'Brien and Mr.
Parnell.

CHAPTER XXXIII.

THE BOULOGNE CONFERENCE.

THE details of that conference were, at the instance of Mr. Parnell, kept secret, and that secrecy was the cause for over a year of many disputes, for while one faction gave its version of what they believed took place and insisted upon its truth, the other one was equally emphatic in denial of its accuracy. The conference was held on Thursday afternoon, December 30, 1890, and the parties present were the Redmonds, Kenny and Clancy, O'Brien, Gill, and Parnell. It was not until the 10th of November, 1891, that the truth of what took place at that conference was published. On that date, Mr. William O'Brien published a long letter in the *Freeman's Journal*, denouncing the conduct of Messrs. Redmond and Harrington in trying to deceive the Irish public by pretending, on the strength of their hope that he had lost Mr. Parnell's letter, that it disclosed some dark treachery towards Mr. Parnell or their Liberal allies. Mr. O'Brien now gives the letter to the world, together with his own reply—the only letter he wrote to Mr. Parnell during the

Boulogne negotiations and not yet published. Mr. Parnell's letter to Mr. O'Brien recounts at length what had already been done, and, as new proposals, suggests that Mr. McCarthy interview Mr. Gladstone and get a written memorandum, embodying assurances already given, anent land and police, transferred to the custody of O'Brien; that if the memorandum was satisfactory to both Mr. Parnell and Mr. O'Brien, the former would announce his retirement from the chairmanship; that the terms of the memorandum should not be disclosed until the Home Rule Bill was introduced, and not then unless the bill was unsatisfactory, but that after the passage of a satisfactory bill Mr. Parnell should be permitted to publish the memorandum. Instead of a two years' limit within which the constabulary should be disarmed and converted into a civil force, Mr. Parnell agreed that the time might be extended to five years, but he said it was of vital importance that some limit should be fixed. The letter in conclusion gives Mr. O'Brien permission to show it to the Redmond brothers and Mr. Gill.

Mr. O'Brien says that on receiving this letter he telegraphed it to Mr. Harrington, who replied that Mr. Parnell's proposals were subject to Mr. O'Brien's accepting the chairmanship. At the same time Mr. O'Brien wrote to Mr. Parnell to the effect that the proposals were feasible, provided Mr. McCarthy continued as chairman;

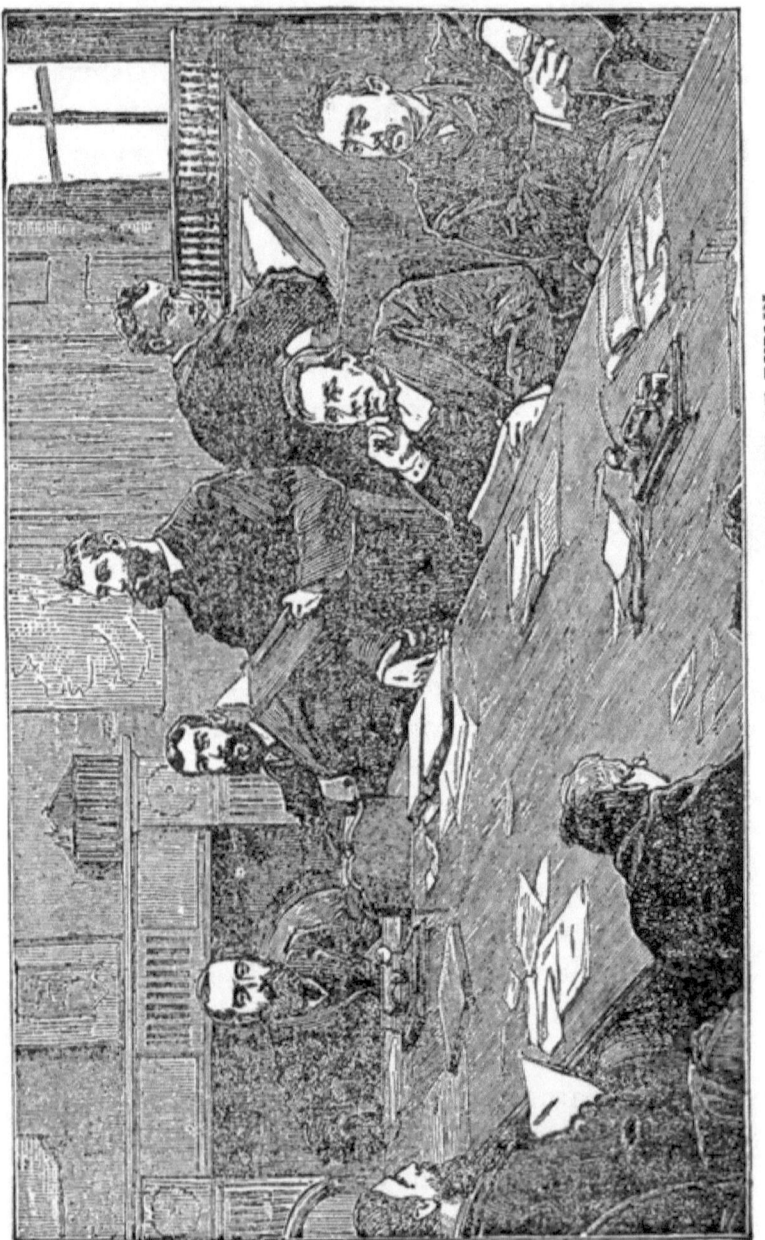

MEETING OF THE LAND LEAGUE COMMITTEE AT DUBLIN.

otherwise, as the Hawarden plan involved the
employment of Mr. McCarthy in a painful trans-
action, they would raise a formidable difficulty.
Mr. O'Brien concludes with an expression of the
belief that they would be able to devise some
other equally satisfactory plan. In a postscript,
he says he consulted Mr. Redmond's Bill, and all
agreed that, when they meet next May, they will
be able to arrange a *modus vivendi.*

Mr. O'Brien now contends that the foregoing
disposes of the Parnellite plea that Mr. Parnell's
retirement was to be a sham, and that he was to
have the right of veto in connection with the
Home Rule Bill.

Mr. O'Brien declares that he no more represented the Liberal Party in the Boulogne negotiations than he did the Mikado. He did not possess
a shadow of authority in the matter, except from
his American brother delegates.

Mr. O'Brien and Mr. Parnell held two conferences at Boulogne Sur Mer, in the Hotel Du
Louvre, on January 6th and 7th, 1891. What took
place at those and the previous conferences Mr.
O'Brien's letters tell plainly and unequivocally.

The Irish Parliamentary Party's differences
were as far as ever from a satisfactory solution,
and the split became of such a pronounced character that Parnell's friends and foes very often
attacked one another in open meetings. Each
party denounced the other, and each faction set

up its own candidates for Parliament. For the purpose of sustaining his campaign, at this juncture, Mr. Parnell sent as envoys to this country James O'Kelly, John Redmond, John O'Conner, and Henry Harrison. Their stay here was brief, but they were successful in raising a large sum of money.

On Wednesday, March 11, 1891, a largely-attended convention was held in Leinster Hall, Dublin, to which 115 organizations sent delegates and ninety other organizations sent letters assuring the convention that they would stand by it in its decisions. The "Irish National Federation" was then formally organized and an executive committee appointed, consisting of McCarthy, Condon, Davitt, Deasy, Dickson, Murphy, McCartan, Arthur O'Connor, Sexton, Sheehy, Sullivan, Webb, Dillon, and O'Brien. The first branch of that organization in this country was formed in Philadelphia at a meeting held in Independence Hall. Dr. Joseph Fox, M. P. for Kings county, is now on a tour of the United States as the propagandist of the new departure. He reports that it is eminently successful, and I have no doubt whatever of the truth of his statement.

MR. PARNELL MARRIES MRS. O'SHEA.

On the evening of March 13, 1891, Mr. Parnell issued an address to the Irish in America,

MRS. O'SHEA PARNELL.

calling upon them for assistance and concluding with the words: "with a confidence even greater than in 1880, I appeal to you once more to assist me in quelling this mutiny and disloyalty to Ireland; to help me in securing a really independent Parliamentary party, so that we may make one more, even though it be our very last effort to win freedom and prosperity for our nation by constitutional means."

At ten o'clock on Friday morning, June 26, 1891, Mr. Parnell and Mrs. O'Shea were married at Steyning, by the registrar, who was enjoined in the most strict manner not to give any information about the marriage. He promised to preserve the closest secrecy in regard to the matter. The only witnesses to the ceremony were two servants from Mrs. O'Shea's house at Walsingham Terrace, Brighton. Mr. Parnell had procured a special license on the preceding Tuesday, setting forth that the marriage would occur within two months. The Associated Press cablegram relating the circumstances attending the ceremony says that "an order was given to have a solitary one-horse phaeton in readiness at six o'clock this morning, instead of the usual order for horses or a carriage for exercise, as was customary when Mr. Parnell was stopping at Brighton. When the conveyance was ready, Mr. Parnell and Mrs. O'Shea entered the phaeton and orders were given to the coachman to drive to

the westward.   After the party had left Brighton
behind them, the driver was directed to proceed
to Steyning, by a circuitous route. Steyning was
reached at nine o'clock, at which time a heavy
rain was falling.   Upon entering the town, Mrs.
O'Shea, who was familiar with the place and
knew the situation of the registrar's office, re-
lieved the coachman of the ribbons and drove
direct to the office herself."

For months subsequent to this event a hot and
bitter contest was waged all over Ireland for political supremacy.   Day by day the Parnellites lost
ground but they manfully fought their opponents
to the last ditch, and now, although but a hand-
ful of them is left, they seem as determined and as
vigorous as when they first began the fight under
Mr. Parnell's leadership.

One of the prime causes of dispute amongst the
contending clans is the distribution of what is
known as "the Paris Fund."   This "Paris Fund"
was made up entirely of moneys contributed in
the United States and the Canadas, as well as in
Great Britain and Ireland and the Australian
colonies, for the relief of evicted tenants.   It
has been placed in the hands of Munroe & Co.,
a celebrated banking firm of Paris, France.   The
London newspapers, always on the alert to
foment discord among the banks of the Irish
party, have published statements to the effect
that Mrs. Kate Parnell, and John Howard Par-

nell, as the heirs of Charles Stewart Parnell, could claim the distribution of half the deposit belonging to the "Paris Fund." These statements so exasperated Healy and other members of the majority faction that they have been saying very bitter and cruel things about Mrs. Kate Parnell. Healy has been especially severe, so much so that Mr. MacDermott, a nephew of Mr. Parnell, gave him a sound thrashing for his misconduct. Healy was not daunted by the beating he received, for he reiterated his uncomplimentary remarks about Mrs. Parnell at a public meeting held twenty-four hours afterwards. The "Paris Fund" having been placed in bank subject to the joint order of Justin McCarthy and Charles Stewart Parnell, Mr. Parnell's death has complicated the situation. Mr. John Munroe, who is the head of the banking firm, in speaking to a friend of mine who was in Paris on October 13, 1891, said: "I shall not part with the fund or any part of it until I am satisfied by my solicitors that I will carry no responsibility. I shall wait until a judicial decision is arrived at, which will remove all responsibility from my shoulders. Personally, I have no interest in the matter and I am not called upon to decide with either party. I am simply its temporary custodian; a custodian who would be very glad to get rid of his charge." Mr. Munroe declined to state the exact amount of the fund, but intimated that it consisted mainly of

American securities, the interest accruing on which has been duly drawn by the two depositors, and that the real value of the fund had varied from time to time, but that at present it was about £40,000.

CHAPTER XXXIV.

THE LAST SAD SCENE.

A ND now I bring this work to a close with the story of the funeral of "The Uncrowned King." On Sunday, October 11, 1891, Charles Stewart Parnell was laid to rest in the famed Glasnevin Cemetery. The Dublin *Freeman*, in describing it, says that "the monster funeral procession, which was the most impressive feature of the obsequies, was worthy of the great Irish Chief and the people for whom he labored and suffered and died. As an expression of national sorrow it stands unequalled. No greater upheaval of emotion has ever been witnessed in Ireland. It was the most imposing public cortege that has passed for half a century through the metropolis, which has during that time seen many a remarkable political funeral procession—the Thomas Davis, the O'Connell, the Terence Bellew McManus, the Manchester Martyrs, the John O'Mahony, the Color Sergeant McCarthy and the Kickham funerals, for instance, to mention only a few. The Parnell Funeral has admittedly transcended all these demonstrations in significance, in grandeur,

and in solemnity.   And there were, indeed, many
reasons why it should be what it was—an intense,
a touching and a pathetic demonstration of general sorrow.   The unexpected news of Mr. Parnell's death fell on Ireland like a stunning blow,
producing stupor, amazement and consternation.
This sudden, untimely, tragic ending of a great
and noble life awakened the profoundest grief
among all parties, classes and creeds of Irishmen.
The reviling tones of hatred, calumny and abuse
—and even the voice of just and fair criticism—
were, with just two insignificant exceptions in the
Irish press, hushed, and, let us hope, hushed forever so far as Parnell is concerned, in the eternal
silence of the grave.   He was remembered only
as the Parnell of old—as one of the greatest
patriots we have ever known—as the leader,
and not alone the leader, but the very idol of the
Irish race.   The memory of his former greatness,
and of all he suffered and endured for Ireland,
only remained.   His fallen fortunes—his eclipse
during the past few sad and terrible months, were
remembered but to add an additional touch of
poignancy to the overwhelming grief and bereavement of the nation.   Edmund Burke complained once of the hunt of obloquy which pursued him through life.   So it was, too, alas! with
Charles Stewart Parnell.   From the very opening
to the very close of his public career he had to
endure envy, calumny, hate and pain.   But it is
all over now.

"'How peaceful and how powerful is the grave that hushes all!' as the poet sings. Nothing was heard on Sunday from that mighty mass of people which followed the dead chief to his last resting place but expressions of uncontrollable grief—the subdued sobbing and weeping of strong men and the loud wailing of women. The fascination of that impenetrable, inscrutable and mysterious personality ended not with his death. During life Parnell was, eminently, a man to enkindle enthusiasm and command devotion. The same potent influences rise even from his ashes, as the demonstration on Sunday proves. It was as pathetic a picture of mingled affection, devoted loyalty and desolate bereavement as the streets of Dublin have ever witnessed. It was, indeed, a memorable funeral procession. Who that saw it will ever forget it? 'I was at Parnell's funeral,' shall be a proud yet melancholy boast in days to come. It was a singular, strange and impressive event, the funeral of Mr. Parnell—from its opening in Brighton at noon on Saturday to its close on Sunday evening at six o'clock. Dublin was astir before morning dawned on Sunday. The silence of the streets was broken by the tramp of men at a very early hour. Crowds converged on Westland row from all points of the city and suburbs, though a cutting wind and a drizzling rain prevailed. The train conveying the body from Kingstown was more than an hour late,

owing to a delay in starting the mail boat at
Holyhead and an exceedingly rough passage;
but the people waited patiently, notwithstanding
the discomfort of the morning, in Westland row
and Great Brunswick street. At last, at eight
o'clock, the sad strains of "The Dead March,"
played by a brass band, announced the arrival of
the *cortege*, and as the hearse, with a body guard
of Gaels with *camans* draped, and followed by
Mr. Parnell's Parliamentary colleagues, passed
between the thick files of people, every hat was
raised, and cries and sobs of anguish rent the
air. On the melancholy procession marched in a
drenching downpour of rain to St. Michan's
Church, Church street. In the vaults of this
sacred edifice the Brothers Sheares, who were
executed in '98, are interred, and in the grave-
yard attached are buried Charles Lucas, the
founder of the *Freeman's Journal*, and one of the
first of the Irish constitutional patriots, and Oliver
Bond, who sought in '98 by other methods to
restore the freedom of Ireland. It is said the
uninscribed tomb of Emmet is there also. Here,
then, in this sacred edifice, rich with Irish National
associations, the prayers for the dead, according
to the ritual of the Protestant Church, were recited by the Rev. Mr. Fry, Rector of All Saints,
Manchester. Is there any church in Dublin in
which this sacred function could have been

more appropriately discharged for the dead Irish Tribune?

The lying in state of the body of Mr. Parnell in the large circular room of the City Hall, to which it was conveyed after the services in St. Michan's Church, was another very impressive ceremonial. The coffin was placed on a low bier just below the massive statue of O'Connell by Hogan, the base of which was draped with the well-worn and tattered colors of the two regiments of Volunteers raised by Sir John Parnell, the incorruptible Chancellor of the Irish Exchequer, in Wicklow, and brought up from Avondale for the melancholy occasion. The coffin was entirely covered with the wreaths, artistically arranged by loving hands, and at its feet was raised the floral offering of Mr. Parnell's colleagues, a Celtic cross five feet high. To the right of the coffin was the statue of Charles Lucas, to its left the statue of Henry Grattan and the bust of Denis Florence M'Carthy, and inscribed on a white ground, hanging in graceful Venetian folds from the heavily draped pillars of the hall, were the last words of Mr. Parnell—

"Give my love to my colleagues and to the Irish people."

The hall, which was open to the public from ten till one o'clock, was visited by 30,000 persons. Meanwhile, from a far earlier hour than ten o'clock, preparations for the funeral procession were afoot.　Special trains crowded with deputations, accompanied by bands, arrived from North, South, East, and West, at the various termini of the metropolis, and poured their thousands on the streets.　The weather continued inclement, yet even during the early forenoon the city was thronged with people who moved about the streets unheeding the bitter wind and the rain, and the mud and slush below.　The shadow of a deep desolation seemed to hang over all.　The walls of the city were extensively placarded with huge posters, in heavy mourning borders, the letterpress of which was headed with the lines—

FUNERAL
OF THE
IRISH CHIEF,

in large black letters, followed by particulars as to the order of the procession.　Another poster also heavily bordered in black, which attracted considerable notice, was the following:

HIS LAST WORDS.

"My love to my colleagues and to the Irish people."

"If I were dead and gone to-morrow, the men who are fighting against English influence in Irish public life would fight on still; they would

still be independent Nationalists ; they would still
believe in the future of Ireland a nation ; and they
would still protest that it was not by taking orders
from an English Minister that Ireland's future
could be saved, protected or secured.

        " CHARLES STEWART PARNELL.

          "At Listowel, September 13, 1891."

   While the deputations were assembling in pro-
cessional order in St. Stephen's green, and in the
neighboring streets, every possible position that
could afford a view of the procession along the
line of route was occupied. The windows were
crowded, the footways were thronged. The
streets through which the procession was to pass
from the City Hall to Glasnevin were literally
swarming with men, women, and children—curious,
interested, and sympathetic—every one, almost,
wearing the emblem of the mourners, a piece of
crape set off with green ribbon, and eagerly
awaiting the appearance of the *cortege*. Street
vendors did a roaring trade in portraits of the
Dead Patriot, and in ballads singing his virtues.

   From many windows hung green flags trimmed
with mourning; from others floral wreaths were
suspended ; and in the poorer portions of the city
through which the procession passed, in Thomas
street, James' street, and along the Northern line
of quays—pictures of Mr. Parnell were liberally
displayed. The depth, reality, and intensity of

27

the sorrow felt by the people—spectators as well as processionists—for the death of their Chief was unmistakable. As the monster procession, starting from the City Hall at a quarter past two, wended its slow, sad, and solemn way, to the mournful cadences of forty bands, through serried files of people—up Lord Edward street, past Christ Church Cathedral, along Thomas street, James' street, down Steevens lane, crossing the Liffey at Kingsbridge, proceeding along the northern line of quays, re-crossing the river over Grattan bridge, advancing up Parliament street, passing the City Hall again, proceeding down Dame street, past "the Old House in College green," through Westmoreland street, over O'Connell bridge, up O'Connell street, through Rutland square, along Blessington street, over Berkeley road, through Phibsborough, and thence to Glasnevin Cemetery—the keening and clapping of hands of the women were frequently heard: heart-rending sobs burst from many a man, and tears were seen on the cheeks of not a few. As the hearse approached every hat in the throng on each side was doffed, and prayers for the dead were muttered. It was, indeed, a spectacle to touch the most callous heart to see the hearse—a splendid vehicle drawn by four sable horses, with outriders in mourning costumes—the coffin on top, completely hidden by floral wreaths, and the crushed and bruised and sorrow-stricken colleagues of the

heroic, the militant, the kingly Irishman who lay
dead inside, surrounding it as pall-bearers.   The
demeanor of the people throughout the trying day
was magnificent for its solemnity, dignity, good
order, and sobriety.   It was apprehended, it is
true, that evil and angry passion would be
aroused, and that the laying to rest of the Great
Irish Leader who is gone from us for ever would
be marred by riot and bloodshed.   Thank
Heaven, there was nothing of the kind.   Thank
Heaven that not the slightest violation of the
law—that not the least infraction of the public
peace marred this solemn and mournful occasion ;
and the only way the services of the police were
brought into requisition was in the aiding of the
marshals and stewards to clear the way and preserve unbroken the march of the procession.
From the opening of the sad proceedings to their
close no hitch occurred ; no disturbance took
place, no accident happened, and neither jarring
note nor a word of anger nor imprecation was
heard.   It was half-past five before Glasnevin
Cemetery was reached, and then, at six o'clock,
just as the shades of night were falling, with the
gathering gloom lighted up by a half moon in a
cloudless sky, after prayers had been recited, the
dull thud of the earth clods on the coffin of
Charles Stewart Parnell was heard amid mur-
murs of sorrow from the multitude thronging
round.   The tragedy of that terrible moment to

the devoted colleagues of the Dead Chie. may
be imagined but it cannot be described."

> " Dead, our mighty Leader lies,
>   Weep not for him with useless cries,
>   Mourn for him as true men ought."

CHAPTER XXXIV.

WILLIAM EWART GLADSTONE.

The history of William Ewart Gladstone is the history of England for fifty years. Beginning as "the rising hope of the stern, unbending Tories," he has come to be the standard-bearer of advanced Liberalism, almost Radicalism. In this process of evolution he has figured conspicuously in every important movement in English national life. Mistakes he has made. False steps he has taken; some of them terribly wrong. But he has had the English people largely with him through them all; and no other man has been so constantly and so perfectly an individual exponent of the aims, the feelings and the very soul of England as he. His history, indeed, is in great measure the history of the whole world for an important half century, for in that time Great Britain has been involved in relations, hostile or friendly, with all other nations, and upon those relations the impress of Mr. Gladstone's character is invariably to be found. In the compass of a few pages it is impossible to present more than a meagre outline of his life-work, or more than a slight hint of the principles that have guided this illustrious statesman, theologian, orator, and

author through a career which has scarcely a rival
in modern history.

"Who is this Mr. Gladstone?" inquired an
elector of Newark, England, one day in December, 1832, when he was asked to vote for him to
represent that borough in the House of Commons. "Who is this Mr. Gladstone?" Not
many of the Newark electors could have answered
the question. It was addressed, however, to the
steward of the Duke of Newcastle, and he made
reply: "Mr. Gladstone is a young man, the son
of a millionaire merchant of Liverpool, who was a
friend of Canning; and he is the *protege* of the
Duke of Newcastle." That meagre biography
was sufficient for electoral purposes, and Mr.
Gladstone was elected. "Vote for Gladstone,"
the Duke practically said to his tenants, "or I
will turn you out of doors." Under this miserable rotten borough system was sent to Parliament the man who was destined in future years
to sweep that system away forever. He was then
twenty-three years old, having been born at Liverpool, December 29, 1809, the son of Sir John
Gladstone. The family is of purely Scottish
origin, and in early generations was connected
with royalty itself. With almost boundless wealth
behind him, the future Prime Minister enjoyed
the best educational advantages England afforded.
He spent six years at Eton; then studied privately under Dr. Turner, afterward Bishop of

Calcutta; and finally spent three years at Christ Church College, Oxford, being graduated in 1831, with the highest honors of the class. He then went to Italy on a pleasure tour, and for the good of his health, which was then delicate. While he was there the Reform Act of 1832 was passed, and the Duke of Newcastle summoned him home to stand for Newark in the ensuing election. His authentic ancestry may be traced briefly from William Gladstone, a brewer, of Biggar, who died in 1728. He left three sons and a daughter. One of these sons left eleven children, one of whom was named Thomas. Thomas Gladstone had sixteen children, the eldest of whom was John, afterward Sir John Gladstone, the father of the subject of this sketch. John Gladstone built up his great fortune chiefly through the slave trade and the products of slave labor in America. He accepted the abolition of slavery with good grace, however, and thereafter continued greatly to increase his wealth. The friendship of Canning and the patronage of the Duke of Marlborough got him into Parliament as Member for Woodstock, a pocket-borough of Marlborough's, and he was still a member of the House when his son, William Ewart, was elected as his colleague from Newark.

The first important act of the Parliament to which Mr. Gladstone was first elected was the abolition of slavery. This was effected in 1833.

In the debates on this topic Mr. Gladstone made his first parliamentary speech. He was not opposed to emancipation, but he demanded that it be done gradually, and that slave-owners be indemnified for their losses. To any such thing as immediate and absolute abolition of slavery he was strongly opposed. In other debates that year he displayed his prowess, and he was made by Peel, in 1834, a Junior Lord of the Treasury. It is, by the way, an odd circumstance that while Mr. Gladstone throughout his public career has especially excelled as a financier, he was when in school the dullest of dullards in arithmetic. A few months later the Tories were turned out of office, and Mr. Gladstone retired for some years to the Opposition benches. Peel returned to power, however, in 1841, and made Mr. Gladstone Vice-President of the Board of Trade and Master of the Mint. That Ministry was one of the most notable in modern English history, and in its important work Mr. Gladstone took a leading part. It was he who prepared the revised Tariff schedule, which largely abolished duties on imports and inaugurated the era of British free-trade. He soon succeeded Lord Ripon as President of the Board of Trade, and in that capacity secured the abolition of restrictions on the exportation of machinery. The next year, 1844, he carried his railway laws, which compelled railways to run cheap trains, established a system of electric telegraphs, and provided for the purchase of railways by the Government—a provision which has never been executed.

The achievement of these important measures within three years marked Mr. Gladstone as the coming leader of British politics. They showed, too, that Tory as he was, he possessed a spirit of independence above party trammels, and was inspired with ideas of advancement and reform that must in time make him a Liberal. The Liberal party of later years was not then in existence, and as between the Tories and the Whigs there was little for a reformer to choose. Meantime Mr. Gladstone had paid much attention to ecclesiastical as well as fiscal politics, and had published two works, "The State in its Relations with the Church" and "Church Principles Considered in their Results." The ideas expressed by him in these were not in harmony with the bill for the endowment of Maynooth College, introduced by the government in 1845, and he accordingly resigned his office. He held the view, since abandoned, that it was the business of the government to uphold "the true religion," by which he meant the Church of England. Maynooth was a Roman Catholic college, and toward Romanists and Dissenters alike Mr. Gladstone would show no favor. In 1845 he favored customs discrimination against slave-grown sugar. Then the Corn Law question came up. His free-trade notions made him favor

their repeal. But his patron, the Duke of Newcastle, to whom he owed his Newark seat, opposed
repeal. So he resigned his place in the Commons
and went back to private life, powerfully aiding,
however, by voice and pen, the campaign for the
repeal of the obnoxious laws. When that campaign was finally triumphant he was re-elected to
Parliament as member for Oxford University.
He still ranked as a Tory, but day by day showed
that he was drifting hopelessly away from that
party. He favored the removal of the political
disabilities of the Jews, thus directly opposing the
Tory policy. He also spoke and worked strongly
for the repeal of the navigation laws and for a
reformed system of colonial administration. In
1850 he made a speech on the Greek question,
which fixed his reputation as one of the three or
four greatest parliamentary orators of Europe.

Sir Robert Peel had begun as a protectionist
and a Tory, and had now become a free-trader
and practically a Whig. Mr. Gladstone had accompanied him through this transformation, and
was now a conspicuous member of that small but
able body of men known as Peelites. That body
was broken up by the death of Peel in July, 1850,
and thenceforth Mr. Gladstone's progress towards
Liberalism was more marked and rapid than ever.
In 1851 he visited Italy again, and observed the
tyranny of the King of Naples. What he saw
stirred him to the core, and he wrote a number of

letters to Lord Aberdeen, passionately appealing
to the common humanity of the world against
such brutalities. "I have seen and heard," he
said, "the strong and true expression used:
'This is the negation of God erected into a system of government.'" These letters greatly
aroused public sentiment against the tyrant, and
hastened the revolution led by Garibaldi. The
next year (1852) he first faced squarely his great
rival, Disraeli, who was a member of the government under Lord Derby. Mr. Disraeli brought
forward a Budget, and Mr. Gladstone attacked it
so vehemently and convincingly that it was rejected by the House, and the Ministry thereupon
resigned.

In the Coalition Ministry which was then formed
Mr. Gladstone was of course made Chancellor of the
Exchequer. He signalized his accession to this
important office by bringing forward another great
scheme of financial reform. This was nothing less
than a plan for reducing the national debt. It was
adopted, and worked admirably until the Crimean
war broke out. He was still earnestly moving
for free trade, which had not yet been established
to his satisfaction, and his first Budget made
sweeping reductions and abolitions of duties,
amounting to more than $25,000,000. Mr. Glad-
stone has generally been regarded as *particeps
criminis* in the terrible iniquities of the Crimean
war, and so strong was public opinion to that

effect that he was constrained to publish an apology for his conduct in that crisis. He accepted office under Lord Palmerston after the fall of the Aberdeen Ministry, but soon resigned because Lord Palmerston would not oppose Mr. Roebuck's motion for an investigation into the mismanagement of the war. This was one of Mr. Gladstone's great blunders, the first of the series. Although a professed opponent of war, he helped lead the nation into the Crimean conflict, and identified himself with the shameful mismanagement that marred the honorable fame of England. Then he resigned his office because his chief would not shield him from an investigation.

Mr. Gladstone arrayed himself against Lord Palmerston in 1857 on the Chinese question, and led against him a motley band of Tories, Radicals and Peelites, who had nothing in common but their hatred of the Prime Minister. Lord Palmerston was defeated; but he appealed to the country and was returned to office stronger than ever. The next year, however, he was beaten on another measure and resigned office. Lord Derby succeeded him, and Mr. Gladstone was again a supporter of the government, though not a member of it. The great India bill, transferring the government of India from the old company to the Crown, was now adopted, and Mr. Gladstone succeeded in getting into it a clause forbidding the use of Hindoo soldiers outside of their own

GLADSTONE PRESENTING THE HOME RULE BILL, 1886.

country, except by special permission of Parliament. In November, 1858, Mr. Gladstone was sent to Corfu by Lord Derby as High Commissioner Extraordinary to the Ionian Islands, and a few years later those islands were formally united to Greece. At about this time, too, Mr. Gladstone published his great work entitled "Studies on Homer." In this he argued vigorously that Homer was an actual personage, that he was the author of the works ascribed to him in their entirety, and that the events related in the poems were real and not fabulous. He has been all his life a careful student and constant reader of the great Greek epics.

Mr. Gladstone again entered Lord Palmerston's Cabinet in 1859, as Chancellor of the Exchequer, and was enabled to carry out still further his free-trade principles. He assisted Mr. Cobden in negotiating an important commercial treaty with France, and still further reduced and abolished duties on imports. He proposed to do away with the paper duty, but the House of Lords refused to sanction this part of his scheme. Thereupon he introduced and secured the passage of a resolution in the House of Commons, declaring that the right of granting supplies to the Crown is vested in the House of Commons alone. This was the first of his battles with the House of Lords, which have grown steadily more bitter and have now come to a determination on his part, if possible, either to remodel and reconstruct that Chamber or do away with it altogether. In 1861 he founded the Post Office Savings Bank system, which has been of incalculable benefit to the people of England. In the Budget of this year the paper duties were abolished, despite the opposition of the Lords, Mr. Gladstone embodying this and all other financial propositions in one bill, and presenting only the alternative of passing the whole or none. If the Lords would not agree to abolishing the paper duties, the Commons would vote no supplies for carrying on the government. For a time a serious constitutional conflict seemed imminent, but at last the Lords yielded to Mr. Gladstone's compulsion. During the three or four years that followed, Mr. Gladstone steadily removed duties and lightened taxation.

Soon after the outbreak of the rebellion in America, in 1861, Mr. Gladstone committed the second big blunder of his life, and one for which, like the first, he was afterwards compelled to apologize and express contrition. In a public address at Newcastle he exultingly declared that " Jefferson Davis had created a nation," and predicted the irretrievable dissolution of the American Union. Thenceforward his sympathies and his influence were altogether on the side of the South.

It is not profitable to speculate upon his motives in thus siding with slaveholders against freedom.

Doubtless his heart warmed for the Confederates because of their emphatic free-trade principles. Free trade in America would, he thought, be greatly to England's commercial advantage; and the breaking up of the Great Republic would in many respects inure to England's benefit. That so great a man, and one so full of love for humanity, should be swayed by such mercenary motives, is a fact to be remembered only with pity and regret. In taking this position Mr. Gladstone differed not only from his opponent, Mr. Disraeli, but also from his close friends, Mr. Bright and Mr. Forster, all of whom were steadfast friends of the Union.

At the general election in 1865 Mr. Gladstone stood again for Oxford, but was beaten by Mr. Gathorne Hardy. He obtained a seat in the House, however, from South Lancashire. Lord Palmerston died soon after, and Earl Russell became Prime Minister, with Mr. Gladstone as Chancellor of the Exchequer and Leader of the House of Commons. His Budget in 1866 showed a surplus of $6,500,000, and further reduction of taxation followed. He then brought in a sweeping Reform bill, intended to extend the franchise to about 400,000 more electors. After its second reading the bill was defeated by a motion of Lord Dunkellin, and the government resigned after less than a year's existence. Lord Derby formed a new ministry, Mr. Disraeli succeeding Mr.

Gladstone in the Exchequer; and a year and a half later Mr. Disraeli became Prime Minister, reaching that coveted goal in advance of his great rival. But although in opposition, Mr. Gladstone, during this time, exercised an important influence on legislation. He and Mr. Bright largely shaped the Reform bill of 1867, which enacted household suffrage, pure and simple, in the boroughs. His bill abolishing compulsory church rates was adopted in 1868; and after a long debate his resolutions declaring for the disestablishment of the Irish Church were carried by a heavy majority. Then he brought in a bill putting these declarations in effect. It was adopted by the House of Commons but rejected by the Lords, whereupon Parliament was dissolved. On the appeal to the country a great Liberal majority was returned, Mr. Disraeli resigned, and Mr. Gladstone became Prime Minister for the first time, December 9, 1868. Backed up by an overwhelming majority in the Commons, he was able to do much as he pleased, and a period of great legislative activity ensued. The most important measure passed by this government was the Education act, for which credit is due chiefly to Mr. Forster. The Irish Church was disestablished in 1869 and the Irish Land act became a law in 1870. When the Franco-German war broke out, Mr. Gladstone declined to define the attitude of England, and thereby provoked much dissatisfaction. In 1871

28

the royal warrant abolishing the system of pur-
chasing army offices was issued, and the treaty
of Washington, for settling by arbitration the
disputes with America, was concluded. These
disputes were finally settled by the arbitrators at
Geneva in 1872, and England was mulcted in a
heavy sum of damages, a just result, but one which
gave Mr. Gladstone much unpopularity at home.
Other laws passed in this and the following years
were the Ballot bill; acts protecting the public health,
prohibiting adulteration of food and medicines,
and regulating the management of mines; and
an Education act for Scotland. The government
tried to settle the Irish University question in 1873,
but were beaten by the narrow margin of three
votes. Thereupon they resigned, but resumed
office again on Mr. Disraeli's refusing to form a
ministry. Cabinet dissensions followed, and in a
fit of temper Mr. Gladstone in 1874 unexpectedly
dissolved Parliament. The ensuing elections gave
the Conservatives a large majority in the House
of Commons, and Mr. Gladstone resigned office,
and was succeeded by Mr. Disraeli. He also resigned the leadership of the Liberal party, and
was temporarily succeeded by the Marquis of
Hartington.

In his retirement from politics he now busied
himself with theology, writing an "Essay on Rit
ualism," and a sharp pamphlet on "Vaticanism,"
in which he vigorously attacked the doctrine of

Papal Infallibility. These utterances involved him in a spiritual controversy with Cardinal Newman. The outrages perpetrated by the Turks in Bulgaria, in which the British government declined to interfere, called him back to politics. At great public meetings throughout the country he scathingly arraigned the government for its inhumanity; he denounced as unconstitutional the bringing of Indian troops to Malta; the Anglo-Turkish treaty he declared to be insane; the purchase of the Suez Canal shares he pronounced an act of madness, in which he made another mistake, as that investment has proved to be in all respects one of the best ever made by any government; he condemned the Afghan war; and generally criticised the policy of the government in the severest possible manner. In 1880 Parliament was dissolved, and Mr. Gladstone, as member for Mid-Lothian, came into the new Parliament with a great Liberal majority, and became for the second time Prime Minister.

Irish affairs largely monopolized attention now. A stringent Coercion act was passed, the Land League was ruthlessly suppressed, and the Irish parliamentary leaders were imprisoned wholesale. Lord Frederick Cavendish, Irish Secretary, was murdered, and a most harsh and arbitrary act for the prevention of crimes was adopted. A second Land bill was passed after a third battle with the Lords, and an Arrears act, both intended to ameliorate the condition of the Irish peasants.

An Affirmation bill, to admit Mr. Bradlaugh, the
infidel, to the House without the customary oath,
was advocated by Mr. Gladstone vigorously, but
was rejected.   Important laws were passed relating
to tramways in Ireland, bankruptcy, emigration,
and agricultural holdings.   The Franchise bill,
establishing almost universal suffrage, was passed
after a struggle with the Lords that at one time
threatened a revolution; and a bill redistributing
parliamentary seats so as to reorganize the House
of Commons entirely, followed.   Foreign affairs
gave much trouble.   A war was begun in Egypt,
Alexandria was destroyed by bombardment, and a
number of battles were fought, which were mere
massacres of Arabs.   These operations have been
generally condemned as a needless waste of life
and treasure, and Mr. Bright resigned from the
Cabinet to mark his detestation of them.   General
Gordon was sent to Khartoum and there abandoned to his fate, the government shamefully
breaking its promises to him and calling down on
its head, at his death, a storm of execration.   In
Afghanistan, Russia made great aggressions, and
a war seemed imminent, but it was averted by the
simple policy of yielding to all of Russia's insolent
demands.   Finally the government was defeated
on their Customs and Inland Revenue bill, and
resigned in June, 1885.

The new election under the Franchise and
Redistribution acts took place that fall, and Mr.

Gladstone was again returned for Mid-Lothian, with a large Liberal majority in the House. Lord Salisbury held on to his office for a time, but was unable to command a working majority, so he resigned, and Mr. Gladstone became Prime Minister for the third time on February 6, 1886. He soon put forward his scheme for Home Rule in Ireland, which caused a revolt in the party. Lord Hartington, Lord Selborne, Sir Henry James, Mr. Bright, Mr. Goschen, Mr. Chamberlain and other great Liberal leaders opposed him and formed the Liberal Unionist party. Thus his scheme was rejected by the House, and Parliament was soon dissolved. The new election resulted in an overwhelming majority against Mr. Gladstone, who thereupon resigned in July, 1886, and has since been the leader of the Opposition in the House of Commons. His political activity has been very great since his retirement from office, and he has made numerous valuable contributions to the periodical literature of the day.

Mr. Gladstone, by the unanimous verdict of critics, is the greatest English orator of our time. He is gifted with a marvellous voice and an unfailing command of words. Wordiness, indeed, sometimes becomes his fault; and he was once characterized by his great political opponent as "a sophistical rhetorician, intoxicated with the exuberance of his own verbosity." His noble countenance and intense manner make his speeches most effectual when listened to ; but on account of their involved construction they do not read well, and can never be quoted to advantage. He is not a successful party leader, because of his dogmatic and arbitrary ways and his lack of tact in dealing with men. He possesses great wealth, and lives at Hawarden Castle, a fine estate in Wales. He has outgrown the delicate health of his youth, and enjoys a robust and vigorous old age; delighting in intellectual labor and physical outdoor exercise, felling trees being his favorite recreation. His personal popularity with a great portion of the English people is very great. Years ago he was sneeringly called "The People's William." Of late years his devotion to the cause he deemed right, and the splendid vitality of his declining years, have given to him the popular title by which he will doubtless always henceforth be known—"The Grand Old Man."